A Sister's Secret

OTHER BOOKS BY WANDA E. BRUNSTETTER:

DAUGHTERS OF LANCASTER COUNTY SERIES
The Storekeeper's Daughter
The Quilter's Daughter
The Bishop's Daughter

DAUGHTERS OF LANCASTER COUNTY SERIES
A Merry Heart
Looking for a Miracle
Plain and Fancy
The Hope Chest

NONFICTION
The Simple Life
Wanda E. Brunstetter's Amish Friends Cookbook

A Sister's Secret

WANDA E. BRUNSTETTER

Sisters of Holmes County
Book One

BARBOUR
PUBLISHING

© 2007 by Wanda E. Brunstetter

ISBN 978-0-7394-8424-1

All scripture quotations, unless otherwise noted, are taken from the King James Version of the Bible.

All German-Dutch words are taken from the *Revised Pennsylvania German Dictionary* used in Lancaster County, Pennsylvania.

Cover Design: The DesignWorks Group, www.thedesignworksgroup.com

Published by Barbour Publishing, Inc., P.O. Box 719, Uhrichsville, OH 44683,

Our mission is to publish and distribute inspirational products offering exceptional value and biblical encouragement to the masses.

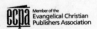
Member of the
Evangelical Christian
Publishers Association

Printed in the United States of America.

DEDICATION/ACKNOWLEDGMENTS

In memory of the precious Amish children
whose lives were taken in the October 2, 2006,
schoolhouse shooting in Lancaster County, Pennsylvania.
And to the victims' families,
who showed the world what God's love
and true forgiveness are all about.
My thoughts and prayers continue to be with you.

For the Lord GOD will help me;
therefore shall I not be confounded:
therefore have I set my face like a flint,
and I know that I shall not be ashamed.
ISAIAH 50:7

Chapter 1

A chill shot through Grace Hostettler. Stepping outside the restaurant where she worked, she had spotted a redheaded English man standing near an Amish buggy in the parking lot. He wore blue jeans and a matching jacket and held a camera in his hands. Something about the way he stood with his head cocked to one side reminded her of Gary Walker, the rowdy Englisher she had dated for a while during her *rumschpringe*, her running around years. But it couldn't be Gary. She hadn't seen him since—

Grace pressed her palms to her forehead. Her imagination was playing tricks on her; it had to be. She forced her gaze away from the man and scanned the parking lot, searching for her sister. She saw no sign of Ruth or of her horse and buggy. *Maybe I should head for the bakeshop and see what's keeping her.*

Grace kept walking, but when she drew closer to the man, her breath caught in her throat. It was Gary! She would have recognized that crooked grin, those blazing blue eyes, and his spicy-smelling cologne anywhere.

He smiled and pointed the camera at her. A look of recognition registered on his face, and his mouth dropped open. "Gracie?"

She gave one quick nod as the aroma of grilled onions coming from the fast-food restaurant down the street threatened to make her sneeze.

"Well, what do you know?" He leaned forward and squinted. "Yep, same pretty blue eyes and ash blond hair, but I barely recognized you in those Amish clothes."

Grace opened her mouth to speak, but he cut her off. "What happened? Couldn't make it in the English world?"

"I–I–"

"Don't tell me you talked Wade into joining the Amish faith." He slowly shook his head. "I can just see the two of you traipsing out to the barn to milk cows together and shovel manure."

Grace swallowed against the bitter taste of bile rising in her throat. "D–don't do this, Gary."

He snickered, but the sound held no humor. "Do what? Dredge up old bones?"

Grace wasn't proud that she'd gone English during her rumschpringe or that she'd never told her folks any of the details about the time she'd spent away from home. All they knew was that she had run off with some of her Amish friends, also going through rumschpringe, so they could try out the modern, English world. Grace had been gone two years and had never contacted her family during that time except for sending one note saying she was okay and for them not to worry. They hadn't even known she was living in Cincinnati, or that—

"So, where is Wade?" Gary asked, halting Grace's runaway thoughts.

She shivered despite the warm fall afternoon and glanced around, hoping no one she knew was within hearing distance. The only people she saw were a group of Englishers heading down the sidewalk toward one of the many tourist shops. "Wade's gone, and. . .and my family doesn't know anything about the time I spent living away from home, so please don't say anything to anyone, okay?"

He gave a noncommittal grunt. "Still keeping secrets, huh, Gracie?"

His question stung. When she'd first met Gary while waiting tables at a restaurant in Cincinnati, she hadn't told him she was Amish. It wasn't that she was ashamed of her heritage; she'd just decided if she was going to try out the English world, she should leave her Amish way of life behind.

But one day when a group of Amish kids came into the restaurant, Grace spoke to them in German-Dutch, and Gary overheard their conversation. He questioned her about it later, and she finally admitted that she was from Holmes County, Ohio, and had been born and raised Amish. Gary had made light of it at first, but later, as his quick temper and impulsive ways began to surface, he started making fun of Grace, calling her a dumb Dutch girl who didn't know what she wanted or where she belonged.

When Wade came along and swept Grace off her feet with his boyish charm and witty humor, she'd finally gotten up the courage to break up with Gary. He didn't take to the idea of her dating one of his friends and had threatened to get even with her. Had he come to Holmes County to make good on that threat?

"Wh–what are you doing here, Gary?" Her voice sounded raspy, almost a whisper, and her hands shook as she held her arms rigidly at her side.

"Came here on business. I'm a freelance photographer and reporter now." He jiggled his eyebrows. "Sure didn't expect to see you, though."

Grace heard the rhythmic *clip-clop* of horse's hooves and spotted her sister's buggy coming down the street. "I–I've got to go." The last thing she needed was for Ruth to see her talking to Gary. Her sister would no doubt ply her with a bunch of questions Grace wasn't prepared to answer.

Gary lifted his camera, and before Grace had a chance to turn her head, he snapped a picture. "See you around, Gracie."

She gave a curt nod and hurried away.

Ruth squinted as she looked out the front window of the buggy. What was Grace doing in the restaurant parking lot, talking to an English man with a camera?

She guided the horse to the curb, and a few minutes later, Grace climbed into the buggy, looking real flustered. "H–how was your interview?" she panted.

"It went fine. I got the job."

"That's good. Glad to hear it."

"Who was that man with the camera?" Ruth asked as she pulled slowly away from the curb and into the flow of traffic.

Grace's face turned red as she shrugged. "Just. . .uh. . .someone taking pictures of Amish buggies."

"It looked like you were talking to him."

"*Jah*, I said a few words."

"Were you upset because he was trying to take your picture?"

Grace nodded.

"Some of the English tourists that come to Berlin and the other towns in Holmes County don't seem to mind snapping pictures without our permission. Either they don't realize we're opposed to having our pictures taken, or they just don't care." Ruth wrinkled her nose. "I feel such *aeryer* when they do that."

Not even Ruth's comment about feeling vexed provoked a response from Grace.

"Guess it's best if we just look the other way and try to ignore their cameras."

"Uh-huh."

As Ruth halted the horse at the second stoplight in town, she reached across the seat and touched Grace's arm. "Are you okay? You look like you're worried about something."

"Just tired from being on my feet at the restaurant all day."

"You sure? That frown you're wearing makes me think you're more than tired."

"I'll be fine once we get home." Grace smiled, although the expression seemed forced. "Tell me about the bakeshop. What will you be doing there?"

Ruth held her breath as the smell of manure from a nearby dairy farm wafted through the buggy. "Mostly waiting on customers while Karen and Jake Clemons bake in the other room," she said, clucking to the horse to get him moving again when the light turned green. "Some days, I'll be working by myself, and others, I'll be with my friend Sadie Esh."

"Are you wishing you could help bake?"

Ruth shook her head and turned the horse and buggy down the back road heading toward their home. "Not really. I'll be happy to keep waiting on customers until I get married some day. Raising a family is my life's dream." Ruth glanced over at Grace. "Of course, I'll have to find a husband first."

"What about Luke Friesen? You think things might get serious between the two of you?"

"I don't know, maybe. For now I'm going to concentrate on my new job." Ruth smacked her lips. "Just thinking about all those delicious pastries and pies at the bakeshop makes me hungry."

"I'm sure Mom will have supper started by the time we get home, so you'll be eating soon enough."

"Speaking of Mom, I heard her mention the other day that she'd like for the two of you to get busy on your wedding dress soon."

Grace nodded and turned toward the window. Was she staring at the vibrant fall colors on the trees lining the road, or was she trying to avoid conversation?

"Do you still want me to help with the flowers for your wedding?" Ruth questioned.

"Jah, sure."

"You'll need several fresh arrangements on the bridal table, and I'm thinking maybe one big bouquet in the center of each of the other tables would look nice."

"Uh-huh."

"Will you want some candles, too?"

Grace nodded.

"Since Cleon's mother and sister make beeswax candles, I'm sure they'll want to provide those."

"Maybe so."

"I hope Cleon knows how lucky he is to be marrying my big sister."

"I–I'm the lucky one." Grace picked at her dark green dress as if she noticed a piece of lint, but Ruth didn't see anything. Of course, she couldn't look too closely as she had to keep her eyes on the road. Just last week, a buggy coming down one of the hills on this stretch of road between Berlin and Charm had run into a deer.

Grace sighed, and Ruth gave her a sidelong glance. If something was bothering Grace, she would talk about it when she was ready. In the meantime, Ruth planned to enjoy the rest of their ride home. Shades of yellow, orange, and brown covered the birch, hickory, and beech trees, and leaves of red and purple adorned the maple, oak, and dogwood. A dapping of sunlight shining through the trees gave her the feeling that all was right with the world—at least her little world.

Cleon Schrock stepped up to the counter near the front of the restaurant where Grace worked and smiled at Sarah, the owner's daughter. "I came to town on business about my bees, so I decided to stop and see Grace. Would you tell her I'm here?"

Sarah shook her head. "Sorry, but Grace got off work about ten minutes ago. Said something about meeting her sister, who had an interview at the bakeshop."

"Okay, thanks." As Cleon turned toward the door, he felt a keen sense of disappointment. He hadn't seen Grace since the last preaching service, and that had been over a week ago. "Have a good evening, Sarah," he called over his shoulder.

"You, too."

Cleon opened the front door, and just as he stepped out, he bumped shoulders with a tall, red-haired English man. The fellow held a fancy-looking camera in one hand and a notebook with a chunky green pen clipped over the top in the other. "Sorry. Didn't realize anyone was on the other side of the door," Cleon said with a shake of his head.

"Not a problem. As long as you didn't ruin this baby, no harm was done." The man lifted his camera. "She's my bread and butter these days."

Cleon stood, letting the man's words sink in. "Are you a newspaper reporter?"

"Nope. I'm a freelance photographer and reporter, and I've written for several publications." He smiled, revealing a set of straight, pearly white teeth. "The pictures I submit often bring in more money than my articles."

Cleon gave a quick nod; then he started to turn away.

"Say, I was wondering if you'd be willing to give me a quick interview. I'm trying to find out some information about the Amish in this area, and—"

"Sorry, not interested." Cleon hurried down the steps and onto the sidewalk. The last thing he wanted was for the Englisher to start plying him with a lot of questions about the Amish way of life. He'd read a couple of articles about his people in the newspaper recently, and none of them had been accurate. Cleon rushed around back to the parking lot, untied his horse from the hitching rail, and climbed into the buggy. If he hurried, he might catch up with Grace and Ruth on their way home.

Chapter 2

As Cleon headed down the road in his open buggy, all he could think about was Grace and how much he wanted to see her. He was excited to tell her about the latest contacts he'd made with some gift stores in Sugarcreek and Berlin, and if he didn't spot her buggy on the road, he would stop by her folks' place before going home.

The horse arched its neck and trotted proudly as Cleon allowed his thoughts to wander back to the day he'd first seen Grace Hostettler. It was almost four years ago—the day after he and his family had moved here from Lancaster County, Pennsylvania. He'd met Grace during a preaching service that was held at her folks' house. She'd seemed kind of quiet and shy back then, but after a while, they'd become friends and were soon a courting couple.

He'd wanted to ask her to marry him sooner but had waited until his beekeeping business was going strong enough to help support a wife and family. Besides, Grace hadn't seemed ready for marriage until a year ago. She had told him that she'd been gone from the Amish faith for a time before joining the church and that she'd only been back in Holmes County a few months before they'd met. Cleon had tried a couple of times to ask about her rumschpringe years, but Grace didn't seem to want to talk about them, so he'd never pressed the issue. What Grace had done during her running around years was her business, and if she wanted to discuss it, he figured she would.

A horn honked from behind, pulling Cleon's thoughts back to the present, and he slowed his horse, steering the buggy closer to the shoulder of the road to let the motorist pass. He gritted his teeth. At this rate, he would never catch up to Grace's carriage.

Once the car had passed, Cleon pulled back onto the road and snapped the reins to get the horse moving faster. The gelding flicked his ears and stepped into a fast trot, and several minutes later, Cleon caught sight of a black, closed-in buggy. Since no cars were in the oncoming lane, he eased his horse out and pulled up beside the other buggy. He saw Grace through the window on the left side, in the passenger's seat, and Ruth on the right, in the driver's seat.

"Pull over to the side of the road, would ya?"

Ruth did as he asked, and Cleon pulled in behind her rig. He climbed out of his buggy, sprinted around to the side of the Hostettler buggy where Grace sat, and opened the door. "I went by the restaurant hoping to see you, and when Sarah said you'd already left, I headed down the road, hoping to catch up with you."

Grace offered him a smile, but it appeared to be forced. Wasn't she glad to see him?

"I was hoping I could give you a ride home so we could talk."

Her face blanched, and she drew in a shaky breath. "Talk about what?"

"About us and our upcoming wedding."

"Wh–what about it?"

Cleon squinted as he reached up to rub his chin. "What's wrong, Grace? Why are you acting so *naerfich*?"

"I–I'm not nervous, just tired from working all day."

"She's been acting a bit strange ever since I picked her up in the restaurant parking lot," Ruth put in from the driver's seat. She leaned over and peered around Grace so she was looking right at Cleon. "If you want my opinion, I think my big sister's feeling anxious about the wedding."

"I am not." Grace's forehead wrinkled as she nudged Ruth's arm with her elbow. "If you don't mind, I think I will ride home in Cleon's buggy."

Ruth shrugged. "Makes no never mind to me, so I'll see you at home."

15

As Grace climbed into Cleon's buggy, her stomach twisted as though it were tied in knots. Had Cleon met Gary while he was in town? Could Gary have told him things about her past? Is that why Cleon wanted to speak with her? Maybe he'd decided to call off their wedding.

"Are you okay?" Cleon reached across the seat and touched Grace's arm. "You don't seem like yourself today."

"I'm fine. What did you want to say to me concerning our wedding?"

"I wanted you to know that I lined up a few more honey customers today, and if my business keeps growing, eventually I'll be able to stop farming for my *daed*." Cleon smiled. "Once we're married, you can quit your job."

A feeling of relief swept over Grace. Cleon must not have spoken to Gary or learned anything about her past, or he wouldn't be talking about her quitting her job after they were married.

He picked up the reins and got the horse moving down the road.

Grace pushed her weight against the back of the leather seat and tried to relax. Everything was okay—at least for now.

They rode in silence for a while. Grace listened to the steady *clip-clop* of the horse's hooves as the buggy jostled up and down the hilly road, while she thought about Cleon's attributes. He was strong and quiet, and ever since she'd met him, she'd appreciated his even temper and subtle sense of humor. He was the opposite of Wade, whose witty jesting and boyish charm she'd found appealing. But Wade had never seemed settled, which could have accounted for the fact that he'd worked as a cook for five different restaurants during the time they'd been together.

As they passed an Amish farmer's field, the rustle of corn blowing in the wind brought her thoughts back to the present, and she sighed.

"You sure you're okay?" Worry lines formed above Cleon's brows. "We're almost at your house, and you haven't said more than a few words along the way."

In an effort to keep him from knowing how upset she was over Gary coming to town, Grace forced a smile. "I was thinking how lucky

I am to be betrothed to someone as *wunderbaar* as you."

"I'm the lucky one," he said, reaching over to gently touch her arm. "And it's you who's wonderful, my blessed gift."

If Cleon knew the secret I'm keeping, would he still think I'm wonderful?

Cleon turned the horse to the right and guided it up the graveled driveway past her father's woodworking shop. A few minutes later, her folks' white, two-story house came into view. He pulled back on the reins and halted the horse and buggy in front of the hitching rail near the barn. "Here we are."

"Would you like to stay for supper?" she asked. "I'm sure that, whatever Mom is fixing, we'll have more than enough to go around."

He gave her a dimpled smile, and the flecks of gold in his brown eyes seemed brighter than usual. "I'd be happy to join you for supper. Afterwards, maybe we can sit on the porch awhile and talk about our wedding."

Grace glanced around the kitchen table. Ruth sat to her right, with their younger sister, Martha, on the left. Mom's seat was at the end of the table closest to the stove, Dad sat at the opposite end, and Cleon was seated across the table from Grace and her sisters.

Grace was pleased that she'd invited Cleon to stay for supper. The conversation and joke telling around the table had helped her feel a little more relaxed, and it was nice to see how well Cleon got along with her family. Dad had said several times that he was happy with Grace's choice for a husband, but she wondered what he and Mom would have thought about Wade. She was sure they wouldn't have approved of the way he hopped from job to job, but they might have enjoyed his lighthearted banter and playfulness.

Those qualities of Wade had attracted Grace from the moment he had showed up to interview for a position as cook at the restaurant where she'd worked in Cincinnati. If her parents had known Grace had once been married to an Englisher, she was sure they would have been upset.

"How are things with your woodworking business, Roman?" Cleon asked Grace's father.

Dad reached for the bowl of mashed potatoes and smiled. "Been real busy here lately."

"Guess it's a good thing you hired Luke Friesen as your helper, then."'

"Luke's a good-enough worker," Dad said with a nod. "Unfortunately, the two of us have butted heads a few times."

"About what?" Ruth asked in a tone of concern. She and Luke had only been courting a few months, and Grace was certain her sister didn't want to hear anything negative about him.

Dad shrugged his broad shoulders. "It's nothing for you to worry about, daughter. Luke just needs to learn who the boss is and what I will and won't tolerate."

Ruth opened her mouth as if to say something more, but Martha spoke first.

"Say, Dad, I was thinking that if you're too busy to build a kennel for my dogs, I could see if Luke would have the time."

Dad frowned at Martha and shook his head. "Luke's got plenty of other work he needs to do, but I'll get your kennel built as soon as I can."

"If you need any help with that, I might be able to lend a hand," Cleon spoke up.

"This is a busy time of year, what with the harvest and all," Dad said. "I'm sure between helping your daed and *bruders* on the farm, working with those bees of yours, and trying to get your and Grace's new house done, you've got your hands plenty full right now."

"You've got a point." Cleon glanced over at Grace. "I'm hoping to have our house done by the time we're married, but with everyone being too busy to help me right now, I'm concerned that it won't get done on time."

"Would you rather postpone the wedding?" she asked as a feeling of dread crept into her soul. If she and Cleon didn't get married in December because the house wasn't finished, would they have to wait until next fall? Most Amish couples in their community got married in

October, November, or December when the harvest was done. Grace didn't think she could stand waiting another year to become Cleon's wife.

"Not to worry. You and Cleon can live here after you're married and stay as long as it takes to complete the house." Dad smiled across the table at Mom and gave his full brown beard a couple of pulls. "Isn't that right, Judith?"

"Oh, jah, that won't be a problem at all," she said. "And since their new house is being built on the backside of our property, it will be easy for both you and Cleon to work on it during whatever free time you have."

Grace glanced back at Cleon to gauge his reaction and was relieved when he smiled and said, "That's just fine by me."

Chapter 3

Despite the pleasant evening she'd had with Cleon the night before, Grace awoke the following morning feeling tired and out of sorts. She'd had trouble sleeping, unable to get Gary out of her mind. All during breakfast, she fretted over his sudden appearance, wondering how long he would remain in Holmes County, questioning if he was really a freelance reporter, and worrying that he wouldn't keep quiet about her past. By the time they'd finished eating and Dad had gone out to his shop, Grace had developed a headache. She dreaded going to work for fear of seeing Gary again and hoped no one she knew would have an opportunity to speak with him.

"Are you feeling all right this morning, Grace?" Mom asked as she ambled across the room with a pile of dirty dishes. "You were so quiet during breakfast and hardly ate a thing."

"I didn't sleep well last night, and now I've got a splitting headache, which has my stomach feeling kind of queasy." Grace filled the sink with hot water and took the plates from her mother's hands.

"I'm sorry to hear that," Mom said with a worried expression.

"Why don't you let me wash the dishes?" Ruth suggested, stepping up beside Grace. "Martha can dry while you sit at the table with Mom and have a cup of tea. Maybe by the time we're ready to leave for work, your headache will be gone."

Grace glanced across the room to Martha, who was sweeping the floor. "Would you like me to take over so you can help Ruth with the dishes?"

Martha shook her head. "That's okay. I'm almost done. You'd better do as Ruth suggested and have a cup of tea."

"All right." Grace headed to the stove to get the simmering teakettle, but her mother got there first. As Mom lifted the teakettle, Grace removed two cups from the cupboard, grabbed a box of chamomile tea and a bottle of aspirin, then took a seat at the table.

While Ruth and Martha did the dishes, Martha chattered about her dogs and how she couldn't wait for Heidi, the female sheltie, to give birth to her first batch of puppies. Grace sipped her tea and tried to tune out her sister's prattle but was unsuccessful.

"Can't you think of anything to talk about except those *hund*?" she snapped. "There are more important things in this world than how many *hundlin* Heidi will have and how much money you might make when it's time to sell them."

Martha turned from the cupboard where she'd put the clean plates and blinked. "It may not be important to you, but it is to me. Just because you don't care for dogs so much doesn't mean you have to make my business venture seem like it's of no great concern."

"Sorry for snapping." Grace took another sip of tea. "I'm not feeling like myself this morning."

Martha wrinkled her nose. "You seemed all right last night when Cleon was here. What happened between now and then to make you so edgy?"

"Nothing. I just don't feel so well."

Mom's blue eyes squinted as she reached over and patted Grace's shoulder. "Maybe you should stay home from work today and rest."

"I agree with Mom; you should go back to bed," Ruth put in from her place at the sink.

Grace shook her head. "I don't want to leave the restaurant short-handed." She popped two aspirins into her mouth and washed them down with some tea. "I'm sure I'll be fine once these take effect."

As Ruth and Grace headed toward Berlin in their buggy, Ruth's concern for her sister escalated. Grace hadn't said a word since they'd left home, and when she leaned her head against the back of the seat and closed her eyes, her breathing came out in short little rasps.

"Does your head still hurt?" Ruth asked, reaching over to touch her sister's arm.

"A little."

"Want me to turn the buggy around and take you home?"

"No. I'm sure I'll be fine by the time we reach Berlin."

"Is something bothering you besides the headache?"

"Just feeling tired and a little jittery is all."

"You know what I think you need?"

The buggy jostled as they descended a small hill, and Grace opened her eyes. "What's that?"

"Some fun in the sun before our beautiful fall weather turns cold."

"What kind of fun did you have in mind?"

Ruth smiled. At least she had her sister's full attention. "This Saturday coming, Sadie and I are planning to meet Luke and Toby at the pond for some fishing and a picnic supper. Why don't you and Cleon join us?"

"That sounds like fun, but I have to work this Saturday." Grace yawned and covered her mouth with the palm of her hand. "How are things with you and Luke? Do you think he might be the man you'll marry some day?"

Ruth shrugged as she flicked the reins to get the horse moving up the hill. "We've only been courting a few months, so it's too early to tell."

"But you like him, right?"

"Jah."

"He must like you, too, or he wouldn't ask you to go places with him."

"Maybe he's just being nice because he works for our daed and wants to keep on his good side."

"From what Dad said last night, it doesn't sound like Luke's doing so well keeping on Dad's good side."

Ruth bristled. "I think maybe it's more Dad's fault than Luke's."

"What makes you say that?"

"You know how picky our daed can be. If it's not done his way, then it couldn't possibly be right."

"I guess either Luke will have to learn to keep his opinions to himself or Dad will have to let some of what Luke says roll off his shoulders."

Ruth nodded. "I hope things work out. It's nice to have Luke working nearby, where I can see him more."

Grace lifted her gaze toward the top of the buggy. "Have you forgotten that you're starting your new job this morning? Most days you'll probably be headed for work before Luke arrives at Dad's shop."

Ruth's dark brows drew together. "I hadn't thought of that. I hope he doesn't take an interest in Martha since she's at home all day and he'll see more of her than he does me."

"I don't think you have anything to worry about. Martha doesn't have anything on her mind these days except raising hund."

After donning his overalls, gloves, and veil, Cleon lit some wood chips in the steel smudge pots with leather bellows. He puffed air through the bottom of the smoldering fuel, and it gave off a cool white smoke that quieted the bees so he could take their honey.

As Cleon worked, he thought about supper the night before with Grace and her family. How grateful he was that he'd not only be getting a wonderful wife when he married Grace, but a great family, as well. He seemed to get along well with all of them, especially Roman.

Cleon had just pulled another honeycomb from one of the bee boxes when his younger brother Delbert showed up, announcing that their father was ready to begin harvesting the cornfields and needed Cleon's help.

"Pop's got the help of half the men in our community this morning. He surely doesn't need me," Cleon protested.

Delbert's gray-blue eyes narrowed into tiny slits. "Pop needs all the help he can get, and he pays you to work for him, so you'd better get out to the fields *schnell.*"

"Jah. I'll be there as fast as possible. I need to finish up here first."

"Sure don't see why anyone would want to mess around with a bunch of buzzin' bees." Delbert sauntered off before Cleon could respond.

After Cleon took the honeycombs inside to Mom so she could cut them into small pieces, mash them, and heat them on the stove to extract the honey, he headed out to the cornfields. They should finish by suppertime, and then he hoped to pay Grace a call.

Grace glanced at the clock on the wall above the restaurant's front counter. It was almost three—quitting time for her today. They'd been busier than usual at the restaurant during the breakfast and lunch hours, and she was glad her shift was almost over. Her feet ached something awful. Fortunately, Ruth's hours at the bakeshop today were the same as hers, so she figured her sister would be here soon, ready to head for home.

"Can you take that customer who just came in?" asked Grace's coworker Esther. "I've got an order to put in and one that needs to be picked up."

"Sure."

"Thanks. I appreciate it." Esther nodded in the direction of the booth where a red-haired man sat with his head down as though studying something, and then she hurried off toward the kitchen.

Grace grabbed a menu, an order pad, and a pencil before moving over to the booth. When she arrived, she saw what the man was looking at, and her heartbeat picked up. Several pictures of Amish buggies and Plain People lay on the table, and even before he looked up, she knew the man was Gary. Drawing in a quick breath to help steady her nerves, she placed the menu on the table on top of his pictures.

"Hey, watch it! I don't need any of these prints getting ruined." Gary frowned as he looked up, but his frown quickly faded. "Well, well. I didn't expect to see you again—at least not so soon. Have you worked here long, Gracie?"

Ignoring his question, she pointed to the menu. "Today's special is pork chops and sauerkraut."

He wrinkled his nose. "Not one of my favorite dishes, but that's okay because it's too early to be thinking about supper. I just came in to take a load off my feet and go over these prints before I send them off to a publisher."

"So you don't want to order anything?"

"I didn't say that." He picked up the menu, thumbed through it quickly, and handed it back to her. "I'll have a cup of coffee and a hunk of pie."

"What kind of pie?"

"Why don't you surprise me?"

Grace clutched the edge of her apron and gritted her teeth. The man was impossible! "I'm not allowed to choose for the customer. You need to pick something yourself."

He drummed his fingers along the edge of the table in an irritating *tat-a-tat-tat*. "How about a slice of apple? Have you got any of that?"

"I believe so." She turned to go, but he reached out and snagged her wrist, holding it firmly with his cold fingers. "Don't run off. I'd like to talk to you a minute—get caught up on each other's lives, maybe reminisce about our dating days."

She tried to pull away, but he held firm as his thumb brushed her arm in a slow, deliberate movement. "Those were fun days we had together. Don't you miss 'em, Gracie?"

Grace's pulse pounded in her temples. She thought she'd resolved her guilty feelings for leaving the Amish faith for a time and keeping her past a secret from her family, but now, with Gary looking at her with such intensity, guilt rushed back like raging floodwaters. If only she'd felt free to tell her parents the truth about where she'd been living and what had transpired during her rumschpringe years.

But she was certain they wouldn't have understood, especially Dad, who had mentioned several times how angry he was about his only sister leaving the Amish faith and marrying an English man, then never contacting her family again. Just the mention of anyone leaving the faith, whether they'd joined the church or not, caused her father to become irritable for days. If he had known the details of Grace's rumschpringe, he would have been angry with her, even though she hadn't been a church member when she'd left home.

"Gracie, did you hear what I said?" Gary asked, releasing his grip on her arm.

She took a step back and nodded. "I'll turn in your order, and one of the other waitresses will bring it to you in a few minutes."

His forehead creased. "I thought you were my waitress."

"My shift is almost over. I'm just covering for someone who's too busy to wait on you right now."

"If you'll be off duty soon, why don't you have a seat, and we can have a cup of coffee together." He nodded at the bench across from him, apparently not the least bit put off by her cold reception. Of course, he never had known when to take no for an answer.

"I can't. My sister will be here to pick me up soon. Besides, I'm betrothed, and it wouldn't look right for me to be seen having coffee with another man—especially one who isn't part of the Amish faith." Grace winced. She couldn't believe she'd blurted out that she was engaged to be married.

He shook his head. "Gracie, Gracie, Gracie, you sound like such a puritan. Whatever happened to the fun-loving, spunky little gal I used to date?"

"I'm not going through rumschpringe anymore," she said through tight lips. "I've been baptized, have joined the Amish church, and—"

"Yeah, I figured that much. You wouldn't be dressed in those plain clothes if you hadn't gone Amish again." He stared at Grace so hard it made her skin crawl. "The last time I heard from Wade, he said the two of you were happily married. What happened? Did he get bored with his Plain little wife and leave you for some other woman?"

Grace's ears burned, and the heat spread quickly to her face. "Wade is dead."

His face blanched. "Really?"

She nodded.

"How'd it happen?"

"One foggy night, an oncoming truck came into Wade's lane when he was on his way home from work." She paused to swallow around the lump lodged in her throat. "I figured you would've heard about it."

"I moved to Indianapolis soon after you and Wade got married." He shook his head. "I'm sorry for your loss, Grace."

She studied his face, wondering if Gary felt any compassion for her. When she'd been dating him, he'd never said he was sorry for anything.

"So after Wade died, you moved back here and joined the Amish church?"

She nodded. *Does Gary know anything else about my life? Does he know—*

She leaned closer to the table. "Promise you won't say anything to anyone about me being married to Wade?"

He held up his hand. "As I told you the other day, I'm working freelance, and I came to Holmes County to take some pictures and get a few good stories about the Amish here, not tell tales about an old flame."

Grace wanted to believe him, and she hoped he was telling the truth. But Gary had never been trustworthy, and she wasn't sure she could believe anything he said. She didn't even know if he was telling the truth about being a reporter. She was about to question him when she caught sight of Ruth entering the restaurant. "My ride's here. I have to go."

She pivoted away from the table and rushed over to Esther, handing her the order pad. "That customer you asked me to wait on wants some apple pie and a cup of coffee. My sister's here, so I've got to go."

"No problem. I'll take care of it right away." Esther's forehead wrinkled. "Are you okay, Grace? Your face is flushed, and you're sweating like it's a hot summer day."

"I'm fine—just tired and hot from working all day. See you tomorrow, Esther." Grace hurried off before her coworker could comment. She needed to get away from Gary and his probing blue eyes. She needed to go home where she felt safe.

Chapter 4

"What's that you're working on?"

Martha looked up from her embroidery work and smiled at her mother, who leaned over the kitchen table with a curious expression. "I'm making a sampler to give Grace as a wedding present. I'll include her and Cleon's names and leave enough room so Grace can add the names of the children they'll have someday."

Mom's blue eyes twinkled like fireflies in the heat of summer. "I'm sure they'll appreciate such a thoughtful gift."

"I considered giving them one of Heidi's puppies because they'll be born soon and should be weaned in plenty of time for the wedding." Martha shrugged. "Since Grace isn't much of an animal lover, I figured she probably wouldn't welcome it."

"I think you're right about that." Mom pulled out a chair beside Martha and sat down. "In all your sister's twenty-four years, she's never had a pet." She frowned. "At least, not to my knowledge. No telling what she did when she was gone those two years during her rumschpringe."

Martha nodded. Her sister's running-around days were not a topic for discussion. Martha had been twelve and Ruth fifteen when Grace left home for a time. Whenever Martha and Ruth were around, Mom and Dad had avoided the subject of their strong-willed daughter and her desire to try out the English way of life. Martha figured her folks probably worried that their other two daughters might follow in their older sister's footsteps, so the less said the better regarding Grace's rumschpringe.

When Grace finally came to her senses and returned home, she was welcomed without question, just like the prodigal son in the Bible had been. Of course, things might have been different if Grace had been a member of the Amish church at the time. But since she hadn't been baptized or joined the faith before she'd gone English, the community didn't shun her, and she didn't need to confess when she returned home.

"Would you like a cup of hot cider or some lemonade?" Mom asked, pushing Martha's thoughts to the back of her mind.

Martha's mouth watered as she thought about the delicious apple cider Dad made every fall. "Jah, sure. Some cider would be real nice."

Mom pushed her chair aside and headed to their propane-operated refrigerator. She withdrew a jug of cider and ambled back across the room, where she poured some of the amber-colored liquid into a kettle and set it on the stove to heat. "Want some crackers and cheese to go with the cider?"

"I'd better not. Don't want to fill up on snacks now and be too full to eat lunch."

"Guess I'll just stick to hot cider, too." A few minutes later, Mom placed a mug of cider in front of Martha. "Here you go. Enjoy," she said before moving over to the counter across the room.

"Aren't you going to join me?"

"I'll drink mine while I make your daed a sandwich. It'll be time for lunch soon, so I'll take it out to his woodworking shop when I'm done."

"Won't Dad be coming up to the house to eat?" Martha asked as she threaded her needle with rose-colored thread.

"He's got a backload of work and doesn't want to take the time for a big meal at noon." Mom opened the breadbox and pulled out a loaf of whole-wheat bread she'd made. "Even with Luke helping him, he's still way behind."

Martha set her embroidery aside and reached for her mug. The tantalizing scent of apple drifted up as a curl of steam rose from the hot cider. She took a sip and smacked her lips. "Umm. . .this is sure good."

"Jah. Your daed makes some of the best apple cider around."

"Say, Mom, I was wondering if you've noticed anything different about Grace lately."

"Different in what way?"

"Ever since she came home from work on Monday, she's been acting kind of odd—like she's off in her own little world or might be worried about something."

Mom shuffled back to the refrigerator, this time removing a package of trail bologna, a head of lettuce, and a jar of mayonnaise. "Maybe she's just tired. Working as a waitress and being on my feet all day would tucker me out."

Martha took another sip of cider. "When we headed for bed last night, I asked Grace if everything was okay."

"What'd she say?"

"Said things were fine and dandy."

Mom was on the other side of the room again, slathering mayonnaise on four slices of bread. "Then they probably are."

Martha shrugged and pushed her chair aside. "Think I'll head out to the barn and check on Heidi. Her time's getting close, and I want to be sure everything goes all right when she gives birth to those pups."

"Jah." Mom reached for the package of bologna. "I'll be in the shop with your daed for a while, in case you need me for anything."

"Would you mind making a delivery for me?" Roman asked Luke. "I promised to have those tables and chairs ready for Steven Bates this week. He's always been a picky customer, and I need to make good on that promise."

Luke pushed some dark hair off his forehead and wiped the sweat away with the back of his hand. "Jah, sure. I can do that right now if ya like."

"That's fine, but don't take too long getting there." Roman grimaced as he rubbed at a kink in his lower back. "And don't dillydally on the way back like you did on the last delivery you made."

Luke shrugged. "Just didn't see any need to run the horse too hard."

"Jah, well, let's get that furniture loaded, and you can be on your way."

Half an hour later with the furniture placed in the back of the wagon, Luke headed down the road, and Roman resumed work on a set of kitchen cabinets he was making for their bishop, Noah King. He'd just started sanding the doors when a gray-haired, middle-aged English man stepped into the shop, holding a notebook.

"Are you the owner of this place?" the man asked.

Roman nodded. "I am."

"Do you own just the woodworking shop or the house and land it sets on, too?"

"Own it all—fifty acres, to be exact."

The man thrust out his hand. "My name's Bill Collins, and I'm scouting out some land in the area, hoping to buy several acres to develop over time."

Ignoring the man's offered handshake, Roman squinted. "Develop?"

"That's right. I want to build a tract of new homes, and I'm also thinking of putting in a golf course, so I—"

"My land's not for sale."

Mr. Collins rubbed his chin as he leaned against Roman's desk. "Come now, Mr. Hostettler—"

"You know my name?"

"The sign on your shop says 'HOSTETTLER'S WOODWORKING.' "

Roman gave a curt nod.

"Anyway, I was hoping you'd be interested in hearing what I have to say. I'm prepared to offer you a decent price for your land."

"Not interested."

"Oh, but if you'll just give me a chance to—"

"One of my neighbors wanted to buy my land once, but I said no, so I'm sure not going to sell it to you."

"Mr. Hostettler, I assure you—"

The door opened again. Judith entered the room carrying a jug of cider and Roman's lunch pail in her hands.

He breathed a sigh of relief, glad for the interruption.

"I know it's not quite noon, but I brought your lunch," she said, offering him a pleasant smile. "Where do you want me to set it?"

"On my desk—if you can find the room, that is." He nodded when Judith pushed some papers aside and set the lunch pail down.

She glanced at the land developer, who hovered near the desk as though he was looking for something. "I hope I'm not interrupting anything," she said.

The man opened his mouth as if to comment, but Roman spoke first. "You're not interrupting a thing. Mr. Collins is on his way out."

"Give some consideration to what I said. I'll drop by again soon and see if you're ready to hear my offer." With that, Bill Collins turned and sauntered out the door.

"What was that all about?" Judith asked when the door clicked shut.

Roman moved away from the cabinets he'd been sanding. "The fellow wanted to buy our land."

Her eyes widened. "Whatever for?"

"Said something about wanting to build a bunch of houses and a golf course, of all things." He flicked some sawdust off his trousers. "I told him I wasn't interested in selling, and if he comes back, I'll tell him the same."

"I would hope so." Judith nodded toward the door. "On my way down from the house, I saw Luke heading out with a wagonload of furniture." She sat in the chair behind Roman's desk. "Is he making a delivery for you?"

"Jah. He's taking a table and some chairs over to Steven Bates's place. He'd better not be late getting back to the shop like he was last time." Roman shook his head. "That young fellow's a fair enough worker, but he's got a mind of his own. Makes me wonder how things are going with him and Ruth since they've begun courting."

"I'm sure they're going fine, or Ruth would have said something. She's not one to keep her feelings bottled up the way Grace has always done."

Roman grunted in reply and moved over to the desk. He had no desire to discuss their oldest daughter and her refusal to talk about things. In many ways, Grace reminded him of his sister, Rosemary, only Grace had finally returned home where she belonged. Rosemary hadn't.

"I'm glad your business is doing so well," Judith said, leaning her elbows on the desk and staring up at him. "When that English fellow John Peterson moved into the area a few months ago and opened a woodworking shop, I was afraid you might lose some of your customers to him."

Roman shook his head. "Nope. Hasn't seemed to bother my business one iota." He lifted the lid of his lunch pail and peered inside. "What kind of sandwich did you make today?"

"Trail bologna and baby Swiss cheese, and I made two in case you're really hungry. I put some of your favorite double crunch cookies in there, as well."

He smacked his lips. "You spoil me, *fraa*."

"That's the part I enjoy the most about being your wife." She grinned and pushed back the chair. "Guess I should head up to the house and let you eat your lunch in peace."

"Why don't you stay awhile and visit? I'd enjoy the company." He grabbed one of his wooden stools and pulled it over to the desk. "What's our youngest daughter up to today? Has she been combing through the ads in the newspaper to see if anymore hund are for sale?"

Judith sighed. "I wish Martha would forget about raising dogs and find herself a real job, like our other two girls have done."

"Let me pray, and then we'll talk about it."

Judith nodded and bowed her head, and Roman did the same. After a few seconds of silent prayer, he opened his eyes and reached into the lunch pail to retrieve one of the sandwiches. "I think we should give Martha the chance to see if she can succeed in her business venture, don't you?"

"I suppose."

He pulled out the second sandwich and handed it to her. "I don't really need two of these, so if you haven't eaten already, you may as well join me."

"*Danki*. I haven't eaten yet."

They sat in companionable silence for a time.

"Martha's concerned that something might be bothering Grace," Judith said, breaking the silence. "Have you noticed anything unusual about the way she's been acting lately?"

Roman squinted as he contemplated her question. "Well, she didn't have a whole lot to say during supper last night, but as you know, Grace is often moody and quiet."

Judith gave a slow nod. "Leastways, she has been since she returned to Holmes County four years ago."

"Maybe she's just feeling naerfich about her upcoming wedding."

"I suppose she could be nervous." She inhaled deeply and released a quick breath, causing the narrow ties of her white *kapp* to flutter. "I'll keep an eye on things, and if I notice her getting cold feet, I'll have a little talk with her."

Roman snapped his lunch pail shut and handed it to her. "Sounds like a good idea. It took Grace some time to settle down and find a good man, so we wouldn't want her to change her mind about marrying Cleon at this late date."

Judith's head moved slowly from side to side. "No, we surely wouldn't."

Chapter 5

The following day as Grace approached the booth where one of her customers sat, she glanced out the window and caught sight of Gary standing on the sidewalk in front of the gift store across the street, talking to Cleon. She flinched. Maybe Gary knew she planned to marry Cleon. He might be trying to turn Cleon against her by spilling her secrets. Maybe she wouldn't marry Cleon in two months, after all.

Grace gripped the water pitcher in her hands so tightly that her fingers turned numb. She ordered her runaway heart to be still. She was doing it again—worrying about things that probably hadn't happened. Knowing Gary, he was most likely making small talk with anyone willing to listen, the way he used to do when they were teenagers. Or maybe Cleon had stopped to ask if Gary knew the time. He often did that whenever he'd forgotten his pocket watch.

Grace felt relief when Cleon finally turned and walked away. The water in the pitcher sloshed as she hurried across the room, knowing she needed to wait on the young English couple who had taken a seat in her section of the restaurant. *I'm sure it was nothing to fret about,* she told herself. *Oh, I pray it was nothing.*

Grace had just finished taking the English couple's order when she spotted Cleon entering the restaurant. He took a seat in a booth near the front door, which was in her section.

When she hurried over to the booth, he looked up at her, his dark eyes crinkling at the corners as he smiled. "It's good to see you, Grace."

35

"It. . .it's good to see you, too."

"I came to town to deliver some honey, and I've also been seeking some new outlets for the beeswax candles Mom and my sister Carolyn make."

"I see." Grace shifted her weight from one foot to the other, wondering how to ask why Cleon had been talking to Gary without arousing Cleon's suspicion.

"Will you be getting off work anytime soon?" he questioned.

"In another half hour."

"That's good, because I'd like to treat you to a late lunch if you haven't already eaten."

"No, I haven't." She tapped her pencil against the order pad in her hand. "Isn't that why you're here—to eat lunch?"

He chuckled and shook his head so hard some of his dark hair fell across his forehead. "I'm done with business for the day now, so I figured I'd come in here, drink a cup of coffee, and wait for you."

"Since this is Saturday and Ruth has the day off, I rode my bike into town, rather than driving one of our buggies. Guess if I leave it parked out behind the restaurant I can pick it up after we're done eating. Unless of course, you'd like to stay here for lunch."

"You eat here enough, don't you think?"

"Guess that's true," she said with a nod.

"Since I drove my larger market buggy today, I can put your bike in the back and give you a ride home after lunch. How's that sound?"

"That's fine with me." At least Cleon hadn't mentioned his conversation with Gary. If Gary had said anything about knowing Grace, she was sure Cleon would have said so by now.

"Where would you like to eat?" he asked, reaching out to touch her gently on the arm.

She smiled. "Why don't you choose?"

"How about the Farmstead Restaurant? Haven't eaten there in a while, and they serve some real tasty Dutch apple pie."

She nodded at the menu lying before him. "We have that dessert here, too."

"Nothing against the food here," he said in a whisper, "but in my opinion, nobody serves a better Dutch apple pie than the Farmstead."

"All right, the Farmstead it is." Grace glanced out the window and caught sight of a man across the street standing near Java Joe's Coffee Bar. Thinking it might be Gary, she stopped talking to take another look.

"What are you staring at?" Cleon asked, turning toward the window.

"Oh, nothing much." Relieved to see that the man wasn't Gary, she focused her attention on Cleon again. "I. . .uh. . .saw you talking to an English man with red hair a while ago. I'm curious what he said to you."

"Said he's a freelance photographer and reporter and that he sends his work into some magazines and other publications. From what I gathered, he's lookin' to write some stories about the Amish in our area." Cleon grimaced. "He cornered me the other day, wanting me to answer some questions, but I said no. Then he asked again today, and I told him the same thing. Wouldn't let him take my picture, either."

"He didn't say anything else?"

Cleon shook his head. "After I turned down his offer to interview me, he headed on down the street, snapping pictures of some buggies that were passing by."

Grace sighed. If Gary found out she was betrothed to Cleon, he might cause trouble. And if Cleon found out she had once dated Gary, she would face some serious questions.

"Why so concerned about this picture-taking fellow? Has he been bothering you or some of the others who work here?" Cleon asked with squinted eyes.

"Not really. I—I just know how bold some reporters can be with their fancy cameras, tape recorders, and nosey questions. It will be good when he's gone." Grace thought about the day when Gary had taken her picture without her permission. She didn't see the need to mention it to Cleon, though. She would have to admit that she'd spoken with Gary, and more questions would likely follow. She hoped Gary wouldn't use that picture in any of his magazine articles, for she didn't want anyone to think she had willingly posed for it.

"I'll take that cup of coffee now if you're not too busy."

Grace jerked her attention back to Cleon. "Oh, sorry. I'll see to it right away."

He touched her hand in such a gentle way that it caused shivers to spiral up her arm. "No hurry. I've got a whole half hour to wait until you get off work."

She smiled and hurried off, thinking how fortunate she was to be betrothed to someone as kind and good-natured as Cleon. A lot of men weren't so easygoing. Some, like Gary, could be downright mean.

"I'm thankful for the beautiful fall weather we're having, and in my opinion, this is the perfect spot to have our picnic," Ruth commented to her friend Sadie Esh as the two of them stepped down from their buggies.

"Jah. I've enjoyed visiting the ponds in our area ever since I was a girl." Sadie's luminous blue eyes twinkled in the sunlight, making Ruth wish she'd been blessed with blue eyes instead of brown. "Sure hope the fellows show up soon. Since they like to fish so much, I figured they would have been here by now."

"Like as not, they'll be here soon." Ruth reached into her buggy and withdrew the wicker basket she had packed with a variety of picnic foods. "I don't know about Toby, but I'm pretty sure the reason Luke's not here yet is because Dad must have asked him to work later than they'd planned. They've been really busy at the woodworking shop these past few weeks."

Sadie pulled a quilt from the under the backseat of the buggy. "It's good that your daed's business is doing so well. That must be why he hired Luke to help him, huh?"

"I suppose." Ruth's sneakers squished through a pile of red and gold leaves as she made her way toward the pond. "How about Toby? Is he working hard at the lumber store?"

"Toby's always been a hard worker, but he doesn't work at his job on Saturdays. I'm thinking he may have had some chores to do at home."

Ruth set the picnic basket on the ground, and as soon as they had the quilt spread out, they both took seats. "It won't be long before winter will be upon us, so we'd better enjoy this sunshine while we can," she said as she closed her eyes and let the sun's warming rays seep into her upturned face. Come next summer, she might not appreciate the heat so much, but right now she felt as if she could spend the rest of the day sitting here, soaking up the sun, listening to the birds chirp, and smelling the aroma of drying wheat shafts from the fields not far from their picnic spot.

"Too bad Grace and Cleon weren't free to join us."

"I did ask, but that was before I realized Grace had to work today." Ruth smiled. "I'm glad I'm not expected to work any Saturdays with my new job."

"Speaking of the new job, are you happy working at the bakeshop?"

Ruth opened her eyes and glanced over at her friend, who sat with her knees bent and her hands clasped around the skirt of her long blue dress. "I like working there, and it's nice that the owners of the bakeshop have a small corral behind the shop where I can keep my horse and buggy." She patted her stomach. "The only drawback is that it's tempting to sample some of the pastries, cookies, and pies. Thanks to you, I'll probably gain weight just from looking at those fattening pastries."

Sadie plucked a blade of grass and twirled it around her fingers. "You've been thin as a reed ever since I've known you, so I don't think you have anything to worry about."

"Jah, well, if I can't control my cravings, I'll have you to blame for getting me the job."

The nicker of a horse followed by the rumble of buggy wheels interrupted their conversation. Ruth turned. Toby King, the bishop's youngest son, hopped down from his buggy and secured his horse to a tree. "At least one of our fellows is finally here."

Sadie jumped up and scurried over to greet Toby, but Ruth stayed seated on the quilt. A few minutes later, the giggling young couple joined her.

"Where's your fishing pole, Toby?" Ruth asked. "I thought you'd have it with you."

Toby motioned to his buggy. "Left it in there, figuring we'd eat before we fished." He looked around. "Say, where's Luke? He passed me on the road a couple miles back, and I figured he would beat me here."

"Luke hasn't shown up yet." Ruth's forehead wrinkled. "Are you sure it was him?"

Toby took a seat on the grass, removed his straw hat, and plunked it over one knee. "I know it was him because he was drivin' an open buggy. I saw his face plain as day, uh-huh." He pulled his fingers through the sides of his reddish-blond hair as his eyebrows furrowed. "This makes no sense to me."

"Don't tell me he suddenly disappeared." Sadie poked Toby's arm. "Maybe an *auslenner* from outer space came down and snatched Luke away."

Toby snickered and reached out to tweak her freckled nose. "What would you know of aliens and outer space?"

"I know what I've read in the newspaper."

He wiggled his fingers in front of Sadie's face. "Maybe Luke's learned how to make himself invisible, like one of those magicians I saw at the county fair last fall."

"You two can make all the jokes you want, but I'm getting concerned." Ruth pushed herself to her feet. Normally, she didn't fret over things, but Luke should have arrived long ago, and she couldn't help but be a little worried.

Sadie stared up at her with a curious expression. "Where are you going?"

"I think we should look for Luke. He could have been in an accident."

Toby shook his head. "Don't ya think I would have seen his rig if it had been smashed up or lying by the side of the road?"

"His buggy could have ended up in the bushes. Maybe you missed seeing it," Sadie said. "I think Ruth's right. We should search for Luke."

The thought of Luke having been involved in an accident sent a pang of trepidation through Ruth. As she hurried to her buggy, she heard Sadie's quick footsteps right behind her.

"Wait up," Toby called. "We can take my rig." He untied his horse, backed him away from the tree, and hitched him to the buggy. He was about to help the girls inside when Luke's horse and open buggy whipped into the clearing, kicking up a cloud of dust.

"Whoa! Hold up there, Gid!" Luke called, pulling back on the reins.

The horse came to an abrupt stop, and Luke hopped down from the buggy. His cheeks were quite red, and his straw hat was slightly askew. Ruth rushed toward him, but before she could get a word out, Toby sprinted over to Luke and hollered, "Where have you been? You had us all worried."

"I had to work a little later than I'd planned." Luke glanced over at Ruth and grimaced. "Sorry if I caused you to worry."

"I'm just glad you're okay," she said, smiling in return. "I was afraid you might have been in an accident or something."

Luke opened his mouth as if to say something, but Toby cut him off. "As I'm sure you must know, you passed me on the way over here, so you should have been ahead of me, not ten minutes behind." He put his hand on Sadie's shoulder. "*Mei aldi* thought you'd been snatched into the outer limits by some evil space invader."

Sadie slapped his hand away. "Your girlfriend was only kidding, and you know it."

Luke shifted from one foot to the other, looking as if he'd been caught in the middle of something he didn't want anyone to know about. "I. . .uh. . .had one stop I needed to make," he mumbled.

"What stop was that? There ain't no places to stop between here and where you passed me on the road." Toby's cheeks flamed, and Ruth was sure it wasn't caused by the warm fall weather.

"Just had to check on something in the woods, that's all."

Toby's dark eyebrows lifted. "Where was your buggy while you were in the woods, huh?"

"I pulled it off the road behind some bushes."

"What were you doing in the woods?" Toby persisted.

"That's none of your nosey beeswax." Luke unhitched his horse and led him over to a tree—the same one Toby's had been tied to earlier. Then he marched back to his buggy, reached inside, and grabbed his fishing pole. "Are we gonna stand around all day yammering about nothing, or did we come here to fish?"

Feeling the need to smooth things over, Ruth stepped up to Luke and touched his arm. "We thought maybe we'd eat first, if that's all right with you."

Toby grunted. "Shouldn't matter what he thinks. He got here late and won't tell us where he was or what he was doin'. As far as I'm concerned, he's got no say in what we do now. I vote we eat first and then fish. Everyone in agreement, raise your right hand."

Sadie's hand popped up, and she looked over at Ruth.

Ruth couldn't believe how bossy Toby was being, and she glanced at Luke to get his reaction. He shrugged, so she lifted her hand, too.

"It's unanimous, uh-huh," Toby said with a nod. "Now let's eat ourselves full!"

Toby and Sadie led the way back to the quilt, and Ruth and Luke followed. Ruth was glad Luke had finally arrived, but she had a niggling feeling that something was amiss. But Luke pushed her doubts aside when he leaned close to her ear and whispered, "Say, what'd ya bring to eat? I'm starving."

"I had a good time with your folks when I ate supper at your place the other night, but it's sure nice having this time alone with you," Cleon said as he leaned forward in his seat across from Grace in a booth at the Farmstead Restaurant.

She nodded and smiled. "I'm enjoying it, too."

"If I can finish building our house in the next couple of months, we can be alone every night once we're married."

"True, but even if you're not able to get it done, I'm sure my family will respect our privacy and give us time alone."

He reached for her hand. "I can't wait to make you my wife, Gracie."

Grace pulled her hand back, feeling like she'd been stung by a bee. In all the time she'd known Cleon, he'd never once called her Gracie.

"What's the matter?" His dark eyebrows furrowed. "Did I say something wrong?"

"What made you call me 'Gracie'?" she squeaked.

He grinned at her. "It just popped into my head, so I said it, that's all. Hasn't anyone ever called you Gracie as a nickname before?"

Only Gary, she thought ruefully. *And because of it, I've never liked the name.* "I'd rather you not use it."

He shrugged. "Okay."

Grace's hands shook as she reached for the glass of water the waitress had placed on the table soon after they were seated. When she lifted the cold glass, she lost her grip, and the glass tipped over, splashing water all over the front of Cleon's shirt.

"I–I'm so sorry." She grabbed her napkin off the table and handed it to Cleon. "Will you forgive me for being such a *dappich dummkopp*?"

"You're not a clumsy dunce," he said with a shake of his head. "It was just an accident, and there's nothing to forgive."

Grace sat in stunned silence, watching as Cleon blotted the water on his shirt, the whole time smiling at her as though she'd done nothing wrong. This little episode had once again reminded her of what a kind, forgiving spirit he had, and it made her wonder if she'd been foolish to withhold the truth from him about her past. Maybe she could tell him her secret without any consequences or judgmental accusations. It might be that their relationship would be strengthened if Cleon knew the truth. Then again, if he didn't respond well to Grace's story, her world would shatter. While Cleon might have a forgiving spirit over a glass of water being splashed on his clothes, it didn't guarantee he would forgive something as big as her secret.

When Cleon excused himself to go to the men's room in order to better dry the front of his shirt, Grace leaned back in her seat and closed her eyes as she gave the matter careful consideration. She wouldn't risk spoiling the afternoon by revealing her secret to Cleon, but perhaps the next time they were together, she would find the courage to tell him the truth.

Chapter 6

I'm going out to the barn to check on Heidi," Martha called to her mother early Monday morning. She pushed an errant strand of chocolate-colored hair away from her face, where it had worked its way loose from her bun, and rushed out the back door.

"Be back in time for lunch." Judith glanced over at Betty Friesen, who sat at her kitchen table sharing a cup of tea, and clicked her tongue against the roof of her mouth. "That girl's in such a hurry to get outside that I doubt she even heard what I said."

"My Luke's the same way. He's always got his mind on something other than what I'm saying." Betty chuckled. "Maybe we should get the two of them together since they seem to have that in common."

Judith reached for her cup and took a drink. "I don't think Martha's interested in finding herself a boyfriend right now. All she talks about is raising puppies. Besides, from what I understand, Luke and Ruth have been seeing each other." She paused, wondering if she'd shared information that Betty didn't yet know.

Betty nodded. "I did hear that Luke had gone fishing on Saturday with Ruth and a couple of their friends, but I wasn't sure if that meant they were actually courting."

"As far as I can tell, they are."

"I don't know why, but Luke's been kind of moody lately. With yesterday being an off-Sunday from preaching, I figured he would want to do some visiting with the rest of his family." Betty frowned. Deep wrinkles etched her forehead. "But all Luke wanted to do was laze around in the hayloft all day. I hope it won't be long before he decides to get baptized and joins the church. Maybe once he does, he'll be ready to settle down to marriage."

Judith grimaced. She hoped Ruth wouldn't think about marrying Luke if he had a moody disposition and seemed lazy at home, but she thought it best not to mention that to Betty. Luke had only been courting Ruth a few months, and as far as she knew, things weren't serious between them.

"Getting back to Martha," Betty said, "someday things will change for her, and she'll want to raise *kinner* instead of hundlin."

"I hope you're right, but at the moment, my youngest daughter doesn't have time to think about children. She has only one thought on her mind: getting her kennel business going."

"Guess you and your oldest daughter must be busy getting things ready for her upcoming marriage to Cleon Schrock, jah?"

Judith nodded. "We'll be shopping for the material for Grace's dress soon."

"She must be excited."

"I believe so, but I think she's also kind of naerfich about things. The last couple of days, she hasn't been acting quite right."

"*Ach*, she'll be fine once they tie the knot."

"I'm sure you're right. She and Cleon are so much in love, things are bound to work well for them once they're married."

Betty reached over and snatched an oatmeal cookie from the plate in the center of the table. "Say, did you hear about the outhouses that got overturned at a couple of schoolhouses up near Kidron?"

"Can't say that I did."

Betty ate the cookie and washed it down with some tea, then leaned forward, resting her elbows on the table. "My Elam told me about it. Said he read it in the newspaper this morning."

"Did your husband give you any details?"

"Said it must have happened sometime during the night because the teachers discovered the damage when they got to their schoolhouses the next morning." Betty shook her head. "It was probably some rowdy English fellows out for a good time."

"Or it could have been Amish boys kicking up their heels during their rumschpringe."

"Maybe so, but they should know better."

Judith took a cookie and dipped it into her cup of tea, then popped it into her mouth, savoring the sweetness. "Seems like there's always something going on, either with English kids playing pranks or Amish fellows sowing their wild oats."

"Sure am glad none of my kinner ever got involved in anything like that."

Judith bit back a reply. If Betty wanted to believe none of her eight boys had ever pulled any pranks, that was her right. Judith was just thankful the good Lord had given her only girls. Grace had been the only one of her daughters to really experience rumschpringe, but thankfully, she'd come back home after living a couple of years in the English world and had settled right down.

Martha stepped into the barn and drew in a deep breath. Dad must have cleaned the horse stalls that morning, because they smelled of clean, sweet hay.

She hurried to the back of the building where she'd made a bed from a wooden crate for her female sheltie and the pups she would give birth to soon. Fritz, the male sheltie she'd bought for breeding purposes, was kept in an empty stall on the other side of the barn during the night and outside on a rope during the day. Eventually, Dad would get around to building a kennel with separate sections for her to house each of her dogs, but in the meantime, the empty barn stalls would have to do.

"Here, Heidi. Where are you, girl?" Martha called when she discovered that the dog wasn't in the crate. Since the sheltie wasn't due to have her pups for a few more days, Martha figured she was probably outside somewhere or had found herself another place to take a nap. If the animal had been nearby, surely she would have answered Martha's call.

Martha headed to the other side of the barn and had just touched the door handle when it swished open. Luke stepped in.

"Whoa! Didn't think anyone would be standing inside the door. We could've bumped heads."

She took a step back. "I—I didn't expect to find you standing there, either."

"Just came to get a couple of cardboard boxes your daed needs. He said I'd find some stacked inside one of the empty horse stalls."

"I can show you the place if you like," Martha offered.

He jiggled his eyebrows playfully. "Might be a good idea. I could get lost in this old barn."

"*Puh!* You're such a tease. I don't know how my sister puts up with you." She turned on her heels and led the way to the horse stalls.

"Ruth tends to be a little more serious than I am," Luke said. "I make her laugh, and she helps me remember that life isn't a dish full of strawberry ice cream. That gives us a healthy balance, wouldn't ya say?"

"I guess it does."

"Last Saturday when Ruth and I met Toby and Sadie for a picnic at the pond, I had them all laughing with my new fishing pole trick."

"What trick was that?" she asked over her shoulder.

"I wasn't paying close enough attention to what I was doing and ended up snagging the top of Ruth's kapp while I was trying to cast my line into the water. Sure got razzed about that little mistake from Toby and Sadie."

Martha chuckled as she stepped into the unused horse stall and lit the gas lamp hanging from the rafters. "All kinds of things are stashed in here, including what you came for." She motioned to the cardboard boxes stacked against one wall.

"Looks like a couple of 'em are just the size I'm needing." Luke reached for the boxes, then halted. "Hey! What's this?"

"What's what?" Martha peered around his outstretched arm and gasped. "Heidi! Why she's gone and had her hundlin inside that old box."

Luke nodded. "That's what it looks like all right."

"I guess she didn't care much for the wooden crate I fixed up for her on the other side of the barn."

"Dogs are like humans in some ways," he said in a tone too serious for someone like Luke. "They're as picky about their birthing boxes as we are about choosin' our mates."

Martha wasn't sure how to respond since she hadn't given much thought to choosing a mate. Truth was, she didn't have a whole lot on her mind these days except getting her kennel business going. "I suppose it would be best to just leave her be since she's picked this place and seems nicely settled in."

He nodded and stared into the box. "How many pups does she have in there, can ya tell?"

Knowing it wouldn't be a good idea to touch any of the puppies yet, Martha squinted and tried to count each little blob. That's what she thought they looked like, too—squirming, squealing blobs with tiny pink noses. "I think there are five," she announced. "Could be more scrunched in there, though."

"Sure are noisy little critters. Are you planning to keep any?"

She nodded. "I might keep one for breeding purposes, but I'll sell the rest because I need the money."

He tipped his head as though studying her. "You're quite the businesswoman, aren't you?"

"I'm trying to be." Martha moved away from the box. "Guess I'll head back inside and see if Mom needs my help getting lunch on the table. Heidi would probably like to be left alone with her brood, anyway."

Luke reached for two of the empty boxes. "I'd better get back to your daed's shop before the impatient fellow comes looking for me."

With no comment on her father's impatience, Martha turned down the gas lantern and followed Luke out the door. She felt good knowing that Heidi had given birth to a litter of pups. At last, she was well on her way to what she hoped would be a successful business venture.

Roman looked up from the paperwork he was doing when Luke stepped into the shop carrying two cardboard boxes. "Took ya long enough," he grumbled. "Couldn't you find the stall I told you about?"

"Found it just fine." Luke set the boxes on the floor. "Martha and I discovered that her sheltie had given birth to five hundlin in a cardboard box inside the stall."

"I'll bet my daughter was happy about that. She didn't think the pups would be born for a couple more days." Roman nodded toward a stack of finished cabinets sitting along one wall. "The set of cabinets Steven Bates ordered for his wife's birthday are ready to go, so I'd like you to deliver them today."

"Sure, I can do that. Want me to go now or wait 'til after lunch?"

"Now would be better. You can eat lunch when you get back."

"Okay."

Roman pushed his chair away from the desk. "I'll help you get them loaded and tied onto the wagon, and then I need to get busy and finish up the paperwork I started this morning."

"I'm sure I can manage to tie 'em in place on my own," Luke said, moving toward the cabinets.

"Okay, but you'd better be certain they're tied on good and tight. Steven's a picky customer, and he won't stand for any scratches or dents."

"I'll make sure everything's firmly in place."

They soon had the cabinets set in the back of the wagon Roman used for hauling, and as Luke began to tie them in place, Roman headed back to the shop. A short time later, he heard the buggy wheels rolling and Luke calling for the horse to "get-a-moving."

"Sure hope he doesn't get that horse moving too fast," Roman mumbled as he reached for his ledger to begin making entries again. "That kid is either running late or moving too fast. No happy medium where Luke's concerned."

For the next hour and a half, Roman worked on the books. Every now and then, he glanced up at the clock on the far wall to check the time. He figured Luke should have been back by now—unless he stopped somewhere to eat his lunch.

The sound of a car door slamming brought Roman to his feet. A few seconds later, Steven Bates entered the shop, looking madder than a bull chasing a dog around the pasture.

"What's wrong? Didn't you like the cabinets Luke delivered? He did deliver them, I hope."

"Oh, yeah. He got 'em a few feet from my driveway, and they slid off the back of your wagon and landed in the street—in several pieces."

Roman's face heated up. "How'd that happen?"

"Guess you didn't get 'em tied on good enough." Steven grunted. "Tomorrow's my wife's birthday, and now I'm in big trouble because our kitchen remodel isn't done."

Roman struggled to keep his temper from flaring. He should have insisted he help Luke tie on those cabinets, and he shouldn't have trusted the kid to do them alone. "It'll take me a few weeks, but I'll make good on the cabinets," he promised.

Steven shook his head. "Don't bother; I'm done."

"Done? What do you mean?"

Steven squinted his beady brown eyes as he rubbed the top of his balding head. "You've been late with work I've contracted you to do before, your work's not the quality I expect, and now this! I'll be taking my business down the road from now on." He turned on his heels and marched out the door, slamming it with such force that the windows rattled.

Roman rushed to the door, but by the time he got there, Steven's car had peeled out of the driveway, sending gravel flying in all directions.

A short time later, Luke showed up, looking more than a little sheepish. "Sorry to be telling you this, but—"

Roman held up his hand. "I already know. Thanks to you, I won't be getting any more of Steven's business."

"I—I thought I had those ropes tied real good, and I can't figure out how it happened."

"Jah, well, what's done is done, but now I'm out the money Steven owed me, so I'll be takin' it out of your pay to make up for what I lost today."

Luke's face turned bright red. "But those cabinets weren't cheap. It'll take me several weeks to pay you back."

Roman gave a curt nod. "And you'll work twice as hard as you've been workin', too."

Luke opened his mouth as if to say something more, but then he closed it with an audible click. "What have you got for me to do now?" he asked, turning toward the workbench.

"You can start by sweeping the floor in the back room, and when you're done with that, I'd like you to clean the front windows."

A muscle on the side of Luke's neck quivered, but he just grabbed the broom from the closet and headed for the other room.

"Always trouble somewhere," Roman muttered under his breath. "I knew I shouldn't have hired that irresponsible fellow."

The door to Roman's shop opened again, and this time Martin Gingerich stepped into the room.

"Can I help you?" Roman asked as he turned to face the young man with light brown hair.

Martin nodded and glanced around the room as if he might be looking for something. "I. . .uh. . .came by to see if you'd have the time to make something for me."

"All depends on what it is."

Martin removed his straw hat and fanned his face with it a couple of times. "My folks' anniversary is coming up soon, and I was hoping to give them something nice."

"Did you have anything particular in mind?" Roman asked as he headed for his desk and took a seat in the chair behind it.

Martin followed and continued to fan his face while he stood on the other side of the desk, facing Roman. "Thought maybe they might like a new rocking chair."

Roman leaned forward, his elbows resting on the desk. "I'm not braggin', mind you, but I think the rocking chairs I make are pretty nice—real comfortable, too."

"Can you have it ready in three weeks?" Martin asked.

Roman nodded. "Jah, sure. Shouldn't be a problem."

"Danki." Martin's gaze dropped to the floor, and he twisted the brim of his hat in his hands.

"Is there anything else I can help you with?"

"Uh. . .no, not really."

Roman pushed his chair aside and stood. "Okay then, I'll put a card in the mail to let you know when the chair's ready."

Martin's head came up. "Oh, no! Better not do that, or my folks will know about my surprise gift." He shuffled his feet a few times. "I'll just plan on dropping by here once a week to check on it."

"Sounds good to me. I'm sure I'll have it done in plenty of time for their anniversary."

Thinking the young man would head out, Roman moved toward the front door. Martin followed, but when he got to the door, he halted and turned to face Roman again. "I. . .uh. . .heard that Ruth got a job in Berlin working at the bakeshop." His voice sounded raspy, almost a whisper.

"Jah, she sure did."

"Does she like it there?"

"I guess so." Roman grinned. "Who wouldn't like working around all those sweet-tasting pastries and pies?"

Martin nodded and glanced around the room again. "Heard you hired Luke Friesen a few months back, but I don't see him anywhere. Does that mean he's not workin' for you anymore?"

Roman nodded toward the back room. "He's doing some cleanup."

"I see. Well, I'd best be on my way, I expect. See you soon."

Roman shook his head as Martin headed out the door. That fellow was sure the nervous type. Nothing like Luke, who never seemed to think twice about what he said or did.

Chapter 7

Cleon pulled into the Hostettlers' place, halted his buggy in front of the hitching rail, and climbed down. As soon as he had his horse put in the corral, he skirted around to the back of the buggy and lifted his bicycle out. Today was another beautiful Saturday with clear blue skies and plenty of sunshine, despite the drop in the temperature that typically came with fall weather. Even though he knew Grace had worked until three this afternoon, Cleon figured they had time to go for a bicycle ride before the sun went down.

He parked his bike near the barn and hurried around the house to the back door, where he found Judith sitting on the porch with a pan of plump, golden apples in her lap and a paring knife in one hand.

"It's good to see you, Cleon," she said, smiling up at him as he stepped onto the porch.

"Good to see you, too." He glanced toward the door. "I'm here to take Grace for a bike ride. Do you know if she's ready to go?"

"She's upstairs changing her clothes, so if you'd like to have a seat and keep me company for a while, that'd be real nice." Judith nodded toward the wicker chair that sat beside her own.

"I believe I will." Cleon liked the way Grace's mother always took time out to visit with him. Not like his mother, who stayed busy from sunup to sunset. But then, Judith didn't have a home-based business where she had to feed several groups of hungry, curious tourists several times a week. Mom also had her candle-making business, and even though she had the help of Cleon's sister with both jobs, she had very little time to sit and visit.

"It's a fine day for a bike ride, jah?"

Cleon nodded. "What are your other two daughters up to this afternoon?"

"Martha's out in the barn hovering over her dogs, like usual, and Ruth went for a walk with her friend Sadie." Judith's lips puckered as she lifted her knife and began to peel one of the apples in the bowl. "Ruth was supposed to go somewhere with Luke this afternoon, but Roman asked him to work today, so she made other plans, which might be a good thing in the long run."

"What makes you say that?"

She shrugged. "If Luke's giving Roman a hard time in the shop, then he might not be the best choice as a suitor for Ruth. She tends to be quite sensitive, and I'm not sure a headstrong man like Luke is what she needs."

The back door swung open, and Grace stepped onto the porch, saving Cleon from having to respond.

"Ready to go?" he asked, feeling a sense of excitement at the prospect of being alone with her again.

Grace nodded and smiled. "Just don't expect me to go speeding down the road. My legs are tired from work, and I'm not sure how far I can go without my strength giving out."

"Would you rather we not ride our bikes? We could go for a buggy ride instead."

She shook her head. "That's okay. I need the fresh air, and the exercise my legs will be getting is different from walking or standing."

"Okay then." Cleon smiled at Judith. "I'll have your daughter home in plenty of time for supper."

Judith's eyes twinkled. "You're welcome to stay and eat with us if you like."

"I might take you up on that offer." Cleon lifted his hand in a wave and hurried down the steps after Grace.

"I can't believe how well this weather is holding out," Ruth commented as she and Sadie turned off the main road and headed onto a wide path into the woods not far from the pond where they'd had a picnic with Luke and Toby the week before.

"Winter will be here soon, which is why we need to do some fun things before it gets too cold."

Ruth poked Sadie gently on the arm. "There are plenty of fun things you can do in the cold, you know."

"Right. Sledding, ice skating, and snowball fights." Sadie swung her arms as they clipped along at a steady pace. "Too bad Toby and Luke weren't free to join us today."

"My daed has a backload of work right now, and he needed Luke's help today."

Sadie nodded. "Since tomorrow's church service will be held at Toby's house, he had to help his brothers get the benches they'll need."

Ruth stopped walking and pointed to a shiny black pickup parked behind a clump of bushes. "I wonder whose truck that is. I don't recall seeing it before, do you?"

Sadie shook her head. "No, but the last time we came to the pond, we never walked back into the woods."

"You're right." Ruth squinted as they moved closer to the truck. "It's empty, and I don't see anyone else around but us."

"Maybe it's abandoned."

"Or maybe someone hid it here."

"Why would anybody do that?"

Ruth's hands went straight to her hips. "Some fellows going through rumschpringe have vehicles they don't want anyone to know about. You ought to know that."

Sadie's blue eyes widened. "You think some Amish fellow owns this truck?"

"Maybe so."

"It's not a new vehicle, but it's clean and polished." Sadie touched the chrome mirror. "I'd say whoever owns it feels a bit of *hochmut* and takes pleasure in keeping it nice."

"If it belongs to an Amish fellow, then he's not supposed to feel pride." Ruth pursed her lips. "I hope he doesn't like having a truck so much that he decides to leave the faith so he can continue to drive it."

Grace's legs were about to give out, and she was on the verge of asking Cleon to stop so she could rest when he pulled his bike to the side of the road and signaled her to do the same. "This hilly road is starting to get to me, and I'm feeling kind of tired," he huffed. "Why don't we push our bicycles awhile? That will make it easier for us to talk, too."

She smiled in appreciation and climbed off her bike.

"I'm glad you were free to spend the afternoon with me, since this is the last chance we'll have to be together for a week or so."

"Oh, why's that?"

"Didn't I tell you that my family and I are leaving for Rexford, Montana, on Monday morning to attend my cousin Sarah's wedding? We'll be gone a week."

She shook her head. "I don't remember you saying that." Of course, lately, she hadn't paid much attention to anything that had been said to her. All she could think about was Gary showing up in town, and whether she should tell Cleon the truth about her past. After another restless night of tossing, turning, and mulling things over, Grace had concluded that it might be best if she revealed her secret now before Gary had a chance to say anything. If Cleon was as understanding as she hoped he would be, then maybe it would give her the courage she needed to tell her folks about it, too.

They walked in silence for a while as Grace tried to decide the best way to broach the subject of her rumschpringe days. Maybe it would be good if she led into it slowly, to see how he felt about things.

"Let's get off the main road and head into the woods," Cleon said, nodding toward a path on the right. "I think this leads to the pond near the Wengerds' place."

Grace pushed her bike off the shoulder of the road and onto the wide dirt path, deciding to wait until she was walking by his side before she spoke again. "Uh. . .Cleon, there's something I want to talk to you about."

His eyebrows drew together. "You look so serious. Is there something wrong? Are you having second thoughts about marrying me?"

Grace moistened her lips with the tip of her tongue and halted her bike. This was going to be harder than she thought. "I'm not having second thoughts, but I think you should know that—"

"Hey, what are you two doing out here?"

Grace whirled around at the sound of her sister's voice. "Ruth, you scared me!"

Sadie chuckled. "I can tell she did. Your eyes are huge as buggy wheels."

"I—I just didn't expect to see either of you here," Grace stammered. It was a good thing she hadn't revealed her secret to Cleon. What if Ruth and Sadie had overheard their conversation? The last thing she needed was Sadie knowing anything about her personal business, because she tended to be a blabbermouth.

"Sadie and I cut through the woods and spent some time at the pond," Ruth said. "It's beautiful there this time of the year." She nodded at Grace. "Is that where you two are headed?"

"Jah," Cleon spoke up. "We were riding on the shoulder of the road but decided to walk our bikes awhile."

Ruth glanced at the diminishing sun filtering through the trees. "It'll be getting dark soon, so I wouldn't stay too long if I were you."

"She's got a point," Cleon said. "Maybe we should head back before we lose our daylight."

"Okay." Grace felt a mixture of relief and disappointment. If they headed for home now, and Ruth and Sadie tagged along, she wouldn't be able to tell Cleon what was on her mind. Still, the girls coming along when they did might have been a good thing, especially if Cleon's response had been negative. Maybe it would be best to wait and tell Cleon sometime after he got back from Montana. That would give her another whole week to think it through and decide the best way to word things to him.

Chapter 8

"Sure were a lot of folks missing from church today," Mom said as she walked toward the house beside Grace, with Ruth, Martha, and Dad following. "Martin Gingerich, Sadie Esh, and Abe Wengerd were sick, I understand."

"Luke was out with the flu," Ruth put in.

"Leastways that's what his mamm said." Dad grunted. "Truth be told, he was probably lazing in bed because I worked him so hard last week after he wrecked that set of cabinets that was supposed to be for Ella Bates's birthday. Steven was hoppin' mad about that, and he said from now on he won't be giving me any more business."

"I'm sure tired this afternoon," Mom said, making no reference to Dad's problems at work, which he'd already told them about.

He yawned noisily. "Jah, me, too. *Ich bin mied wie en hund.*"

"If you're as tired as a dog," Martha put in, "you're very tired indeed. I'm going out to the barn to check on Heidi and her pups as soon as I change out of my church clothes."

Grace couldn't help but smile at her sister's exuberance. It seemed that all Martha talked about anymore were those dogs of hers.

"You can spend the rest of the day in the barn with your hundlin if you want to," Dad said, "but I'm gonna take a nap."

Mom nodded. "I think I'd better take one, too."

As they stepped onto the back porch, Grace noticed that the door hung slightly open. Dad must have noticed it too, for he turned and gave them a curious stare. "Which of you was the last one out the door

58

this morning? And how come you didn't close it?"

"It wasn't me," Grace was quick to say.

Ruth shook her head. "Nor me."

"I may have been the last one out," Martha admitted, "but I'm sure I didn't leave the door open."

"Well, someone did." Dad pushed the door fully open and entered the house, grumbling about all the flies that had probably gotten in.

Grace and her sisters stopped in the hallway, but Mom had already entered the kitchen. "Someone's been in here," she shouted. "Ach! They've made such a mess!"

The others rushed into the kitchen. Mom stood in the midst of chaos—pots and pans littered the floor, chairs were overturned, and several items of food from the refrigerator lay in the middle of the table.

They stood for several seconds in stunned silence. Then Dad groaned and shook his head. "Weren't no critter that sneaked into the house and did all this. Had to be done by human hands—that's for certain sure." He turned on his heels with a huff.

"Where are you going?" Mom called with a panicked expression.

"To check out the rest of the place, what do you think?"

She rushed to his side. "If whoever did this is still in the house, then what?"

"If he is, then we'll have ourselves a little heart-to-heart talk."

Martha bent down and picked up a rolling pin from the floor. "Maybe I'd better go with you."

Mom moved like she was going to stop Martha, but Grace got to her first. "Just what do you think you're doing?" She grabbed the rolling pin and placed it on the counter. "I hope you're not considering using that as a weapon."

"I—I wasn't going to hit anyone, just scare 'em a bit is all."

Dad pointed to the floor. "You'd better stay here and help your mamm clean up while I look through the other rooms." He rushed out of the kitchen before anyone could argue the point.

Grace's hand trembled as she bent to retrieve one of her mother's frying pans. *Who could have done this, and why would they do such a thing?*

59

"Never in all the years your daed and I have been married has anything like this ever happened to us," Mom said in a shaky voice.

"I—I wonder if anything's been stolen." Ruth's dark eyes were huge, and her face had turned chalky white, making her brunette hair appear even darker.

"I hope not," Mom said, "but we need to remember that nothing we own is really ours. It's all on loan from God."

Grace moved closer to the hallway door and craned her neck. She couldn't see anything, but she could hear her father's footsteps as he moved through the living room. "Dad, are you all right?"

"I'm fine. Just checking things out in here."

"Has that room been vandalized, too?"

He stepped into the hall and shook his head. "Nothing appears to have been disturbed in the living room. Next, I'm going to check upstairs."

Grace gripped the edge of the door and clenched her teeth. *What if someone's been in my room? What if they went through my things? What if. . .*

"I hope everything's okay upstairs," Mom said, breaking into Grace's disturbing thoughts. "I wish your daed had let one of us go with him."

"I'm sure he'll be down soon." Ruth managed a weak smile.

It seemed obvious to Grace that they all felt uneasy about this break-in, and she wouldn't rest easy until she knew if anything had been taken from her room.

"I'll be right back," Martha said, scooting toward the back door.

"Where are you going?" Mom called to her.

"To the barn to check on my dogs." Martha's shoulders lifted, and her breath came out in little spurts. "I want to be sure they're okay."

"Not without your daed, you're not. Whoever broke into the house could be hiding in the barn." Mom shook her head firmly.

Martha raised her chin as if she might argue, but Grace knew her determined little sister would not get her way on this matter.

"We must be patient and wait for Dad," Ruth said, reaching for the jar of dill pickles that had been dumped on the table.

When Grace heard her father's heavy footsteps clomping around upstairs, she glanced into the hallway again.

"Let's try to remain calm and wait and see what he discovers upstairs," Mom said as she wet a dishrag at the kitchen sink and began to wash off the table.

For the next few minutes, Grace and her mother and sisters bustled around the kitchen, picking things up and cleaning off the table. They were nearly finished when Dad showed up again, squinting his dark eyes and scratching the side of his head.

"What's wrong, Roman?" Mom asked, stepping up to him. "Was everything all right upstairs?"

"There's nobody there, and nothing was disturbed in any of the rooms except for Grace's."

"How odd." Mom's forehead wrinkled. "If they messed up one room, you'd think they would have done the same to the others."

"Maybe Heidi or Fritz sensed something was amiss and started barking, scaring anyone off before they could do more damage," Martha suggested.

"That could be," Dad agreed as he reached up to rub the bridge of his nose. "Or maybe it was done randomly, with no rhyme or reason as to which rooms got messed."

Grace stood for several seconds, trying to piece everything together. With a little gasp, she dashed from the room.

"Would you like me to run down to the phone shed and call the sheriff's office?" Martha asked her father.

"I'll go with her," Ruth put in.

Firmly, he shook his head. "We won't involve the sheriff, and I wouldn't press charges even if he was notified and found the person who made this mess."

"I know that, but—"

"I'm sure it was just some pranksters—probably the same ones who turned over those outhouses near Kidron last week."

"So we just allow them to get away with this?" Martha motioned to the remaining items on the table. "I think they need to be stopped, or else they might do the same thing to other folks."

Mom touched Dad's arm. "Our daughter has a point. Maybe we should let the sheriff know about this."

"We'll do what others in our community have done whenever the rowdy English kids have played their pranks. We'll look the other way, turn the other cheek, forgive, and forget." Dad sighed. "Now let's get on with the business of living and forget this ever happened."

Martha made a sweeping gesture with her hand. "How can we forget it happened when our kitchen is such a mess and Grace is upstairs trying to deal with whatever they did to her room?" She moaned. "This isn't right. It's not right at all."

"We can forget it happened by making the choice to put it out of our minds. That's how we'll deal with it." Dad folded his arms in a stubborn pose.

"Do you think Grace is going to forget that a stranger came into her room while we were at church?" Martha nodded toward the door leading to the upstairs.

Before Dad had a chance to answer, Ruth spoke up. "I'm going to see how she's doing. No doubt, she'll need some help cleaning up the mess."

Grace entered her room and skidded to a stop in front of the bed. Articles of clothing were strewn everywhere—white kapps, choring aprons, a pair of black sneakers, and some dresses that had been torn into shreds.

Her heart thudded. Her hands sweat. Her knees nearly buckled. With a sense of dread, she made her way over to the cedar chest at the foot of the bed and flipped open the lid, dipping both hands deep inside and feeling around to see if anything was missing. When Grace's fingers touched the scrapbook she'd kept hidden away, and then she discovered that her faceless doll was still there, she breathed a sigh of relief.

"Are you all right? Has anything been stolen?"

Grace slammed the lid shut and spun around. "Ruth! I didn't hear you come in."

"I came up to see if there was anything I could do to help." Ruth stepped forward and pointed to the mess on Grace's bed. "Oh, sister, I'm so sorry. I can't understand why anyone would do such a thing. It makes no sense why they would mess up the kitchen and your room yet not bother with any of ours."

"I—I don't understand it, either, but to my knowledge, nothing was taken." Grace stood on trembling legs and clenched her teeth, trying to stop the flow of tears.

"Maybe Martha's right about either Heidi or Fritz hearing the intruder and scaring him off before he had time to ransack the other rooms." Ruth glanced around. "It does seem odd that nothing is missing, though."

Before Grace could respond, Martha rushed into the room, her face flushed and her eyes wide with obvious concern. "Did they break anything? Have any of your things been stolen?"

"Not that I can tell." Grace pointed to her bed. "They threw some of my clothes on the bed and tore up a couple of my dresses."

"Look over there!" Martha pointed to the desk on the other side of the room. "They emptied everything out of the drawers onto the floor. Looks like some of your papers have been shredded, too."

Grace pivoted. She'd been so concerned about the things in her cedar chest that she hadn't even noticed the desk. Tears burned her eyes, and she nearly choked on the lump lodged in her throat. Who could have done this? Who could hate her enough to rummage through her room and make such a mess?

She froze as an image of Gary Walker popped into her head. Could he be responsible for this? He'd said he would get even with her someday for breaking up with her. Had he finally made good on his threat?

Chapter 9

It was difficult for Grace to go to work the next day, but she had no legitimate reason for staying home other than feeling traumatized over the break-in at their house. She wished she could tell Cleon about the break-in, but she knew he and his family had left for Rexford, Montana, to attend a cousin's wedding. In all likelihood, they wouldn't be back for a week.

When Grace arrived at the restaurant, she was surprised to learn that Esther was out sick with the flu. That meant Grace was needed more than ever, confirming that she'd done the right thing by coming to work.

She donned her apron, grabbed an order pad and pencil from behind the counter, and headed for the dining room. She'd only taken a few steps when she halted. There sat Gary in a booth in her section, looking as smug as always. Grace had no choice but to wait on him.

Her legs felt like two sticks of rubber as she slowly made her way across the room. When she reached Gary's table, she placed the menu in front of him, avoiding his piercing gaze. "Would you like a cup of coffee?"

"Sure, that'd be great."

"I'll take your order when I bring the coffee." Grace turned and walked away before he could respond.

When she returned a few minutes later, she had calmed down some. She'd decided to come right out and ask if he had anything to do with the break-in at their house when she spotted a notebook lying on the table beside his camera. That's when she remembered that Gary had said he was some kind of reporter. If she mentioned the break-in and he wasn't the one involved, he might want to do a story about it, and seeing a story about their break-in in some publication would make her father furious. Maybe it would be best if she didn't say anything—at least for now. No point in letting Gary know how upset they had all been.

"Are you going to stand there staring at the table all day, or did you plan to give me that cup of coffee you're holding?"

Grace drew in a deep breath and placed the cup on the table; then she reached into her apron pocket and withdrew her order pad and pencil. "What would you like for breakfast?"

He jiggled his eyebrows and gave her a quick wink. "Is a date with you on the menu?"

She moaned. Apparently Gary hadn't changed. He'd always been a big flirt, which she'd been attracted to at first. But when she got to know him better, she'd come to see how moody he could be.

"Aw, come on, Gracie," he drawled. "Don't look so down-in-the-mouth. You and I had something special together once, remember?"

Of course she remembered. Remembering was the easy part. The hard part was forgetting. If Grace had it to do over again, she never would have dated anyone outside her faith during her rumschpringe, and she certainly wouldn't have dated anyone as arrogant as Gary.

He touched her arm, and the contact of his sweaty, hot fingers made her cringe. "You're bound and determined not to warm up to me, aren't you?"

Grace jerked away, feeling like she'd been stung by one of Cleon's honeybees. She could hardly believe she used to enjoy this irritating man's touch or that she'd been sucked in by his smooth talking. Not anymore. She was older, wiser, and more cautious. "Are you going to order or not?" she asked through tight lips.

He grinned up at her and tapped the menu with his pen. "I'll have two eggs over easy, a side of hash browns, and a cinnamon roll to make me sweeter."

If a cinnamon roll would make you sweeter, I would bring you ten.

Grace picked up the menu and turned away, but she'd taken only a few steps when he called out to her.

"Better make that two cinnamon rolls, Gracie. Today, I'll be interviewing several people who work with the Amish, and I might need a little extra energy so I can sweet-talk 'em into telling me what I want to know."

Grace hurried across the room to put in his order. She figured the best thing was to ignore his catty remarks. If he really was a reporter and had only come to Holmes County to get a story on the Amish, then hopefully he would be gone in a few days.

Ruth had just finished waiting on a customer when Luke walked into the bakeshop. "I'm surprised to see you," she said as he stepped up to the counter. "I figured you'd be working for my daed today."

"I am. Just came into Berlin to deliver a table to Paul Hendricks. Last week, he and his wife opened a new bed-and-breakfast across town."

"I heard about that. With all the tourists who come into the area, I guess we need another place for them to stay."

"Jah." Luke leaned against the counter and studied the pastries Ruth had put into the case when she'd arrived at work this morning. "Think I'll buy myself a donut or something. Any suggestions?"

"Normally, I'm kind of partial to cream puffs, but since I have no appetite today, I'd better let you decide."

"What's wrong with your appetite? You're not comin' down with the bug that's been going around, I hope." He lifted his shoulders in a brief shrug. "I felt kind of under the weather yesterday. That's why I wasn't in church."

"Are you doing better now?"

He nodded. "Guess a lot of folks are still sick, though."

"The flu's not my problem," she said with a shake of her head, "but I am a bit *loddrich* after what happened yesterday."

"What happened that's got you feeling shaky?"

"Didn't my daed tell to you about the break-in at our place

yesterday while we were at church?"

"He never said a thing. So why don't you fill me in?"

Ruth glanced around the room to be sure there were no other customers in the store, and then she quickly relayed the details of the break-in. She sniffed and swallowed hard in an effort to hold back the threatening tears. "I know others have been the victims of break-ins and vandalism in the past, but we've never had anything like that happen to us, and it made everyone in the family feel loddrich."

Luke leaned on the counter. "Did your daed phone the sheriff?"

Ruth shook her head. "Dad thinks it was probably a bunch of English kids having some fun. He said we should try and forget it ever happened." She drew in a deep breath and released it quickly. "Of course, that's easier said than done."

"Roman's probably right about it being some English fellows. A group of 'em dumped over some outhouses not long ago. Did you hear about that?"

"It wasn't confirmed that they were English, though, right?"

"Well, no, but—"

"Who's to say that it wasn't some Amish kids going through rumschpringe?"

"Right." Luke shifted from one foot to another, then stepped away from the counter. "Well, guess I'd better be going."

"What about that donut you wanted?"

He turned and lifted his hand in a backwards wave. "Some other time, maybe. I've got things to do and places to go."

As Luke left the store, Ruth's thoughts took her to the day she and Sadie had gone to the pond to meet Luke and Toby. When Luke had shown up late, he'd acted kind of odd, too.

She grabbed a tray of donuts from the shelf behind her and slipped them into the display cabinet, knowing she needed to keep busy so she wouldn't have to think about yesterday's break-in or Luke's strange behavior.

A few minutes later, another customer entered the store. This time it was Donna Larson, their middle-aged English neighbor, who often drove for them when they needed to go places that were too far to travel by horse and buggy.

"I heard you were working here now," Donna said as she stepped up to the counter and pushed a wisp of grayish-brown hair away from her face.

Ruth nodded and pointed to the pastries inside the glass. "We're having a special on donuts today, if you're interested."

"I haven't had time to do much baking lately, so I think I will take a few of those with chocolate glaze." Donna snickered. "Better make that half-a-dozen chocolate and half-a-dozen lemon. Ray has a sweet tooth, and he'll probably eat all the chocolate ones himself."

Ruth smiled, but her heart really wasn't in it. Truth was, she wished she and Grace could have stayed home from work today, since they'd both felt shaky after yesterday's break-in.

"For a young woman with a new job, and a good-smelling one at that, you sure look down in the dumps today," Donna commented.

Ruth wondered if she should tell Donna what had happened at their place. Maybe whoever had broken in had vandalized some of the neighbors' homes, as well. She waited until she had Donna's donuts put in a box and had rung up her purchase, then she leaned across the counter and said, "Did anything unusual happen at your place yesterday?"

"Let's see now, Ray fixed us some omelets for breakfast." Donna grinned and fluttered her eyelashes. "That's pretty unusual for him."

"No, I meant did anything *bad* happen yesterday?"

"Not really. Unless you count Ray falling asleep in the middle of me trying to tell him about the letter I got from my sister the other day."

Ruth grimaced. Beating around the shrubs wasn't getting her anywhere, so she guessed she might as well come right out and say it. "Your house wasn't broken into, was it?"

Donna tipped her head to one side and squinted at Ruth, her gray-blue eyes narrowing into tiny slits. "Of course not. Why do you ask?"

Ruth cleared her throat and lowered her voice to a whisper. "While we were in church, someone broke into our house."

Donna's eyes opened wide. "Was anything taken?"

"No, but they made a mess in a couple of rooms." She leaned closer to Donna. "Did you hear or see anything unusual yesterday?"

"No, I didn't, but then I was inside most of the day watching Ray sleep while I worked on a crossword puzzle." Donna's eyes narrowed again. "Did you notify the sheriff?"

Ruth shook her head. "Dad said no to that idea. Even if he had let the sheriff know, he wouldn't have pressed charges if they'd found the person responsible."

"I understand that's not the Amish way."

"No, it's not. Dad also thinks it was probably a bunch of kids out for a good time and that it isn't likely to happen again."

"He could be right, but I'll tell Ray to keep an eye out just the same. He's always got those binoculars of his trained on the trees in our yard, watching for different birds. I'll ask him to check things out over at your place whenever he gets the chance." Donna plucked the box of donuts from the counter and glanced at her watch. "I'd better run. I've got a hair appointment in ten minutes, and I don't want to be late." With a quick wave, she hurried out the door.

"How are you doing today, Heidi?" Martha asked as she stared into the box where the mother sheltie lay nursing her pups.

The dog responded with a faint whimper but didn't budge from her spot.

She patted the top of Heidi's head. "You're a good *mudder*, and I'm glad you and your little ones weren't bothered by whoever broke into our house yesterday." Just thinking about anyone disturbing her dogs made Martha feel sick to her stomach.

The barn door clicked open, then slammed shut, and she jumped. "Who's there?"

"It's only me," Mom called. "Came out to tell you that I'm taking some lunch to your daed soon. I thought if he's not too busy I would eat with him, and I wondered if you'd like to join us."

Martha waited until her mother was closer before she responded. "Will Luke be there, too?"

"I don't rightly know. Probably so, unless he's planning to go home for lunch today. I guess he does that from time to time." Mom laid a hand on Martha's shoulder. "Why do you ask?"

Martha shrugged. "Just wondered, is all."

"So, did you want to join us?"

"Think I'll spend a little more time with Heidi and her brood, and then I'll take my lunch out back and sit by the creek awhile."

Mom leaned over and looked into the box. "Those puppies are sure cute. I'll bet it's going to be hard for you to part with them after they're weaned."

Martha sighed. "Jah, but I'm raising them for the money, so except for one pup I might keep for breeding, I'll be selling the rest."

"Are you still planning to buy some other breed of dogs to raise?"

"I hope so. If and when I can afford it."

Mom patted Martha's arm. "Be patient, dear one. Only barns are built in a day, and that's because there are so many workers to help with the building."

Martha chuckled. It appeared that her mother had calmed down after yesterday's scare, for her sense of humor had obviously returned.

"Guess I'll head back to the house and gather up the lunch I fixed," Mom said, turning to go. "Come on out to the shop if you change your mind about eating with us."

"Okay."

Mom closed the door behind her, and Martha dished up some dog food for Heidi. When she was done, she dropped to a bale of hay and let her head fall forward in her hands. "Dear Lord," she prayed, "please protect our family, and don't let anything like that awful break-in happen to anyone else we know."

"You're sure late getting back. What took you so long?" Roman grumbled as Luke stepped into the shop with his face all red and sweaty and his straw hat tilted to one side.

"Had a little trouble with the delivery wagon." Luke grimaced. "Guess it was more your horse that gave me problems than the wagon."

Roman set aside the piece of sandpaper he'd been using to sand a table leg and moved over to the window. "What's the problem with Sam?" He peered though the glass and spotted his delivery wagon parked near the stable, but there was no sign of the horse.

"He tried to run away with the wagon when Paul Hendricks and I were unloading his table. I had quite a time gettin' that skittish animal settled down."

"Didn't you have him tied up?"

Luke nodded and hung his straw hat on a wall peg near the door. " 'Course I did, but he broke free, and I didn't realize it 'til the wagon started moving."

Roman thumped the side of his head and groaned. "Don't tell me you lost the table in the street like you did with those cabinets for Steven Bates. If you did, it'll be more than a few days pay you'll be docked for this time."

Luke shook his head, and his face turned even redder. "Me and Paul had just taken the table out of the back when the wagon started moving, and we had to set the table down in order to chase after the horse."

"Where's Sam now?"

"I gave him a good rubdown and turned him loose in the corral. He acted kind of spooky on the way home and was pretty lathered up by the time we got here."

Roman moved back to his sanding job. "I thought he was acting a bit jumpy this morning when I took him out of his stall, but I figured he'd settle down once he was harnessed up."

"Maybe you should have the vet check him over," Luke suggested. "It's not like Sam to carry on like that."

"I'm wondering if it has something to do with what happened yesterday." Roman gave the table leg he'd been working on a couple of swipes. "I didn't mention this earlier, but someone broke into our house while we were at church."

"I heard about that."

"Who told you?"

"Stopped by the bakeshop to say hello to Ruth when I was in

Berlin. She told me about it." Luke grabbed a hunk of sandpaper and started working on one of the other table legs that had been lying on the workbench.

"The womenfolk were pretty shook up when we got home and discovered the kitchen had been ransacked." Roman grunted. "Whoever did it made a mess in Grace's bedroom, too, although nothing appeared to have been stolen."

"Ruth said you had decided not to notify the sheriff."

Roman nodded. "I'm sure this was just a prank—probably done by whoever tipped over those outhouses not long ago."

Luke squinted. "You think that's got something to do with the way your horse acted this morning?"

Roman stopped sanding long enough to reach up and scratch the side of his head. "I'm not sure, but maybe the person who broke into the house went out to the barn and bothered the horses."

"Was anything in the barn disturbed?"

"Not that I could tell."

"Did any of the other horses act jumpy this morning?"

"Nope. Just Sam." Roman gave his earlobe a couple of sharp pulls. "Guess I'll never know what all went on during the break-in, but I'm thankful nothing was stolen and that none of the animals were hurt."

Luke opened his mouth as if to comment, but the door opened, and Judith stepped into the room. "Ready for lunch, Roman?" she asked, lifting the lunch pail she held in her hands.

Roman nodded, grateful for the interruption. He didn't want to give any more thought to yesterday's happenings, much less talk about them.

Chapter 10

As Roman headed to his woodworking shop the following Monday morning, thoughts about the break-in flitted through his mind. During the past week, he'd checked with some Amish families who lived close by to see if they'd had any problems, but apparently no one else had been bothered. If it was some rowdy English boys running amuck, then they probably wouldn't stop with just a prank or two.

Roman slipped his key into the lock and swung the shop door open. He froze. Even without the gas lamps lit, he could see the devastation. Broken tools littered the floor, a couple of tables had been dumped over, and the distinctive odors of lacquer thinner and stain permeated the room.

"*Was in der welt?* What in all the world was someone thinking? Who's responsible for this?" Since the front door had been locked, he knew the only way anyone could have gotten in was through one of the windows or the back door.

Cautiously, he stepped through the mess, making his way to the back room. The door there was slightly ajar, and he saw immediately that the lock had been broken.

He lit the nearest lamp so he could see better. Anger boiled in his chest when he realized how many of his tools and supplies had been ruined. After a thorough search through the cabinets where more tools were kept, he discovered several items were missing—a gas-powered saw, a sander, and his two most expensive hammers.

He bent over to set one of the tables in an upright position. "I don't need this kind of trouble. No one does."

The door swung open just then, and Ruth stepped into the room. "Dad, I came to tell you that breakfast is ready." Her mouth dropped open, and she motioned to the mess on the floor. "Ach, my! What's happened here? It looks like a tornado blew through."

Roman shook his head and grunted. "More like a bunch of *diewe*. Besides making a mess of the place, the thieves stole some of my tools."

She drew in a couple of shaky breaths. "Do you think it could be the same ones who broke into our house a week ago?"

"Don't know. Probably so."

"Are you going to let the sheriff know about this?"

"No need to involve the law. Even though I'm not happy about this, no one was hurt, and I'm turning the other cheek just like the Bible says we should do."

Ruth bent down and picked up a chair that had been overturned. "If it is some rowdy English fellows, it's not likely they'll stop until someone catches them in the act and they're put in jail."

"I know that already, but I'm not going to bother the sheriff."

"Okay." Ruth nodded toward the house. "If we hurry and eat, we can all come back to the shop and help you clean up before it's time for Grace and me to leave for work."

He motioned to the floor. "After seeing this mess, I've lost my appetite. You go on up to the house and eat. I'll get something after I've cleaned things up in here."

Ruth shrugged and headed out the door.

Ruth shivered as she started for the house, and she knew it wasn't from the chilly morning air. Had the same person who'd ransacked their house broken into her father's shop? Why would anyone do such a thing?

Stepping into the kitchen, she told the rest of the family, "Dad's shop has been broken into." She drew in a quick breath. "Broken pieces of furniture are all over the floor."

Mom's face blanched, and she grabbed hold of the cupboard as though needing it for support. "Oh, no, not again."

Martha set the plate she'd been holding onto the table. "Maybe now Dad will notify the sheriff."

Ruth shook her head. "He says no. He'll turn the other cheek as the Bible says we're to do."

"But what harm could there be in letting the sheriff know? It doesn't mean Dad will have to press charges or anything."

Mom walked across the room as if she were moving in slow motion, removed her shawl from a wall peg, and opened the back door.

"Where are you going?" Ruth called.

"Out to speak with your *daed*."

Martha pulled out a chair and sank into it with a groan. "Mom won't get anywhere with Dad; she never does. Whatever he says, she's always in agreement with, so he won't be phoning the sheriff."

"Is Grace still in her room?" Ruth asked.

Martha nodded. "She hasn't come down yet. Why do you ask?"

"I need to see if she'll ask Cleon to speak to Dad about this."

"Why Cleon?"

"Dad thinks highly of him, and if anyone can convince Dad to notify the sheriff, it will be Cleon."

Later that morning as Grace traveled down the road in her buggy toward the Schrocks' place, she prayed they would be back from their trip and that Cleon would agree to speak to her father. She also prayed that Dad would listen. At Ruth's suggestion, she'd agreed to take a separate buggy so that she could stop by to see Cleon before she headed to work. Passing a phone shed on the way, she felt tempted to pull over and call the sheriff herself but thought better of it. If Dad found out she'd done that, she would never hear the end of it. No, it would be better if Cleon convinced Dad to contact the sheriff.

A short time later, Grace pulled her rig into the Schrocks' driveway. Cleon's twenty-year-old brother, Ivan, was out in the yard. "I'm glad you're home from Montana. When did you get back?" she called as she stepped down from her buggy.

"Got home late last night."

"Is Cleon here?"

"Jah. He's checking on his bee boxes right now." Ivan nodded his blond head in the direction of the meadow out behind the Schrocks' three-story home. "What brings you by so early this morning?"

"I'm on my way to work, but I wanted to speak with Cleon about something."

"Does it pertain to your wedding?"

She shook her head and tied her horse to the hitching rail near the barn.

"Want me to go fetch him?"

"That won't be necessary. I'll head out to the meadow myself. I'd like to see how things are going with his bees."

"Jah, okay. See you later then, Grace."

Grace lifted the edge of her skirt as she stepped carefully over the cow flops in the pasture, then traipsed through the tall grass leading to the open space where Cleon kept his bee boxes. The newly risen sun had cast a beautiful orange haze on the sky, and she could smell the distinctive, crisp odor of fall in the air. If she hadn't been so upset, she might have felt a sense of peace from the scenery.

When she reached the first grouping of bee boxes, she stopped and stared at the bees buzzing around one of the boxes as though looking for a way to get in. She wondered if the bees felt trapped once they were inside the box. That was certainly how she felt—trapped. And there seemed to be no way out. No way to forget the past or make her family feel safe in their own home again.

Grace spotted Cleon across the field, and her frustrations abated some. His easygoing mannerisms and genuine smile made her feel safe and loved. Drawing in a deep breath, she rushed over to him.

"Grace! What a surprise. I was planning to come by your place after you got off work today, but I sure didn't expect to see you here this morning."

"I took my own rig and left the house early. I'll be heading to work soon, but I wanted to speak with you first thing."

He drew her close to his side. "What's wrong? You're trembling. Are you upset about something or just cold?"

She leaned her head against his chest, relishing the warmth of his jacket and finding comfort in the steady beating of his heart. "I'm upset. We're all upset."

"Why's that?"

"There have been two break-ins at our place in the last week—the first one at the house last Sunday, and then this morning, my daed's shop was vandalized."

Cleon held her at arm's length, and a muscle on the side of his face quivered. "Is everyone all right?"

"We're fine, but some of Dad's tools were taken, and lots of other things were ruined."

"What's your daed planning to do about this?"

"Nothing. He thinks it was probably done by whoever turned over outhouses at the schoolhouses near Kidron a few weeks back." Grace swallowed hard in an effort to dislodge the lump in her throat. She wanted so desperately to share her suspicions about Gary with Cleon, but fear of his reaction kept the words in her throat. "Dad thinks it won't happen again and says if we involve the sheriff and he finds whoever did it, we'll be expected to press charges."

"Roman wouldn't do that. It goes against our beliefs."

She nodded. "Even if we can't press charges, don't you think the sheriff should be told so he can keep an eye out for trouble and hopefully catch the person responsible?"

Cleon reached up to rub the bridge of his nose. "I suppose it might be good if the sheriff knew what happened. Maybe there have been some other break-ins in the area, and he might have a better chance of catching whoever did it if he knew what all had been done. Could be some kind of a pattern these kids are using."

She tipped her head and stared up at him. "What do you mean?"

"Maybe they strike once or twice in one area, then move on to some other place and pull a few pranks there."

"What they did to our house and Dad's shop was more than a prank, Cleon."

"You're right, and it could get even more serious if they're not stopped."

"So you'll talk to my daed and offer your opinion?"

He nodded. "Not sure how much influence I have with him, but I will give my two cents' worth."

Grace sighed with relief. If Gary was the one responsible and the sheriff caught him, then even without her father pressing charges, she figured Gary would be hauled off to jail. That would get him out of Holmes County and away from Grace and her family. Then she would never have to worry about revealing her secret.

Ruth had just placed a pan of fresh cinnamon rolls into the bakery case when the bell on the front door jingled. A customer walked in. He was English—the same man she'd seen Grace talking to a few weeks ago in the restaurant parking lot. Ruth recognized his wavy red hair and the haughty way he held himself, like he thought he was something special.

The Englisher stepped up to the counter and stared at Ruth so hard it made her squirm.

"Can I help you?"

"Well, now, that all depends." He raked his fingers through the sides of his hair, and a spicy fragrance permeated the air, causing Ruth to sneeze.

He wrinkled his nose. "Have you got a cold? Because if you do, you shouldn't be working around food."

"I don't have a cold. I think I must be allergic to something." She motioned to the glass case that separated them. "Cinnamon rolls just came from the oven. Would you like to try a sample?"

He shook his head, blinking his eyelids. "I didn't come here for anything to eat."

"What did you come for then?"

"I need some information."

"If you want to know anything about the town of Berlin, the Chamber of Commerce would be your best source."

"I've been there already." He reached into his shirt pocket and pulled out a small notebook. "The people who work there can't give me the kind of firsthand information I'm needing."

She tipped her head in question.

"Personal details about the Amish who live in Holmes County and the outlying areas." He winked at her. "I can see that you're Amish by the way you're dressed, so I thought you'd be a good person to ask."

Ruth glanced over her shoulder, hoping Karen or Jake Clemons, the owners of the bakeshop, might come out of the kitchen and rescue her, but they were still busy baking in the back room.

The man extended his hand across the counter. "My name's Gary Walker. I'm a freelance photographer and reporter. Awhile back I did a pretty big article for a new magazine called *Everyone's World*. Have you heard of it?"

She shook her head. "I don't read many magazines."

"I guess the Amish newspaper is probably more your style, huh?"

"I do read *The Budget*." Ruth glanced toward the front door, hoping another customer would come in and wishing this was Sadie's day to work with her at the bakeshop. "If you already know some things about the Amish, why not write that?"

"I'm not interested in basic facts. I want to know what's going on in the lives of the Amish people in this area compared to what I've learned about Amish settlements in other parts of the country."

"Do people who read your stories want to know that kind of thing?"

"You'd be surprised what curious readers want to know." Gary removed the cap of the pen with his teeth and grinned at her. "So what can you tell me—what'd you say your name was?"

Her cheeks warmed. "Ruth Hostettler."

He started to write it down but lifted his pen and stared at her in a most peculiar way. "Say, you wouldn't be related to Grace Hostettler, would you?"

She nodded. "Do you know my sister?"

"Let's just say we've met a time or two."

"A few weeks ago, I saw you talking to Grace in the parking lot of the restaurant where she works. Were you asking her questions about the Amish, too?"

"As a matter of fact, I was." His forehead wrinkled. "She didn't tell me much, though. Not a very friendly one, that sister of yours."

Ruth bristled. *I'm not about to tell this man anything, either.*

"Have there been any attacks made against the Amish around here?"

Her mouth dropped open. She leaned against the counter, not knowing what to say. Did the man know about the break-ins at their place? Was he hoping she would give him details?

He tapped his foot and glanced around as though growing impatient. "I know of some Amish communities in other parts of the country where the Plain People have been taunted by outsiders trying to make trouble, so I wondered if anything like that has ever happened here."

Ruth wasn't about to give him any information, and she felt relief when another customer came into the bakeshop. "You'll have to excuse me. I need to wait on this lady."

Gary stepped away from the counter and folded his arms. "I can wait."

Ruth shook her head, feeling a little braver now that she wasn't alone with the persistent man. "If you're not here to buy baked goods, then there's nothing more to be said."

"Look, if it's that little remark I made about your sister not being friendly, I'm sorry. I tend to say stupid things when I'm around pretty women."

Ruth's face grew hot, and she turned from Gary and focused on the English woman who had stepped up to the bakery case. "May I help you?"

"I'd like half a dozen cream puffs, two cinnamon rolls, and an angel food cake."

"I'll get those for you right away."

Gary cleared his throat, and when she glanced his way again, he gave her a quick wink and sauntered out the door.

Ruth breathed a sigh of relief. *No wonder Grace didn't want to answer that man's questions. He's pushy and arrogant. I hope he gets done with his stories soon and leaves Holmes County.*

Grace drew in a deep breath and whispered a silent prayer as she carried a tray full of food out to the restaurant's dining room. Her hands shook so badly, she didn't know how she would make it through the day. Ever since she'd heard about her father's shop getting broken into, she'd been a nervous wreck. She hoped Cleon would find time today to talk to her father about notifying the sheriff, and she hoped Dad would listen.

Grace gripped the tray tighter. If only they knew who was responsible for the break-ins. Could the same person who broke into their house have vandalized her father's shop, or were they two separate incidences? Were some rowdy English boys the culprits, or could it have been Gary?

She glanced out the restaurant's front window. No sign of the arrogant man, at least. For the last two weeks, he'd been going from shop to shop, asking people questions about the Amish and snapping pictures whenever he felt like it—even some close-up shots of Amish people. Grace knew this because some of her friends had mentioned that a redheaded Englisher with a fancy camera was nosing around. Grace figured that, after this many days, Gary should have gotten enough information to write ten articles, so it made no sense that he was still hanging around. She'd heard that he'd been seen in Walnut Creek on Saturday, taking more pictures and interviewing anyone willing to talk to him.

As Grace approached an English couple whose order she'd taken earlier, she gritted her teeth with a determination she didn't feel and carefully set their plates of food in front of them. "Will there be anything else?"

The elderly woman smiled. "I'd like another cup of coffee, please."

"One for me, too," the man said with a nod.

"I'll see to it right away."

"Are you okay?" Esther asked as she joined Grace in front of the coffeepot moments later. "Your hands are shaking."

"I'm feeling a little nervous this morning," Grace admitted. "My daed's shop got broken into sometime during the night, and it has us all plenty worried."

Esther's forehead wrinkled, and she patted Grace's arm in a motherly fashion. "That's terrible. I understand now why you're shaking. You have every right to feel nervous."

"I didn't say anything about this before, but someone broke into our house a week ago, too," Grace whispered.

Esther's pale eyebrows lifted high on her forehead. "How come you didn't tell me this sooner?"

"Dad said he thought it was a one-time thing, and since nothing was taken at that time, I saw no point in mentioning it."

"Do you have any idea who might be responsible, and do you think both incidents were done by the same person?"

"We don't know, but Dad suspects it might be some rowdy English fellows." Grace wasn't about to tell Esther whom she suspected.

Esther slowly shook her head. "Let's hope it doesn't happen again—to your family or to anyone else in our community."

Grace nodded and headed back to the dining room with her customers' coffee. Having Gary Walker back in town was hard enough to deal with. Now she had the added worry of whether another break-in would occur.

Chapter 11

"I t's good you could meet me and Ruth after work today," Grace said to her mother as the three of them headed down the sidewalk toward the quilt shop, where a variety of fabric was sold.

Mom nodded. "I thought if we looked at some material for your wedding dress, it might take our minds off this morning's break-in."

"Did Dad get everything cleaned up?"

"Jah. He and Martha worked on it while Luke made some deliveries."

Ruth pursed her lips as she slowed her steps. "I don't suppose he changed his mind about calling the sheriff?"

"He says he will turn the other cheek, just like before."

"What if it happens again?"

"Then we'll have to deal with it."

Grace clenched her fingers around the straps of her black handbag. *How do we deal with it?* She wanted to scream out the question but knew it was best to keep silent. When Ruth had met her after work, she'd mentioned that Gary had come into the bakeshop asking questions. It made Grace feel more anxious than ever. What if Gary didn't leave Holmes County? What if he decided to stay and torment her indefinitely? What if more break-ins occurred?

"Oh, there's Cleon's mamm, Irene." Mom pointed to the dark-haired Amish woman who'd just gotten out of her buggy across the street. "If the two of you would like to go inside the quilt store and start looking around, I'll join you in a few minutes. I want to see how the Schrocks' trip to Rexford went and speak to Irene about making some beeswax candles for your wedding."

"Sure, Mom, we can do that," Ruth said as the two of them moved toward the door of the shop.

Ruth nudged Grace's arm as they began looking through some bolts of blue material. "I'm so happy for you and Cleon. I'll bet you can hardly wait for the wedding."

"I am looking forward to it," Grace admitted, "but it's hard to concentrate on wedding plans with what's been going on lately."

"You mean the break-ins?"

"Jah."

"Like Dad said, maybe it won't happen again. Maybe whoever broke into his shop got what they wanted when they stole his tools."

Grace wished she could believe it wouldn't happen again, but she had a terrible feeling that the break-ins were only the beginning of their troubles. If Gary had come here to make good on his threat to get even with her, then there could be more attacks. Should she tell her folks who Gary was—that she'd dated him during her rumschpringe years? Would that be enough to convince Dad that he needed to notify the sheriff?

She cringed. If she told her folks about Gary, wouldn't that lead to more questions? Should she tell them the truth about her marriage to Wade, or would it be better to keep quiet and see what happened with Gary?

"Grace, are you listening to me?" Ruth nudged Grace's arm again.

"Wh–what was that?"

"Do you think there will be more attacks?"

"Oh, I hope not." Grace pulled a bolt of blue material off the rack and held it up. "I think this is the one I want."

"Should we look for some white to make your apron now?"

"Okay." Grace followed Ruth to the other side of the room. Several shelves near the front of the store were stocked with bolts of white material, and she glanced out the window to see if Mom was still talking to Cleon's mother. She didn't see any sign of either woman. "I wonder what could be taking Mom so long," she said, turning to face her sister. "I don't see her anywhere, and I'm getting worried."

"She and Irene probably went into one of the other stores. You know how gabby our mamm can get whenever she's with one of her friends."

Grace nodded. "Jah, she does like to talk."

"What do you think of this?" Ruth asked, as she handed a bolt of white material over to Grace.

"It's nice, but I'd like to keep looking awhile."

"Want me to hold it out in case you decide it's the best one?"

"Sure." Grace looked out the window again, and she nearly dropped the bolt of material she held when she saw her mother standing on the sidewalk talking to Gary.

"What's wrong, Grace? Your face has gone pale as goat's milk," Ruth said in a tone of obvious concern.

"It. . .it's that reporter. He's talking to Mom, and I've got to stop him." Grace thrust the material into her sister's hands and rushed out the door.

Judith heard Grace holler even before she saw her running down the sidewalk, frantically waving her arms.

"What is it, Grace? What's the matter?"

Grace gulped in a quick breath and grabbed hold of Judith's arm. "I—I thought you were with Irene."

"I was, but she was in a hurry to get home, so she left a few minutes ago." Judith turned to the English man she'd been talking to and smiled. "My daughter's choosing the material for her wedding dress today, and she's real excited."

"Is she now?" Gary looked over at Grace and offered her a wide grin. "Who's the lucky man?"

"Mom, are you coming?" Grace gave Judith's arm a little tug, and their elbows collided. "Sorry."

"No harm done. I'll come with you as soon as I've answered this man's questions."

"He's some kind of a reporter, Mom. Dad wouldn't like it if

anything you said was put in some publication for the whole world to read." Grace gripped her mother's arm, and Judith noticed a look of fear in her daughter's eyes.

The man stared at Grace, and his auburn-colored brows drew together. "Say, haven't we met before?"

Grace's eyes darted back and forth, and her face turned crimson. "Mom, let's go."

Judith had never seen Grace act in such a strange manner. She seemed afraid of the man. Did the thought of being asked a few questions make her that nervous, or was she still feeling jumpy about the break-ins?

Judith turned to the reporter and smiled. "I think we'd best be on our way."

He gave her a quick nod. "Sure. I've got some business that needs tending to, anyway."

Judith hurried off toward the quilt shop with her distraught daughter beside her.

"What did you tell that fellow?" Grace asked before they entered the store. "You didn't mention the break-ins, did you?"

"Of course not. If your daed doesn't want the sheriff to know, he sure wouldn't want such news put in some magazine or newspaper for everyone to read."

"What kind of questions did he ask, and what did you tell him?"

Judith shrugged. "He wanted to know my name and how long I've lived in Holmes County. Then he asked me a couple of questions about our family."

Grace halted in front of the shop door. "What kind of questions?"

"Just wondered how many children I have and what type of work my husband does for a living. They were simple questions, and I saw no harm in answering."

"If he tries to talk to you again, I hope you won't answer."

Judith gave her daughter's arm a gentle squeeze. "Why do you fret so much? Why can't you be more like your sister Martha? *Sie druwwelt sich wehe nix.*"

Grace frowned. "What do you mean, 'She doesn't worry about

much of anything'? Martha worries about those dogs of hers more than you realize."

"Maybe so, but she doesn't worry about everything the way you do." Judith nodded toward the store. "Shall we go inside and choose your material now?"

Grace nodded, but her wide eyes revealed fear as she watched the reporter cross the street and begin talking to an Amish man.

"You all right? You seem awfully naerfich this afternoon."

"I'm fine."

"I think you overreacted to that reporter, don't you?"

Grace didn't answer; she just opened the shop door and followed her mother inside.

Roman had just stepped outside his shop to load the rocking chair Martin Gingerich had asked him to make for his folks' anniversary into Martin's market buggy when a truck rumbled up the driveway. It halted a few feet from where he stood, and when the driver got out, he recognized him immediately—Bill Collins, the land developer who'd expressed interest in buying Roman's land.

"Afternoon," Bill said, lifting his hand in a wave.

Roman merely grunted, and Martin, who stood beside his buggy, gave him a strange look.

"I was in the area and thought I'd stop by and see if you've changed your mind about selling your land."

"Nope, sure haven't." Roman glanced over at Martin, thinking the young man didn't need to be in on this conversation. "The chair's secure in your buggy now, so you can be on your way."

Martin hesitated but finally climbed into the driver's seat and took up the reins. As he directed the horse down the driveway, he stuck his head out the window and hollered, "I'll let you know what the folks had to say about the chair, and danki for getting it done early for me."

"You're welcome." Roman turned back to Bill Collins. "As I said before, I'm not interested in selling my land to you or anyone else."

"You sure about that?"

"Very sure." When Roman headed for his shop, Bill followed so close he could feel the man's warm breath blowing on the back of his neck.

"I hope you'll at least take a look at these figures," Bill said, holding a notebook in front of Roman's nose.

Roman scanned the paper quickly, and his spine went rigid. The man was offering a tidy sum. Even so—

"If you'd like to discuss my offer with your family, I'd be happy to leave you a copy of these figures." Bill started to tear off the piece of paper, but Roman stopped him with a shake of his head.

"Don't bother. My place isn't for sale, plain and simple." He pushed past the man. "Now if you'll excuse me, I have work waiting."

"You won't get an offer like this every day," Bill called. "I would suggest that you think on it some more."

Roman gave no reply. Six months ago, the Larsons had asked about buying his property as an investment. He had told them no, too, so he sure wasn't about to sell off his land to some money-greedy land grabber who wanted to turn it into a development of fancy English houses with electricity. And a golf course was the last thing their Amish community needed!

As Martha stood at the kitchen sink peeling potatoes for their supper, she thought about the break-in of her father's shop that morning. Ruth had said that Dad seemed real upset at the time. Yet he'd refused to talk about the incident when Martha had taken some lunch out to him later that afternoon.

Martha knew what the Bible said about forgiveness, turning the other check, and loving one's enemies, but she still wondered if the sheriff should be notified.

Forcing herself to concentrate on the matter at hand, she placed the potatoes on the cutting board and cut them into hunks, then dropped them into a kettle, filled it with cold water, and set it aside. She wouldn't start cooking them until her sisters and Mom came home, and the ham she'd put in the oven a short time ago would be okay until then, too. Maybe she would take a book and go sit on the back porch to relax and read awhile.

She hurried up to her room, grabbed the historical novel she'd borrowed from Ruth a few days ago, and headed down the stairs. When she entered the kitchen, she placed the book on the table and opened the oven to check on the ham.

As she closed the oven door, she heard a sound. What was it? A creak? A bump? Hair prickled on the back of her head as she peered out the window. Nothing out of the ordinary, at least not that she could see.

She turned away from the window and had just picked up her book when a deafening crack split through the air. The kitchen window shattered, and a brick flew into the room, landing with a thud on the floor.

Martha let out a bloodcurdling scream, and with no thought for her safety, she dashed out the back door.

Chapter 12

Martha stepped onto the back porch. Cold, damp air sent a shiver rippling through her body. She scanned the yard but saw no one. "Someone had to have thrown that brick; now where did they go?" she muttered.

Taking the steps two at a time and ignoring how cold and wet the ground felt on her bare feet, she sprinted across the yard. Looking around, she listened for any unusual sounds. Nothing was out of the ordinary.

Needing to know if Heidi and her puppies were safe, Martha raced for the barn, her heart pounding like a herd of stampeding horses.

She had almost reached the door when she noticed a straw hat lying on the ground. It didn't look like any of her father's hats, and she bent to pick it up, wondering if he might recently have purchased a new one. *I'd better take this out to Dad's shop when I tell him about the brick, but not until I've checked on Heidi and her brood.*

Martha opened the barn door, lit the lantern hanging from a beam overhead, and peered cautiously around, allowing her breathing and heartbeat to slow. She saw no one and heard nothing but the gentle nicker of the two buggy horses inside their stalls and the cooing of some pigeons in the loft overhead.

She hung the straw hat on a nail near the door and started toward the back of the building, but she'd only taken a few steps, when a mouse darted in front of her. She let out a yelp, screeched to a halt, and drew in a shaky breath as the tiny critter scurried under a bale of straw. *I'm okay.*

It was only a maus. *There's nothing to be nervous about.*

With another quick glance around, she rushed over to the box that had become the temporary home for Heidi and her puppies. A feeling of relief washed over her when she discovered that the pups were nursing and Heidi was sleeping peacefully.

"I'll check on you again after supper," Martha whispered, patting the top of the dog's silky head.

She made her way quickly back to the place where she'd lit the lantern, extinguished the flame, and lifted the straw hat from the nail.

Once outside, Martha scoured the yard one more time; then seeing no one in sight, she dashed for her father's shop.

"You sure have sold a lot of honey lately," Cleon's brother Ivan commented, as the two headed home from town in one of their family's closed-in buggies. After they'd finished helping their father and younger brothers, Willard and Delbert, in the fields earlier that day, the two of them had made some honey deliveries and taken a few orders.

Cleon smiled. "I'm doing real well here of late."

"Think you'll ever quit helping Pop on the farm and go out on your own with the honey business?" Ivan's dark eyes looked full of question as he tipped his head.

"I hope so. Never have liked farming that much. I'll have to find more customers for my honey than just a few stores in the towns around here and a handful of people from our community, though."

"Looks to me like you've got more customers than just a handful." Ivan tapped Cleon's arm. "We delivered twenty quarts of honey this afternoon, and you met with five others who want to become regular customers."

"I'm glad for that, but it's still not enough to make a decent living."

"You'll be gettin' married soon, so I can see why you might need some extra cash."

Cleon nodded. "The wood for the house I'm building on the

acreage behind the Hostettlers' place is costing a lot more than I'd figured, so it's taking longer than I'd planned."

"Building materials aren't cheap anymore, that's for sure."

"Nothing's cheap nowadays."

"So, what'd Grace want when she came by to see you this morning?" Ivan asked. "I got so busy helping Pop with chores all morning, I forgot to ask."

Cleon grimaced. "The Hostettlers had a break-in at their house after church last Sunday, but we didn't hear about it because we left for Montana early the next morning."

"That's too bad. Was anything stolen?"

"Not until this morning."

"They had another break-in this morning?"

"Not at the house, but Roman's shop got broken into. Grace said whoever did it made a mess of things, and some of her daed's tools were stolen, too."

"That's a shame. You think it could have been done by whoever dumped over those outhouses some weeks ago?"

Cleon shrugged. "Could be, but that was several miles from here."

"You've got a point, but there was some cowtipping done at the bishop's place awhile back, too."

"I'm sure that was done by some pranksters."

"Do you have any idea why someone would want to target Grace's family like that?"

"Nope. None at all."

"Well, hopefully, it won't happen again."

"Sure hope not. The Hostettlers don't need this. No one does."

"Changing the subject," Ivan said, "you mentioned before that you thought Grace felt nervous about getting married. I was wondering if you're feeling that way, too."

"Not really. I love Grace a lot, and I'm sure we're going to be happy living together as husband and wife."

"You plannin' to start a family right away?"

Cleon shrugged. "Kinner will come in God's time, not ours."

"Jah, well, I know for a fact that our mamm's lookin' forward to bein' a *grossmudder*, so she'll be real happy when you do have some kinner."

Cleon thumped his brother's arm. "Maybe you ought to find yourself an aldi and get married, too. That way you can take an active part in giving Mamm a bunch of *kinskinner*."

Ivan wrinkled his nose. "I'm in no hurry for that. Besides, women have too many peculiar ideas to suit me."

Cleon grimaced as a vision of Grace came to mind. She'd been acting kind of peculiar herself lately. He hoped she wasn't getting cold feet about marrying him. His whole being ached with the desire to make Grace his wife, and he didn't think he could stand it if she broke things off.

Ivan leaned closer to Cleon. "Say, you'd better watch out for that hilly dip we're coming to. Last week my friend Enos hit a deer standing in the road."

"I'll be careful." Cleon guided the horse up the hill and started down the other side. They had just reached the bottom of the hill when he spotted a black pickup in his side mirror coming up behind them at a pretty good clip. The driver, wearing a pair of sunglasses and a baseball cap, laid on his horn, and Cleon steered the horse toward the shoulder of the road, glad he had one of their more docile mares today. With no traffic coming in the opposite direction, he figured the truck would have plenty of room to pass. Apparently the driver didn't think so, because he nearly sideswiped Cleon's buggy as he whipped around him and raced down the road.

"Whew, that was too close for comfort," Cleon said, sweat beading on his forehead and rolling onto his cheeks. "I wish people wouldn't drive so fast on these back country roads."

"Makes me wonder if that fellow was trying to run us off the road on purpose," Ivan grumbled.

Cleon gripped the reins a bit tighter and directed the horse back onto the road. "What would make you think that?"

"Last week, Willard and I were heading home from a singing, and a truck nearly sideswiped our open buggy. It was dark out, and we couldn't see the color or make of the vehicle, but we knew it was a truck." Ivan's dark brows drew together in a frown. "Willard was driving, and boy, *waar er awwer bees.*"

"I can imagine just how angry he was, but it's not likely that it was the same truck. Whoever was driving wasn't trying to hit you on purpose any more than that fellow was trying to hit us just now. Some Englishers get in too big of a hurry and drive too fast, that's all."

"Humph!" Ivan folded his arms and stared straight ahead. "Some English don't think we have a right to be on the road with our buggies, and they don't like the road apples our horses leave, either. It's almost like they're singling us out because we're different."

Cleon thought again about the break-ins that had occurred at the Hostettlers' and wondered if they'd been isolated incidents or if the family might have been singled out. He needed to have a talk with Roman as he'd promised Grace he would do.

"Mind if we stop by the Hostettlers' before we go home?" he asked his brother. "I want to speak with Roman about those break-ins."

Ivan shrugged. "Makes no never mind to me. Maybe the brothers will do our chores if we don't get home on time."

Cleon grunted. "Jah, right. That's about as likely as a heat wave in the middle of January."

"It's past quitting time," Roman said when Luke returned to the shop after loading some cabinets for Ray Larson, their nearest English neighbor. "You're free to go whenever you want."

"You sure about that? We've still got several pieces of furniture that need fixing."

"They can wait until tomorrow. We've both put in a long day, and I'm exhausted."

Luke nodded. "I'm kind of tired myself."

"Sure was nice of John Peterson to come by this afternoon and loan us some tools," Roman said as he put a final coat of stain on a straight-backed chair.

"I hope you don't mind that I mentioned your break-in to John when I went home for lunch and found him visiting my daed." Luke nodded toward the shelf where the hammer and saw lay that John had dropped by shortly after lunch.

"Why would I mind?"

"I know you don't want the incident reported to the sheriff, so I figured you might not want anyone else knowing about it, either."

Roman shrugged. "We live in a small community, and I've told some of my Amish neighbors. I'm sure the news would have gotten out soon enough."

Luke opened his mouth as if to comment, but the shop door opened, and Martha rushed into the room, interrupting their conversation.

"Dad, you'll never believe what happened a few minutes ago!"

A look of fear covered his daughter's face. "What is it, Martha? What's happened?"

"I was in the kitchen getting supper started, and a brick flew right through the window."

"What?" Roman dropped the rag he'd been using to stain the chair and hurried to her side. "Are you all right? Did the brick hit you?"

"I'm okay. It just shook me up a bit."

"Did you see who did it?" Luke asked.

Martha shook her head. "I ran outside right away, but whoever threw the brick must have been a fast runner, because no one was in sight." She lifted the straw hat in her hand. "I went out to the barn to check on Heidi and her pups and found this lying on the ground outside the barn door."

Luke grabbed hold of the hat. "That's mine. I must have dropped it as I was putting my horse in the corral when I got here this morning."

"Are you sure you weren't wearing it when you went outside to load those cabinets for Ray? Maybe you dropped it then."

"I'm sure I didn't have it on." Luke plunked the hat on his head. "Want me to take a look around the place before I head home? Maybe whoever threw the brick is still lurkin' about."

Roman groaned. "I'm guessing the culprit took off like a shot as soon as that brick hit the window."

"I believe you're right, Dad." Martha touched his arm. "I know you won't press charges, but don't you think it's time to notify the sheriff?"

He shook his head. "Psalm 46:1 says, 'God is our refuge and strength, a very present help in trouble.' "

"If someone's out to get us—and it seems like they are—I'm worried that the next attack could be worse." Martha's chin trembled. "If this keeps up, someone's likely to get hurt."

The truth of her words sliced through Roman like a knife. The thought of someone in his family getting hurt gave him the chills, but he had to keep believing and trusting that God would protect his family. He was about to say so when his shop door opened again and in walked Cleon and his brother Ivan.

"I see you made it back from Montana," Roman said. "Did you have a good trip?"

Cleon nodded. "We got back last night." He glanced around the room and grimaced. "Grace stopped by our place on her way to work and told me about the break-ins that happened at your house last week and then here this morning."

"Make that three acts of vandalism," Martha said. "Someone tossed a brick through our kitchen window a short time ago."

Cleon's mouth dropped open. "Was anyone hurt?"

Martha shook her head. "Sure scared me, though."

"Any idea who could have done these things?"

Roman shrugged. "I'm guessing it's some rowdy fellows—maybe the same ones who dumped over those outhouses near Kidron."

"I heard a couple of cows got tipped over awhile back in Bishop King's field," Ivan put in. "One of the bishop's sons saw some English fellows running through their land, so he's pretty sure it was them who pushed the cows over."

"Dumping outhouses and pushing over cows doesn't compare to breaking into someone's home or place of business," Cleon said. "Makes me wonder if someone has a grudge against you. What do you think, Roman?"

Roman contemplated Cleon's question a few seconds. He guessed there might be a few people who weren't too happy with him right now: Luke, because Roman had docked his pay; Steven, because his wife's birthday present had been ruined; and Bill Collins, because Roman refused to sell his land. Even so, he didn't think any of them would resort to vandalism. Of course, he didn't know the land developer personally, so he guessed it might be possible that the determined fellow could resort to scare tactics in order to get Roman to agree to his terms.

"What does the sheriff have to say about all this?" Cleon asked, breaking into Roman's swirling thoughts.

"Haven't told him," Roman muttered, staring at the floor where a blob of stain still lingered.

"How come?" The question came from Ivan this time.

"Saw no need. I wouldn't press charges even if we knew who'd done it. I'm turning the other cheek and relying on God's protection, like the Bible says we should."

Cleon leaned against Roman's desk. "Has anyone else in the community been bothered?"

"Not that I know of."

"If we hear that anyone has, what will you do?" Martha asked.

"I'll get with the others, and we'll have a talk with our church leaders and see how they think it should be handled." Roman put his arm around his daughter's trembling shoulders. "In the meantime, we need to be more watchful while we pray for God's protection over our friends and family."

Chapter 13

Grace awoke the following morning with another pounding headache. Hearing about Martha's scare with the flying brick had about done her in, and she'd gone to bed early.

With great effort, she pulled herself out of bed and padded over to the window. It was a sunny day, yet she felt as if a dark rain cloud hung over her head—the whole house, really. She continued to struggle with the need to tell her folks she suspected Gary might be out for revenge. However, her fear of them finding out about her previous life kept her from saying anything.

Grace moved away from the window, frustration bubbling in her chest. Maybe it would be best either to tell Gary what she suspected or to ask him to leave Holmes County. She clenched her fists and held her arms tightly against her sides. Unless Gary had changed, it wasn't likely that he would be willing to leave the area simply because she asked him to. If he could be cruel enough to break into her home, what else might he be capable of doing?

A knock on the bedroom door brought Grace's thoughts to a halt. "Mom has breakfast ready, and we're going to be late for work if we don't eat soon," Ruth called from the other side of the door.

"I'll be down in a minute." Grace didn't feel up to going to work, but she didn't want to leave her employer shorthanded. Besides, the only chance she had of seeing Gary was in town.

She hurried to get washed and dressed, then took two aspirins for her headache and headed downstairs.

"Are you okay, Grace?" Mom asked, turning from her place at the stove and squinting. "You look awful *mied* this morning. Didn't you sleep well?"

Grace went to the refrigerator and removed a quart of grape juice. "I am a bit tired, and I woke up with a headache, but I'll be okay."

"Are you sure about that?" Ruth, who had been setting the table, clicked her tongue. "Your face is paler than a bedsheet, sister."

"Maybe you're coming down with that achy-bones flu that was going around," Mom said with a look of concern. "Might be good if you stayed home and rested today."

Grace shook her head. "I'll be fine once I've had some breakfast." She glanced around the room. "Where are Dad and Martha?"

"Your daed's still out doing his chores, and Martha went to check on Fritz, Heidi, and the hundlin."

"Those two dogs and the puppies are all our little sister thinks about anymore." Ruth's forehead wrinkled. "What she needs is a boyfriend."

"Martha's only eighteen." Mom broke a couple of eggs into the frying pan and glanced over her shoulder. "She has plenty of time to find the right man."

Ruth placed the last glass on the table and turned to face Grace, who was pouring juice into each of the glasses. "I guess what Mom says is true. Look at how long it took you to find a man and decide to get married."

Grace winced, even though she was sure Ruth wasn't trying to be mean. *What would my family say if they knew my secret? How would Cleon deal with things if he knew? Is it time to tell him the truth?*

The back door flew open, and Martha rushed into the room. Her lips were compressed, and her eyes looked huge. "The pups are all alone in their box crying for their mamm's milk, and I couldn't find Heidi anywhere." She hurried over to their mother. "What am I going to do? Those puppies are too young to make it on their own."

Mom pushed the frying pan to the back of the stove. "Calm down and take a deep breath. I'm sure Heidi is somewhere nearby. Probably just needed a break from her pups, or maybe she went outside to do her business."

99

"Mom's right," Grace put in. "Heidi will return to her puppies soon; you'll see."

"Are you sure you're up to going to work today?" Ruth asked again when she noticed how Grace was gripping the buggy reins with clenched fingers and a determined set to her jaw. She didn't know which sister to be the most concerned about this morning—Grace, who looked like she should be home in bed, or Martha, who had refused to eat breakfast so she could hunt for her missing dog.

"I need to go to work," Grace said with a nod.

"You could have gone to the phone shed to let your boss know you weren't feeling well."

"My headache's eased some, and I saw no need to stay home. Besides, it would have left them shorthanded at the restaurant, and I know from experience how hard that can be on the other waitresses."

Grace stared straight ahead, gripping the reins so tightly that the veins on the back of her hands stood out.

"You've been acting awful strange for the past couple of weeks. Is it the trouble we've had at our place that has you so *engschderich*?" Ruth questioned.

"I'm not anxious, just concerned."

"We all are."

"First the break-in at the house, followed by Dad's shop being vandalized. Then a brick thrown that could have hit Martha, and now her dog is missing."

"I'm sure Heidi's not really missing. I'll bet by the time we get home from work Martha will be all smiles because Heidi's back in her box with the puppies again."

"Maybe so, but that won't undo what's already been done." Grace's voice cracked as she guided the horse to the side of the road.

"Why are we stopping? Aren't you worried we'll be late for work?"

"I need to tell you something, but you must promise not to repeat to anyone what I'm about to say." Grace's blue eyes flickered, and her chin quivered slightly. "Do I have your word on this?"

Ruth gave a quick nod as she reached over to squeeze her sister's hand. She couldn't imagine what Grace might tell her that she didn't want to have repeated.

Grace leaned forward and massaged her forehead. "You know that reporter in town?"

"The one who says he's doing stories on the Amish here and has been asking all kinds of questions?"

"Jah."

"What about him?"

"His name is Gary Walker, and I went out with him for a while when I first moved away. It was during a time when I lived in Cincinnati."

"You. . .you did?"

"Jah. I thought he was cute and fun at first, but then he started acting like he owned me." Grace lifted her head, and when she looked over at Ruth, tears filled her eyes. "Gary had a temper, and when I refused to go out with him anymore, he said I would be sorry and that he'd make me pay for breaking up with him."

Ruth let her sister's words sink in. If the reporter had been angry because Grace broke up with him, was it possible that he'd come here to make good on his threat? "Oh, Grace, do you think he might be the one responsible for the damage that has been done at our place?"

Grace nodded. "If I see him in town today, I'm going to ask if he's the one."

"Maybe it would be best if I'm with you when you speak to him."

Grace picked up the reins and gave them a snap. "I appreciate your concern, but this is something I must do alone."

Throughout Grace's workday, she kept an eye out for Gary, but he never came into the restaurant, and she didn't notice him outside whenever she looked out the window. Maybe he'd gone to one of the nearby towns to do his research. Or maybe he'd left the area altogether. She hoped that was so, but a niggling feeling told her otherwise. If Gary had come to Holmes County to make her pay for running off with Wade, then he probably wasn't done with her yet.

By the time Grace got off work, her headache had returned. She was glad she'd told Ruth that she would walk over to the bakeshop after work. It would give her time to think. She hoped the fresh fall air would help clear the throbbing in her head, as well.

She'd only made it halfway there when someone called her name. She whirled around and spotted Gary leaning against an Amish buggy parked next to the curb.

Grace's heart pounded so hard she felt it pulsate in her head as she made her way over to where he stood. *I've got to do this. I need to confront him now.*

"Hey, Gracie," he said with a lopsided grin. "Haven't seen you around in a while. Have you changed your mind about going out with me?"

Grace shook her head vigorously. "I'm surprised to see that you're still in Holmes County. I figured you would have enough information to write ten stories about the Amish by now."

He chuckled. "You're right. I do. But I've decided to stick around the area awhile longer and do a couple of stories about some of the events that will be taking place here, as well as in Wayne and Tuscarawas counties, during the next few months."

"The next few months? How can you afford to stay here that long?"

"My granddaddy died six months ago and left me a bundle." He winked at her. "So I've got enough money to stay here as long as I want."

"If he left you so much, then why do you have to work at all?"

"Let's just say I enjoy the work that I've chosen to do. It makes me feel in the know."

She tipped her head. "Are you really a freelance reporter?"

"Of course." He lifted the camera hanging from the strap around his shoulder. "Is it so hard to believe I'm gainfully employed?"

Grace shrugged. When they had been teenagers, Gary had been kind of lazy. While the other kids they'd hung around with all had jobs, he'd been content to take money from his dad, who seemed to have more than he needed. It was hard to imagine Gary holding down any kind of job—much less working on his own as a photographer and reporter. Of course, some people changed when they matured. Grace was living proof of that.

"So, how about the two of us going somewhere for a cup of coffee?" Gary asked.

"I told you before that I'm—"

"I know. I know. You're soon to be married."

"Jah."

"Jah? What's this jah stuff, Gracie? I'm English, remember? So I'd appreciate it if when we're together you would speak English."

"Sorry," Grace mumbled. She was losing her nerve, and if she didn't say what was on her mind soon, she might never say it. "Some. . .uh. . . unusual things have been going on at our place lately. I'm wondering what you know about it."

His forehead creased. "If you're trying to say something, Gracie, then spit it out and quit croaking like a frog."

She glanced around to be sure no one was listening. "The thing is. . .we've had a problem with—"

"With what? What kind of problem are you having?"

She felt his hot breath blowing against her face and took a step back. "Someone broke into our house a week ago, and then yesterday morning my dad discovered that his woodworking shop had been ransacked." She paused to gauge his reaction, but he simply stared at her with a stoic expression. "As if that wasn't enough, someone threw a brick through our kitchen window while my youngest sister was fixing supper last night, and this morning, one of her dogs went missing."

A muscle in the side of Gary's face quivered slightly, but he said nothing.

"Do you know anything about this?"

He shook his head. "What kind of crazy question is that? How would I know anything about some break-ins at your place?"

A sense of frustration welled in Grace's soul. Had she really expected he would admit what he'd done?

"Look, Gracie," he said in his most charming voice. "I don't know anything about any break-ins, but I do appreciate the information."

Her mouth dropped open. "You. . .you appreciate it?"

He nodded.

"Why is that?"

Gary pulled a notebook from his shirt pocket. "Because this will make one great story."

Chapter 14

"A re they accepting the little bottle with the formula we made up?" Judith asked as she stepped into the barn and found Martha bent over a box, trying to feed Heidi's puppies.

Martha looked up and offered a weak smile. "They're eating some, but not as well as they would if their mamm was here feeding them."

Judith gave her daughter's shoulder a gentle squeeze. "Even if Heidi doesn't come home, I'm confident that the pups will live; you'll see to it."

"I spent the whole day searching for Heidi. Luke and Dad even helped me look during their lunch hour, but it was a waste of their time." Martha frowned. "If Dad would only let the sheriff know about the things that have been happening to us lately, maybe he could find out who's doing this and why."

"Your daed believes the things that have happened were merely pranks, and he sees no need to notify the sheriff." Judith reached into the box and stroked one of the whimpering pups with the tip of her finger. "Just pray, dear one. That's the best we can do."

When Martha left the barn sometime later, she noticed a gray SUV pulling into their yard. John Peterson opened his door and stepped down, and to her surprise, Toby King climbed out of the passenger's side, holding a cute little sheltie in his arms.

"Heidi!" Martha raced down the driveway and scooped the dog out of Toby's arms. "Where have you been, girl? I was worried about you."

"I found her wandering along the side of the road near my house," Toby said. "I knew you had a couple of shelties, and I decided to bring her over and see if she was yours."

"I was heading to town and saw Toby walking alongside the road, so I gave him a ride," John put in.

"I appreciate that." Martha stroked the top of the dog's head. "Heidi gave birth to a batch of pups not long ago, and she's still nursing. When she went missing this morning, I was afraid she'd been stolen."

John's eyebrows furrowed as he pulled his fingers through the sides of his dark, curly hair. "She probably just went for a run and lost her bearings."

"But she knows where she lives, and she's always come straight home before."

"Maybe she forgot." John tipped his head, making his slightly crooked nose look more bent than usual. Martha figured he'd probably broken it sometime—maybe when he was a boy. She didn't think it would be polite to ask, so she averted her gaze and focused on the trembling dog in her arms.

John pointed down the driveway toward her father's shop. "When I brought some of my tools for your dad to borrow, he said he thought the incidents that had happened to your family were probably done by some rowdy English kids. Does he still think that?"

Martha nodded soberly.

"Luke's been hanging around with some English fellows. I wouldn't be surprised if he wasn't in on some of those pranks." Toby gave one quick nod.

Martha pursed her lips. "I doubt Luke would take part in anything like that, but if I could prevent more pranks from happening to us or anyone else, I surely would."

John shook his head. "You'd best not do anything foolish, girl. I told your dad I would keep my eyes and ears open, and if I hear or see anything suspicious, I'll be sure to let him know."

Martha almost laughed at John referring to her as a girl. He wasn't much more than a boy himself—maybe in his mid-twenties.

"I'll keep a lookout for things, too," Toby said. "And if I find out Luke had anything to do with it, I'll inform my daed."

Martha was on the verge of telling Toby there would be no need for him to tell his bishop father anything, but she figured the less said about Luke, the better.

"I should get Heidi back in the box with her brood." She smiled at the young men. "Thanks for returning her to me."

"Glad we could help," they said in unison.

Grace leaned against the buggy seat and closed her eyes. She was glad Ruth had been willing to drive home, because after the encounter she'd had with Gary awhile ago, she probably couldn't have kept her mind on the road if she'd been the one in the driver's seat.

Ruth reached over and touched Grace's arm. "Does your head still hurt?"

"Jah."

"Sorry about that. Was the restaurant real busy today?"

"No more than usual."

"Things were sure hectic at the bakeshop. Seemed like everyone wanted a dozen donuts, all at the same time. At one point, there must have been twenty customers milling around the store, and even with Sadie's help this afternoon, I could barely keep up."

Grace nodded. She didn't feel like talking right now. All she wanted to do was go home, take a couple of aspirin, and lie down.

"I've been mulling over what you told me on the way to work this morning," Ruth said. "I think you should tell the folks about that reporter fellow."

Grace opened her eyes and blinked a couple of times. "No." The word was nearly a whisper. "I don't want them to know. At least, not yet."

"Why not? It isn't as if you're running around with the Englisher now. You were only a teenager when you dated him, and it was during your rumschpringe, so Mom and Dad should understand."

Grace inwardly cringed. There was a lot more to the story than she'd told Ruth, and if her folks found out everything, she was sure they wouldn't understand. She knew she should have told them that she'd married Wade and that a year later he'd been killed in a car accident. But if she'd told them that much, she might have had to reveal other details she'd rather not talk about.

Grace's thoughts went to Cleon, the way they always did whenever she reflected on her past. If she had only known him when she was a teenager, she might not have run off with her friends to try out the English world. Too bad his folks hadn't moved from Pennsylvania to Holmes County a few years sooner than they did. The love she felt for Cleon was strong—not based solely on physical attraction or having fun, the way it had been with Wade. With Cleon, she felt an assurance that he would always be there for her, through good times and bad. *If that's so, then why haven't I found the courage to tell him the truth?*

"If you won't tell Mom and Dad about the English reporter, then at least let me go with you when you speak to him," Ruth said, breaking into Grace's thoughts.

Grace's eyes snapped open. "Uh. . .I saw Gary this afternoon when I was walking to the bakeshop to meet you after work."

"Why didn't you tell me about this before now?"

"My head hurt, and I—I didn't want to talk about anything unpleasant."

Ruth pulled back on the reins.

"What are you doing?"

"I'm pulling over to the shoulder of the road so we can discuss this some more."

Grace shook her head. "Better keep on driving. There's no point in us being late and worrying Mom. She's had enough to worry about lately."

"That's true." Ruth glanced over at Grace. "What did Gary say when you talked to him? Did you come right out and ask if he's responsible for the awful things that have been done at our place?"

Grace moistened her lips with the tip of her tongue. "I did, but he denied knowing anything about it."

"Do you believe him?"

"No."

"Did he say when he would be leaving Holmes County?"

Grace clenched her fists as she relived the anxiety she'd felt during that conversation. "He says he's got lots of money and plans to stay here longer and write more stories."

"That's not good."

"No, it's not, and there's more. After I told Gary about the break-ins and the brick that was thrown through the kitchen widow, he said it would make a great story. I—I think he's planning to tell the whole world about the troubles we've been having."

Ruth gasped. "Oh, Grace, that would be *baremlich*. Dad will have a conniption fit if this gets written up in some magazine or newspaper."

"I know it would be terrible, and now I'm wishing I had never mentioned it to Gary. Nothing good came from it, since I couldn't get him to admit that he's involved."

"If you're not planning to tell the folks about this, then what are you going to do?"

Grace shrugged. "I don't know."

"Maybe Gary will decide he's got enough information on the Amish, leave the area, and never come back."

Grace pursed her lips. After seeing the determined look on Gary's face today, she felt certain that he would write the story. The only questions remaining were how soon until he found a publisher, and when would the story be released?

Chapter 15

For the next several weeks, life was quiet at the Hostettlers'. Grace felt grateful that her family hadn't been attacked again, and she figured if Gary was behind the earlier incidents, he was lying low so as not to cast suspicion on himself. If he'd written an article about their break-ins, either it hadn't been published or none of the Amish in the area had seen it, because no one had mentioned it.

Since Grace didn't have to work at the restaurant this Saturday, she decided it would be a good opportunity to hem her wedding dress and get the apron and cape made. Ruth and Martha had gone shopping in Berlin; Mom was visiting her friend Alma Wengerd; and Dad would be working in his shop most of the day. The house would be quiet, and Grace would have no interruptions.

As she checked the kitchen table to be sure it had been wiped clean after breakfast, her thoughts went to Cleon. *I've got to find a good time to tell him what's on my mind, and I need to come up with the right words to say,* Grace thought as she spread the white material for her apron on the table.

She hadn't seen much of Cleon lately, between him working on their house, helping his dad and brothers on the farm, caring for his bees, and making honey deliveries.

Her fingers trailed along the edges of the soft white fabric she would wear over her wedding dress. Would it be best to wait and tell Cleon the truth after they were married, or should she keep the secret she'd been carrying for the last four years locked in her heart forever?

Grace picked up the scissors. If she could only cut out her past as she was about to cut out her wedding apron, things might go better for all.

A knock on the back door brought Grace's thoughts to a halt. "I wonder who that could be."

She opened the door. Cleon stood on the porch with a jar of amber honey is his hands. "*Guder mariye*," he said. "This is for you."

"Good morning to you, too, and danki for the honey. It's always so sweet and tasty, and I enjoy putting some in my tea." Grace took the jar and motioned Cleon inside. "I didn't expect to see you today. I figured you'd be helping your daed and bruders on the farm."

"Now that the corn has been harvested, we're pretty well caught up with things, so I decided to use today to make some deliveries to the stores in Berlin that sell my honey." He smiled and leaned so close to Grace that she could smell the minty odor of the mouthwash he must have used that morning. "Thought maybe you'd like to ride along if you're not busy with other things."

Grace nodded toward the table. "I was working on the cape and apron for our wedding, but I can finish up with that later on."

"You sure?"

"Jah." Grace would never pass up an opportunity to spend time with Cleon. "Just give me a minute to clear the table, and we can be on our way."

As Ruth and Martha left the market with their sacks of groceries, Ruth noticed a few more Amish buggy horses had been tied to the hitching rail since she and her sister had arrived. She wrinkled her nose as the sweaty scent of the horses greeted her and wondered as her horse nuzzled the one next to him what these animals would have to say if they could talk.

"Say, isn't that Luke over there with those English fellows?" Martha pointed to the other side of the parking lot, where several cars were parked.

Ruth turned to look. Sure enough, Luke stood beside two young

Englishers dressed in blue jeans and white T-shirts. They leaned against a fancy red sports car and seemed to be engrossed in conversation.

Martha nudged Ruth's arm with her elbow. "I wonder what Luke's doing in town. I figured he would be working for Dad today."

Ruth nodded. "I thought so, too, but maybe he had a delivery to make and stopped by the market to buy something for lunch."

Martha opened the door of the buggy and set her paper sack in the back. "I didn't see anything in his hands, did you?"

"Maybe he hasn't gone into the store yet."

"If you'd like to go over and say hello, I'll wait here with the buggy."

Ruth was tempted to follow her sister's suggestion, but she and Luke hadn't been courting very long, and she didn't want him to think she was throwing herself at him. She placed her own sack of groceries in the back of the buggy and shut the door. "I don't want to interrupt his conversation."

"He'd probably like to introduce you to his friends since you're his aldi and all."

Ruth stared across the parking lot and squinted. "You think those Englishers are Luke's friends?"

"The other day when Toby brought Heidi home, he mentioned that Luke's been hanging around some English fellows, and if they weren't his friends, then why would they be gabbing away like there's no tomorrow?"

Ruth shrugged. "I don't know, but I've never seen either one of them before. If they are Luke's friends, wouldn't you think I would have met them, or at least seen them around Berlin somewhere?"

Martha shrugged. "You'll never know what's up until you go over there."

Ruth hesitated a moment, and when she caught Luke looking her way, she decided it would be rude not to at least say hello. "You're welcome to come with me," she told her sister.

"You wouldn't mind?"

"Not a bit. I'll be less nervous if you're by my side."

Martha chuckled. "Jah, right."

Ruth walked beside her sister, and when they reached the spot where Luke and the Englishers stood, she halted. "Hello, Luke. I'm surprised to see you here. Did you come to town to make a delivery for my daed this afternoon?"

He shook his head. "Uh. . .no. I'm not workin' for him today."

"But I thought Dad was getting behind on things."

"Maybe so, but he said he didn't need me today."

"Oh, I see."

One of the English fellows, whose curly blond hair reminded Ruth of a dust mop, snickered and nudged the other fellow, whose straight, black hair looked like it hadn't been combed in several days. His clothes smelled of smoke, and she turned her head to avoid sneezing.

The other Englisher mumbled something under his breath, but Ruth couldn't make out the words.

When Luke made no move to introduce her, she backed slowly away. "Well, I. . .uh. . .guess we'd best be on our way. It was nice seeing you, Luke."

"Right. See you around, Ruth." He offered her sister a half smile. "You, too, Martha."

"I wonder what's gotten into Luke," Martha said once they had climbed into their buggy. "He sure was acting *kariyos*, don't you think?"

Ruth nodded. "I thought he acted a bit odd, too. Maybe it was because he was with those English fellows and didn't want to let on that I'm his girlfriend." She clutched the folds in her dark blue dress. "But then, if he cares for me, why would he be too embarrassed to let anyone know we're courting?"

"Luke hasn't joined the church yet, and since he's still going through rumschpringe, I'm sure he feels he has the right to run around with those Englishers."

"It's not the Englishers I have a problem with," Ruth murmured. "It's the fact that he didn't bother to introduce me. He barely acknowledged he knew me at all, much less that I'm his aldi."

"Guess you'll have to ask him about it."

"I might the next time we're alone."

"Changing the subject, is there anyplace else you'd like to stop while we're in town, or did you want to head for home now?" Martha asked as she gathered up the reins and backed the horse out of her parking spot.

"Let's stop by the bakeshop," Ruth suggested. "I'll treat you to a lemon-filled donut."

Martha smacked her lips. "Sounds good to me."

Grace and Cleon traveled along the hilly road toward Berlin in his buggy. "The other day when we went bike riding," Grace said, "I was going to discuss something with you, but we got interrupted when Ruth and Sadie came along."

He glanced over at her and smiled. "What was it you wanted to discuss?"

She gulped in a breath of fresh air and blew it out quickly, hoping to steady her nerves. "I have an aunt who moved away from Holmes County and never returned."

"Which aunt is that?"

"Her name is Rosemary, and she's my daed's only sister."

Cleon's forehead wrinkled. "I've never heard your daed mention having a sister. I thought he only had brothers."

"Dad probably wouldn't mention Aunt Rosemary. He rarely speaks of her, and when he does, it's always with a tone of regret."

"How come?"

"From what I've been told, Aunt Rosemary fell in love with an Englisher and left the Amish faith almost thirty years ago."

"I see."

"In all that time, she's never once come home for a visit or contacted any of her family."

Cleon stared straight ahead as he clucked to the horse.

"My daed's whole family was hurt by this—Dad most of all. I don't think he's ever really forgiven her for leaving."

"I can understand why he would be hurt. The fact that his sister went English and left the faith would be hard to take."

Grace's pulse pounded in her temples, and she turned her head away so Cleon wouldn't see her tears.

They rode along quietly for a while, the only sounds being the steady *clip-clop* of the horse's hooves and an occasional *whirr* of an engine as a car whizzed past. Grace hated keeping her secret from Cleon, but if he felt the way Dad did about an Amish woman marrying an Englisher, no good could come from telling him the truth. He would probably call off the wedding, and Grace loved Cleon too much to jeopardize their relationship. The best thing she could see to do was to continue keeping the painful secret to herself. She could only hope it wouldn't be revealed by someone else.

Chapter 16

Grace could hardly believe her wedding day had finally arrived. Sitting at the kitchen table and drinking a cup of tea, she reflected on the day before. Several of their Amish friends and relatives, some of whom would be table waiters during the wedding meal, had showed up early to help out. The bench wagons from both their home church district and from a neighboring district were brought over to the Hostettlers' because they would need more seating at the wedding than during a regular Sunday church service. Much of the furniture had been removed from their house and stored in clean outbuildings, while smaller items were placed in the bench wagons after the men had unloaded the benches, unfolded the legs, and arranged them in the house.

Many hands had prepared the chickens that would be served at the wedding meal as well as mounds of other food items. The four couples assigned as "roast cooks" had divided up the dressed chickens and taken them home to roast in their ovens. Aunt Clara, Mom's oldest sister, was an excellent baker and had made several batches of doughnuts. Some of the other women had made a variety of cookies, and there were three large, decorated cakes, one of which had been purchased at the bakeshop where Ruth worked.

"Guder mariye, bride-to-be," Ruth said as she stepped into the kitchen wearing a smile that stretched ear to ear. "You look like you're a hundred miles away."

"Good morning," Grace said. "I was just thinking about yesterday and all the help we had getting ready for today."

"We sure did." Ruth moved across the room and pulled out a chair at the table. "How are you feeling this morning? Are you naerfich?"

"I am a little nervous," Grace admitted.

"I'm sure I'll be nervous when I get married someday, too." Ruth took a seat beside Grace and reached for the teapot sitting in the middle of the table. "Cleon's a good man, and I'm glad the two of you will be living here until your house is finished."

Grace nodded. "At least our new home is close by so it will be easier for Cleon to work on it when he's not busy with his bees or helping his daed."

"It's obvious that he loves you, and I think you two will have a good marriage."

"I hope we can be as happy as Mom and Dad have been all these years."

"I think one of the reasons they have such a good marriage is because they see eye to eye on so many things." Ruth reached for one of the empty mugs sitting near the teapot and poured herself some tea. "Mom told me once that she believes the most important ingredient in marriage, besides loving the person you're married to, is honesty."

"Honesty?" Grace repeated as a sinking feeling made her stomach feel tied in knots. Years of regret tugged at her heart, and a twinge of guilt whispered to her that she wasn't worthy to marry Cleon—wasn't worthy to bear his children.

"Mom said from the moment she and Dad started courting, she made a promise to herself that she would never intentionally lie or keep secrets from him."

Grace inwardly groaned. She was about to begin her marriage to Cleon with a secret between them—one that could change the way he felt about her and could destroy her relationships with her parents and sisters, as well.

She set her empty mug in the sink and glanced out the kitchen window. It was a cold, crisp day in early December, but at least no snow covered the ground. Her stomach flew up when she noticed several buggies were already lined up in the yard. She knew some of their

English friends and neighbors had also arrived because a couple of vans and several cars were parked outside. It wouldn't be long before the bishop and other ministers arrived, and soon after that, the wedding service would begin. It was too late to tell Cleon her secret. That would have to wait until sometime after they were married, if at all.

Feeling the need to think about something else, Grace focused on the six teenage boys, known as the "hostlers," whose job it was to lead the horses into the barn and tie them up. For the next hour or so, those young fellows would be kept plenty busy, and during the afternoon, they would see to it that all the horses were fed.

"What are you doing in here?" Dad asked, stepping up beside Grace and placing his hand on her shoulder.

"Oh, just watching the goings-on outside."

He chuckled. "There's a lot of activity out there, all right. I imagine the bishop will be here most any time, so it might be good if you headed to the other room and got ready for the service, don't you think?"

Grace nodded and smiled, even though her stomach was still doing little flip-flops. She wanted so much to become Cleon's wife, yet she was full of apprehension and misgivings.

"I'm glad you and Cleon will be living nearby," Dad said. "It would be hard on your mamm if you were to move too far away."

Grace wondered if her father was referring to the time she'd been gone during her rumschpringe. She knew how much it had hurt her parents when she'd moved to Cincinnati and not kept in touch. When she returned home two years later without a word of explanation, they hadn't asked any questions, just welcomed her with open arms. From that day on, Grace had tried to be the perfect daughter, helping out at home without question and adhering to the church rules. Now all she had to do was be a good wife to Cleon, and everything should be fine.

Glancing down at her dark blue dress draped with a white cape and apron, Grace grew more anxious by the moment as she sat rigidly in her seat. Most of their guests had arrived, including two other ministers, but Bishop King was late, and she was getting worried. What if something had happened to him? What if someone had tried to detain the bishop and his family along the way?

Her thoughts went to Gary. Would he stoop so low as to try and stop her from marrying Cleon? Did he even know that this was her wedding day? Since he was a reporter, he might have finagled that information from someone in the community.

"I think I'd better get my horse and buggy and go looking for the bishop," Deacon Byler announced as he headed for the door.

"I'll go with you," Mose Troyer, one of the ministers, said.

Grace glanced across the room to where Cleon sat straight and tall, wearing a white shirt, black trousers, and a matching vest and jacket. Did he feel as nervous as she? Was he having second thoughts? His stoic expression gave no indication of what he might be thinking.

If she'd told him about her previous marriage and everything that had transpired after that, would he have forgiven her for keeping the truth from him? She loved Cleon, but did it really matter if only she knew the details of her rumschpringe days? After all, that was in the past. Shouldn't it stay that way?

Grace clenched her teeth so hard her jaw ached. She wished she could quit thinking about this. She had to get ahold of herself, or the entire day would be ruined.

Since the wedding wouldn't start until the bishop arrived, everyone left their seats. Some of the women went to the kitchen, some sat in groups around the living room, and most of the men went outside to mill around and visit.

Half an hour later, the bishop and his family showed up. He offered his apologies for being late, explaining that one of his carriage wheels had fallen off.

Grace breathed a sigh of relief. At last, the wedding could begin.

The ceremony, which was similar to a regular Sunday preaching service, began with a song from the Amish hymnal, the *Ausbund*. Grace did fine during the first part of the song, but as the time drew closer for her and Cleon to meet with the bishop and other ministers for counseling, she became more apprehensive.

As the people began the third line of the hymn, the ministers stood and made their way up the stairs to a room on the second floor. Grace and Cleon followed, but their attendants—Grace's sisters and two of Cleon's brothers—waited downstairs with the others.

Upstairs in the bedroom that had been set aside for the counseling session, Grace sat in a straight-backed chair, fidgeting with a corner of her apron as she listened to the bishop's admonitions and instructions on marriage.

The counseling session consisted of several scripture references and a long dissertation from Bishop King on the importance of good communication, trust, and respect in all areas of marriage. He reminded the couple that divorce was not an acceptable option among those of their faith, and he emphasized the need to work through any problems that might arise in their marriage.

When Cleon and Grace returned to the main room a short time later, they took their seats again, and the congregation sang another song. The ministers reentered the room during the final verse and also sat down. Next, a message was given by Mose Troyer, followed by a period of silent prayer and the reading of scripture. The bishop rose and began the main sermon.

Grace glanced over at Cleon, and he flashed her a grin, which helped calm her nerves and offered her the assurance she so desperately needed.

The bishop called for the bride and groom to stand before him, and Grace joined Cleon at the front of the room. "Brother," Bishop King said, looking at Cleon, "can you confess that you accept this, our sister, as your wife, and that you will not leave her until death separates you? And do you believe that this is from the Lord and that you have come thus far by your faith and prayers?"

With no hesitation, Cleon smiled at Grace and answered, "Jah."

The bishop then directed his words to Grace. "Can you confess, sister, that you accept this, our brother, as your husband, and that you will not leave him until death separates you? And do you believe that this is from the Lord and that you have come thus far by your faith and prayers?"

"Jah."

The bishop spoke to Cleon again. "Because you have confessed that you want to take this, our sister, for your wife, do you promise to be loyal to her and care for her if she may have adversity, affliction, sickness, or weakness, as is appropriate for a Christian, God-fearing husband?"

"Jah."

The bishop addressed the same question to Grace, and she, too, replied affirmatively. He then took Grace's hand and placed it in Cleon's hand, putting his own hands above and beneath theirs. "The God of Abraham, the God of Isaac, and the God of Jacob be with you together and give His rich blessing upon you and be merciful to you. To this I wish you the blessings of God for a good beginning, and may you hold out until a blessed end. Through Jesus Christ our Lord, Amen."

At the end of the blessing, Grace, Cleon, and Bishop King bowed their knees in prayer. "Go forth in the name of the Lord. You are now man and wife," the bishop said when the prayer was done.

Grace and Cleon returned to their seats, and one of the ministers gave a testimony, followed by two other ministers expressing agreement with the sermon and wishing Cleon and Grace God's blessings. When that was done, the bishop made a few closing comments and asked the congregation to kneel, at which time he read a prayer from the prayer book. Then the congregation rose to their feet, and the meeting was closed with a final hymn.

Grace drew in a deep breath and blinked back tears of joy. In a short time, the wedding feast would begin, and so would her new life as Mrs. Cleon Schrock. Maybe now she could finally leave her past behind.

As several of the men set up tables for the wedding meal, Cleon reflected on the somber expression he'd seen on his bride's face as they'd responded to the bishop's questions during their wedding vows. Grace had taken her vows seriously, which reassured him that everything was as it should be between them.

Once the tables had been put in place and covered with tablecloths, the eating utensils were set out. Foot traffic was heavy and continuous from the temporary kitchen that had been set up in the basement to the eating areas, which included the living room and upstairs kitchen. Food for all courses was soon placed on the table, beginning with the main course, which included roasted chicken, bread filling, and mashed potatoes. They were also served creamed celery—a traditional wedding dish—coleslaw, applesauce, pies, doughnuts, fruit salad, pudding, bread, butter, jelly, and coffee.

As soon as everything was ready for the meal, the bridal party made its entrance, beginning with the bride and groom, followed by Ruth, Martha, Ivan, and Willard, entering single file.

As Cleon and Grace took their seats, she commented about the jars of select celery that had been spaced at regular intervals on each of the tables so the leaves formed a kind of flowerlike arrangement. There were also several bouquets of flowers Ruth had put together.

"Everything looks real nice," Cleon said, leaning close to her as they sat at the corner table known as the "*Eck.*" "You and your family did a fine job decorating for our special day."

"Your mamm and sister did well with the candles, too." Grace touched the tablecloth adorning their corner table where the bride and groom traditionally sat. "This is from my hope chest, and two of the three decorated cakes were contributed by friends."

He smiled and licked his lips. "They look real tasty."

"The most elaborate cake, we bought from the bakeshop where Ruth works," she said. "Did you notice what's written in the center of that cake?"

Cleon read the words out loud. "*Bescht winsche*—best wishes, Cleon and Grace." He reached for her hand and gave it a gentle squeeze. "I hope we'll always be this happy."

Tears pricked the backs of her eyes. "Jah, me, too."

Chapter 17

Grace couldn't believe she and Cleon had been married a little over two months already, and as she stood in front of the sink one Saturday afternoon, peeling potatoes for the stew they would have for supper, she reflected on how things had been since their wedding day. She and Cleon were enjoying married life and getting along well at her folks' place, although Grace looked forward to the day when their own house would be done and they could move into it.

During December and January, they'd had several days of snow, and Cleon had taken time out from his honey deliveries and working on the house in order for them to do some fun things together. They had frolicked in the snow, taken a sleigh ride, sat by the fire sipping hot chocolate, and played board games with the rest of her family.

Grace felt happier than she had ever dreamed possible, and she was grateful there had been no more attacks on her family. She was certain this was because Gary Walker had left Holmes County. Esther had told her that Gary had come into the restaurant where Grace used to work and mentioned that he was leaving for Lancaster County, Pennsylvania, to do some stories on the Amish who lived there. Grace hoped Gary never returned to Ohio.

Now, if they could just get their house finished, things would be nearly perfect. It wasn't that she minded living with her folks, but it wasn't the same as having a place of their own. Grace was anxious to set out her wedding gifts, as well as the things she had in her hope chest. Cleon had said the other day that he hoped the house would be finished in a few months, but since he'd gotten so busy with new honey orders, he'd spent less time working on it.

Grace had wanted to do some work on the house herself since she'd quit her job at the restaurant as soon as they were married, but she didn't know a lot about carpentry. Even if Grace had, Cleon made it clear that building the house was his job, and with the help he got from other family members, including Grace's father, Grace knew their home would be finished in due time, so she needed to be patient.

She glanced out the kitchen window and noticed the dismal-looking gray sky. Between that and the drop in temperature, they were sure to have more snow.

Grace had just finished with the potatoes when she heard a knock on the front door. *That's strange. Hardly anyone we know uses the front door.*

She left the kitchen, hurried through the hall, and opened the door. A tall, middle-aged man wearing a dark green jacket and a pair of earmuffs stood on the porch. He held the hand of a petite little girl whose dark brown hair was pulled back in a ponytail. The child wore blue jeans and a puffy pink jacket with a hood, and as she looked up at Grace with a quizzical expression, her clear blue eyes blinked rapidly.

"Can I help you?" Grace asked, thinking the man had probably stopped to ask for directions like other English tourists did when they got lost.

He cleared his throat. Seconds ticked by as they stared at each other. "Grace Davis?"

Her mouth went dry, and she glanced around, relieved that she was alone. She hadn't been called by that name since—

"Is this the Hostettler home?"

She could only nod in reply. Who was this man, and how did he know her previous married name?

"Are you Grace?"

She nodded again as she studied him closer. They might have met before, but she couldn't be sure. Could he have been one of her customers at the restaurant or maybe someone from one of the

English-owned stores in town? But if that were so, how did he know her last name used to be Davis?

Grace glanced at the little girl again. She was certain she'd never met her, yet there was something familiar about the child. "Have. . . have we met before?" she asked, returning her gaze to the man.

He nodded. "Just once—at my son's funeral."

Grace's heart slammed into her chest with such force, she had to lean against the doorjamb for support. The man who stood before her was Wade's father, Carl Davis. She looked down at the little girl standing beside him, and goose bumps erupted on her arms.

"This is your daughter." Carl touched the child's shoulder. "Anna, this is your mother. As I told you before, you'll be living with her from now on."

Anna's eyes were downcast, and her chin quivered slightly.

Grace clung to the door, unsure of what to say or do. She was glad her long skirt hid her knees, for they knocked so badly, she could barely stand. She'd never expected to see Anna again, much less have her show up on her doorstep like this.

"How did you find me? Where have you been all this time? Why are you here?" Grace's head swam with so many unanswered questions she hardly knew where to begin.

"May we come inside?" Carl motioned to Anna. "She's tired from the long plane ride, and it's cold out here."

"Oh, of course." Grace held the door open for them and, on shaky legs, led the way to the living room.

Carl pulled off his earmuffs and took a seat on one end of the sofa, lifting Anna into his lap. Grace seated herself in the rocking chair across from them, fighting the urge to gather the girl into her arms and kiss her sweet face. Anna looked so befuddled, and Grace didn't want to frighten or confuse her anymore than she obviously was.

"Before I answer your questions," Carl said, removing Anna's jacket and then letting her turn and nestle against his chest, "I need to explain a few things."

Grace nodded in reply, never taking her eyes off Anna—the precious little girl she'd been forced to give up four years ago.

"When Wade married you without inviting us to the wedding, my wife was devastated."

"Where is Bonnie?"

"I'm getting to that." Carl leaned over and placed Anna on the other end of the sofa. Her eyes had closed, and her steady, even breathing let Grace know she'd fallen asleep. "When Wade finally called and told us he had moved to Cincinnati and had gotten married, Bonnie insisted that he tell her everything he knew about you—where you were from, what your background was, and why you had convinced him to elope with you and not include us in the wedding."

"But. . .but I didn't convince him," Grace sputtered. "Eloping was Wade's idea, and none of our parents were invited to the wedding." She stared down at her hands, clenched tightly in her lap. "My folks don't know I was ever married to your son or that we had—" She drew in a quick breath. "Go ahead with what you were about to say."

"Wade told us soon after you were married that you'd grown up in the Amish faith and that you had lived here in Holmes County, somewhere between Berlin and Charm. He said your last name had been Hostettler, and that you'd left your faith in order to marry him."

"Actually, I hadn't been baptized or joined the church yet."

"I see. Well, since I knew your family's last name and the general area where they lived, I was able to track you down."

A lump formed in Grace's throat. "I tried to call you and Bonnie soon after you left with Anna, but your phone had been disconnected. I wrote several letters, but they all came back with a stamped message saying you had moved and there was no forwarding address."

"Bonnie thought it would be better if you had no contact with Anna." Carl shifted on the sofa. "So we moved from our home in Michigan to Nevada, where we had some friends, and left no forwarding address."

"Why are you here now after making no contact with me these past four and a half years?"

"Bonnie had a sudden heart attack a few days after Christmas and died."

"I–I'm sorry." Even though Grace had only met Wade's folks when they'd come to his funeral, she'd taken an immediate dislike to his mother. Still, she took no pleasure in knowing the woman was dead.

"I've had my own share of health problems lately, and because of that, I won't be able to continue caring for Anna on my own." Carl swiped his tongue across his lower lip and grimaced. "I want you to know that I never felt good about taking your baby from you. It was Bonnie's idea. She felt we could give Anna a better home."

Too little, too late. Why couldn't you have stood up to your wife back then? Why couldn't you have offered me some financial support instead of taking my child?

Grace lifted her hands to her temples and massaged them with her fingertips. "I was so young, and. . .and I knew I couldn't provide properly for a baby. I was grieving over my husband, and I didn't know what was best for me or Anna at the time." She paused and drew in a quick breath to help steady her nerves. "I wanted to take my little girl and go home to my folks, but I—I was afraid of their rejection."

He opened his mouth as if to comment, but she rushed on. "Ever since the day you took Anna, I've felt guilty for letting someone else raise my daughter and for not having the courage to tell my family about my marriage or that I'd had a baby girl. I was too ashamed to admit I'd given up my rights as her mother, and since I didn't think I would ever see Anna again, I decided it would be best to keep my marriage and my daughter a secret."

He glanced around the room. "Where are they now—your family?"

"My dad's out in his woodworking shop, Mom went to visit a friend, and my two sisters are in town shopping."

Carl leaned slightly forward. "As I said before, I can't take care of Anna myself, so I've brought her to you. You're her mother and should have been the one caring for her these past four years, not me and Bonnie."

Grace closed her eyes as the memory of Wade's funeral and all that had happened afterwards rose before her. It had been enough of a shock to learn that Wade had been killed, but when his parents showed up for the funeral and said they wanted to take Anna, Grace's whole world had fallen apart.

She remembered how Bonnie had insisted that Grace let them raise the child, saying they could offer her more than Grace possibly could. When Grace refused, Bonnie threatened to hire a lawyer and prove that she was an unfit mother, unable to provide for Anna's needs. Bonnie and Carl had promised Grace visiting rights, saying she was welcome to see her little girl anytime she could make the trip to Michigan. But that hadn't happened because they'd moved, and Grace had given up all hope of ever seeing her daughter again.

Grace's eyes snapped open as the reality of the situation set fully in. Wade's father was offering her the chance to raise Anna—something she should have been doing all along. But the child didn't know Grace, and it would be a difficult transition for both of them. Not only that, but agreeing to keep Anna would mean Grace would have to reveal the secret she'd kept from her family and Cleon. She would need to explain why she had hidden the truth.

Grace rose from the chair and knelt on the floor in front of the sofa, reaching out to stroke her daughter's flushed cheeks. "Oh, Anna, I've never forgotten you." She gulped on a sob. "I've never stopped loving you, either."

Carl cleared his throat. "Are you willing to take her? Because if you aren't, I'll need to make other arrangements."

Other arrangements? Grace had already lost Anna once and couldn't bear the thought of losing her again. Regardless of her family's response, she knew what she had to do. "I think God might be offering me a second chance," she murmured.

"Does that mean Anna can stay?"

She nodded. "I will never let her go again."

"I wouldn't expect you to." Carl rose. "I packed some of Anna's winter clothes, and her suitcase is in my rental car. I'll get her things and be on my way before she wakes up." He smiled at his granddaughter as tears welled in his eyes. "It'll be better that way."

Grace started to get up, but he waved her aside. "No need to see me out. I'll just get the suitcase, bring it inside, and head back to the airport."

For the next hour, Grace sat on the floor in front of the sofa, watching her daughter sleep and thanking God for the opportunity He'd given her to be with Anna again.

When the back door slammed shut, Grace jumped, and when she heard the unmistakable sound of her father's boots clomping across the linoleum in the kitchen, she cringed. Her secret was about to be revealed. She could no longer hide the truth.

Chapter 18

Is anybody home?" Dad called.

Grace's heart took a nosedive. She couldn't let him see Anna without explaining things first. Guilt clung to her like a spider's web to a fly. If only she could undo the past. Oh, how she wished she hadn't kept this secret from her family.

"Grace, are you here?"

She jumped up and rushed out of the room, meeting him in the hallway outside the kitchen door.

"I figured you were here, but I wasn't sure about your mamm and sisters. Are they home yet?" Dad asked.

"No, and I—I don't expect them until closer to suppertime." Grace took hold of his arm. "Uh, Dad, we need to talk."

"Sure, I've got time for a little break. Just came in to refill my thermos with something to drink." He nodded toward the living room. "Should we go in there?"

She shook her head. Panic threatened to overtake her. "Let's go to the kitchen. I'll pour you a glass of goat's milk, and we can sit at the table."

"Sounds good to me."

Grace followed her father down the hall. When they entered the kitchen, he pulled out his chair at the head of the table and took a seat, stretching his arms over his head. "Didn't realize how tired I was until I sat down. I've been working too many long hours lately."

Grace took down two glasses from the cupboard and poured some milk.

130

As she handed a glass to her father, his forehead wrinkled. "Your hands are shaking. Is there something wrong? There hasn't been another break-in, I hope."

She shook her head and sank into the chair across from him. "We had a visitor awhile ago—an English man with a little girl."

He took a drink from his glass and wiped his mouth with the back of his hand. "Oh? Did they come in a car?"

"Jah."

"I'm surprised I didn't hear it pull into the yard. Of course, I've been hammering and sawing much of the day, so most outside sounds would probably have been drowned out." He took another drink. "Who were the English visitors?"

Grace's throat felt so dry and swollen she could barely swallow. She took a sip of milk and nearly choked as the cool liquid trickled down the wrong pipe.

"Are you okay?" Dad jumped up and thumped her on the back. "Take a couple of deep breaths."

She coughed and sputtered, finally gaining enough control so she could speak. "There's. . .uh. . .something I must tell you."

"What is it, daughter? Your face is as pale as this milk we're drinking."

"I think you'd better sit down again. What I have to say is going to be quite a shock."

"You're scaring me, Grace." He lowered himself into the chair with a groan. "Has something happened to your mamm or one of your sisters?"

She shook her head. Tears clouded her vision. "The man who was here is Carl Davis. When I was living among the English, I—I married his son, Wade."

Dad sat, staring at Grace in a strange way. "Is this some kind of a joke? You're married to Cleon, remember?"

"It's not a joke. Wade was killed in a car accident, and I returned to Holmes County soon after his funeral."

His eyebrows furrowed, nearly disappearing into the wrinkles of his forehead. "Does. . .does Cleon know of this?"

She shook her head.

"How come you never mentioned it before now?"

Grace gulped in some air. "I was afraid you wouldn't understand."

He opened his mouth as if to respond, but she held up her hand to stop him. "There's more. I've been keeping another secret these past four and a half years, as well."

"What other secret?"

She glanced toward the door leading to the hallway. "There's a little girl asleep on the sofa in our living room. Her name is Anna, and she. . .she's my daughter."

Dad's mouth dropped open, and his eyes narrowed into tiny slits. "Your what?"

"Anna's my little girl. She was only six months old when her daed was killed. Then Wade's parents took her from me and moved away." She gulped on the sob rising in her throat and steadied herself by grabbing the edge of the table. "I was unable to contact them by phone or mail, so I finally realized I needed to be here with my family and not living in the English world on my own."

The color drained from Dad's face, and he slowly shook his head.

"I know it was wrong to keep this from you and Mom." Grace reached out to touch his arm. "I was so ashamed that I'd given up my baby, and I didn't think I would ever see Anna again, so I—"

"You're just like your aunt Rosemary, you know that?" Dad's fist came down hard, scattering the napkins that had been nestled in a basket in the center of the table. "How could you have done such a thing, Grace? Ach, it's bad enough that you ran off and married an Englisher, but how could you have given up your own flesh and blood?"

"I—I didn't want to, but Wade's mother was so mean and pushy. She insisted that Anna would be better off with them, and she threatened to hire a lawyer and prove I was unfit to raise Anna on my own."

"Were you unfit, Grace?"

Their gazes connected, and Dad's pointed question was almost Grace's undoing. "I was so young, and the only job I'd ever had was working at a restaurant as a waitress. I knew I couldn't make enough money to support myself and Anna, and I thought—"

"You could have come home and asked for help. Surely you knew we wouldn't have let you or your daughter starve. If Rosemary had come home, she would have been welcomed, too."

Silence filled the air in the wake of her father's reproof, and the tears Grace had fought so hard to hold back spilled onto her cheeks and dribbled down her chin. She didn't understand how he could forgive whoever had broken into their home and his shop yet not forgive his sister or his own flesh-and-blood daughter. "You have every right to be angry with me," she said with a sniff. "But no one could be any angrier than I am with myself."

He continued to stare straight ahead, a muscle in his cheek quivering.

"Wade's mother is dead now, and his father's health isn't good, so he brought Anna to me and asked that I raise her."

Dad blinked rapidly, and he tapped his fingers against the tablecloth in quick succession. "Where is this man now?"

"He left soon after Anna fell asleep. Said it would be better that way."

"I see."

"Would. . .would you like to meet your granddaughter?"

He shook his head. "I need time to think about this. I need to understand why you would lie to your mamm and daed—why you would follow in your aunt's footsteps."

"I know it was wrong to keep the truth from you, but I—" Grace bit her lower lip to stop the flow of tears and pushed her chair away from the table. All she wanted to do was hold Anna and promise that she would never let her go again.

Grace left the kitchen, hurried back to the living room, and dropped to the floor in front of the sofa, where her daughter lay sleeping. Her heart thumped with fury and remorse. *I should never have let Wade's folks take Anna from me, no matter what they threatened to do. I should have packed up our things and brought my baby girl home with me, regardless of the consequences. Things would have gone better if I'd told Mom and Dad the truth right away. I should have told Cleon about Wade and Anna, too.*

Grace hiccupped on a sob. Regrets wouldn't change anything, and she knew she had to find a way to deal with her new situation. If only Dad had shown some understanding or offered a bit of support when she'd told him about Anna instead of comparing her to Aunt Rosemary, whom she'd never even met. Would Cleon respond the same way when she told him?

She glanced at the door leading to the hallway. Should she go back to the kitchen and try to talk to her father again? Would it do any good if she tried to explain things better?

Anna stirred, and Grace held her breath, waiting to see if her daughter would wake.

The child sat up, yawned, and looked around. "Poppy? Where's Poppy?" she asked in a small, birdlike voice.

Grace searched for words that wouldn't be a lie. "Your grandpa went home, but he'll come back to visit sometime, I'm sure." She smiled, hoping to reassure the child.

Anna's eyes opened wider. "Poppy left?"

Grace nodded. "He wants you to stay with me now because he can't care for you any longer." She moved closer to Anna and reached out her hand. "I'm your mother. Your grandpa said he told you about me."

Anna scrambled off the couch and raced for the front door. "Come back, Poppy! Come back!"

Grace rushed to her daughter's side, gathering the child into her arms. "It's going to be all right. You're safe here with me."

Roman sat at the kitchen table, trying to let Grace's news sink into his brain. He felt betrayed and didn't understand why she'd kept her first marriage a secret or why she'd hidden the fact that she'd had a baby and had given the child to someone else to raise. The one thing Roman knew was that he was a *grossdaadi*, and that his *grossdochder* was sleeping in the next room.

His shoulders sagged, and he dropped his head into the palms of his hands. This news would affect the entire family. And what of Grace's new husband? How would Cleon deal with things?

His thoughts shifted to a silent prayer. *Dear God, haven't we been through enough these past few months with the break-ins we've had? Must we now endure the shame of our daughter's deception?*

The back door opened and clicked shut, interrupting Roman's prayer. He lifted his head as his wife entered the room.

"*Wie geht's?*" Judith asked with a cheery smile.

He groaned. "I'm not so good, and my day was going along okay until I came into the house awhile ago."

A look of alarm flashed across her face, and she hurried across the room. "Was there another break-in or something else to upset things?"

"Oh, there's an upset all right. Only it's got nothin' to do with any break-ins."

"What is it, husband? You look so *uffriehrisch.*"

"I am agitated, and you had better sit down." He motioned to the chair across from him. "What I have to tell you is going to be quite *schauderhaft.*"

She sank into the chair, her eyes full of question. "You're scaring me. Please tell me what is so shocking."

"We've got a grossdochder."

Judith blinked as she let her husband's words sink into her brain. "Is Grace in a family way? Is that what you're trying to say?"

He shook his head. "I'm not talking about a granddaughter we might have someday; I'm talking about the one we have now."

Her forehead wrinkled. "What are you saying, Roman? We have no grandchildren yet."

"Jah, we do. She's in the living room, asleep on the sofa."

The muscles in Judith's face relaxed, and she poked her husband on the arm. "You always did like to tease, didn't you?"

His expression turned somber as he leaned forward in his chair. "I'm not teasing. There really is a little girl in our living room, and she's Grace's daughter."

Judith sat rigid in her chair, her mouth hanging slightly open. "What?"

"It's true. Grace was married during the time she lived among the English, and she. . .she had a baby girl."

"But how can that be?"

"I just told you she was married before and—"

She held up her hand. "This makes no sense. If Grace is already married, then how could she marry Cleon?"

"Her husband's dead. Died in a car accident, Grace said." Roman pulled his fingers through the back of his hair and grimaced. "Guess her husband's folks came to the funeral and took Grace's baby to raise."

As Judith tried to digest her husband's astonishing story, her head began to throb. These last four and a half years, Grace had never said a word about having been married—or that she'd given birth to a baby girl. "Why would she do that, Roman? Why would our daughter let someone else raise her child?"

He shrugged. "She said it was because she was young and scared and didn't think she could support the child."

"But she could have come home, let us help raise the baby."

Roman squeezed his fingers around the edge of the table so hard his knuckles turned white. "Grace said she was afraid we wouldn't understand." He slowly shook his head. "She's right—I don't. I think she's got my sister's blood in her; that's what I think."

"What are you saying?"

"Hearing Grace's story brought all the pain back that my family felt when my own sister left the Amish faith. Then Rosemary made things worse by marrying that Englisher who ended up taking her away from her family for good." He squeezed his eyes shut. "Nearly broke our mamm's heart, it did."

Judith stared at a dark spot on the tablecloth and struggled to keep her voice steady. "You can't compare what our daughter did with your sister's act of defiance. Rosemary left home and never returned or made any effort to contact your family or come home for a visit." She swallowed a couple of times. "At least Grace returned home and joined the church, and she's—"

Roman's eyes snapped open, and his fist came down hard on the table, clattering the two glasses sitting there, nearly knocking them over. "She's been lying to us all this time, Judith! Our daughter kept her marriage to an English man and the child she bore a secret, and I doubt Grace would have ever told the truth if her dead husband's father hadn't shown up on our doorstep with her daughter today."

"Is. . .is the man still here?"

He shook his head. "Grace said he left soon after the child fell asleep on the sofa. His wife is dead, and he's not well, so he brought his granddaughter here for Grace to raise."

Judith pushed her chair aside and stood.

"Where are you going?"

"To meet our grossdochder. Wouldn't you like to come along?"

Deep wrinkles formed on his forehead as he released a moan. "I do want to meet her; I'm just not sure I can."

"Of course you can." She held out her hand. "You can't sit here all evening, fretting because Grace kept this secret from us. What's done is done, and we need to put it to rest because we have a granddaughter to help raise."

"But. . .but what will I say to the child—or to Grace?"

Judith shrugged. "I don't know. The words will be on your lips when you need them, same as mine." She moved toward the door. "Are you coming or not?"

He grunted and pushed away from the table.

Anna wiggled free from Grace's embrace and pulled on the door handle. "Leave me be! I wanna go home! I want Poppy!"

Before Grace could react, her mother and father stepped into the room. "What's going on? What's all the shouting about?" Mom asked with a worried expression.

"Oh, Mom, I've made such a mess of things." Grace nodded at Anna, who stood with her little body pressed up to the door, trembling from head to toe. "This is my daughter, Anna, and—"

"I know already. Your daed told me everything." Mom knelt in front of Anna and reached out to wipe the tears from her cheeks. "I'm your grandmother, Anna."

"Grandma's gone away and will never come back. Poppy said so."

"I'm your other grandmother. My name is Grandma Hostettler." She motioned to Grace's father. "That's Grandpa Hostettler."

"Poppy went home! He. . .he's never comin' back."

"That's not true," Grace was quick to say. "I'm sure he'll write you letters and come visit whenever he can."

Anna's lower lip quivered. More tears flooded her eyes. The sorrow Grace saw on the child's face tore at her heartstrings, but she didn't know what she could say or do to make things better—for her or Anna.

Mom stood and reached for Anna's hand. "Why don't we go out to the kitchen for some cookies and milk? Does that sound good to you?"

"Got any chocolate ones?" the child asked with a hopeful expression. It was the first indication that she might calm down, and for that Grace felt some relief.

"I have chocolate chip and peanut butter cookies," Mom said with a smile.

Anna sniffed and quietly nodded.

Mom touched Grace's shoulder, and Grace found a measure of comfort in the gesture. "If we put our trust in God, He will see us through this, just as He helped us through those acts of vandalism awhile back."

As soon as Mom and Anna left the room, Grace turned to face her father, her stomach lurching with nervous anticipation. "I'm sorry for keeping the truth from you. I know how disappointed you must be in me."

"You're right, I am disappointed and feeling more than a little *verhuddelt* right now."

"We're all confused. Anna most of all."

His gave a short nod and then headed for the door. "Luke's gone for the day, but I'm going back to work for a while." He rushed out of the house.

"You've been awful quiet since we left town," Martha commented to

Ruth as their horse and buggy rounded the bend a short distance from home.

"I've just been thinking, is all."

"What about?"

"Luke. He's been acting awful strange for a couple of months, and as time passes, he seems more tense and sometimes unfriendly toward me. It makes me wonder if he wants to break up with me, but I haven't had the nerve to ask."

Martha clicked her tongue and shook the reins to get the horse moving faster. Her stomach had been growling for the last couple of miles, and she was anxious to get home and eat supper. "If Luke were my boyfriend, I'd ask him why he's been acting so peculiar. If he really cares about you, he should be willing to share whatever's on his mind."

Ruth sighed. "I've tried talking to him about his strange behavior a couple of times, but he always changes the subject."

As they pulled into their yard, Martha was glad to see her mother's buggy parked near the barn. She was probably getting the evening meal started. Martha's stomach rumbled again, as she thought about the good food they'd soon be having.

"I'll help you put the horse away," Ruth offered. "That way we can get into the house quicker and help Mom and Grace get supper on the table."

"Danki, I appreciate that."

After the horse had been rubbed down and put into his stall, Martha and Ruth headed for the house. When they opened the back door, Martha was disappointed that no tantalizing aromas greeted them. "Guess Grace and Mom must not be at home after all," she said. "Otherwise we'd smell something."

"Maybe we're having cold sandwiches tonight," Ruth commented.

"Jah, maybe so."

When they stepped into the kitchen a few seconds later, Martha was surprised at the sight. Mom sat at the table with a young English girl. They each had glasses of milk, and the child nibbled on a cookie.

"Wie geht's?" Martha called to their mother. "Who's your little friend?"

Mom looked up and smiled, but the child kept eating, only giving Martha and Ruth a quick glance. "This is Anna, and she's going to be staying with us."

"Just 'til Poppy comes back," the child said around a mouthful of cookie.

Martha looked at Ruth, who merely shrugged. She turned back to Mom. "Who's Poppy, and where's Anna from? Don't think I've ever met her before."

Mom nodded toward the door leading to the hallway. "Grace is in the living room with your daed. It might be best if you let her explain."

Chapter 19

As Cleon headed down the road toward the Hostettlers', he glanced over at the cardboard box sitting on the seat beside him. Inside were six jars of clover honey. He'd had some extra this week and wanted to share it with his in-laws as a thank you for letting him and Grace stay with them while their house was being finished.

A horn blared behind Cleon's buggy. He looked over his shoulder and noticed several cars behind him, so he guided his horse to the shoulder of the road to let them pass. As soon as the cars went by, he pulled onto the highway again and let the horse trot for a bit.

"If only things could stay nice and calm," Cleon murmured, thinking about the Hostettlers again. He was glad they hadn't had any more problems at their place, and he hoped the troublemaker who had destroyed some of their property and stolen Roman's things never struck again.

A short time later, Cleon pulled up to Roman's barn, hopped down, and tied his horse to the hitching rail. Then he reached into the buggy, grabbed the box full of honey, and headed to the back of their house. When he stepped into the kitchen a few minutes later, he spotted Judith sitting at the table with a little English girl.

"I brought you some honey," he said, nodding at the box in his arms.

"That was. . .uh. . .real nice of you." Judith glanced over her shoulder and cleared her throat a couple of times.

He placed the box on the counter nearest the door. "Didn't realize you had company. There was no car in the driveway."

"No. . .uh. . ." Judith's forehead wrinkled. "I think you need to speak with Grace."

Cleon couldn't imagine why he would need to talk to Grace about why there wasn't a car in the driveway, but eager to be with his wife, he nodded. "Where is she?"

"In the living room."

"Okay." Cleon smiled at the young girl sitting at the table, but she never made eye contact with him. He left the room wondering why Judith was acting so strangely.

"I wish you would have told us this sooner," Ruth said, reaching over to take Grace's hand. Grace had just informed her sisters about her marriage to Wade and how she'd allowed her in-laws to take her baby girl.

Martha nodded. "We could have helped you through this, sister."

Tears welled in Grace's eyes. "I know how strongly Mom has always felt about having children, and I was afraid if she knew I had allowed someone else to raise my child, she wouldn't have understood. I was ashamed of what I'd done and thought if no one knew my secret it would be easier to deal with the guilt." She sniffed. "The way Dad reacted to my news only confirms what I suspected. He's still hurting over his sister leaving home when she was a young woman, and he's upset with me now, too."

"I really believe it would have been easier for you to deal with things if you'd had the support of your family," Ruth said.

Grace swallowed hard. "I'm not so sure. You should have seen how upset Dad was with me. I think he and Mom feel that I've cheated them out of knowing the granddaughter they should have met long before now." She drew in a quick breath. "I cheated myself—and Anna, too. Now my little girl sees me as a stranger, and I don't know if anything will ever be right for any of us again."

"You need to give your daughter some time to adjust. We'll help in any way we can. Isn't that right?" Martha asked, turning to Ruth, who sat between them.

Ruth nodded. "Of course we will."

"I'm not sure. . . ." Grace forced herself to complete her thought. "I'm not sure what I've done will be overlooked by the ministers or anyone else in our community."

"But you weren't a member of the church when you went through rumschpringe and married an Englishman, so you won't be shunned," Martha reminded.

"That's right," Ruth agreed. "You were legally married, your husband died, and you returned home and joined the Amish church."

"But I gave away my daughter and kept my previous marriage a secret. If I can't forgive myself, how can I expect others to accept what I've done?" Grace released a deep moan. "And what of Cleon? How's he going to take the news when I tell him the secret I've been keeping?"

"What secret is that, Grace?"

Grace jumped at the sound of her husband's voice, and when he strolled into the room, her heart almost stopped beating. "Cleon. I—I didn't know you were home."

"I came in the back door and stopped in the kitchen to give your mamm some honey. She said you were in here."

Grace's throat felt so swollen she could barely swallow. Had Cleon met Anna? Had Mom told him the whole story? Was that why he looked so befuddled?

Ruth stood and reached for Martha's hand. "I think we should get out to the kitchen and help Mom with supper, don't you?"

"Jah, sure." Martha glanced over her shoulder and offered Grace a reassuring smile. Then both sisters exited the room.

As soon as they were gone, Cleon took a seat on the sofa beside Grace. "There was a little English girl sitting at the kitchen table, but I didn't recognize her as one of your neighbors."

"Didn't Mom introduce you?"

He shook his head.

"Then I guess I need to explain."

"Explain what? Is she a friend of your family?"

"No, uh—"

"Where are her parents?"

Grace squeezed her eyes shut, praying that the right words would come. When she opened them again, Cleon was looking at her in a most disconcerting way.

"What's wrong, Grace? You look so unsettled."

"The little girl's name is Anna," she said in a near whisper. "I–I'm her mother."

Cleon sat with his forehead wrinkled. "What was that?"

"Anna's my daughter."

"Are you joking?"

She shook her head as tears threatened to escape. Her heart thumped furiously.

"I don't understand. How can that English girl be your daughter?"

"When I was going through my rumschpringe, before your family came to Holmes County, I moved to Cincinnati with some other Amish girls who wanted to try out the English world for a while. During the time we were living there, I worked as a waitress in a restaurant, and I. . .well, I dated an English fellow." She gulped in some air. "It was that reporter who was in town for a while, asking questions so he could write stories about our people."

"You. . .you married the reporter?" Cleon's face blanched, and his voice raised a notch.

Grace shook her head vigorously. "I finally broke up with him because he had a temper and acted like he owned me."

"Then who's the *daadi* of the little girl in the kitchen?"

"Wade Davis. He was one of Gary Walker's friends, and the two of us started dating soon after I broke up with Gary."

"So you married this Wade fellow?"

She nodded, unable to speak around the lump in her throat.

"Did your folks know about this?"

Grace shook her head. "I never told any of my family where I was during that time or that I'd gotten married and had a baby." She paused long enough to gauge Cleon's reaction. He sat stony-faced and unmoving. "A year later, Anna was born, and six months after that, my husband was killed in a car accident."

A muscle on the side of Cleon's face quivered. "Where's your daughter been all this time?"

"When Wade died, his parents came to the funeral, and the next day they took Anna away to live with them." Grace's voice trembled. "Bonnie, Wade's mother, said I was an unfit mother, and she threatened to hire a lawyer and take Anna from me if I didn't agree to let them raise her." She drew in another quick breath. "Bonnie insisted that she and Carl could give Anna a better life."

Cleon's eyebrows lifted high on his forehead. "So you gave up your child because your husband's parents said they wanted her?"

She sniffed and swiped at the tears coursing down her cheeks. "I was confused and afraid I wouldn't be able to support Anna. I was afraid my folks wouldn't understand or accept me back if I had a child."

"And your daughter's been living in Cincinnati all this time?"

Grace shook her head. "Wade's folks lived in Michigan at the time, and soon after they took Anna, I changed my mind about letting them have her. I wanted to take my little girl and go home, hoping my folks would accept me back and help raise her."

"Why didn't you?"

"I tried to contact Wade's folks, but their phone had been disconnected. The letters I wrote came back with a stamp that said they'd moved and there was no forwarding address."

"Then what did you do?"

"I moved back home but was too ashamed and too frightened of my family's reaction to admit what I'd done, so I kept the secret from everyone."

He gave a quick nod. "Including me—the man you're supposed to love and trust."

"I was afraid if I told you the truth you wouldn't understand and might not marry me."

"I thought our relationship was built on trust." He stared at the floor, slowly shaking his head. "I was sure wrong about that."

"I'm sorry, Cleon. I never meant to lie to you, but—"

He lifted his gaze and leveled her with an icy stare. "But you didn't love me enough to be honest with me? Isn't that what you're saying?"

"No. I do love you, and after Gary showed up in town, it made me rethink my decision to keep my previous marriage and daughter a secret." She choked on a sob. "I was planning to tell you, but I just couldn't do it."

"Why not?"

"When I told you about my aunt who went English, you said you could understand how my daed felt, so I assumed you would react the same way Dad did when he found out his sister married an Englisher."

Cleon's face turned bright red, and sweat darkened the sides of his hair. "So you were never going to tell me the truth?"

"I don't know."

He stood and headed for the door but then whirled around to face her again. "I can't talk about this anymore. I need time to try to figure out what to do about all this."

Grace was tempted to throw herself into his arms and beg him to stay and talk things out, but she knew Cleon well enough to realize that he needed time alone to deal with his feelings. Maybe a few hours from now they could talk about this again. Maybe by then he'd be willing to forgive her deception.

Chapter 20

As Martha and Ruth helped their mother with supper, Martha kept looking over at little Anna. She'd finished her cookies and milk and sat at the table staring at her folded hands in her lap and looking as forlorn as a lost puppy.

An idea popped into Martha's head. "Would it be all right if I take Anna out to the barn to see Heidi's hundlin?" she asked, leaning close to her mother's ear.

Mom nodded. "Jah, sure, that's a good idea. Ruth and I can finish getting the meal ready. It won't be done for another half hour or so, and that should give you plenty of time to take Anna to the barn. Oh, and if you see your daed out there, tell him supper will be on the table in about thirty minutes."

"Okay." Martha hurried over to the table and bent down so she was eye level with the child. "How would you like to walk out to the barn with me to see some cute little puppies?"

At first Anna shook her head, but then she hopped down from her chair. "Can I hold 'em?"

"Of course you can." Martha extended her hand. "We'll be back in time for supper," she called to Mom as the two of them went out the back door.

Holding tightly to Anna's hand, Martha led the way to the barn. Once inside, she called for her father, but when he didn't respond, she figured he must have gone out to his shop.

Martha directed Anna over to one of the stalls where she had moved Heidi's three remaining puppies. They'd outgrown the box soon after they were born and needed room to run around. Dad had begun working on a dog kennel for her, but it wasn't done.

Anna knelt in the straw with one of the sleepy pups nestled in her arms. Slender and willowy, with a slightly turned-up nose, the little girl reminded Martha of Grace in many ways.

A lump formed in Martha's throat as she thought of how much her sister had missed, knowing she had a daughter, believing she would never see her again, and being afraid to share her secret with them. Everyone in the family had missed out on Anna's babyhood, and it gave Martha a strange sensation to realize that she was an aunt and could have been helping raise this little girl if Grace hadn't been afraid to tell them the truth.

She knelt next to Anna and picked up one of the other puppies. "They're cute little things, aren't they?"

Anna nodded and stroked the pup's furry head. "How come you're wearin' such a long dress?" she asked, tipping her head to one side.

"Because my family and I belong to the Amish church, and we believe women should wear plain, simple dresses, not trousers like men."

Anna squinted and pursed her lips. "Poppy said you dressed different than us."

"That's right, we do, and soon your mother will make you some long dresses to wear; then you'll look like one of us, too."

Anna shook her head. "I don't wanna look like you. I wanna go home and live with Poppy."

Martha patted Anna's shoulder in a motherly fashion, wondering how the child would cope with all the changes she would face in the days to come.

Roman was about to turn down the gas lamps in his shop when the front door opened, and their bishop, Noah King, stepped in. He held a magazine in his hands, and his lips were compressed in a thin line.

"Wie geht's?" Roman asked. "What brings you by so late in the day?"

"I'm here on business, but not the woodworkin' kind," Noah replied with a curt nod.

"What's the problem?"

"This is the problem." Noah held up the magazine and waved it about. "How come you let some reporter write up a story about those break-ins a few months back? Now everyone in the country will know about them, and they'll all get a good look at your daughter, too."

"Huh?" Roman took a step closer to the bishop and squinted. "What's it say in there, and which daughter are you talking about?"

Noah huffed and then handed him the magazine. "See for yourself."

Roman's gaze came to rest on a picture of Grace standing near an Amish buggy that he assumed had been parked in Berlin, because he could see the drugstore and Christian bookstore in the background. His hands shook as he read the article telling about the break-ins that had occurred on their property. "I wonder how the reporter was able to take Grace's picture and get all these facts. And why after all this time is the story coming out?"

"You don't know who gave him the facts?"

"Of course not. What'd you think—that I volunteered all this information?"

The bishop shrugged. "Figured it might have been Grace, since she must have let the man take her picture."

Roman shook his head vigorously. "I'm sure none of my family would give any reporter information such as this, much less pose for a picture."

"Then how'd the article get written up, and how'd the man get this?" Noah's long finger tapped the picture of Grace as he noisily clucked his tongue.

"I have no idea. Someone outside the family must have told that fellow about the break-ins, but I'm sure it wasn't Grace. I'm equally sure she didn't agree to him taking her picture." Roman handed the magazine back to Noah. "How'd you come across this anyway?"

"One of my English neighbors subscribes to the magazine, and he gave it to me." Noah gave his beard a couple of quick pulls. "Sure hope this won't lead to more attacks for you or any of our other people."

Roman's forehead wrinkled. "You think it could?"

"Well, the one who was responsible for your break-ins might read this and decide to do it again because he's getting free publicity. Or someone else might get the idea that if the person who did this got away with it, maybe he can, too." Noah tapped the magazine again. "It says in the article that the sheriff wasn't called, so someone might think they could do whatever they wanted and never get caught."

"You think I should have called the sheriff?"

"*Nee.* I'm only sayin' this article isn't a good thing."

Roman slowly shook his head. "Didn't think this day could get much worse, but it surely has."

"What's wrong? Has there been another break-in?"

"No, but thanks to my oldest daughter and the secret she decided to keep from us these past four and a half years, things are more *verhuddelt* around here than ever."

Noah's bushy eyebrows drew together. "What kind of secret would Grace be keeping from you?"

Roman pulled out the chair behind his desk and another that sat near one of the workbenches. "Have a seat, and I'll tell you about it."

"Where's Anna?" Grace asked, as she rushed into the kitchen, hoping to find comfort in her daughter's arms.

"She's gone out to the barn with Martha to look at the puppies." Mom turned from the stove, where she had poured some green beans into a kettle. "Where's Cleon? Is he still in the living room?"

Grace winced. "He's gone."

"Gone where?"

"I–I'm not sure. Just said he was leaving and rushed out of the house."

"Did you tell him about Anna?" Ruth, who had been setting the table, questioned.

Grace nodded and steadied herself against the cupboard door. "He. . .he didn't take the news well." With a childlike cry, she hurried across the room, burying her face against her mother's chest. "Oh,

Mom, I'm afraid I've ruined things between me and Cleon. I–I'm sorry I didn't tell everyone the truth right away. How I wish I could change the past, for if I could, I would never have let Wade's folks take Anna away. I would have raised her myself, no matter how hard it might have been."

Mom massaged Grace's shoulders as she rocked her gently back and forth, the way she'd done when she was a child in need of comfort. "It's going to be all right; you'll see. We'll get through this together."

"But you didn't see Cleon's face when I told him the news. He looked so angry and hurt."

"I'm sure in time Cleon will realize that you didn't keep your secret in order to hurt him," Ruth interjected.

Grace stepped back and wiped her nose on the handkerchief Mom handed her. "No, I didn't, but that doesn't mean he'll ever forgive me."

"Cleon loves you, Grace, and I doubt he'll stay mad for long. If he's the kind of man he seems to be, then he'll not only forgive as the Bible says we should do, but he'll be willing to help you raise Anna."

Grace tried to smile but failed miserably. She was so happy to have Anna back, but it seemed like nothing in her life would ever be right again.

"Come, have a seat at the table, and I'll fix you a cup of tea," her mother said.

Grace nodded numbly and pulled out a chair. She'd just taken a seat when the back door opened, and her father stepped into the kitchen followed by Bishop King. Her heart pounded. Had Dad told the bishop about Anna? Had he come here to reprimand Grace for keeping such a secret?

"*Gut-n-owed*, Grace," the bishop said, moving across the room to the table.

"Good evening, Bishop King."

"I came by your daed's shop to tell him about an article that has your picture in it."

Dad stepped forward, waving a magazine in the air. "Did you pose for this, Grace?" he asked accusingly. He plunked the magazine on the table, and Grace gasped.

"I—I didn't pose for that picture. The reporter just snapped it without my permission." She swallowed hard. "I didn't know he was going to use it in a magazine article, either."

"Many people take pictures of us Amish without asking, especially reporters." The bishop pulled out the chair next to Grace and lowered himself into it. "Your daed tells me you have a daughter you've been keeping a secret. I came up to the house thinking you might want to talk about it."

Grace nodded as shame and remorse settled over her like a heavy quilt. "I—I know it was wrong to keep such a secret, but I was afraid my folks wouldn't accept the fact that I'd once been married to an English man, and that they wouldn't understand why I had allowed his parents to raise my child after he died."

Grace's mother moved over to the table, placing her hands on Grace's shoulders as if to offer some comfort. But her father stood with his arms folded, leaning against the cupboard door across the room.

"It would have been much better if you'd been up-front about this from the beginning," the bishop said, "but the past is in the past, and nothing's going to change what's been done." He touched Grace's arm. "Since you weren't a member of the church when this all took place, there's no need for a public confession. However, I do hope you've learned a lesson from your mistake and that you'll never lie or keep secrets from anyone again."

"No. No, I won't." Grace's eyes filled with tears, blurring her vision. "I just want my family's support as I try to help my daughter adjust to a new way of life."

"I'm sure you shall have that, and you can call on me or any of the other ministers for counsel should you feel the need."

Dad said nothing, but Mom gave Grace's shoulders another comforting squeeze. Now, if she could just get through to Cleon, she would feel some hope for the future.

For the past twenty minutes, Cleon had been sitting on the floor in the middle of what would soon be their new living room, thinking about the secret Grace had kept from him and wondering what he should do. He felt betrayed, humiliated, and confused. How could she have kept her previous marriage from him? And what about the daughter she'd allowed someone else to raise? What kind of mother would give up her own child and keep such a secret from her family and the man she was supposed to love?

He scooped up a handful of sawdust from the floor and let it sift through his fingers. "If she'd only told me about this before we were married." He winced as the truth slammed into him with the force of stampeding horses. If Grace had told him the truth, he probably wouldn't have married her. It wasn't his job to raise another man's child—especially a man who didn't share their faith.

He stood and began to pace, going from the front window to the stone fireplace and back again. What he really wanted to do was run away from this problem, but where would he go—back home to live with his folks? What would he tell them? That his wife had a child she'd been keeping from him, and that he felt betrayed and wasn't sure he could forgive her? Cleon knew that divorce wasn't an option and that he needed to figure out a way to deal with Grace's deception, but he also knew it wouldn't be easy.

The back door opened and shut, and he whirled around. Grace entered the room. Her face was red, and the skin around her eyes looked puffy as though she'd been crying. Under different circumstances, he would have reached out to her and offered comfort.

"I was hoping that I would find you here," she said, moving toward him.

He took a step back.

"We need to talk."

"I think we've already said all that needs to be said."

She reached her hand out to him. "I need you to understand why I kept the truth from you about Anna."

"I don't care about your reasons. You obviously don't love me enough to be truthful."

"That's not true. I do love you, Cleon." Grace's voice broke, and she swiped at the tears running down her cheeks. "I—I was afraid of how you would respond, and the way you're acting now tells me what your reaction would have been if I'd told you sooner."

Cleon shook his head. "I'm reacting to you not telling me about your secret."

"So you're not upset about me having been married before or having a daughter you knew nothing about?"

He turned away. "I'm very upset, and I can't talk about this now."

"But we need to talk things through. We need—"

"I want to be left alone." He moved toward the door and pulled it open. "I'll be spending the night here, so you may as well go home to your folks—and your daughter."

"Cleon, please—"

Once more, he shook his head. "I don't want to talk about this right now. Please, just go."

Grace gulped on a sob, turned, and fled from the room.

Chapter 21

It was difficult for Grace to get ready for church the next morning, but she knew she must. When she'd put Anna in bed with her last night, the child had cried herself to sleep. Cleon had apparently followed through on his intention to spend the night in their unfinished house, because he'd never returned to her folks' home.

"Anna, wake up. It's time to get dressed and ready for church." Grace leaned over the bed and gently shook the child's shoulders.

Anna moaned but didn't open her eyes.

"You need to get up and have some breakfast."

Anna finally opened her eyes, which looked red and swollen. "Poppy. I want Poppy," she murmured.

"I know you do, but your poppy had to go home. He's sick and can't take care of you now, so he brought you to me."

Before putting the child to bed, Grace had tried to explain to Anna about her father dying and Grace agreeing to let his parents raise her baby girl because she was young and confused. The look of bewilderment on Anna's face told Grace that the child didn't fully understand, but with time and patience, she hoped to gain her daughter's approval.

Grace opened Anna's suitcase. Carl had packed plenty of winter clothes—several pairs of jeans, some sweaters, blouses, underwear, a pair of tennis shoes, snow boots, white patent leather shoes, slippers, a nightgown, and two pretty dresses—nothing suitable for an Amish child to wear to church. *But she's not really Amish*, Grace reminded herself. *It will take some time for her to feel as if she's one of us.*

155

"Anna, I believe your grandma is making pancakes for breakfast this morning. So let's hurry downstairs so we can have some."

Anna jerked the covers over her head. "Grandma's gone. Poppy said so."

Grace pulled them gently aside. "I was talking about my mother, Grandma Hostettler."

Anna just lay staring at the ceiling as her eyes filled with tears.

Grace wanted to take the child in her arms and offer comfort, but she'd tried that last night and Anna had become hysterical. So she just stood there feeling as helpless as a newborn calf. When a knock on the bedroom door sounded, Grace hurried across the room, hoping it was Cleon. Martha stood in the hallway.

"I came to see if Anna wants to help me feed Heidi and Fritz," Martha said, peering around Grace and into the room.

Anna shot out of bed before Grace could offer a reply. "Can I hold one of the puppies again?" Her pink flannel nightgown edged with fancy lace hung just below her knees, exposing her bare legs and feet, and her long brown hair was a mass of tangles. But for the first time, Grace saw a hopeful expression on her daughter's face.

Martha leaned down so she was at eye level with the child. "As soon as we're done feeding the dogs, you can hold a puppy."

"Let's go then!" Anna started out the door, but Grace caught her arm. "You can't go outside dressed like that. It's cold, and you need to put some clothes on first."

Anna hurried back across the room, flipped open her suitcase, and removed a pair of jeans and a turtleneck sweater.

While the child dressed, Grace stepped into the hallway to talk to Martha. "I looked through the clothes Anna's grandfather packed for her, and she's got nothing to wear to church except for some fancy dresses and blue jeans. I wish I still had some of the dresses I wore as a child, but they were passed on to Ruth after I outgrew them, and if they were still in good condition, they became yours."

Martha tipped her head. "All my childhood clothes are gone. Once I couldn't wear them anymore, Mom gave them to one of our younger cousins."

"I guess she'll have to go to church wearing one of her fancy dresses," Grace said, "but tomorrow I'll get busy and make her a few plain dresses."

When Cleon stepped into the Hostettlers' kitchen, he realized that they'd already eaten breakfast and that Grace and her mother were doing the dishes.

Grace turned to look at him, her eyes puffy and rimmed with dark circles. Apparently, she hadn't slept any better than he had last night. Cleon had bedded down on the floor of their unfinished living room, using the sleeping bag he'd kept there for times when he'd been working late on the house and had decided to spend the night. Besides the fact that the floor was hard and unyielding, his only source of heat had come from the stone fireplace that had been completed a few weeks ago.

Cleon had lain awake for hours, mulling things over and fretting about the secret Grace had kept from him. When he'd finally succumbed to sleep, he'd slept fitfully and much longer than he should have. Since today was Sunday, and he would be expected to be at the preaching service at the home of Mose and Saloma Esh, he had to go to the Hostettlers' in order to get cleaned up and dressed for church. He'd also intended to get some much-needed breakfast.

"We've already had breakfast, but I'd be happy to fix you something to eat," Judith offered, making no mention of where he'd spent the night. Why hadn't Grace offered to fix his breakfast? She was his wife, after all.

"I'll just have some coffee and toast, but I can get it myself," he mumbled.

Judith shrugged and turned back to the sink, but Grace didn't say a word. Was she angry with him for sleeping at their new house? Well, he was the one who had a right to be angry, not her. If it weren't for Grace's deception, everything would be fine, and they would have slept warm and toasty in their bed together last night.

Cleon glanced around the room. "Where are the others?" What

he really wanted to know was where Grace's English child was. He'd had such a brief encounter with her last evening, he couldn't even remember if he'd been told her name.

"Roman's out in the barn getting a horse hitched to the buggy, Ruth is upstairs changing into her church dress, and Martha's helping Anna get ready."

Cleon pulled his fingers through the beard he'd begun growing since his marriage and ambled to the stove. He didn't know how he could go to church and act as if everything was okay when his world had been turned topsy-turvy, yet he had no legitimate excuse for staying home. So he would do the right thing and drive his wife and her daughter to church, but he didn't have to like it.

The ride to church seemed to take forever, and it wasn't because the Eshes lived far away. Fact was, Mose Esh's place was only a couple miles from the Hostettlers', but the tension Grace felt between Cleon and her made the trip seem twice as long. Her husband kept his gaze straight ahead as he guided their horse and buggy down the road. He didn't say a word. Except for an occasional deep sigh, followed by a couple of sniffs, Anna was quiet, too.

Grace wasn't sure what she should say to others in their community about the daughter they didn't know she had, and she didn't know how well they would accept Anna or how well Anna would accept them. When they pulled up to the Eshes' barn, she climbed down quickly and reached for Anna. Then, forcing a smile, she took the child's hand and led her toward a group of women who stood on the front porch talking with Mose's wife, Saloma.

"Now who's this little girl?" Saloma asked as Grace stepped onto the porch with Anna.

"She. . .she's my daughter."

"Your what?" Saloma's mouth dropped open, and several of the other women gaped at Grace as if she'd taken leave of her senses.

Grace needed to explain Anna's appearance, but she didn't want to do it front of the child. She was relieved when she spotted Ruth and

Martha talking to some of the younger women nearby. "Excuse me a minute," she said, stepping off the porch with Anna in tow. "Would you two look after Anna until church starts?" she whispered in Ruth's ear.

"Don't you think it would be best if she stayed with you?"

Grace shook her head. "Not while I explain to Saloma and the other women who Anna is."

"She can come with me," Martha spoke up. "I'll introduce her to Esta Wengerd and some of the other children who are close to her age."

Grace blew out a sigh of relief. At least one problem was solved.

Chapter 22

As Grace stood in the hallway outside Martha's open door, staring at her sleeping daughter, a lump formed in her throat. Anna had been with them almost two weeks, and she still hadn't accepted Grace as her mother. The child barely looked at her and spoke only when spoken to. Yet Anna seemed to have accepted Martha fairly well, even sleeping in Martha's room and spending all her free time in the barn with Martha and the puppies.

Anna continued to ask for her poppy and often complained because she wanted to watch TV and wear blue jeans instead of the plain dresses Grace had sewn for her, but she'd done better in church yesterday than she had two weeks ago. She hadn't squirmed so much on the hard benches and had even frolicked around the yard after the noon meal with her new friend, Esta, and some of the other children.

Grace had been relieved that the other women at church had been kind and understanding about the situation when she explained it to them. If only her husband and father could be that accepting.

She released a heavy sigh. It didn't seem fair that the two men she loved most seemed so unforgiving, and it wasn't fair that due to Anna's unwillingness to accept her, she was still being deprived of her daughter's love. Grace's only consolation was that Anna was here and didn't cry for her Grandpa Davis as often. Maybe in time, the child would adjust to her new surroundings and learn to love Grace. Maybe with prayer, Cleon and Dad would decide to forgive her, too.

For the last two weeks, Cleon had kept his distance—going to his folks' place to tend his bees early every morning, making honey deliveries the rest of the day, and sleeping on a mattress in the middle of the living room floor in their future home, rather than at the Hostettlers' house with Grace. She wondered if anything would ever be right between them again.

When Grace entered the downstairs hallway a few minutes later, she met Ruth, who had just come in through the back doorway.

"Shouldn't you have left for work by now?" she asked her sister.

"I was getting ready to head out when Cleon stopped me." Ruth handed Grace an envelope. "He wanted me to give you this."

"What is it?"

"I don't know. He said he was on his way to town and asked if I would see that you got it."

Grace's heart raced with hope. Maybe Cleon had forgiven her. Maybe he wanted to make things right between them.

"Well, I'd better go, or I'll be late getting to the bakeshop." Ruth gave Grace a hug and went back out.

Grace stood in the doorway and watched Ruth guide the horse and buggy down the driveway. Then she took a seat on the sofa and opened Cleon's note.

Dear Grace,

I've spent the last two weeks thinking about our relationship and wondering why you didn't love me enough to tell me about your previous marriage and the child you had given up. I can't say how I would have responded if I'd known the truth sooner, but I know how I'm feeling now. I feel betrayed, hurt, and angry. I need more time to deal with this, and I can't do it here where we see each other every day.

I have an opportunity to expand my honey deliveries to some places in Pennsylvania, so I've decided to catch a bus and head there. Ivan will care for my bees while I'm gone, and it will give me a chance to think things through.

As Always,
Cleon

Grace gulped on a sob as she crumpled the letter into a tight ball. What if Cleon never came back? What if—

"Daughter, what's wrong? Why are you crying?"

Grace looked up and saw her mother standing over her, a worried expression knitting her brows.

Releasing more sobs between every couple of words, Grace shared the letter Cleon had written. "I'm afraid I may have driven him away, and now nothing in my life will ever be any good."

Mom took a seat on the sofa and gathered Grace into her arms. "God brought your daughter back to you, and that's a good thing."

Grace nodded.

"After your visit with the bishop the night Anna arrived, he offered you words of comfort and acceptance."

She nodded again.

"The people in our community have been friendly to Anna and tried to make her feel welcome."

"Jah."

"You need to trust God with Cleon. I'm sure that in time your husband will come around, too."

"I—I hope so." Grace sniffed. "Anna may have been returned to me, but she doesn't accept me as her mother. She doesn't seem to want anything to do with me."

"She needs more time to adjust and get to know you better."

Grace reached for the box of tissues sitting on the table next to the sofa. She dabbed her eyes and blew her nose. "That doesn't solve things between Cleon and me. I'm afraid he might decide to leave the Amish faith and begin a new life in the English world without me."

"That's ridiculous. Cleon would never leave the faith or risk a shunning by deciding to do something so unthinkable as to dissolve your marriage." Mom gently patted Grace's back. "He's strong in his beliefs, and I'm sure that deep down, he loves you. Just give him some time to sort things out, and soon he'll be home again."

Grace moaned. "Dad's angry with me, too—not only because of the secret I kept from you, but because he blames me for that magazine article Gary Walker wrote."

Mom shook her head. "Now how can that be your fault?"

"I'm the one who told Gary about our break-ins. I figured he'd forgotten about it because I'd heard he had gone to Pennsylvania to write some stories about the Amish there."

"I see."

"I was as surprised as anyone when that story came out, and when Dad told us about the article and picture the bishop showed him, I believed it would be best to admit that I'd spoken to the reporter." She lifted the tissue to her face and blew her nose again.

"But there were details in the article that you never mentioned to the reporter, right?"

Grace nodded. "That's true, but if Gary is the one responsible for our break-ins, he would have already known everything that happened to us."

"Or someone else might have told him."

"Like who?"

Mom shrugged. "I don't know, but others in our community knew about the break-ins. One of them might have spoken to the reporter and told him the details you left out."

"Maybe so. All I know is when someone makes a decision about something important, the way I did when I allowed Wade's folks to take Anna, it can change their life forever." Grace slowly shook her head. "That's what happens when people don't think about the effect their decisions will have on others. If I'd known that giving up my little girl and keeping it a secret would have affected my family so much, I would have done things differently."

"That's how life goes—we learn and grow from our mistakes."

"And hope we don't make them again," Grace murmured.

"We shouldn't merely hope. We need to ask God to guide us in all our decisions."

Grace nodded. She knew Mom was right, for if she'd sought God's will in the first place, she wouldn't be in the mess she was in right now.

"Martha's gone to Kidron with your daed to look at a pair of beagles, so why don't we hire a driver to take us to the Wal-Mart store in Millersburg and get your daughter some appropriate shoes?"

Grace shook her head. "I don't feel like going anywhere, Mom. Why don't you and Anna go? It'll give you a chance to get better acquainted."

"I don't think staying home feeling sorry for yourself is going to solve anything. I really wish you'd come along."

"I'd rather not."

Mom shrugged. "All right then. Maybe some time alone is what you need."

A short time later, Judith and Anna were on their way to Millersburg in Donna Larson's car. As soon as they entered the Wal-Mart, Anna pointed to the mechanical horse inside the entrance. "I wanna horsey ride!"

Judith gave the child's hand a gentle tug. "Maybe on our way out." She'd hoped, as Grace had suggested, that this would be a chance for her and Anna to get better acquainted.

"I wanna ride the horsey now."

"Not until we finish our shopping." Judith grabbed a shopping cart, scooped Anna into her arms, and placed her inside the cart.

"I don't want new shoes. Let me out. I want out!"

"You might get tired if you walk. It's better that you ride inside the buggy."

Anna scrunched up her nose and crossed her arms.

Judith sighed and headed for the shoe department. Anna needed a sturdy pair of dress shoes, and they had to be plain and black. The other day, they'd looked at the boot and harness shop run by their friend Abe Wengerd but found nothing in Anna's size.

A short time later, Judith found a pair of appropriate-looking black shoes for the child and was about to move on to do some other shopping when Anna shouted, "I don't want these shoes! They're ugly, and I won't wear 'em."

Judith drew in a deep breath and prayed for patience. "I know you're upset about the shoes, and I understand that being left with strangers has been hard on you, but I won't tolerate such outbursts, Anna." She bent over so she was at eye level with the child. "Do you understand?"

Anna nodded but said nothing. She sat like a statue with her arms folded, staring straight ahead.

Judith gritted her teeth and maneuvered the cart down the toothpaste aisle. When she finished the rest of her shopping, she went to the nearest checkout stand, paid for her purchases, and pushed the shopping cart toward the door. They'd no sooner left the checkout counter when Anna started hollering, "Horsey! Horsey! I wanna ride the horsey!"

"Shh. I told you before you mustn't yell." Judith wondered what the other shoppers must think seeing a child dressed in plain clothes carrying on in such a manner. Amish children were taught at an early age to behave in public. But of course, none of the people staring at them had any idea Anna hadn't grown up Amish. How different things might have been for all of them if the child had been a part of their family from the time she was a baby.

When an ear-piercing buzzer went off, Anna let out a yelp. Judith halted outside the first set of doors where the scanners were located. She figured the security alarm had been triggered because the clerk who'd rung up her purchases had forgotten to remove the security strip from one of the items. A few seconds later, a clerk rushed over, demanding to see Judith's receipt and then searching her packages. Throughout the entire process, Anna fussed and cried for a horsey ride, which only caused Judith further embarrassment.

When the clerk found nothing in any of the packages, she turned to Judith and said, "You'd better let me see that purse you're holding."

Her forehead wrinkled. "Why would you need to see this? I didn't buy it here. It was a gift from my sister who lives in Indiana, and I was carrying it when I came into the store."

"Our scanners are set up to check for security strips on things going out of the store, not coming in," the clerk said. "Now, are you going to let me see that purse, or do I need to call my supervisor?"

Judith's head began to pound, and as Anna's screams increased in volume, she felt as if she could shriek at someone herself. Gritting her teeth, she handed over the purse.

The clerk snapped it open, and after a few seconds of rummaging around, she said, "I found the problem." She held up a small metallic strip. "This was stuck to the lining of your purse and must not have been removed when your sister purchased it. Since it's full of your personal things, it's obviously yours."

Judith sighed in relief, and miraculously, Anna stopped crying.

"I'm sorry for your trouble, ma'am," the clerk said with a sheepish-looking smile. "This kind of thing doesn't happen often, but we need to check things out to be sure nothing leaves the store that hasn't been paid for."

"I understand." On shaky legs, Judith pushed the cart toward the front door, anxious to get out to the car where Donna waited. Before she could exit the last set of doors, Anna stood up in the cart and hollered, "Horsey ride! Please, Grandma."

Judith halted and reached over to give the little girl a hug. Something good had come from this otherwise stressful shopping trip: Anna had called her "Grandma." Maybe the child would call Grace "Mama" soon. Oh, how she hoped so.

"Anna's asleep," Martha said, as she entered the kitchen later that evening.

Grace looked up from the letter she'd been writing and frowned. "I tried to get her to sleep with me tonight, but she cried and insisted on sleeping in your room again. It doesn't look like she's ever going to accept me as her mother."

Mom, who sat across from Grace drinking a cup of tea, shook her head. "I think you're wrong about that. I didn't say anything before because I didn't want to embarrass Anna in front of everyone during supper, but this afternoon as we were leaving Wal-Mart, she called me 'Grandma.' "

Grace set her pen aside and reached for her own cup of tea, letting the warmth of it seep through her cold fingers. "I'm glad to hear that, but just because Anna seems to have accepted you as her grossmudder and Martha as her *aendi* doesn't mean she will ever accept me."

Martha pulled out the chair next to Grace and sat down. "You need to remember that the only mother Anna's ever known was her grandma Davis. Now that the woman is dead and her grandpa left her with people she'd never met before, the poor little thing doesn't know where she belongs or who she can trust."

"I think your sister's right about that," Mom said with a nod. "I believe you need to work at gaining Anna's trust. If you spend as much time with her as you can, she'll learn that she can trust you, and eventually she'll begin calling you 'Mama.' "

Martha poured herself a cup of tea. "The only reason Anna has taken to me is because of the hundlin. She enjoys playing with them, and it's given us something to do together."

"Speaking of puppies," Grace said, "how'd things go with you and Dad in Kidron? Did you see any dogs you liked?"

Martha nodded, and her blue eyes fairly sparkled. "Found me a pair of beagle hounds for breeding. The male is named Bo, and his mate's name is Flo."

"They sound more like twins than mates."

Martha chuckled. "I think Anna will like the beagles as much as she does Heidi, Fritz, and the pups. "

Tears trickled down Grace's cheeks, and she plucked a napkin from the wicker basket on the table and wiped them away. "It hurts so much to know that Anna's accepting you but not me."

Mom reached over and touched Grace's arm. "Maybe if you can find something Anna's interested in, it might do the trick."

"Jah, maybe so. It doesn't look like I'll be spending my free time with Cleon anymore." Grace choked back a sob. "He gave Ruth a note for me this morning, and it wasn't good news."

"What'd it say?" Martha asked.

"He said he was catching a bus and would be going to some places in Pennsylvania where he wants to sell his honey."

"I'm sure he won't be gone long," her sister said.

"I agree," Mom put in. "Cleon will be back before you know it."

"As I'm sure you know, he's been sleeping on the floor in our unfinished house because he's still upset that I didn't tell him the truth about Wade and Anna sooner. I'm afraid he left because of that more than a need to sell honey." A sense of hopelessness welled in Grace's soul.

"I knew he'd been sleeping there," Martha said, "but I thought it was because he wanted to work on the place late at night and early in the morning. I never dreamed it was to get away from you."

"Cleon said he needs time to think about things, and I guess he feels he can't do that here where he would see me and Anna every day."

"Oh, Grace, I'm so sorry. Why didn't you say something about this sooner?"

Grace sniffed, picked up the napkin again, and blew her nose. "I told Mom about Cleon's letter this morning, but I haven't mentioned it to anyone else because I didn't think Anna needed to hear things she wouldn't understand."

Martha placed her hand in the small of Grace's back and gently massaged it. "Maybe it's good that Cleon will be gone awhile. It will give you more time to spend with Anna. I'm sure that after he's had a chance to think things over, he'll realize his place is here with you."

"I hope you're right." Grace stood up and walked toward the hallway.

"Where are you going?" Mom asked.

"Upstairs to check on Anna."

"I told you she's asleep," Martha said.

"I just want to be sure she's okay."

"Will you join us for some popcorn and hot apple cider afterward?" Mom called. "Your daed will be joining us when he's done with his chores in the barn."

Grace gave a quick nod, then rushed out of the room.

Chapter 23

"It's been awhile since I've ridden in your buggy," Ruth said as she and Luke headed down the road in his open courting buggy. It was a brisk, windy evening, and she felt grateful for the quilt wrapped around her legs.

Luke looked over at her and smiled. "I'm glad you were free to go with me this evening."

"Me, too."

"Your daed says things are hectic at your house right now, what with Grace's secret daughter showing up and all."

She nodded. "That's why I haven't felt free to go anywhere with you. I wanted to be around home every evening so I could get to know Anna better and help Grace deal with things. It's been quite a shock to have her daughter show up the way she did."

"I imagine."

"Almost every day Anna asks about her other grandpa, wondering when he's coming back for her."

"He's not, though, right?"

"Maybe for a visit." Ruth sighed. "Even though Anna seems to be adjusting in some ways, she doesn't like doing without some of the modern things she's used to. She isn't accepting Grace as her mamm very well, either."

"I'm sure in time she'll be okay."

"I hope so." She lifted her gaze toward the starry sky. It was a clear winter night, and the stars looked so bright and close she felt as if she could reach out and touch them.

"Your daed told me that you've had no more break-ins at your place, but he's worried there might be more because of the magazine article about the troubles you had."

"I think Dad's more concerned about the article bringing attention to the Amish in this area than he is with trying to find out who attacked us."

"Maybe it's best that he doesn't find out."

"What do you mean?"

"If someone in your family started snooping around, trying to play detective, somebody might end up getting hurt."

Ruth blinked as a feeling of dread crept up her spine. She knew Grace had been trying to find out if the English reporter might have been responsible for the break-ins, but the last she'd heard, Gary was gone, so Grace would no longer be asking him questions and putting herself at risk.

"Your daed's a stubborn man; that much I know," Luke said. "We've butted heads about the way I do my work, and he won't listen to reason when I try to show him something new I'd like to try. He's gotten upset with me for being late to work a couple of times or taking longer to get a delivery made. Even docked my pay once because he blamed me for some cabinets that fell off the wagon and got busted." He grunted. "Makes me wonder if I shouldn't try to find another job."

"Has someone offered you a better job?"

"Not yet, but I'm good with my hands, and I'm sure somebody would be willing to hire me as a carpenter."

Ruth hated to think of Luke quitting work for her father, but if he decided to go, she couldn't do much about it. "Let's talk about something else, shall we? This is supposed to be a fun evening, and discussing my daed's business isn't much fun."

Luke reached for her hand. "You're right. Your daed's not my favorite subject, either."

Her face flamed. "I didn't say that—"

He let go of her hand and slipped his arm around her shoulder.

"Getting back to that reporter fellow, do you have any idea who gave him the information he used in that article or how he got Grace's picture?"

She shrugged. "Grace admitted that she'd told him a few things, but she never posed for the picture. He took it without her permission. She believes he might have gotten the rest of his story from someone else in our community."

"Like who?"

"I have no idea."

"Who else knew about the break-ins?"

Ruth pursed her lips. "Let me see. Dad told Bishop King and a couple of our Amish neighbors about them. Grace told Cleon, and then I mentioned it to one of our English neighbors when she came into the bakeshop." She looked over at Luke. "Of course, you knew."

"I never talked to that reporter, so I hope you're not accusing me of anything." Luke's voice raised a notch, and he gave the reins a quick snap, causing the horse to pick up speed. "Giddy-up, there, boy."

"I wasn't accusing you."

"Sure sounded like it to me."

"You asked who else knew about the break-ins, and I answered."

He frowned. "Jah, well, I thought maybe you didn't trust me, that's all."

"Of course I trust you." Ruth flinched as the words rolled off her tongue. For some time she'd felt uneasy whenever she was with Luke. She wasn't sure if it was mistrust or simply confusion because he acted so odd at times. It was almost as if he was hiding something, but she didn't know what it could be.

She thought about the day she and Sadie had met Toby and Luke for a picnic, and how Luke had been late but wouldn't explain why. She thought about that morning when she and Martha had seen Luke outside the market in Berlin talking to a couple of English fellows. He'd acted strange then, too, not even bothering to introduce her.

"I've been wondering about something," she said, gathering up her courage.

"What's that?"

171

"A few months ago when Grace and I saw you outside the market talking to a couple of English fellows, you seemed kind of edgy and acted like you barely knew me."

His forehead wrinkled. "I don't know what you're talkin' about. Fact is, I barely remember the incident. I'm sure I wasn't acting edgy or said I didn't know you."

"I said you *acted* like you barely knew me."

He removed his arm from around her shoulders and gave the reins another snap. "I was busy, and you probably interrupted my conversation."

Ruth looked away, feeling like a glass of water had been dashed in her face. The passing scenery became a blur as tears stung the back of her eyes. "I wish you would slow down, Luke. The road could be icy, and it makes me naerfich to be going this fast."

"I'm a good driver. There's nothing to be nervous about."

"There have been too many buggy accidents on this road, and the way you're driving could set us up for one."

"You're turning out to be just like your sister Grace, you know that?"

"What's that supposed to mean?"

"You both worry too much."

Ruth folded her arms and compressed her lips. She had a good mind to tell Luke to turn his buggy around and take her home. And if he said one more unkind thing, that's exactly what she would do.

They rode in silence for the next several miles; then Luke reached for her hand and gave her fingers a little squeeze. "I'm sorry for snapping at you. I know most women tend to worry about things—my mamm most of all."

"I never used to worry so much," Ruth admitted. "But when the vandalism went on at our place, I began feeling anxious about many things."

"Guess that's understandable."

Ruth moistened her lips and decided to bring up the previous subject again. "Mind if I ask what you and those English fellows were talking about in the parking lot that day?"

He stared at her in such a strange way it sent chills up her spine. "I can't believe you're bringing something up that happened months ago."

"I wanted to talk to you about it before, but every time I started to, you changed the subject."

He shrugged.

"So I'm asking now, and I'd really like an answer."

"I'd rather not say."

"Why? Is it because you have something to hide?"

Luke's face turned bright red. "I've got nothin' to hide."

"Then why won't you tell me what was being said?"

"Because it's not important."

"What about that day at the pond with Sadie and Toby?"

"What about it?"

"How come you acted so strange and said you were late because you'd stopped in the woods? What did you really stop for, Luke?"

He slowed the horse and released a grunt. "Promise you won't say anything to anyone?"

She nodded, although it made her feel uneasy to make such a promise. What if Luke had been doing something wrong? If she knew about it and kept quiet, wouldn't that mean she was doing something wrong, too?

"If you really must know, I bought myself a truck last summer, and I've been keeping it hidden in the woods so my folks won't know."

Ruth compressed her lips tightly together. So that must have been Luke's truck she and Sadie had seen the day they'd been walking in the woods.

"Now, don't give me that face," he said, wagging his finger. "I'm still in rumschpringe, and I've every right to drive a motorized vehicle if I want to."

"If you think it's fine and dandy, then why hide it from your folks?"

Luke stared straight ahead and shrugged.

"Are you planning to leave the Amish faith?" Ruth dared to ask. She had to know what his plans were, for it could affect their relationship.

He shrugged again.

"Luke, would you please answer my question?"

"Haven't made up my mind yet."

Ruth leaned against the narrow seat and closed her eyes. This whole evening had gone sour, and from the looks of things, it wasn't going to get any better. "I think it would be good if you took me home now," she muttered.

"Whatever you say." Luke directed the horse to make a U-turn.

They rode the rest of the way in silence, and when they pulled into Ruth's yard, she turned to him and said, "I think it would be best if we don't see each other anymore."

His eyebrows lifted high on his forehead. "Now what brought that on?"

"If you don't care enough for me to answer my questions, then I think—"

"I did answer your questions. Well, most of 'em, anyway."

"If you decided to go English, we'd have to break up because I could never leave the Amish faith."

A spot on the right side of his face twitched, and he looked away. "Maybe you're right. Maybe we should go our separate ways before someone gets hurt."

"Jah, I agree. *Gut nacht*, Luke."

"Good night."

Ruth stepped down from the buggy onto the frost-covered grass and shivered. It wasn't until she reached the back porch that she allowed her tears to flow. It had been a mistake to let someone like Luke court her, and she almost felt relief that it was over.

Grace sank into a chair at the kitchen table, where Martha sat with their parents. Dad was reading *The Budget*; Mom had the newest issue of *Country Magazine*; and Martha was doing a crossword puzzle. A bowl of popcorn sat in the center of the table, and they each had cups of hot cider.

"Was Anna asleep when you checked on her?" Martha asked.

Grace nodded with a weary sigh. "I wish she was willing to sleep in my room. Anna, my own flesh-and-blood daughter, wants as little to do with me as possible. She talks more to her new friend, Esta, than she does me."

She blinked, willing her tears not to spill over. She'd shed enough tears since the little girl had come to live with them—tears over Anna not accepting her as mother, tears over Cleon's refusal to forgive her, tears over her own shame and regrets.

"It will get better in time—you'll see," Mom said with a look of understanding.

"I don't think anything will ever be better for me." Grace's head ached, her emotions were spent, and a sense of despair threatened to pull her down. "I–I'm afraid Cleon's never coming back."

Dad's head came up. "Why would you say something like that? Have you heard from him again?"

"I got a letter this morning."

"What'd it say?"

"He's asked his brother Ivan to check on his bees and collect the honey because he's going to be on the road a few more weeks, trying to line up several new customers."

"That makes sense to me," Martha put in. "Someone's got to take care of the bees while he's gone."

"But what if Cleon never comes back? What if—"

"He'll be back. He's just trying to drum up more business so he can provide better for you and Anna," Mom said.

Grace shook her head as tears coursed down her cheeks, despite her effort to keep them at bay.

Mom patted Grace gently on the back. "I'm sorry for your pain."

"Cleon might not have gone if you'd been honest with us in the first place." Dad's chair scraped against the linoleum as he pushed away from the table. "If your husband leaves the Amish faith and never returns, it will be your fault."

Grace trembled as her father's sharp admonition pierced her soul, but as much as his words hurt, she knew they were true.

"Roman, don't be so harsh." Mom set her magazine aside and

joined him at the sink, where he'd gone to put his empty cup.

He groaned. "Nothin's been right around here for months. Not here at home or even with my business. Why, the other day when I was in town, I saw Steven Bates at the drugstore, and the fellow snubbed me. Acted like I didn't even exist. I think he's still put out over those cabinets that broke, and I wouldn't be surprised if he hasn't been bad-mouthing me to others so I'll lose some business."

"I know I'm not to blame for that," Grace said tearfully, "but I do feel responsible for what's happened between me and Cleon, and now me and Anna."

Martha offered Grace a sympathetic smile. "None of us can do anything about Cleon except pray that he'll come home soon. However, we can all pitch in and do whatever we can to help make Anna feel more at ease."

Mom nodded and turned to Dad. "You always seem to be busy in your shop, but couldn't you make a little time to spend with your granddaughter?"

He shrugged and gave the end of his beard a quick tug. "I suppose I could. I've been wantin' to crack some of those walnuts I've had stashed away, so maybe I'll take Anna out to my shop and show her how to do it."

"That's a fine idea," Mom said with a hopeful-looking smile. "Don't you think so, Grace?"

Grace nodded, as the lump in her throat grew tighter. "I guess I haven't found the right thing to do with her yet."

"You'll think of something. Maybe you could—"

Martha's sentence was halted when Ruth entered the room, her lips turned down at the corners and her eyes swimming with tears.

"What's wrong?" Mom asked, rushing to Ruth's side. "Have you been crying?"

Ruth opened her mouth, but all that came out was a little squeak.

Dad stepped forward and grabbed hold of her arm. "What's the problem? Has there been another attack?"

She shook her head. "It's. . .it's Luke."

"What about Luke? Has he done something to you?" Dad's voice shook with emotion, and a vein on the side of his neck bulged.

"He won't be honest with me about anything, and I'm afraid he may end up going English, so I—I broke up with him." Ruth nearly choked on a sob and bolted from the room.

Grace groaned. Apparently she wasn't the only one in the family with problems.

Chapter 24

I don't wanna crack walnuts," Anna whined as Roman led her into his shop Saturday morning. "I wanna watch TV."

"We have no TV, Anna, and you know it." He glanced over at her and frowned. It seemed like all the child had done since she'd arrived at their house was pout, complain, and cry for her poppy. The hardest part was seeing what the little girl's sudden appearance had done to Grace and her relationship with Cleon.

Roman grimaced. Truth was, he'd felt just as hurt and betrayed as Cleon when Grace's secret had been revealed. If only she'd told them sooner, when she'd first returned home after living among the English. If they'd known about Anna then, maybe they could have helped Grace get her back. They surely would have offered their support.

Would you have been supportive or judgmental? a little voice niggled at the back of his mind.

He flinched. In all likelihood, he wouldn't have taken the news of her marriage well, and he wouldn't have been happy that Grace had allowed someone else to raise her child. This whole episode continued to remind him of his wayward sister. Had Rosemary been afraid of her family's reaction to her going English, or didn't she care enough to want to see them again? Did Rosemary have any children? Was she still alive? He feared he might never know the answer to those questions.

"How come there's so much wood in here?"

Anna's simple question pulled Roman out of his musings, and he jerked to attention. "This is where I work. I make wooden things."

She shrugged her slim shoulders and wandered around the room as though scrutinizing everything she saw.

"Come, have a seat at my workbench." Roman pulled out a stool for Anna and lifted her onto it. Then he poured some walnuts out of a burlap sack and picked up a hammer. "In my opinion, this is the best way to split open a walnut." *Crack!* The hammer came down, and the walnut shell split in two. "Now, it's your turn." He handed the hammer to Anna, but she stared at the smashed walnut, her eyes filling with tears.

"You killed it!"

"No, Anna, it's—"

"It's dead, just like my grandma."

"Your grandma isn't dead; she's back at the house, probably fixing lunch by now."

"Grandma's dead, and Poppy's gone away." Tears trickled down Anna's cheeks in little rivulets.

Roman looked around helplessly, wishing Judith or Martha were here. They seemed to have better luck at calming the child than he did. "Let's forget about the walnuts for now," he said. "You can sit at my desk while I do some work."

Anna's eyebrows furrowed, and her lower lip jutted out like a bullfrog. "I don't want to. I don't like it here."

"Fine! You can go back to the house, and that will give me the freedom to go somewhere I need to go." Roman set the hammer aside and reached for Anna's hand. So much for them getting to know each other better.

Judith was about to put the last two quarts of applesauce into the pressure canner when she heard a knock on the front door. *That's strange. It's not likely anyone we know would use the front door.*

"Martha, could you see who's at the door?" she called. Then she remembered that Martha had gone to check on her dogs, and Grace was upstairs resting.

Sighing, Judith dried her hands on a towel, stepped into the living room, and opened the front door. An English man stood on the porch. At first she didn't recognize him, but then she remembered him having gone to Roman's shop when he'd asked about purchasing their land.

"Can I help you?" she asked, stepping onto the porch.

"I hope so." He offered her a crooked smile. "In case you don't remember, my name's Bill Collins, and I was here a few months ago, talking to your husband about the possibility of buying your place."

She nodded curtly. "I remember."

"I'd like to talk to you a minute if you're not busy."

"Actually, I was about to put some applesauce into the canner."

"No problem. I can wait until you're done."

Thinking he might take a seat in one of the wicker chairs on the porch, Judith headed back inside, leaving the door slightly open. She'd just entered the kitchen when she heard a man's voice. She whirled around and was surprised to see the land developer standing inside the doorway.

"I'm hoping you and your husband might have reconsidered my offer about selling this place," he said, leaning against the counter and folding his arms.

"Have you spoken to Roman about this again?"

Mr. Collins shook his head. "I thought I'd talk to you first."

She frowned. "My husband would decide if we were to sell, but I'm sure he hasn't changed his mind in that regard."

"I'm prepared to offer you a fair price for the land."

"That may be so, but we have no plans to sell or relocate."

He grunted. "Money talks, and it's not my style to take no for an answer."

She opened her mouth to comment, but a knock sounded on the front door again. "Excuse me. I need to answer that."

"Sure, no problem."

The man stood as though he had no intention of leaving, so Judith headed for the front door, figuring she would ask him to leave as soon as she saw who was at the door.

She was taken aback to see another man standing on the porch, and she grimaced when she realized it was the reporter she'd talked to in town several months ago.

"Mind if I ask you a few questions?" he asked, reaching into his jacket pocket and withdrawing a tablet and pen.

"You've already done a magazine article about the break-ins we had. Shouldn't that be enough?" Judith surprised herself by the boldness of her words and her cool tone of voice. She was usually more pleasant to strangers—even the nosey ones who wanted information about the Amish.

"I was working on some other stories in Pennsylvania, but I've come back to Ohio to do a follow-up story on the break-ins. So I was wondering if there have been any more acts of vandalism here."

"I'd rather not talk about this if you don't mind."

"How about the law? Do they have any leads on who might have been responsible?"

"We didn't involve the sheriff."

"Mind if I ask why?"

Judith opened her mouth to reply when she remembered her jars of applesauce needing to be put into the canner. Besides, that determined land developer was still in her kitchen. All she wanted was for both men to leave so she could get on with the things she'd planned to do. "If you'll excuse me, Mr. Walker, I have something that needs to be taken care of in the kitchen." She left him on the porch and rushed back to the other room. Mr. Collins was still standing in the same place she'd left him.

"As I was saying," he said, following her across the room, "I'd like to discuss the details of my offer with you."

"It's not my place to talk about this with you, so if you have anything more to say, you'll have to meet with my husband." She nodded toward the window. "He's working in his shop this morning, so I'm sure you'll find him there."

He glanced at his watch and moved toward the back door. "I've got an appointment in half an hour, so I won't have time to talk to Mr. Hostettler right now." He handed her a business card he'd taken from his jacket pocket. "If you have any persuasion over your husband, I'd recommend you try and talk some sense into him." He sauntered out through the doorway.

Judith shook her head and dropped the card to the counter as she made her way to the stove. The water in the cooker was already boiling, so she set the jars of applesauce in place, closed the lid, and checked the pressure valve. When she turned from the stove, she was shocked to see Gary standing inside the kitchen door.

"Ach! You scared me. I thought you'd left."

He nodded at the notebook in his hand. "Didn't get any answers yet."

She released an exasperated groan. "I have nothing more to say."

"You never answered my question about the sheriff and why he wasn't involved."

"We're trusting in God for our protection and leaving it up to Him to bring justice to those who did us wrong."

"Are you saying that even if you knew who had done the break-ins, you wouldn't press charges?" His pen flew across the notebook with lightning speed.

"That's right." She nodded toward the stove. "Now if you'll excuse me—"

Just then the back door flew open, and little Anna darted into the room.

"Back already?" Judith couldn't believe they could have finished cracking all those walnuts so quickly.

"Grandpa killed a nut, and then he got mad and sent me back here."

Judith's gaze went to the back door. She saw no sign of Roman. "Where's your grandpa, Anna?"

"He's going somewhere." The child's chin trembled. "He's not nice like Poppy."

Concern welled in Judith's soul. She needed to speak with her husband and find out what had happened between him and Anna and tell him about the pushy land developer and the incessant reporter. With only a slight hesitation, she opened the back door and rushed onto the porch. When she spotted Roman turning his horse and buggy around by the barn, she ran down the walkway, waving and calling his name.

He halted the horse and leaned out the side opening. "What is it, Judith? I'm in a bit of a hurry."

"What happened with Anna, and where are you heading?"

"Didn't she tell you?"

Judith shivered and stepped up to the buggy. "She said you were mad at her, and that you were leaving."

"That's all?"

"Pretty much. Oh, and she said you'd killed a nut."

Roman grimaced. "All she did was whine and complain, and after I cracked the first walnut, she started to bawl. Then she mentioned her other grandpa and said she wanted to go home." His nose twitched and his eyebrows scrunched together. "I figured I'd never get anything done with her howling like a wounded heifer, so I sent her back to the house."

"I see. And where are you off to now?"

"Going into town to get a few things I need in my shop. Is that all right with you?"

"Of course, but I think you should know that Mr. Collins, that land developer, was here a few minutes ago."

"What'd he want?"

"To get me to convince you to sell our land."

"What'd you tell him?"

"That he'd need to talk to you, but I didn't think you were interested in selling."

"You got that right. If and when he does talk to me again, I'll tell him the same thing I told the Larsons when they asked about buying our place: I won't sell for any amount of money." Roman picked up the reins. "I'm off to town now."

Before she could say anything else, he got the horse moving and steered the buggy down the driveway.

Judith blew out her breath and rubbed her hands briskly over her arms. Spring would be here soon, but it was still too cold to be outside without a shawl or a jacket. "I'd best get back inside and see about Anna." She'd only taken a few steps when she realized that she'd left the child alone with a stranger. *What was I thinking? If only I'd thought to call Grace downstairs before I left the house in search of Roman.* She hurried her steps. *Guess I wasn't thinking straight because I felt so flustered over that land developer's pushy ways, the reporter's noisy questions, and then Anna showing up unexpectedly.*

She stepped onto the porch, and was about to open the door when Gary stepped out. She startled and took a step back, nearly losing her balance.

"Sorry if I frightened you, but I've got to go." He hurried down the steps and toward the driveway. She saw no sign of a car. Surely the man hadn't walked here all the way from town.

She reached for the handle of the screen door and was about to pull it open when a thunderous explosion rumbled through the house. Breaking glass crackled.

Judith's heart thudded against her chest as she raced into the kitchen. "Anna!"

Chapter 25

The vibrating floor beneath Grace's bed caused her to waken, and the rumbling roar made her aware that something horrible must have happened. She scrambled off the bed and without even bothering to put on her shoes, rushed from her room. At the bottom of the steps, she nearly collided with Martha as she dashed into the house.

"What happened, Grace? It sounded like something blew up in here. I heard it all the way out in the barn."

Trembling, Grace shook her head. "I—I don't know. I was upstairs in my room and heard a terrible noise. It shook my bed, rattled the windows, and vibrated the walls." Her gaze went to the kitchen. "You don't suppose—"

Martha made a beeline for the kitchen, with Grace right on her heels. Their mother was kneeling on the floor by the table, her arms wrapped around Anna. On the other side of the table lay several broken jars, with blobs of applesauce splattered everywhere.

Grace's heart pounded, and she rushed to her mother's side. "What happened? Is Anna hurt? Are you okay, Mom?"

"The pressure cooker's gauge must be faulty. It exploded when I was out on the porch." Mom's voice trembled with emotion. "Anna's shaken up, but she seems to be okay." She nodded toward the broken glass. "Thankfully, nothing went past that side of the table."

"Dad put a new gauge on the cooker a few weeks ago," Martha said, stepping around the mess and up to the stove. "Makes no sense that it would go like that."

Grace reached for Anna, but the child wouldn't budge. She clung to Mom, weeping for all she was worth.

"That's what I get for leaving the stove unattended and going outside to see where your daed was heading," Mom said tearfully. "That reporter had me so rattled with all his questions, and then when Anna showed up saying her grossdaadi was mad at her and was going somewhere—"

Grace felt immediate concern. "Reporter? What reporter?"

"The fellow who asked me some questions in town the day we went looking for your wedding dress material." Mom clambered to her feet, pulling Anna to her side. "First that land developer showed up, and he followed me into the kitchen. Then the reporter came to the door, and soon after the land developer left, the reporter came into the kitchen. When Anna ran into the house and said your daed was going someplace, I went outside to see what was up."

"I thought Gary had left Holmes County."

"Said he was back now and doing a follow-up story about our break-ins." Mom glanced toward the door. "Without even thinking, I left him in the kitchen with Anna, but he headed out a few minutes before the explosion."

Grace gritted her teeth so hard her jaw ached. Could Gary have had something to do with the pressure cooker exploding? Could he have tampered with the valve while Mom was outside talking to Dad? She glanced down at her daughter, still whimpering and clinging to Mom's skirts; then she moved quickly toward the door.

"Where are you going?" Mom called after her.

"Outside to see if I can find Gary."

"Not without me." Martha caught up to Grace at the door and pushed it open. "If you do catch up to that curious reporter, you shouldn't be alone with him."

Grace offered her sister a grateful smile. "I appreciate your concern."

As Martha followed Grace down the porch steps, her thoughts raced like a runaway horse. What if her sister was right and the reporter was responsible for the break-ins and other attacks? If they couldn't report it to the sheriff or prove that he'd done it, how would they ever make him stop?

"There's no sign of his car." Grace pointed to the driveway. "Guess that means he's already gone."

"Maybe so, but let's look out by the road, in case he parked his car somewhere nearby," Martha suggested.

"Jah, okay."

They hurried down the driveway, and when they approached the mailbox by the road, they saw him standing across the street with a camera pointed at them. Grace turned her head, but Martha marched boldly across the street until she stood face-to-face with Gary. "What do you think you're doing?"

"Just taking a few pictures to go with the article I'm planning to write." He turned the camera toward her, but she put her hand in front of the lens.

"Don't even think about it."

Gary's eyes widened, and his jaw dropped open. Apparently, he wasn't used to hearing an Amish woman speak so boldly.

Grace joined them. "Wh–what are you doing here, Gary?"

"I'm back in the area again, hoping to do another story or two." He nodded at Grace. "I came by to see if there have been any more attacks at your place."

Martha planted both hands on her hips and stared up at him. "Did you mess with the gauge on our mother's pressure cooker?"

"Of course not. Why do you ask?"

"It blew up minutes after you left our house. Since you were alone in the kitchen—"

He held up his hand. "I hope you're not insinuating that I had anything to do with it."

"My daughter was in the kitchen when the cooker blew." Grace took a step closer to him.

His eyebrows furrowed. "Your daughter? That little girl with the whiny mouth is yours?"

Grace nodded. "My secret's out now, so you have nothing to hold over me anymore."

He scratched the back of his head. "What secret are you talking about?"

Martha stepped between them. "Anna. She's talking about Anna."

"Huh?" Gary looked at Grace, over at Martha, then back at Grace again. "You two are talking in circles. I have no idea what secret you're referring to."

"The one about me being married to Wade and giving birth to his daughter."

"I never knew you and Wade had a kid."

"You said you knew he'd married me."

"Yeah, I knew that much."

"After I broke up with you and started dating Wade, you said you would get even with me."

He shrugged. "Guys say and do a lot of things when they're trying to keep a woman."

"It seems odd that we never had any attacks until you showed up in Holmes County," Martha put in. "And since you've been asking all sorts of questions and pestering Grace to have coffee with you and all, you're our prime suspect."

Gary leaned his head back and howled. "Prime suspect? Who do you think you are—the Nancy Drew of the Amish?"

"Who?"

"Never mind." Gary turned to face Grace again. "You and your little sister are acting paranoid. You have no proof that I'm anything other than a reporter trying to do his job." He pointed to his camera. "Do you honestly think I would be stupid enough to jeopardize my chance to sell a dynamic piece to some big publication?"

She opened her mouth to reply, but he cut her off. "As I said, I'm back in the area to do a few more stories on the Amish, and I might do a couple articles about some of the events happening in the area. So whether you like it or not, I'll be sticking around Holmes County for as long as I want."

Grace's face paled, and her whole body trembled. Martha didn't think it was doing either of them any good to continue arguing with the Englisher, so she took hold of her sister's arm and steered her toward the house. "Let's go, Grace."

"Say, Gracie. Did you and that Amish man ever get married?" Gary called after her.

She gave a quick nod.

Martha glanced over her shoulder as Gary headed for his car parked on the shoulder of the road. She felt certain of one thing: If he was responsible for the things that had happened to them, God would deal with him in His time.

Chapter 26

For the next several days, Grace made every effort to spend more time with Anna. They'd baked cookies together and taken them over to the Wengerds' place so Anna could play with Esta while Grace and Alma visited awhile. The next morning, Anna helped Grace feed and water the chickens in the henhouse. At the moment, Grace was sitting in one of the wicker chairs on the back porch, watching her daughter romp around in the yard with Heidi's rambunctious pups.

Anna seemed to be accepting her new life better these days—accepting Grace better, too.

"Thank You, God," Grace murmured as she took a sip of tea from the mug she held. She closed her eyes and drew in a deep breath. *Bless my husband, Lord, and bring him home soon.*

"Are you sleepin'?"

Grace startled at the sound of her father's deep voice, and she turned to face him. "I was watching Anna play with Heidi's pups."

Dad took a seat in the chair beside her and set his cup of coffee on the small table between them. "Watching with your eyes closed, huh?"

Grace smiled. "Actually, I was talking to God."

"Ah, now that's a good thing. I've been doing a lot of that myself here of late."

"Because of the attacks on our family?"

He shrugged. "There've been no more for some time. I'm sure that trouble is over."

"What about the pressure cooker exploding the other day?"

"That was an accident, plain and simple."

"An accident?" Grace could hardly believe her ears.

"The gauge must have been faulty, or maybe the valve was broken."

"You replaced the gauge with a new one, so I don't see how it could have been faulty."

"Maybe it happened because your mamm left the cooker on the stove too long and it overheated."

She touched his arm. "I'm sure that wasn't an accident, and neither were the other things that have happened to us."

"I know you believe the reporter had something to do with it, but I'm equally sure he didn't. The things that were done before were most likely done by some rowdy English fellows who've probably been the cause of a few other destructive things that have been done in our area."

"I still think Gary might be the one responsible, but since I have no proof, I guess there's not much I can do about it." She released a weary sigh. "I'm just glad no one was hurt when the pressure cooker blew up. It would break my heart if something happened to Anna."

"God was watching over your mamm as well as your *dochder*; there's no doubt about that." He smiled, but a muscle in his cheek quivered, letting her know he was more concerned than he was letting on. "It's silly of us to think it could be this person or that. It's just speculation on all our parts."

"That's true, but—"

"Only God knows the truth, and He will handle things in His way, His time. You'll see." He leaned back in his chair and took a drink of his coffee.

Grace mentally scolded herself for being overly suspicious of Gary, but she shuddered to think what could have happened to Anna if she'd been sitting on the other side of the table. The child could have been cut by the broken glass or burned by the hot steam that shot from the pressure cooker when it exploded. *Thank You, God, for watching out for my little girl.*

Dad motioned in the direction of Cleon and Grace's new home.

"Since Cleon's brothers have been coming over to help me work on your place the last couple of weeks, I believe we'll have it ready for you to move in by the time Cleon gets home."

She stared at the silhouette of the two-story structure sitting near the back of her folk's property—the place she had hoped would be her and Cleon's happy home. "I appreciate all the work you've done on the house, and when it's done, Anna and I will move in, but I'm not sure about Cleon."

Dad frowned. "What do you mean? It's Cleon's home, too, and I'm sure when he returns from his business trip, he'll be glad to find the house has been finished."

Grace nibbled on her lower lip as she contemplated the best way to voice her thoughts. "I'm. . .uh. . .not sure Cleon will ever return home. His last letter let me know how hurt he still is, and he said something that made me think he might decide to leave the Amish faith and go English."

"What did he say?"

"That he's still feeling confused and wonders if maybe he's meant to do something else with his life besides what he'd planned."

"He could have been referring to the honey business. Maybe he's having trouble lining up customers and is thinking about doing some other kind of work." Dad pointed in the direction of his shop. "Cleon's carpentry skills are pretty good. Maybe he would consider coming to work for me."

"You already have Luke working for you, Dad, and I don't think you have enough work right now to keep three men busy, do you?"

He shrugged. "Never know what the future holds."

Grace wrapped her arms around her stomach as she was hit by a sudden wave of nausea. She'd been feeling a little dizzy lately and kind of weak but figured it was because she hadn't been eating much since Cleon left. Then again, it might be caused by stress or a touch of the flu.

Dad placed his hand on her shoulder. "Try not to worry so much. Just pray and leave the situation in God's hands."

Grace squeezed her eyes shut and willed her stomach to settle down. It was easy enough for Dad not to worry; it wasn't his mate who'd gone off to Pennsylvania.

"Say, aren't you one of those Amish fellows?"

Cleon turned to the middle-aged English man who shared his seat on the bus and nodded. "Jah, I'm Amish."

"I thought so by the way you're dressed. And from the looks of that beard you've got going, I'd say you might be newly married."

Cleon scrubbed a hand down the side of his face. "Jah, I'm married."

"Me, too. Been with the same woman for close to twenty years. We've got three great kids—two boys and a girl. How about you?"

"I've only been married a couple of months." Cleon chose not to mention Anna. She was Grace's child, not his. Truth was, he and Grace might never have any children.

"Where you from?"

"I live in Ohio, between Berlin and Charm."

"Holmes County, right?"

"Jah."

"I heard that's the largest Amish settlement in the United States." Cleon nodded.

"So what are you doing in Pennsylvania?"

"I've had business here."

The man studied Cleon intently. "Do you farm for a living?"

Cleon shook his head. "I raise bees for honey, and we also use the wax to make candles."

"Ah, I see. Were you trying to set up some new accounts, then?"

"Jah."

"I'm in sales, too. I sell life insurance." The man stuck out his hand. "My name's Lew Carter, and I work for—"

"I don't mean to be rude, but I've got no use for life insurance."

The man looked stunned. "If you've got a family, then you ought to make some provision for them in case something were to happen to you."

WANDA &. BRUNSTETTER

"The Amish don't buy any kind of insurance. We take care of our own." Cleon turned away from the man and stared out the window at the passing scenery. Maybe it was time to finish up his business here and face his responsibilities at home.

Chapter 27

"Church was good today, jah?" Mom asked as she glanced over her shoulder and smiled at Grace. They were riding home in their buggy with Dad, Mom, and Martha sitting in front, and Grace, Ruth, and Anna in the backseat.

Grace nodded in response to her mother's question. The truth was she'd barely heard a word that had been said during any of the sermons today. She'd been fighting waves of nausea.

"It was hard for me to see Luke at church today," Ruth whispered to Grace.

"I can imagine. Did he say anything to you after the service?"

"He never looked my way." Ruth sighed. "It's probably for the best since he wants to be so close-mouthed and not share things with me."

"Luke was late to work again on Friday; did I mention that?" Dad asked.

Ruth looked stunned, but it was no surprise to Grace that Dad had overheard their conversation. Mom often teased him about being able to hear a piece of sawdust fall if he was listening for it.

"Did he say why he was late?" The question came from Martha.

"Made some excuse about having an errand to run after he left home and it taking longer than he expected."

"Did you believe him?" Ruth asked.

Dad shrugged. "Not sure what I believe where Luke's concerned. He's got a mind of his own, that's for sure. I think he actually believes he knows more than me about working with wood."

"I'm sure Luke's just trying to share his ideas," Martha put in.

Martha's defense of Luke made Grace wonder if her sister might have more than a passing interest in Ruth's ex-boyfriend.

"When Luke finally showed up for work on Friday, I smelled smoke on his clothes." Dad shook his head. "Sure hope he's not messing with cigarettes during his rumschpringe."

"Did you question him about it?" Mom asked.

"Nope. Didn't think it was my place to be askin'.'"

Ruth's cheeks turned pink, and she cleared her throat a couple of times. "I. . .uh. . .think it's possible he's doing a lot of things he shouldn't be."

"How do you know that?" Dad asked.

"Well, he's got a—" She fell silent. "Never mind. It's not my place to be saying."

Dad gave the reins a quick snap to get the horse moving faster, as the animal had slowed considerably on the last hill. "Well, whatever Luke's up to during his rumschpringe, my main concern is his work habits. I made up my mind last week that if he was late to work again I would fire him, and I should have done that on Friday morning."

"Why didn't you, Roman?"

Dad reached over and patted Mom's arm. "Figured you would tell me I ought to give the man one more chance."

She chuckled. "You know me well."

Grace leaned against the seat and tried to relax. She and Anna would be moving into their new house tomorrow morning, but it would be without Cleon. She shivered. All this waiting and wondering if he would ever come home was enough to make her a nervous wreck. No wonder her stomach felt upset much of the time. If it weren't for Anna, she would be utterly miserable.

She reached over and took her daughter's hand, and the child smiled at her. *Thank You, God. Thank You for giving my daughter back to me.*

"Do we have to go?" Anna asked as Grace placed a stack of linens into a box she would be taking over to their new home. "I like it here."

Grace smiled and nodded. "I know you do, but at the new house, you'll have your own room. Won't that be nice?"

The child stuck out her lower lip. "But I'll miss Aunt Martha."

"She won't be far away. She'll come over to see us, and we'll go see her and the rest of the family, too."

Anna's forehead wrinkled. "Poppy never comes to see me like he promised."

"That's because he lives far away, and he's still not feeling well, Anna." Grace gently squeezed the child's arm. "He writes you letters, though."

Anna stared at the hardwood floor. "I miss him."

"I know." Grace drew Anna into her arms, but the child just stood, unmoving. One step forward and one back. If there was only something she could do to put a smile on her little girl's face this morning.

Grace's gaze came to rest on her cedar chest. The faceless doll! Why hadn't she thought of it sooner?

She hurried across the room, flipped open the lid, and dug into the contents of the cedar chest until she located the doll. "Look what I've found, Anna."

"What's that?" The child's eyes opened wide, and Grace was pleased that she'd captured her interest.

"It's the doll I made for you when you were a baby."

Anna's forehead wrinkled as she pursed her lips. "It's got no mouth." She touched the side of her nose. "No nose." She pointed to one of her eyes. "No eyes." She shook her head. "She ain't no doll."

Grace resisted the temptation to correct her daughter's English. Instead, she got down on her knees beside Anna and cradled the doll in her arms. "It's hard for me to explain, but Amish people make their dolls without faces."

"How come?"

"It has to do with a verse from the Bible that talks about not making any graven images."

Anna tipped her head and squinted. Obviously, she had no idea what Grace was talking about.

"It's fun to pretend, don't you think, Anna?"

The child nodded. "Last Sunday after church, me, Esta, and some of the other kids took turns pretending to be a horse pulling a buggy along the road."

"Then let's pretend this doll has a face." She looked up at her daughter to get her reaction, but Anna's expression didn't change.

Grace tried again. "Let's start by naming the doll."

Still no response.

"How about if we call her Sarah?"

"I don't like that name."

"How about Phoebe? I had a friend named Phoebe when I was a little girl, but she moved to Wisconsin."

Anna shook her head.

Grace released an exasperated sigh. "What would you like to call the doll?"

"Martha."

Grace nodded. "Martha it is, then." She touched the doll's face again. "Let's pretend that little Martha has eyes. What color should they be?"

"Blue. Like Aunt Martha's."

"Okay. What color hair should the doll have?"

"Aunt Martha has brown hair."

"True." She extended the doll toward Anna. "Would you like to hold her now?"

Anna reached for the doll and snuggled it against her chest. "I like the doll with no face."

Grace smiled. She might not have completely won over Anna, but she was making a bit more headway every day. And now she could see her daughter cuddling the doll Grace had made for her when she was a baby.

Chapter 28

Roman looked up from sanding a chair and frowned when Luke entered the shop. "You're late again, boy. What's the problem this time?"

Luke stayed near the door as if he was afraid to come in. Was he dreading another lecture or worried that Roman might fire him? That's what he'd planned to do if Luke showed up late again without a good excuse.

"Well, how come you're late, and why are you standing by the door?"

Luke made little circles in a pile of sawdust with the toe of his boot as his gaze dropped to the floor. "I. . .um. . .I'm late because I had an errand to run on the way here."

Roman set his sandpaper aside and straightened. "I warned you about this habit of being late. Said if it happened again, I'd have to let you go."

Luke lifted his gaze. "Are you sayin' I'm fired?"

Roman nodded.

Luke shuffled his feet a few times. "I know you and me haven't seen eye to eye on some things, but—"

"That's true, we haven't." Roman took a step toward Luke, and a whiff of smoke permeated his nostrils. Either Luke had taken up smoking, as Roman had suspected, or the boy had been hanging around someone who did.

Luke's eyebrows drew together. "I know you have a fair amount of work right now, and if I leave, you'll be shorthanded."

"That's my problem. I'll do fine on my own until I can get someone else."

Luke shrugged. "I think you're gonna regret having fired me." He pulled a pair of sunglasses from his shirt pocket, turned on his heels, and headed for the door.

Roman grunted and went back to sanding the chair.

"Now how'd that happen?" Judith muttered as she made her way across the yard to check on her drying laundry. The line was down, and clothes were strewn all over the ground. At first, she thought the towels she'd hung must have been too heavy and caused the line to break, but after closer inspection, she realized that the line had been cut. "Who would do something like this?"

She bent to retrieve one of Roman's shirts and noticed a pair of sunglasses lying on the ground a few feet away. No one in her family wore sunglasses like that, and her heart started to race as she realized that whoever had cut the line had probably lost their sunglasses during the act.

Grabbing up the glasses along with one of the dirty shirts, Judith hurried toward Roman's shop. She found him bent over his workbench, sanding on the legs of a straight-backed chair. "There's been another attack," she panted.

He rushed over to her. "What's happened? Has anyone been hurt?"

She shook her head as she held up his shirt. "My clothesline's been cut, and now everything needs to be washed again."

"That's it—just a broken line—and you're all in a dither?"

"It didn't break on its own, Roman. I checked the line, and it was obviously cut." She showed him the sunglasses. "I found these on the ground not far from the clothes."

He reached for the glasses. "These look like the pair Luke had in his pocket. He put them on as he was leaving my shop."

Judith glanced around the room. "Where'd Luke go?"

Roman shrugged. "Don't know. I fired him."

"Why would you do such a thing?"

"He was late to work again, and I'm getting tired of it. That fellow's been a thorn in my side for some time—coming in late to work, arguing with me about how things should be done. I'm even more convinced that he's been smoking."

Judith's eyes widened. "He's always seemed like such a nice young man."

"Looks can be deceiving." He frowned. "Makes me wonder if that *ab im kopp* might be the one who broke into our house and my shop. That crazy fellow's certainly had opportunity."

"Ach, Roman, surely not."

"Luke hasn't joined the church yet, and from what I've heard, he's been seen with a rowdy bunch of English fellows. You never know what kind of pranks he might decide to play."

Judith slowly shook her head. "The things that were done here were more than pranks, and what reason would he have for singling us out?"

He shrugged. "Can't say for sure, but it could have to do with his broken relationship with Ruth, or he might be nursing a grudge against me because we've butted heads so many times. With me firing him just now, he may have decided to retaliate by cutting your clothesline."

She sank into a chair and released a deep moan. "May the Lord help us all."

Chapter 29

I'm glad you were free to go shopping with me and Anna this morning," Grace said to Martha as they drove their buggy toward Berlin. "It's a nice clear day, and I thought it would be good for us to get some fresh air and time together." She glanced over her shoulder at Anna, asleep on the backseat with her faceless doll in her hand. "She's not completely adjusted, but things are getting better between me and my daughter."

"Glad to hear it."

"She likes the doll I made her when she was a *boppli*. Hardly lets it out of her sight."

Martha smiled. "Once Cleon gets back, you'll be a real family."

Grace swallowed back the wave of nausea that hit her unexpectedly. It wasn't good for her to feel this way—not when she had so much to do and was trying hard to be a good mother while she put her faith in God to make things better.

"Are you okay?" Martha reached across the seat and touched Grace's arm. "You look kind of pale, and your hands are shaking."

"I'm all right. Just a bit tired is all."

"Want me take over driving?"

Grace shook her head. "I'll be okay."

"Are you sure?"

Grace opened her mouth to respond, but before she could get a word out, something went *splat* against the front window.

"What was that?" Martha leaned forward and squinted at the red blob.

"Looks like a tomato."

Splat! Splat! Two more hit the buggy.

"*Ich kann sell net geh*—I cannot tolerate that." Martha pointed to the shoulder of the road. "Would you please pull over?"

"What for?"

"We need to see if we can find out who threw those tomatoes."

"It's probably just some kids fooling around."

"They shouldn't be hiding in the woods, throwing things at buggies. It could cause an accident."

Grace pulled back on the reins and guided the horse to the side of the road, knowing if she didn't stop, she would never hear the end of it. She looked around. "I don't see anyone in the woods, do you?"

"Over there!" Martha pointed to a stand of trees on the opposite side of the road. "I thought I saw the back of some fellow's head bobbing in and out between those trees."

Grace craned her neck. "I don't see anyone."

"He ducked behind that tree."

"What'd he look like?"

"I'm not sure. It looked like he was wearing a baseball cap." Martha opened the door on her side of the buggy.

"Where are you going?"

"Across the road to see what's up."

Grace reached across the seat and grabbed her sister's arm. "Are you kidding? There could be more than one person in those woods, and you might get hurt."

"I just want to talk to them."

"Do you really think anyone mean enough to throw tomatoes at an Amish buggy is going to listen to you?"

"They might." Martha compressed her lips as she frowned. "You don't suppose whoever threw that brick through our kitchen window and broke into the house and Dad's shop could be responsible for throwing those tomatoes, do you?"

Grace glanced over her shoulder and was relieved to see that Anna was still asleep. She didn't think it would be good for her daughter to hear this conversation. It might frighten her. "I doubt it could be the same person, but just in case, we're not going to put ourselves in any danger by going into the woods." She gathered up the reins and got the horse moving again. "We need to get our shopping done so we can help Mom do some cleaning."

Martha nodded. "Sure hope Ruth doesn't have any trouble on her way home from work this afternoon."

Grace shook her head. "I'm sure whoever threw those tomatoes will be long gone by then."

For the rest of the morning, Roman had trouble getting any work done. He couldn't stop thinking about how he'd fired Luke or about the clothesline that had been cut in their yard. What if he'd been wrong about rowdy Englishers committing the break-ins? What if Luke had done all those things because he was angry with Roman?

He was also worried about Judith, who had seemed extremely agitated after the clothesline incident. When they'd gotten the laundry picked up and the line put back in place, she'd gone to the cellar to wash everything again. Roman could tell by the droop of her shoulders and her wrinkled forehead that she was deeply troubled.

"Wish there was something I could do to make things better for everyone," he mumbled as he brushed a coat of stain on a chair. It wasn't right that their lives were in such turmoil. He wondered if his prayers were getting through to God, and if they were, why wasn't God answering?

Maybe I should pay a call on our bishop and see what he has to say about this. Jah, that's what I need to do.

As Grace guided the horse and buggy over their graveled driveway, Martha spotted their mother out in the yard. "Look, Mom's hanging out the wash. That makes no sense, because she was hanging it out when we left for town this morning."

"Maybe she found some other things that needed to be washed," Grace suggested as she halted the horse near the barn.

Anna sat up and yawned. "Are we home yet? I'm hungry."

"Jah, we're home," her mother replied. "We'll have lunch as soon as we get the groceries put away."

"The horse needs to be put in the corral, too," Martha added.

A short time later, Grace, Martha, and Anna headed for the house, but they stopped at the clothesline to speak with Mom.

"How come you're still doing wash?" Martha asked. "I figured you'd be bringing in dry clothes by now, not hanging out wet ones."

Mom frowned. "Someone cut the line. I found clothes all over the place."

"That's terrible! Who would do such a thing?"

Mom pointed to the ground. "I found some sunglasses nearby, and your daed thinks they were Luke's."

Grace stepped forward. "What'd they look like?"

"Metal-framed with dark lenses."

"Gary has a pair of metal-framed sunglasses. He was wearing them the day the pressure cooker blew up."

"So it could have been Gary rather than Luke who cut the line." Martha frowned. "Someone threw tomatoes at our buggy on the way to Berlin. I wonder if it could have been—"

Mom motioned to Anna, who stood beside Grace with an anxious expression on her face. "Can we talk about this later?"

Grace nodded and took her daughter's hand. "Let's go into the house, Anna. You can help me make some sandwiches."

"Can we have peanut butter and honey?"

"Jah, sure. We've got plenty of honey."

"I'm going to check on my dogs, and then I'll see about getting our lunch made," Martha said as Grace and Anna headed up the path leading to their new house.

"Jah, okay."

When Martha drew close to the barn, she heard yipping. It sounded like Fritz, only it wasn't coming from the dog kennel Dad had finally finished. It seemed to be coming from the other side of the house.

Yip! Yip! There it was again.

She hurried around the house and halted when she saw Fritz tied to a tree. The rope had been fastened around the dog's neck and left front leg, so that it was pulled up under the animal. The poor dog's water dish had been placed just out of his reach.

Martha let out a shriek and rushed to the animal's side. "Oh, Fritz, you poor little thing. Who could have done this to you?"

The dog whined pathetically, and Martha's fingers trembled as she undid the knot and removed the rope. "Whoever did this has gone too far. Dad has got to notify the sheriff!"

Roman was about to put the CLOSED sign in his window and head up to the house for lunch when Martha rushed in holding Fritz in her arms. Her face was crimson and glistening with sweat. "What's wrong, daughter?"

"It's Fritz," she panted. "I found him on the side of the house."

"How'd he get there? I thought he was in the kennel with the other dogs."

"All the dogs were in the kennel when Grace, Anna, and I left for town this morning, but when I found Fritz just now, he was tied to a tree, with one leg held up." She paused and gulped in some air. "A watering dish had been placed just out of his reach."

Roman compressed his lips as he shook his head. "Cuttin' your mamm's clothesline is one thing, but cruelty to an animal is going too far."

Hope welled in Martha's soul. "Are you going to notify the sheriff?"

He shook his head. "We have no proof who did it, and even if we did—"

"As I'm sure you know, Grace thinks that English reporter might be trying to get even with her for breaking up with him before she married Anna's daed."

He drew in a quick breath and released it with a huff. "I think she's wrong; I suspect it could be Luke."

"But Luke seems so nice. I can't imagine him doing anything that mean." Martha looked down at the trembling animal in her arms.

"What reason would he have for hurting one of my dogs or for doing any of the other things?"

"You know that Luke and I have butted heads several times. He doesn't like to be told what to do, and when I fired him this morning, he might have been mad enough to get even."

"You. . .you fired him?"

Roman nodded. "I hate to think it could be one of our own, but your mamm did find some sunglasses this morning that looked like Luke's."

"Grace said the reporter had a pair of sunglasses that fit the description of the ones Mom found."

Roman shrugged. "Maybe so, but remember that day when the brick was thrown through the kitchen window and you discovered Luke's hat on the ground near the barn?"

She nodded.

"Doesn't that make him look like he could be guilty?"

"I suppose it does, but if Luke's running with that bunch of rowdy English fellows Ruth and I saw him in town with one day, maybe he thinks playing a few pranks is fun."

Roman's eyebrows drew together. "There's nothing fun about vandalizing someone's property, stealing tools from their shop, or hurting their animals."

Martha rubbed Fritz's silky ear. "He's not really hurt. Just scared a bit—that's all."

He grunted. "Jah, well, the critter could have been hurt if you hadn't found him when you did."

"That's true, and I am upset about what happened. Still, I'm not convinced that Luke's the one who did it."

"We can't solve this problem right now, so why don't you put Fritz back in the kennel with the other dogs, and then we'll go up to the house for some lunch. If Luke shows up to get his sunglasses and I'm able to question him, it might give me a clue as to what's going on. If not, then I may go over to his place and have a little talk with him."

Chapter 30

Martha paced in front of her dog kennels, stopping every couple of minutes to watch Heidi and her remaining three pups frolic on the concrete floor inside the chain-link fence. She had placed another ad in a couple of newspapers, including *The Budget*, hoping to sell the rest of them. So far she'd sold one female pup to Ray and Donna Larson, and a male to an Amish man who lived near Sugarcreek. Flo, the female beagle, hadn't become pregnant yet, but Martha hoped that would happen soon.

Maybe I should go over to the Larsons' after lunch and see how their puppy is doing. It would give me a chance to talk to Donna about the situation here and find out if she or Ray might have heard or seen anything suspicious.

"I invited the folks to lunch at my house," Grace called from the barn doorway. "It's ready now, so are you coming?"

"Jah, okay." Martha took one final look at the dogs and hurried toward the front of the barn. "Did Dad tell you about Fritz?"

Grace nodded with a grim expression. "When he came up to my house a few minutes ago with Mom, he told us the whole story." She touched Martha's arm. "I'm sorry it happened but glad the dog wasn't hurt."

"Dad's trying to blame Luke, but I'm not convinced."

"Me, neither. I've been saying all along that Gary's responsible for the terrible things that have happened to our family." Grace bit her lip and stared at the ground. "Except for the mess I've made with my marriage. That's my fault—no one else's."

Martha slipped her arm around her sister's waist as they started walking up the driveway toward Grace's house. "You made a mistake in keeping the truth from Cleon, but that doesn't give him the right not to forgive."

"Maybe not, but I should have told him sooner, not kept it hidden until Anna showed up."

"No one's perfect, Grace. We all make mistakes."

"I seem to take the prize in that department." Grace stopped walking and drew in a shaky breath. Her face looked pale, and dark circles rimmed her eyes.

"What's wrong? Are you feeling *grank?*"

"I don't think I'm really sick, but I've been having waves of nausea for a couple of weeks."

"Have you missed your monthly?"

Grace nodded soberly.

"Sounds to me like you might be in a family way."

"I-I'm afraid that might be the case."

"It's nothing to look so down in the dumps about. If you're going to have a boppli, that's joyous news."

"It would be if things weren't so verhuddelt around here."

"You're right about things being confused, which is why I'm going over to the Larsons' this afternoon to see if they know anything."

"Why would they know anything? Surely you don't think that nice couple would want to hurt us in any way."

Martha shook her head. "Of course not, but I'm hoping Ray might have seen something with those binoculars he uses for bird watching. Or maybe Donna has heard something from one of the people she drives to appointments."

"I'd feel a lot better if the attacks would stop," Grace said, "but that doesn't solve my problem with Cleon not coming home."

"Have you heard from him lately?"

"Not since he sent that letter saying he was making more contacts for honey sales and didn't know when he might be home."

"Guess you can't write back and tell him you're pregnant, then."

"I haven't seen a doctor yet, so I'm not sure I'm in a family way. Maybe my symptoms are caused from the stress I've been under." Grace halted when they came to the steps leading to her back porch. "Please don't say anything to the folks about this. If I'm still feeling nauseated by the end of the week, I'll make an appointment to see the doctor."

"You promise?"

Grace gave a quick nod.

As Cleon exited the store he'd visited in hopes of soliciting some business, he spotted an English girl skipping down the sidewalk beside her mother. It made him think of Grace's little girl, who was about the same age. After Grace's secret had been revealed, he'd made no effort to get to know Anna, but then, she hadn't seemed that interested in him, either.

A pang of guilt shot through him. Anna might not be his child, but she needed a father. Her own father had died when she was just a baby, and her grandfather—the only father she'd ever known—had left her with strangers to begin a new way of life. Even so, Cleon wasn't sure Anna would ever accept him as her father, and he didn't know if he would ever feel comfortable in that role.

He pulled his gaze away from the English girl and spotted a phone booth down the street. Since his folks had a phone shed outside their home because of Mom's meal-serving business to tourists, he decided to give them a call and let them know he'd be on his way home soon.

Cleon entered the phone booth and dialed his mother's number. Ivan answered. "Cleon, I'm glad you phoned, because I have some bad news."

"Has something happened to Grace? Have there been more attacks at the Hostettlers'?"

"I don't know about that, but there's been one here."

"What's happened?"

Ivan cleared his throat a couple of times. "It's your bee hives—they're gone."

"Gone? What do you mean?"

"They've been destroyed."

Cleon's knees went weak, and he had to brace himself against the phone booth to keep from toppling over. "All of them?"

"Jah. Every last one has been burned. There's nothing left but a pile of ashes."

"Wh-when did this happen?"

"I'm not sure. I hadn't checked on things for a few days, and when I got done helping in the fields earlier today, I decided I'd better see how your hives were doing. That's when I discovered they'd been ruined. Some of the bees were flying around with nowhere to go, but I'm sure a lot of 'em were burned with the hives."

Cleon groaned. With no hives and no bees, he had no more honey to sell. And if he had no honey, he had no job other than farming for his father, which he'd rather not continue to do.

"I can't figure who would do this to you or why."

"Could have been some disruptive kids out for a good time, or maybe it was done by someone who's got something against me."

"Come on, brother. Who would have anything against you?"

Cleon had no answer. "I'll be there as soon as I can."

"Are you going to start up some new hives when you get home?"

"I—I don't know."

"I'm sure Grace will be glad to see you."

Cleon cringed. Despite his anger at Grace, he really did miss her—missed what they used to have together. He knew he'd hurt her by leaving, but she'd hurt him, too, and he wasn't certain he could ever trust her again.

When lunch was over and Grace's folks had left for home, she decided to put Anna down for a nap.

"Are you sure you don't want my help with those?" she asked Martha, who stood near the sink drying the last few dishes.

"No, you go ahead upstairs." Martha waved a soapy hand. "Maybe you should lie down awhile yourself. You're looking even more peaked than before we had lunch."

"I am feeling a bit tired, so maybe I will take a short rest." Grace headed for the door. "See you later, Martha."

A short time later, Grace had Anna situated in her room, so she stretched out on her own bed across the hall. It seemed odd to be living in this house—the home Cleon had started building when they'd first become engaged, the place where they were supposed to be living together.

Tears trickled down her cheeks and splashed onto the dahlia-patterned quilt. *Dear God, I'm so sorry for what I've done to my family and Cleon. Won't You please bring my husband home so I can make it up to him?*

Chapter 31

Y ou critters are sure messy, you know that?" Martha clicked her
tongue, as she hosed out the unpleasant debris that had ac-
cumulated on the concrete floor of the dogs' outside run.

Heidi and her pups ran around one side of the kennel, and Fritz
occupied the other side with a partition between them. Bo and Flo
shared another section of the kennel, which would also be divided
once Flo got pregnant. Dad had built the kennel against the back of
the barn and connected it to an outside run through a small door
Martha could open whenever the dogs needed fresh air or exercise.

Martha thought about Freckles, the pup Donna and Ray had
bought from her, and how well the dog seemed to be doing. When
she'd gone over to the Larsons' the other day, she'd been pleased to
see how much the pup had grown and how well-adjusted it seemed.

Martha had brought Donna and Ray up to date on the attacks
at her home. They seemed shocked and promised to keep an eye out
for anything strange going on, and Ray had said he would notify the
sheriff about the attacks that had already occurred.

Martha felt some measure of relief knowing the sheriff would
finally be told, but it wouldn't set well with her father if he thought
she'd had anything to do with it. Hopefully, the Larsons wouldn't
mention her visit.

As Grace left the doctor's office, her heart swirled with emotions.

What she'd suspected had been confirmed—she was definitely pregnant. She was pleased to learn that she was carrying Cleon's baby, but she was worried about how well she could cope with having another child when everything in her life was so mixed up.

The odor of horseflesh assaulted her senses, and she glanced to the left. Two buggies waited at the stoplight, the horses both pawing at the pavement as though they couldn't wait to go. A car down the street tooted its horn, and an English boy heading up the sidewalk with his mother sneezed. A world where everything seemed normal was going on all around her, while Grace's world had been turned upside down.

When she approached her buggy, parked in the lot next to the doctor's office, she spotted Gary across the street, entering the restaurant where she used to work. How much longer would he be hanging around? Every time she saw him, she was reminded of her past and of her concerns that he might be responsible for the attacks. She wondered if she should confront him again—ask him to stop harassing them, plead with him if necessary.

Grace shook her head. What good would that do? When she'd confronted him before, he'd denied knowing anything about the attacks. Maybe he found pleasure in knowing she and her family were frightened. If she ignored him, he might leave them alone.

Roman had just begun sweeping up a pile of sawdust when John Peterson entered his shop.

"What can I do for you, John?" he asked, setting the broom aside.

John moved closer to Roman and pulled his fingers through the back of his hair. "You've...uh...probably heard that Luke Freisen has come to work for me."

"Jah, I heard."

"Well, I came by to make sure there were no hard feelings over me hiring him."

Roman leaned against his workbench and folded his arms. " 'Course not. It's not like you lured Luke away or anything. He only went to you because I fired him."

John blinked. "Really? I thought—" He shook his head. "Luke said you'd had a difference of opinion and that he figured he'd do better working for someone who used modern equipment."

"What'd you say to that?"

"What could I say? I wouldn't be happy doing the kind of work I do without the electricity and updated equipment I have in my shop." He glanced around the room. "Not that you do poor work with what you use here."

"I hope things go okay between you and Luke," Roman said with a shrug. He didn't want to make an issue of it, but if he were a betting man, he'd bet Luke Friesen wouldn't last more than a few weeks working for John.

"Luke seems like a pretty smart fellow, and from what I've seen, he's a good-enough worker."

Roman grunted. "He likes to do things his own way, and I'll give you a little warning: He tends to be late to work pretty often. Leastways, he was when he was workin' for me."

"I appreciate the tip, and you can be sure that I'll be keeping an eye on him."

Roman glanced at the fancy pair of sunglasses he'd set on the shelf across the room—the ones Judith had found on the ground near the clothesline. He was tempted to mention that he thought Luke might have something to do with the attacks that had been done at their place but decided against it since he had no proof. He supposed he could mention the sunglasses and ask John to take them and see if they belonged to Luke. On the other hand, if they were Luke's, it might be best to let him come and claim them himself.

John moved away from the desk. "I'd better get back to my shop. I left Luke working on a set of cabinets for Dave Rawlings, and I need to be sure he knows how many coats of stain it will take."

"Jah. Thanks for dropping by." When John closed the door, Roman reached for his broom and gave it a couple of hard sweeps across the floor. Now Dave, one of his steady customers, had taken his business elsewhere. Could Luke be saying bad things about Roman's work in order to lure more customers to John?

Roman grabbed a dustpan and pushed the pile of shavings into it as he thought about the conversation he'd finally had with their bishop the other night. "I've got to quit stewing over things and put my trust in God like Bishop King said I should do."

"I'm glad you're home, 'cause I didn't know what to do about all this."

Cleon grimaced as he and Ivan stood in the middle of the clearing where his beehives had once been. "Not a one left, is there?"

"Nope, and I'm sure sorry about this." Ivan shook his head. "I didn't want to make things worse by tellin' you all the details when I spoke with you on the phone the other day, but the shed where you kept your beekeeping equipment was burned, too."

Cleon huffed. Things seemed to be going from bad to worse for him these days. "It wasn't your fault. This could have happened if I'd been here. It isn't possible to keep an eye on the hives all the time."

Ivan touched Cleon's shoulder. "Have you seen Grace and told her about this?"

Cleon shook his head. "I had my driver bring me here as soon as I got off the bus in Dover."

"I'll bet Grace will be happy to know you're home. She looked awful *mied* and *bedauerlich* when I saw her in church a few weeks ago."

Cleon shrugged. Grace wasn't the only one who felt tired and sad. Finding out about her secret had made him feel like he'd been butted in the stomach by a charging bull. Now that his beehives were gone, he didn't even have a job he liked to do.

"You going home soon, then?"

Cleon winced. Was his brother trying to make him feel guilty for being gone so long? Didn't he realize the way things were with Grace?

"Guess I'll have to since I have no other place to go."

Ivan opened his mouth as if to say something more, but Cleon cut him off. "Think I'll speak to Grace's *daed* and see if he'd be willing to hire me in his shop. I'm not the best carpenter in the world, but

I believe I can give him a fair day's work."

"Sounds like a good idea." Ivan made a sweeping gesture of the open field. "You planning to get some more bees soon?"

"I don't know. Maybe." Cleon sighed. "Guess that all depends on how things go when I talk to Roman. I'll need some money in order to buy more bees and boxes, not to mention all the equipment that was burned in the fire."

"I'm sure Pop would loan you—"

Cleon held up his hand to halt his brother's words. "I'd rather do this without Pop's help." He nodded toward their folks' house. "Guess I'll get the horse and buggy I left here and head over to the Hostettlers' place. May as well get this over with."

Ivan's eyebrows lifted high on his forehead, but he said nothing. Truth be told, he probably knew Cleon was in no hurry to see Grace.

Chapter 32

Cleon's boots echoed against the wooden boards as he stepped onto the Hostettlers' porch. He dreaded this encounter with Grace even more than seeing his burned-out beehives. It was hard enough to return home without a job; it would be harder yet to live with a wife he didn't trust.

When he entered the kitchen, Grace's daughter was sitting at the kitchen table with a tablet and a pencil. She looked up and glared at him as though she was irritated with the interruption.

"Hello, Anna," he said. "Is your mother to home?"

The child squinted her blue eyes.

Cleon moved over to the table and pulled out the chair beside Anna. "I need to talk to your mamm—I mean, your mother."

"I know what mamm means, and she's sleepin' in her room right now."

His forehead wrinkled. Why would Grace be asleep in the middle of the day? "Is she sick?"

Anna shrugged.

"Guess I'd better go see." Cleon's chair squeaked against the floor when he pushed away from the table. As he made his way up the stairs, he hoped for the right words to say to Grace.

When he reached her bedroom, he noticed that the door was open. He stepped inside and was surprised to see that Grace wasn't there. For that matter, the house seemed unusually quiet, and he'd seen no one except Anna. Surely the child wouldn't have been left alone in the house.

218

He hurried down the stairs and was headed for the kitchen when the back door opened and Martha entered the house.

"Cleon! When did you get back? Does Grace know you're here?"

He shook his head. "I haven't seen her yet. I just left my folks' place after seeing what's left of my beehives."

Her forehead wrinkled. "What do you mean?"

"They've all been burned."

"Ach! When did that happen?"

"A few days ago, according to Ivan. All my hives, boxes, and equipment are gone, and that means I'm out of a job."

"I'm so sorry. I'm sure Grace will be, too, but I know she'll be glad to see you."

He nodded toward the kitchen door. "Anna said her mamm had gone to take a nap, but Grace wasn't upstairs in her room."

"She's over at your new house. She and Anna moved in there last week."

Cleon tipped his head. "But it's not finished—at least not enough so Grace could move in."

"Jah, it is. When your brothers weren't helping with things on your farm, they came over here and helped my daed get it done." Martha smiled. "They weren't sure how long you'd be gone, and they thought it would be a nice surprise when you got back."

"It's a surprise—that's for sure."

"Your being here will be a surprise for my sister, too. Why don't you go over to the house and say hello?"

He nodded and moved toward the door. "Guess I'd best do that."

As Grace lay on her bed, tossing, turning, and fighting waves of nausea that had kept her stomach churning for hours, her mind rehashed the past. She was still angry with herself for keeping her secret from her family, but she became more upset whenever she thought about her rumschpringe and how she'd wasted so many days dating Gary Walker. She wished she'd never left home to try out the English way of life. But then, if she hadn't married Wade, she wouldn't have Anna now.

She sniffed and swiped at the wetness under her nose. It did no good to dwell on the past. She needed to concentrate on a future with Anna and on the new life she carried in her womb. Last night, she'd told her folks about the baby, and they'd seemed pleased. If only she could be sure Cleon would feel the same way.

The door creaked open, and thinking it must be Anna, she wiped her eyes and sat up. Shock waves spiraled through her when she saw her husband standing inside the door. She scrambled off the bed and rushed toward him but was disappointed when he took a step back.

Grace held her arms rigidly at her sides. "Did you get a lot of honey orders on your trip?"

He nodded. "Trouble is I can't fill any of 'em now."

"Why not?"

"Hives, bees, and all my equipment are gone—burned out—every last one."

"What? How?" Grace could hardly believe her ears, and she wondered why she hadn't heard anything about this until now.

"Ivan said it looked like someone had deliberately set the fires." Cleon huffed. "I sure didn't need this right now."

"What are you going to do?"

"Don't know. Guess I need to find another job, because it will take some time before I can get any new hives going well enough so I'll have some honey to sell." Cleon's eyes looked weary and spent. "Just when I was beginning to think I might be able to make a decent living as a beekeeper."

Grace took a tentative step toward him. She wanted to offer support and let him know how much she cared but was afraid of his rejection. "I'm sorry, Cleon. Sorry for everything."

His broad shoulders shrugged. "Jah, well, it's all part of life, I guess. You think you've got things figured out and you're on the path to happiness. Then everything gets knocked out of kilter."

Grace was sure Cleon was referring to their messed-up marriage. She moistened her lips with the tip of her tongue and decided a change of subject might help. "Were you surprised to see that the house had been finished in your absence?"

He nodded. "Didn't expect anyone to do the work for me."

"My daed and your bruders wanted to surprise you, and they thought it would be good if Anna and I got moved into our new home."

"It looks nice. They did a fine job." He glanced around the room. " 'Course anything that pertains to building would be done well if your daed had his hand in it."

"You did well with your part of the building, too."

"It was all right, I guess."

A sudden wave of weakness washed over Grace, and she sank to the edge of her bed. "Cleon, I think we should talk about us."

"There's nothing to talk about," he said with a wave of his hand. "You kept the truth hidden from me, and that's that."

"It's not as simple as you make it sound. There's more I'd like to explain."

"It's a little late for explaining, don't you think?"

Grace sat trying to decide how best to respond. Should she list the reasons she had kept Wade and Anna a secret, beg Cleon to forgive her, or suggest that they try to forget the past and move on from here?

Before she had the chance to respond, Cleon spoke. "While I was on the road, I did a lot of thinking."

A ray of hope welled in Grace's soul. Cleon had come home, so that was a good sign. She placed one hand against her stomach, wondering if now was the time to tell him about the child she carried—his child, a product of their love. "Cleon, I—"

"Please, hear me out."

She lowered her gaze to the floor.

"After thinking things through, I realized that I have an obligation to you—and to Anna."

"Does that mean—"

"It means I'm back, and I'll provide for your needs. But I'll be sleeping in some other room."

"So our marriage will be in name only? Is that what you're saying?" Grace almost choked on the words.

He nodded.

"Is there anything I can say or do to make you change your mind?"

"Not unless you can undo the past."

"You know that's not possible." Grace clenched her fists as frustration raged within her like a whirling storm. Cleon had come home, but he hadn't forgiven her. They would be living in the same house but not sharing the same bedroom. He was the father of the baby she carried, yet she didn't feel free to tell him. Not now. This wasn't the right time.

"I'm going out to your daed's shop," Cleon said. "I need to speak with him about the possibility of giving me a job."

Grace nodded. When Cleon left the room, she moved over to the window and pulled the curtain aside. *What am I to do, Lord? Cleon and I used to be so close, and now it's as though we're strangers. I know I can't keep the news of my pregnancy from him indefinitely. Sooner or later, he'll have to know.*

She squeezed her eyes shut as tears threatened to escape. When Cleon had walked into the room moments ago, her hopes had soared. Now she was certain that nothing would ever be right in her world again.

Chapter 33

Ruth had just set an angel food cake in the bakery case when Martin Gingerich entered the shop.

"I heard you started working for Abe Wengerd last week," she said as he stepped up to the counter.

"Sure did, and I think I'm going to enjoy learning how to make and repair harnesses. Always did like the smell of leather." A wide smile spread across his face as he motioned to the counter full of pastries. " 'Course, what you're smelling here every day would be a lot better."

"Jah, it's enough to make me feel hungry the whole time I'm working."

"I imagine it would. Fact is, I'm feeling hungry right now."

"Would you like to sample something?"

He shook his head. "Better not. My mamm's fixing stuffed cabbage rolls for supper tonight, and she'd be sorely disappointed if I didn't eat at least five."

Ruth chuckled. She couldn't imagine anyone eating that many cabbage rolls. If Martin's mother made them as big as Ruth's mother did, she'd be lucky to eat two.

"So what can I help you with?"

"Actually, I didn't come to the bakeshop to buy anything."

"You didn't?"

"No, I. . ." Martin's voice trailed off, and he stared at the floor as his face turned a deep shade of pink. Finally, he looked up, although he kept his focus on the pastries inside the case. "I. . .uh. . .heard that you. . ." He paused and swiped at the sweat rolling down his forehead.

"What did you hear?"

"I heard that you and Luke broke up."

"That's true."

"Mind if I ask why?"

Truthfully, she did mind. The last thing she wanted to talk about was Luke and her mistrust of him.

"If you'd rather not say, I understand. It's just that. . .well, I've heard some things, and—"

"What kind of things?"

"Heard he's been hanging around with a bunch of rowdy English fellows, and my daed mentioned that he thinks Luke might have been in on that cow tipping over at Bishop King's place some time ago." Martin lifted his gaze to meet hers. "I thought maybe you knew about it, too, and that's why you broke up with him."

Ruth swallowed hard. Should she share her suspicions with Martin? She'd known him since they were little, but they'd never been close friends. Besides, she wasn't sure what his reaction would be if she told him what she thought Luke might be up to. She couldn't be sure Martin would keep what she said to himself.

"If you don't want to talk about it, I won't press." Martin's hazel-colored eyes held a note of sympathy.

She nodded. "Danki. I'd rather not."

Martin shrugged. "Anyway, finding out why you and Luke broke up isn't the reason I dropped by." He shifted his weight and pulled his fingers through the back of his thick, Dutch-bobbed hair.

"What is the reason?"

"There's going to be a young people's get-together at our place this Saturday evening. We'll be playing some games, and of course, there'll be plenty of refreshments furnished by my mamm."

"Sounds like fun."

"I came by to see if you might be free to come. Your sister Martha's invited, too, of course."

Ruth's first thought was to decline the invitation because she hadn't felt like doing anything fun since she and Luke broke up, not to mention the stress she'd been under because of all the trouble at home. But as she thought about it more, she decided that she and Martha might need an evening of fun with others their age. "I'll speak to Martha this evening and see if she's wants to go."

"Good. I hope to see you on Saturday then." Martin hesitated but finally turned and headed out the door.

Ruth smiled as the door clicked shut behind him. For the first time in many days, she felt a sense of anticipation.

After Cleon went to his house to speak with Grace, Martha decided to take Anna out to the barn. Mom had gone to visit Alma Wengerd, who'd sprained her ankle a few days ago, and Martha figured Mom might stay awhile, which meant she'd probably have to keep an eye on Anna for most of the day.

"Can I play with the puppies?" Anna asked as they neared the end of the barn where the kennel had been built.

"Jah, sure."

Anna grinned up at her. "I like Rose the best."

"Rose?"

"That one right there." Anna pointed to the runt of the litter—the pup no one wanted.

Martha smiled and patted the top of Anna's head. "How would you like to have Rose as your own?"

"You mean it?" Anna's blue eyes lit up like a firefly.

"If your mamm says it's okay."

"You think Mama will let me keep her at the new house?"

Martha was pleased that Anna had referred to Grace as *Mama*. She finally must have accepted Grace as her mother. "You can ask your mamm after supper tonight. How's that sound?"

Anna's smile quickly faded. "Is that man gonna eat supper with us?"

"What man?"

"The one who came to our house today."

Martha nodded. "I think Cleon will be joining us. He was on

a business trip for a while, but his home is here with you and your mamm."

Anna thrust out her chin. "I don't like him. I wish he'd go away again."

Martha was about to reply when she heard the barn door open and shut. She turned and saw Grace heading their way with shoulders slumped and head down. Martha figured things hadn't gone so well between her sister and Cleon.

"I'll get Rose out of the kennel, and you can sit over there and play with her," Martha said, leading Anna to a nearby bale of straw.

"Okay."

Once the child was seated, Martha stopped by Grace. "I'm going to get one of the pups for Anna to play with, and then the two of us can talk."

Grace nodded.

"As soon as Anna and the puppy are settled, I'll meet you in the tack room."

Grace glanced over at her daughter, who sat on the bale of straw with her chin resting in the palms of her hands. "That's fine."

Grace headed for the tack room, and Martha hurried to the kennels at the back of the barn. A few minutes later, Anna had a sleeping pup nestled in her lap.

"Your mamm and I need to talk, but we'll be back soon." She gave Anna's shoulder a gentle squeeze. "Don't leave the barn, you hear?"

"I won't."

Martha hurried to the tack room and found Grace sitting on a wooden stool, her head down. "Why do you look so sad?"

Grace lifted her head. "Cleon's back."

"I know. He came by looking for you, and when I told him your place had been finished and that you were over there, he headed that way." Martha slipped her arm around Grace's shoulders. "Did he speak with you?"

"Jah. He had some bad news."

"You mean about his beehives being burned?"

Grace nodded. "He's going to Dad's shop to see if he might be able to work there."

"I thought he helped with the farm at his folks' place."

"He's never enjoyed farming that much. I think he'd be happier working in Dad's woodworking shop."

"What did Cleon say when you told him about the baby?"

"I—I didn't tell him."

"You didn't tell him you're pregnant?"

"No."

"Why not?"

"He made it clear that he's only staying with me out of obligation." Grace drew in a quivering breath. "From now on, Cleon and I will be sleeping in separate bedrooms. He'll be my husband in name only."

Martha had known Cleon was upset about Grace's secret, but she didn't think he would still be nursing a grudge. She massaged Grace's shoulders and neck, feeling the tension in her sister's knotted muscles beneath her fingers. "What are you going to do about this?"

"There's not much I can do."

"You could start by telling Cleon that you're carrying his boppli. That might make him see things in a different light."

"Or it might make him feel more resentful—like I trapped him on purpose."

Martha's forehead wrinkled. "That's *lecherich*. It's not like you planned to get pregnant."

"It might seem ridiculous to you," Grace said with a catch in her voice, "but Cleon is full of hurt and bitterness right now, and he might think I'm capable of doing most anything."

Martha moved to face Grace. "You can't hide this from Cleon forever. Before long, you'll be showing."

"I know."

"Besides, you've already told our folks. If you wait to tell Cleon and he finds out on his own, he might accuse you of keeping another secret from him. You don't want that, do you?"

Grace shook her head as more tears pooled in her eyes. "I'll tell him tonight after Anna's in bed."

Chapter 34

R oman was about to close up for the day when a customer entered his shop. At least he thought it was a customer until he looked up from his desk and saw Cleon standing inside the door.

"Cleon! It's good to see you. How long have you been back?"

"Got home this morning."

Roman's forehead wrinkled. "This morning? You've been here that long?"

Cleon nodded. "Went over to see the damage that had been done to my beehives; then I stopped in to see my folks."

"What damage was done to your hives?"

"Somebody set fire to 'em. Every last one is gone."

"I'm real sorry to hear that. Do you have any idea who might have done it?"

Cleon shook his head. "Ivan figures it was probably some rowdy fellows out for a good time. Could even be the same ones who dumped over those outhouses near Kidron and were involved in the cow tipping." He moved closer to Roman's desk. "Since I have no bees, hives, or equipment, I'm out of a job."

"But spring is here, and you'll be farming with your daed again, right?"

Cleon's fingers curled through the ends of his beard. "I've never enjoyed farming, and I'd rather do something else." He took a step forward. "I know I'm not an expert carpenter, but I can handle a hammer and a saw fairly well. So I was wondering if you might be able to use an extra pair of hands here in your woodworking shop."

"As a matter of fact, I could use some help. I had to fire Luke for being late to work so many times, and now he's working for John Peterson." Roman nodded at Cleon. "Judging from the work you did on your new house, I'd say I'd be getting more than an apprentice if I hired you."

Cleon shook his head. "I can't take credit for all the work done on my house. You and my brothers helped in the beginning, and from what Grace told me, you finished it up in my absence. I appreciate all your hard work."

"I figured you and Grace would want to get settled into your own place before the boppli is born."

Cleon's eyebrows drew together. "Boppli? What boppli are you talking about?"

"Surely Grace must have told you."

"Told me what?"

"About her being in a family way."

Cleon's face turned red as a cherry, and a vein on the side of his neck bulged. "I just came from talking to Grace, and she never said a word about any baby."

Roman reached up to swipe the trickle of sweat rolling down his forehead. Apparently Grace hadn't learned her lesson about keeping secrets. "I'm sorry you had to hear it from me. Should have been my daughter doing the telling."

"You're right about that." Cleon grunted. "Of course, she seems to be real good at keeping secrets, so I shouldn't be surprised that she's kept this one from me, as well."

"Maybe she was waiting for the right time."

"The right time? And when would that be?" Cleon crossed his arms.

Roman shrugged. He wanted to defend his daughter, but the truth was, he hadn't quite forgiven Grace for not telling them about her English husband and the little girl she'd allowed her in-laws to take. He couldn't blame Cleon for being angry that Grace hadn't told him about the baby she carried. That should have been the first thing out of her mouth when she'd seen him today.

Cleon's lips parted as if he might have more to say, but the shop door opened. Luke stepped into the room.

"I hope you're not here about getting your job back," Roman said, irritation edging his voice. He motioned to Cleon. "You've been replaced."

Luke's face flushed as he shook his head. "Came to see if I left my sunglasses here. I think I had 'em with me that day you fired me, and—"

"Well, it's about time. What took you so long?"

"Huh?"

"Never mind." Roman pointed to the shelf across the room where the fancy pair of sunglasses lay. "They're right over there. My wife found 'em on the ground, not far from where her clothesline had been cut." He squinted at Luke. "You wouldn't know anything about that, would ya, boy?"

The color in Luke's cheeks deepened. "Are you accusing me of cutting your wife's clothesline?"

Roman shrugged. "Not accusing, just asking, is all."

Luke's eyes narrowed into tiny slits. "Now why would I do something like that?"

"I don't know. Why would somebody burn Cleon's beehives, vandalize our house, or steal tools from my shop?"

Cleon's face blanched. "Surely you don't think one of our own had anything to do with those things?"

"I don't know what I believe anymore, and those aren't the only things that have been done to us, either."

"What do you mean? What else has been done?"

Roman looked at his son-in-law, then over at Luke. "Maybe you should ask him."

Luke's eyes flashed angrily. "Ask me what—whether I know what attacks have been done, or if I had anything to do with them?"

"Both."

"I only knew about the break-ins here at the shop and the house. Oh, and also the brick that was thrown through your kitchen window.

I don't know who's responsible for any of those acts, but—"

Jack Osborn, the middle-aged sheriff in their county, entered the shop.

Roman pushed his chair away from the desk and stood. "Sorry, but that rocking chair you asked me to make for your wife isn't ready yet, Jack."

"I'm not here about the chair." Jack glanced around the room as if he was looking for something. "Got a phone call from one of your English neighbors the other day. They said you folks had been having a few problems. I should have come by sooner, but two of my deputies have been out sick, so I've only had time to respond to urgent calls."

Before Roman could formulate a response, Luke dashed across the room and grabbed his sunglasses off the shelf. "I've got an errand to run, so I'd better go." He rushed out the door like a fox being chased by a pack of hounds.

Jack opened his jacket and pulled a notebook and pen from his shirt pocket. "Now why don't you tell me what's been going on here, Roman?"

"Jah, okay." Roman returned to his seat, and Cleon grabbed one of the wooden stools near the workbench.

For several minutes, Roman related the details of the attacks, and Sheriff Osborn took notes. Roman ended his speech by saying, "My son-in-law here recently had his beehives burned, so I'm thinking that whoever's been bothering us might have ruined the hives, as well."

Jack leaned over and placed both hands on Roman's desk. "You think someone's singled out your family?"

Roman gave his left earlobe a couple of pulls. "Thought at first it might be a bunch of rowdy English fellows, but now I'm not so sure."

Jack's bushy eyebrows rose as he leveled Roman with a questioning look. "I know you Amish don't prosecute, but you could have at least let me know what was going on here so I could have investigated and hopefully brought the criminal to justice."

"God is the only judge we need. He knows who did those things, and if it's His will for them to be brought to justice, then He'll do it in His time, His way."

Jack looked over at Cleon as though he hoped he might say something, but Cleon said nothing. Finally, Jack straightened and slipped the notebook and pen back into his pocket. "Have it your way, but I want you to know that I'll be keeping an eye on things for a while."

"Suit yourself."

"If there are any more attacks made on you or your family, I'd appreciate hearing about it. Some who've committed crimes like this against the Amish have done it simply because you're different, and that doesn't set well with me."

"Nor me, but it will be up to our church leaders and the nature of the crime whether it's reported or not."

Jack shrugged and headed for the door. "Let me know when that rocking chair's done," he called over his shoulder.

"Jah, I surely will."

The door clicked shut, and Roman let his head fall forward into his hands as he released a groan. "I wonder which one of our English neighbors phoned the sheriff, and more importantly, who told 'em about the attacks?"

Cleon shook his head. "Could someone in your family have mentioned it?"

"Maybe so, but I need you to do me a favor."

"What's that?"

"Don't say anything about the sheriff showing up here today, or that he plans to keep an eye on things."

"Why not?"

"I don't want the family to get the idea that they're being watched, and I don't want 'em thinking I called the sheriff."

"I won't say a word unless you speak about it first."

"I appreciate that." Roman slid his chair away from the desk. "Now let's go on up to the house and see if supper's ready. Grace and Anna have been taking most of their meals with us since you left, so I'm sure everyone will eat together at our place tonight."

Cleon nodded.

"If you'd like to meet me here at the shop tomorrow morning, I'll give you some woodworking tools and show you what I need to have done."

"I'll be here, bright and early."

Tension had filled the air between Grace and Cleon all during supper, and Grace had even noticed something going on between Dad and Cleon. It was as if they knew something and had decided not to share it with the rest of the family. She'd been tempted to ask about it but figured it might be best to question Cleon later on—if she got the chance.

By the time Grace took Anna home to their house and was getting her ready for bed, she felt ready to go to bed herself. But she knew she couldn't. Not until she'd told Cleon she was carrying his baby.

She slipped Anna's nightgown over the child's head and pulled back the bed covers. "Hop into bed now."

"Aunt Martha says I can have a puppy of my own," Anna said as she nestled against her pillow.

"Are you sure about that?" Grace knew her sister was trying to build up her business, and giving dogs away wouldn't bring in any money.

Anna nodded, her blue eyes looking ever so serious. "She says I can have Rose if it's all right with you, Mama."

Grace stroked her daughter's arm, relishing the warmth and softness of the child's skin. It felt good to hear Anna call her Mama. They'd been drawing closer every day, and Grace wouldn't do anything to spoil things between them. She nodded and smiled. "You may have the puppy on one condition."

"What's a 'condition'?"

"It means you must agree to help take care of the dog."

Anna's eyes brightened. "I will. I've been helpin' Aunt Martha with the puppies ever since I came to live here."

Grace bent over and kissed Anna's forehead. "All right, then. You can call Rose your own."

Anna snuggled beneath the covers with a satisfied smile, and Grace slipped quietly out of the room. The last she'd seen Cleon, he had been downstairs in the living room reading the latest issue of *The Budget.*

Knowing he needed to speak with Grace before she went to bed, Cleon left the living room and started up the steps. He'd just reached the top when he bumped into Grace.

She covered her mouth with the palm of her hand. "Oh! You startled me. I—I was heading downstairs so we could talk."

He nodded. "You're right. We do need to talk. Let's go to the living room so our voices won't be heard."

Once they reached the living room, Cleon took a seat on the sofa, and Grace sat in the rocking chair across from him. No furniture had been in the house when he'd left Holmes County, so Grace's father must have provided it in his absence.

"I know you're pregnant."

"I'm pregnant."

They spoke at the same time, and Cleon repeated himself to be sure she had heard him.

Grace's mouth dropped open. "You know?"

He nodded.

"Who told you?"

"Does it matter? The point is you didn't tell me, and I'm wondering why."

"I—I was afraid you might think I had gotten pregnant on purpose so I could trap you into staying with me."

Cleon slowly shook his head. "That's lecherich. How could you have gotten pregnant on purpose? It's not like we were using any birth control methods."

She dropped her gaze to the floor. "I know, but I've heard of some women who try to time things around their monthly cycle, and—"

He held up his hand to silence her. "I know you didn't get pregnant on purpose, and under normal circumstances, I'd be looking forward to becoming a daed."

"But not now? Is that what you're saying?" Grace's chin trembled, and her eyes filled with tears. He made no move to comfort her.

"Things are so verhuddelt right now I'm not sure how I feel about much of anything."

"I'm sorry for my part in your confusion."

"You want me to forgive you for keeping Anna a secret, yet you keep another secret from me. That makes no sense."

"I—I was scared you would leave and scared you would stay for the wrong reasons."

He grimaced. "I told you earlier today that I would take care of you and Anna."

"I know, but—"

"Until you can learn to be honest with me, I don't see how we'll ever be able to have a real marriage, Grace."

"Are you saying that you don't love me enough to try to make our marriage work? It takes two, you know."

Cleon flinched. Was that what he was saying? "I'll be starting work for your daed tomorrow morning, so I'd better get to bed." He stood and rushed out of the room, knowing if he didn't get away from Grace, he might say something he would be sorry for come morning.

Chapter 35

When Grace awoke the following morning, she felt as if she hadn't even gone to bed. Besides the morning sickness she'd been dealing with for weeks, her head hurt, and her hands shook so badly that, as she cracked eggs, several pieces of shell fell into the bowl. If only Cleon would forgive her. If he could just show some excitement over the baby she carried in her womb.

Soon after Grace and Cleon had become betrothed, they'd begun talking about the family they would have some day. Cleon had said he wanted a large family, and Grace had looked forward to the day when she could hold another baby in her arms and know it wouldn't be taken from her. Now she would have that baby, as well as her five-year-old daughter, but she feared she would never have her husband again. Not in the real sense of the word, anyway.

A knock at the back door halted Grace's thoughts. Since Cleon hadn't come downstairs for breakfast yet, she dried her hands on a towel and went to see who was at the door. Martha stood on the porch.

"Why didn't you come in rather than knocking?"

"I—I wanted to be sure I could talk to you alone."

Noting how pale her sister's face looked, Grace felt immediate concern. "Are you feeling grank this morning?"

Martha shook her head. "Not physically, but I'm sure sick at heart."

Grace's heart pounded against her chest. "Has there been another attack?"

"I'm not sure." Martha stepped closer, and her voice lowered to a whisper. "Where's Anna? I don't want her to hear what I have to say—at least not yet."

"She's upstairs in bed. I figured I would wait until breakfast was ready to wake her." Grace motioned to a couple of wicker chairs sitting on the other end of the porch. "Let's sit over there."

Once they were seated, Martha leaned over and massaged her forehead. "Rose is dead."

"Rose?"

"The puppy I promised Anna she could have if you said it was okay."

"She asked me about it last night, but I'd forgotten that she'd called it 'Rose.' " Grace touched her sister's arm. "What happened? How did the pup die?"

"I'm not sure. I found both kennel doors open when I went out to feed the dogs this morning, and then I discovered them running around the yard." Martha paused. "Except for Rose; she was dead."

Grace covered her mouth.

"I don't know how I'm going to tell Anna. She really liked that puppy and was looking forward to calling it her own."

"I'm her mamm; it's my place to tell her."

"I feel awful enough about losing one of my dogs, but I hope it won't affect how things are with you and Anna."

"I hope not, either. Do you have any idea why the hundli died or how the dogs got out of their kennel?"

"They got out because the doors were open, and I guess the pup could have climbed onto one of the bales of hay that sat near the barn and then fallen off."

"You don't suppose someone did this on purpose, do you? I mean— let the dogs out of their cage and. . .and killed Anna's puppy?"

"I hope that's not the case."

"How do you think the cage doors got open?"

"I don't know. Maybe I forgot to latch them when I fed them last night."

"But you're always so careful when it comes to things like that."

"That's usually true, but I've had a lot on my mind lately, so I suppose I could have forgotten." Martha released a sigh. "Are you sure you don't want me to tell Anna?"

"No, I'll do it after breakfast."

"Guess I'd better go bury the puppy." Martha released a sigh. "I don't want Anna to see it that way."

"No, that wouldn't be good." As Grace rose from her chair, a wave of nausea hit her, and she clutched her stomach.

"Are you okay?"

"I'll be fine. It's just a touch of morning sickness."

"What did Cleon say when you told him about the boppli?"

Grace rubbed her hands briskly over her arms and shivered even though the early spring weather had turned quite warm. "He already knew."

"He suspected it? Is that what you're saying?"

"I guess Cleon learned about it when he went to Dad's shop to see if he would hire him."

"Dad told Cleon you're in a family way?"

Grace nodded. "I'm sure he thought Cleon knew about the baby. He probably figured I'd already told him. Now Cleon thinks I deliberately kept another secret from him, and—" Grace couldn't finish her sentence.

"Didn't you explain why you hadn't said anything yet, and that you had planned to tell him last night?"

"I tried, but Cleon doesn't trust me anymore, and he—"

"He what, Grace?"

Grace took a few seconds to compose herself as she sniffed and wiped the tears from her cheeks. "Cleon didn't show any enthusiasm about the baby. I—I don't think he wants to be a daed. At least not to any of my children."

Martha wore a look of disbelief and slowly shook her head. "I didn't think things could get much worse around here."

"Me, neither. It makes me wonder if God cares how much we're all hurting."

Unable to control her emotions, Grace leaned her head on Martha's shoulder and sobbed.

When Cleon entered the kitchen, he was surprised to discover that it was empty. When he'd first wakened, he thought he'd smelled coffee brewing, so he figured Grace had to be awake. He had tossed and turned most of the night and needed a cup of coffee to clear the cobwebs from his foggy brain.

He spotted the coffeepot sitting near the back of the stove and was about to take a mug from the cupboard, when he noticed a carton of eggs on the counter, a sure sign that Grace must be nearby. Maybe she was using the necessary room or had gone outside for something.

Cleon poured some coffee and was about to take a drink when he heard footsteps coming down the stairs. A few seconds later, Anna entered the kitchen dressed in a long, cotton nightgown.

"Where's Mama?" she asked, rubbing her eyes and looking around the room.

"I'm not sure. She must have been in the kitchen at one time, because breakfast has been started." Cleon motioned to the coffeepot and then to the eggs. "She wasn't here when I came downstairs, and I don't know where she is now."

Anna padded over to the table and climbed onto a chair. "I'm hungry. I wanna eat now so I can play with Rose."

"Who's Rose?"

"My new puppy. Aunt Martha said I could have her if Mama said it was okay." Anna's head bobbed up and down. "Last night Mama said it was all right with her."

Cleon leaned against the counter and studied the child. Her long brown hair hung down her back in a mass of heavy curls, reminding him of how Grace's pale blond hair had looked on their wedding night after she'd taken it down and he'd begun brushing it for her. His heart clenched as he thought about how soft Grace's skin had felt beneath his touch, and how full of love his heart had been for her that night. He ached with the knowledge of her deception. Didn't honesty come with love? Had she ever truly loved him?

"Are you gonna look for Mama so we can eat?"

Cleon's mind snapped back to the present. "Uh, I'll see if she's outside." He headed for the back door, but it opened. Grace stepped in. Her face looked ashen, and her eyes were red and swollen. Had she been crying because of him, or had something else happened?

He stepped aside. "What's wrong? Have you been crying?"

"I—I can't talk about it right now." She glanced over at Anna and grimaced. "I'll deal with it after breakfast."

Cleon shrugged. If she didn't want to talk about what was bothering her, he couldn't do much about it. He took a seat at the table.

Anna looked up at her mother. "I'm hungry."

Grace nodded and hurried to the stove. "I'll have some breakfast on the table real soon."

"Can we go see Rose after we're done eating?"

Grace shook her head.

"You said I could have the puppy." Anna thrust out her lower lip. "I wanna see her now."

"You need to eat breakfast. We can talk about Rose after you've finished your scrambled eggs."

"I wanna see her now."

"Your mamm said after breakfast," Cleon said before Grace could respond. "Now quit whining and sit there quietly until breakfast is served."

Grace glared at Cleon. "There's no need to be yelling at her."

"I wasn't yelling."

"Yes, you were." Anna pointed at Cleon. "Your face is red, too."

A muscle on the side of Cleon's cheek pulsated. He debated whether he should say anything more and finally decided that if Grace chose to ignore the child's sassy attitude, then she could deal with it, not him.

Anna hopped off her chair and raced for the back door.

"Where are you going?" Grace called to her daughter's retreating form.

"To see Rose."

"No! You can't see her now." By the time Grace started across the room, Anna had already opened the door. "Come back here, Anna!"

She reached out and grabbed the child's arm, pulling her back into the house.

"I wanna see Rose!" Anna screamed as she tried to pry her mother's hands off her arm.

Grace's shoulders trembled, but she kept Anna in her grip. Cleon wondered if he should step in and attempt to calm the child or if it would be best to let Grace handle things.

"Anna, listen to me now." Grace knelt down and wrapped her arms around the child, holding her firmly until she finally calmed down. "Rose is dead. Your Aunt Martha found her that way this morning."

Anna stiffened. She pulled away sharply. "Rose can't be dead!"

"I'm sorry, Anna. Maybe Aunt Martha will give you another puppy when Flo has some." Grace reached out to wipe the tears from Anna's face, but the child jerked open the door and bolted out of the house.

Grace rushed after her. Cleon sat too stunned to move.

Chapter 36

The next few days were difficult. Anna mourned the loss of her puppy, and Grace tried to deal with the emotions swirling around in her heart like a windmill going at full speed. Her relationship with Anna had taken a step back. Her relationship with Cleon was strained and formal. Concern for her family's safety weighed on her heavily.

If they could only learn who was responsible for the attacks and make them stop. If they could just go back to the way the things were before their world had been turned upside down.

As Grace finished the breakfast dishes, she stared out the kitchen window at the tree branches swaying in the wind. Cleon had gone to work in Dad's shop, and Anna was upstairs in her room. Thinking it might help the child get her mind off the loss of her puppy, Grace had suggested that they go to the Wengerds' today so Anna could play with her friend Esta, but Anna hadn't wanted to go.

The quiet and solitude of the house would have been a welcome respite on most days, but this morning, Grace felt as if she were suffocating. She wanted to rush outside and scream out her fears. Instead, she grabbed a scouring pad and scrubbed the frying pan clean. "I need to keep busy. If I keep my hands and mind occupied, I won't have time to think about the troubles I'm facing."

When the back door creaked open, Grace turned to see who had come in. Her mother held a gray and white kitten in her hands. "How are you feeling this morning?"

"My stomach's settled down some, but that's about all."

"Things are no better with Anna's grief over the puppy?"

Grace shook her head. "She's not even interested in visiting her friend Esta today."

"I'm sorry." Mom nodded at the squirming kitten. "Martha offered Anna another puppy, but she refused, so I thought maybe I might interest her in one of Callie's kittens."

"Martha shouldn't be giving her pups away, anyhow. She'll never get her business going if she doesn't start bringing in some money." Grace glanced at the door leading to the hallway. "Anna's upstairs in her room. You can offer her the kitten, but I doubt she'll take it."

"It's worth a try." Mom started toward the door but paused. "Your daed says Cleon's working out well in his shop."

"That's good." Grace went back to washing the dishes, figuring her mother would head upstairs to see Anna, but Mom moved over to stand beside her at the sink.

"Your sullen expression tells me there might be something else bothering you besides Anna grieving for her puppy. Are things any better between you and Cleon?"

The lump in Grace's throat refused to let her say a word. She could only shake her head and shed a few more salty tears.

Mom placed the kitten on the floor and gathered Grace into her arms. "Is there anything I can do?"

Grace swallowed a couple of times, hoping to push the lump down. "I don't think there's much anyone can do. Cleon doesn't trust me anymore. We're still sleeping in separate bedrooms."

"But he knows about the boppli, right?"

"Jah."

"And that makes no difference?"

"I guess not. Dad told him the news before I had a chance to say anything, and now Cleon thinks I was trying to keep my pregnancy a secret from him." She inhaled deeply. "I think, more than anything, Cleon's upset that I was married before. I believe the thought of me having had a child with another man is too much for him to bear."

"*Puh!*" Mom waved a hand. "That's just plain lecherich. We know many widows who have married again, and their new husbands don't sleep in separate rooms or act is if the wife has done something wrong because she used to be married."

Grace dried her hands on a towel that had been lying on the counter. "If I'd been married to an Amish man who had died, Cleon would probably be okay with it. I think what troubles him most is that I was once married to an Englisher."

"Has Cleon said he feels prejudiced toward your deceased English husband?"

"Well, no. . .not in so many words, but from some of the things he's said, I've gotten that impression." Grace dropped her gaze to the floor. "He seems to have trouble with forgiveness."

"Then he needs to read his Bible more and start putting into practice the things he hears in church." Mom nodded toward the back door. "Truth be told, your daed has the same problem concerning his sister. Since it's a touchy subject with him, I try to be understanding and don't question his feelings." She patted Grace's arm. "My advice is to put your relationship with Cleon in God's hands."

"I'll try to be a better wife. Maybe if Cleon sees how much I love him, he'll find it in his heart to forgive me."

"I'll be praying that he does." Mom bent to retrieve the kitten. "Guess I'll head upstairs now and see what Anna thinks about this *siess* little ball of fur."

Grace smiled despite her frustrations. "It is pretty sweet, and I hope she likes it."

"Sure am glad I hired you. You've been a big help to me the last few days."

Cleon looked up from his job of sanding a straight-backed chair and smiled at his father-in-law, who stood nearby hammering nails into a set of cabinets. "I appreciate the job."

"I know it's selfish of me," Roman said, "but I wouldn't mind if you decided to forget about beekeeping and stayed right here working for me. I have no sons, so I'll need to pass on the business to someone, and you're a lot more dependable than my last employee."

"I wonder how things are working out for Luke at his new job. Have you heard any complaints from John?" Cleon asked, making no comment about his interest in taking over the woodworking shop someday. He was taking one day at a time, and even if he didn't rely solely on selling honey, he still wanted to do it on a part-time basis.

Roman pursed his lips. "John came by the other day and said he was pleased with Luke's work, but I'm guessin' he won't be for long—not once that lazy fellow starts showing up late for work." He shrugged. "But then I guess it's not my place to judge."

Cleon recoiled, feeling like he'd been stung by one of his bees. Had that remark been directed at him? Did Grace's dad know Cleon hadn't forgiven Grace? Was this Roman's subtle way of trying to make him feel guilty?

Cleon pushed the sandpaper a little harder against the unyielding arm of the chair and grimaced. *Roman doesn't understand the way I feel. He's not the one who wishes he could leave Holmes County and never look back.*

Ruth smiled when she saw her youngest sister enter the bakeshop. "I didn't know you were coming to town today," she said as Martha stepped up to the counter.

"I got a ride from Donna Larson into Sugarcreek this morning so I could stop by *The Budget* and run another ad for Heidi's remaining pups, since I've decided not to keep any. Then we drove to Berlin."

"I'm sorry you lost that little pup the other day."

Martha frowned. "Sure wish I knew how it happened and whether or not it was an accident."

Ruth leaned on the counter. "Who would want to hurt an innocent puppy?"

"It's hard to say, but if whoever did this is the same person who made the other attacks at our place, then I'd have to say they must be a bit ab im kopp."

"You're right, they must be off in the head, and I hope it's no one we know."

Martha glanced around the room, and her voice lowered to a whisper. "Are you thinking of Luke?"

Ruth nodded. "Dad said those sunglasses Mom found near her clothesline belonged to him."

"How does he know that?"

"Luke came by his shop the other day, looking for his glasses."

Martha shrugged. "So the sunglasses were Luke's. That doesn't prove he had anything to do with cutting the line. He may have dropped his glasses when he was heading for his buggy."

"Jah, maybe so." Ruth didn't want to think the worst of Luke, but he'd acted so strangely the last few months of their courtship. Dad had mentioned that Luke had said and done some things at the shop he didn't care for and that he'd put Luke in his place a couple of times. She supposed Luke could be nursing a grudge, but to try and get even—going so far as to kill one of Heidi's pups? It was too much to fathom.

"Are you still going to that young people's fellowship with Martin on Saturday?" Martha asked.

Ruth's mouth dropped open. "I'm not going with Martin. He just asked if I planned to go and said he hoped to see me there."

"What'd you tell him?"

"That I thought it sounded like fun and I'd try to be there."

"What was his response to that?"

"He said he was glad and would look forward to seeing me on Saturday."

Martha snickered. "Sounds like a date to me."

"It's not a date."

"Whatever you say." Martha winked at Ruth. "Martin's kind of shy, but he's also pretty cute. You'd better make sure you're playing on his side of the volleyball net."

"Go on with you now," Ruth said with a wave of her hand. "And you'd better plan on going with me, because you spend way too much time at home with those dogs of yours. You need to get out more and have some fun."

Martha wrinkled her nose. "Caring for my hund seems like fun to me."

"That might be, but you need to be with people your age." Ruth smiled. "Speaking of which, I was thinking that since this Sunday will be an off-Sunday from preaching, the two of us could go to the pond for a picnic."

"That's a fine idea. Maybe we could take Anna along, too. She's been so sad since her puppy died. She wouldn't even accept the kitten Mom offered her. Maybe a day at the pond will help lighten her mood." Ruth smiled. "It might be good for Grace and Cleon to have some time alone, too."

"Sounds good to me. We can go to the young people's gathering on Saturday evening and spend Sunday afternoon at the pond. By Monday morning, maybe we'll all feel a little better than we have here of late."

Chapter 37

"How was the young people's gathering you girls went to last night?" Roman asked, nodding at his two daughters who sat to the left of him at the kitchen table.

"It was all right," Martha said, reaching for a piece of toast.

Ruth just sat there with a dreamy look on her face.

"How about you, Ruth? Did you enjoy the young people's get-together?"

"Jah, it was a lot of fun."

Martha snickered. "Ruth's in love."

Judith's eyebrows lifted in obvious surprise, but Roman looked over at Ruth and frowned. "Did Luke show up there? Are the two of you together again?"

Ruth shook her head. "No, Dad. Luke wasn't there, and we aren't a courting couple."

He breathed out so forcefully that the air lifted a lock of hair from his forehead. "That's a relief. As far as I'm concerned, that fellow can't be trusted."

Martha's forehead wrinkled. "I'm sure Luke's not the one responsible for the attacks against us. He doesn't seem like the type to do something like that."

"Jah, well, you can't always judge a piece of wood by its color."

Judith leaned close to Ruth. "If you're not seeing Luke, then what did Martha mean when she said you were in love?"

Ruth lifted her gaze to the ceiling. "I'm not in love, Mom. I just

248

got to know Martin a little better last night, that's all."

"Martin Gingerich?"

"Jah."

"I talked to Abe Wengerd the other day, and he said he'd recently hired Martin as his apprentice," Roman said.

Ruth nodded. "That's what Martin told me. He said he thinks he's going to like working in the boot and harness shop."

"You should have seen the way Martin looked at Ruth," Martha put in. "If ever there was a man in love, it has to be him."

Ruth elbowed her sister. "Martin's not in love with me any more than I am with him. As I said before, we're just getting to know each other."

"Jah, well, at least Martin's settled down and joined the church. That's more than I can say for Luke, who in my opinion is much too old to still be running around," Roman grumbled.

Martha opened her mouth as if to respond, but he held up his hand. "Enough talk about Luke. Let's get our breakfast finished and decide how we want to spend our day."

"Since this is an off-Sunday from church, I thought it might be nice if we went calling on a few folks," Judith spoke up.

"Martha and I had planned to take Anna on a picnic today," Ruth said.

"We thought it might help take her mind off the puppy she lost," Martha added.

"Besides, it will give Grace and Cleon some time alone together."

"That's a good idea," Judith agreed. "Those two surely need to talk things through. With Anna out of the picture, it might be easier for them."

Roman swallowed some coffee, then said, "If Grace hadn't lied to Cleon, they wouldn't have a problem."

"She didn't actually lie, Roman. She just withheld the facts about her previous marriage and having a daughter."

He grunted. "From what Cleon told me, she didn't tell him about her being in a family way, either."

Judith shrugged, and the girls stared at their plates.

Roman grabbed a piece of toast and slathered it with a glob of apple butter. "I say we forget about Grace and Cleon's problems and finish our breakfast."

Grace paced between the kitchen sink and the table as she waited for Cleon to come downstairs. He'd gotten up long enough to drink a cup of coffee, but then he'd gone back to bed without eating breakfast, saying he had a headache. So Grace had fixed Anna's breakfast and sent her off to spend the day with Ruth and Martha at the pond. She hoped a day of fun might lift her daughter's spirits. Now if something could be done to lift her own.

The sound of footsteps on the stairs drew Grace's attention, and she turned to greet Cleon when he entered the kitchen. "Is your *koppweh* gone?"

He nodded and yawned, stretching his arms overhead. "Can't remember the last time I had a headache like that. A few more hours of sleep finally took it away, though."

"I'm glad." She motioned to the table. "If you'd like to take a seat, I'll fix you something to eat."

He glanced at the battery-operated clock on the far wall as he pulled out a chair and sat down. "It's too late in the day for me to eat a big breakfast. Just a cup of coffee and some of those biscuits we had last night will do."

Grace went to the stove for the coffeepot, then reached into the cupboard to retrieve a mug. After she'd filled it with hot coffee, she set it on the table in front of Cleon and went back to the counter to get the basket of biscuits. "Would you like me to warm them in the oven?"

"They'll be fine the way they are."

She placed the basket on the table, along with a dish of butter and a jar of strawberry jam. "Can I get you anything else?"

He shook his head.

"Ruth and Martha picked Anna up awhile ago, and they're on their way to the pond."

No response.

Grace pulled out the chair beside him and sat down. "I thought the two of us could spend the day together—maybe go for a walk or sit out on the porch swing and talk." She watched his face, hoping to tell what he was thinking. His face was stoic.

He cut a biscuit in two and slathered some butter on both halves. "I'd planned to go over and see my folks today," he mumbled. "Thought maybe I'd talk to Ivan about going in with me on some more beehives."

"I could go along. It's been a while since I visited with your folks."

"I'd rather go alone."

Grace's heart sank. A dozen responses came to mind, but she couldn't gather the presence of mind to verbalize one of them.

"Maybe you can spend the day with your folks," he suggested.

She dared not say anything least she break down and cry, so she stared at a purple stain on the tablecloth until tears blinded her vision. What kind of marriage did they have with him sleeping in another room and the two of them barely speaking? Cleon had made it quite clear that he didn't want to spend any time alone with her. Their marriage was a marriage in name only, just as Cleon had said it would be when he'd come home.

The now familiar churning in Grace's stomach gripped her like a vise, and unable to stand the wall of silence between them, she pushed her chair away from the table and stood. One thing was certain: Only God could mend her broken marriage.

Cleon sat at the kitchen table staring into his empty mug and mulling things over. In his heart, he knew that he still loved Grace, but he felt frozen, unable to respond to her as a husband should respond to his wife. If only he could rid himself of the memory of her lies. How he wished he could erase everything that had happened between them and start over with the day they'd first met. Would Grace have said and done things differently if she'd known how things would turn out between them?

He leaned back in his chair and clasped his hands behind his head, staring at the cracks in the ceiling. The gas lamp hanging overhead hissed softly, and he spotted a fly that had landed in a spider's web in one corner of the room.

That's how I feel, he thought ruefully. *Like a trapped fly.*

Cleon remembered his grandfather saying once that happiness didn't depend on what life dished out to a person but rather on how the person chose to accept whatever came his way.

Guilt lay heavily on Cleon's chest, and tension pulled the muscles in his neck and upper back as he shifted in his chair. It wasn't good for a body to get so worked up, but every time he thought about Grace's deception, it was as though his heart was being ripped in two. As a Christian, he should forgive, but did he have the strength to forget the past and look to a future with Grace and the baby she carried? Could he find enough love in his heart to be Anna's stepfather?

Chapter 38

What a perfect day for a picnic," Ruth said as she and Martha spread a quilt under a leafy maple tree. "The pond looks so clear today. It's almost as blue as the sky above. I'm glad spring is finally here. Makes me anxious for summer."

Martha nodded and glanced down at Anna, who stood off to one side with her arms folded and a scowl on her face. Most children would be excited about going on a picnic, but Anna still grieved for her puppy. Nothing anyone had said or done had helped ease her pain. Maybe today would be different. Maybe something would happen that might make Anna laugh again.

"I thought it might be fun to take a walk in the woods." Martha tapped Anna on the shoulder. "Should we do that now or after we eat our lunch?"

Anna wrinkled her nose. "I'm not hungry."

Ruth placed the picnic basket on the quilt and took hold of Anna's hand. "All right then, the three of us will take a walk now, and we can eat when we get back." She smiled as the thought of the tasty lunch that awaited them made her mouth water. "I'm sure by then you'll have worked up an appetite."

Anna said nothing, but she didn't resist as the three of them walked away.

Martha halted and turned back toward the quilt. "What about our picnic basket? Do you think it's all right to leave it unattended, or should we put it back in the buggy?"

"I'm sure it'll be fine," Ruth called over her shoulder. "No one else is around that I can see, and we won't be gone long. Let's leave it under the tree where it can stay nice and cool."

Martha shrugged and started walking again. If she wasn't careful, she might end up like her older sister—worried about everything.

As Cleon headed to his folks' place on foot, he struggled with feelings of guilt. He'd turned down Grace's offer to accompany him, knowing she wanted them to spend time together. He simply wasn't able to deal with the two of them being alone. He became anxious whenever they were in the same room, and his words often came out clipped or defensive. He knew it was wrong to harbor feelings of mistrust and bitterness, but he couldn't seem to control his emotions where Grace was concerned.

It was an exceptionally warm day for spring, and Cleon reached up to wipe the rivulets of sweat running down his forehead and into his eyes. He wanted to be a father, had wanted it for a long time. This should be a joyful occasion, and he and Grace shouldn't be sleeping in separate bedrooms.

That's your choice, a voice in his head reminded him.

He picked up speed. It was best that he didn't think about this. Maybe he would feel better once he'd talked to Ivan and decided what to do about his beekeeping business.

A short time later, Cleon's folks' house came into view. He found Mom and Pop relaxing on the wide front porch in their rocking chairs, with one of the yellow barn cats sitting at Mom's feet. She kept so busy all the time with her many responsibilities, it was nice to see her doing nothing for a change.

She smiled when Cleon stepped onto the porch. "It's good to see you, son."

"Good to see you, too."

Pop grunted. "You don't come around so much now that your bee boxes are gone and you've begun workin' for Roman."

Cleon took a seat on the top step and swiped at his sweaty

forehead with the back of his hand. "That's one of the reasons I came over—wanted to speak with Ivan about the bees."

"How's Grace and that cute little stepdaughter of yours?" Mom asked. "I'm disappointed you didn't bring them along."

"Anna went on a picnic with Ruth and Martha today."

"And Grace? How come she didn't come with you?"

Cleon winced. Should he tell his folks the truth about his strained relationship with his wife? Should he tell them about her pregnancy? He knew they would find out sooner or later, and he figured the news should probably come from him.

He swallowed hard. "Uh. . .Grace isn't feeling well these days, so I thought it would be best if I came alone."

"What's wrong with her? Is she grank?" Mom's brows furrowed with concern.

Cleon removed his straw hat and fanned his face with it. "Grace isn't sick. She's. . .uh. . .in a family way."

Mom clapped her hands and nearly jumped out of her chair. "Oh, that's wunderbaar!" She nudged Pop's elbow. "Just think, Herman, our first *kinskind* is on the way."

Pop's face broke into a wide smile. "That is good news. Are ya hopin' for a *buwe* or a *maedel?*" he asked, nodding at Cleon.

Cleon shrugged. "Haven't had a chance to think much about whether I'd like a boy or girl. Just found out Grace was pregnant a few days ago." He stood and flopped his hat back on his head. "Is Ivan about? I'd like to talk to him."

"I think Ivan's out in the barn. Said he was goin' to take a nap in the hayloft." Pop chuckled. "Ever since that boy was a kinner, he's liked sleepin' in the hay."

"Okay. I'll see if he's there." Cleon hurried away before his folks could continue discussing the baby.

He entered the barn a few minutes later and tipped his head to stare into the hayloft. "You up there, Ivan?"

No response.

Cleon cupped his hands around his mouth and hollered, "Ivan!"

A muffled grunt, followed by another, came from a mound of

hay. "What's with all the racket?" Ivan peered over the edge of the loft. "Cleon, I didn't know you were comin' over today."

"Since this is an off-Sunday from church, I thought it would be a good chance to drop over and say hello to the folks." Cleon removed his hat and fanned his face with the brim. "Wanted to speak with you about something, too."

"What's that?"

"Why don't you come down here, and we can talk about it. It's kind of hard to carry on a conversation when you have to yell."

"You've got a point." Ivan crawled out of the hay and scrambled down the ladder. When his feet hit the bottom, he shook like a dog, sending pieces of hay flying.

"Hey, watch it!" Cleon jumped back, but not before a couple of stubbles landed on his shirt. He flicked them off and sat on a nearby bale of straw.

"What'd ya want to talk to me about?" Ivan asked as he plunked down on the bale next to Cleon's.

"Bees and honey."

Ivan reached up to pick a chunk of hay out of his hair. "What about bees and honey?"

Cleon pulled out a length of straw and chewed on the end of it as he contemplated the best way to ask his question. "I'm wanting to start up my bee business again, and as you know, I don't have enough cash yet to buy more bees, boxes, and the supplies I'll need."

Ivan nodded. "I still feel bad about you losin' 'em that way."

"I'm making pretty good money working for Roman, but it's gonna be a while before I have enough saved up to start the business again." Cleon reached up to rub his bearded chin. "The thing is, I read an ad in *The Budget* the other day from someone in Pennsylvania who's selling off his beekeeping supplies. So I was wondering if you might be able to loan me enough money to get a start on things. Or maybe you'd like to go halves on the business with me this time around."

Ivan's dark eyebrows drew together. "I do have some money laid aside, but I was plannin' to use it to buy a new buggy horse."

"What's wrong with the one you've got now?"

"Nothing, really. He's just gettin' kind of old and isn't as fast I'd like him to be."

"Ah, I see."

Ivan stroked his clean-shaven chin. "Guess buyin' a new buggy horse can wait awhile, though." He nodded at Cleon. "Don't really want to be your business partner, but I'm willing to loan you whatever you need."

Cleon sighed with relief. If he could get his bee business going again, he'd be earning money from that as well as from working for Roman. Then he not only could pay Ivan back what he'd borrowed, but he'd have enough to pay Roman back for all the lumber and other supplies he'd bought in order to finish Cleon's house. Besides, working with the bees again would give him a good excuse to be away from home when he wasn't at work in Roman's shop. He thumped his brother on the back. "I appreciate the loan, and if Roman doesn't mind me missing a few days' work, I'll head out soon and see about buying what I need."

Martha led the way for Ruth and Anna as they tromped through the woods. Birds warbled from the trees overhead, insects buzzed noisily, and leaves rustled in the breeze. It had turned into such a warm day, but being in the shaded forest made it seem much cooler.

"Should we play hide-and-seek?" Ruth suggested, remembering how the childhood game had always made her laugh whenever she'd felt melancholy.

"That's a good idea." Martha halted and turned around. "I'll close my eyes and count to one hundred while you two hide. Then the first one I find has to hide her eyes next time around."

Anna looked up at Ruth with a hesitant expression. "What happens if I get lost?"

Ruth bent to give Anna a hug. "You won't get lost, because the two of us will be staying close together."

Martha leaned into the nearest tree and closed her eyes. "One. . . two. . .three. . .four. . ."

Ruth grabbed Anna's hand and dashed away in search of a good hiding place. They halted behind a clump of bushes, and Ruth motioned Anna to get down. "Be real quiet. Martha won't find us so easily if she can't hear us."

Anna giggled and covered her mouth with the palm of her hand. Ruth crouched behind her. If Martha found them, she would spot Ruth first. Then Ruth would have to count to one hundred while Martha took Anna off to look for a place to hide. If they kept going like that, Anna would never have to be the one to go looking, and they would know she was safe and couldn't get lost in the woods.

"One hundred!" she heard Martha shout. "You'd better have found a really good hiding place, because here I come!"

Ruth held her breath and squeezed Anna's hand. This reminded her of when she was little, and she and her sisters had run through the woods behind their home playing hide-and-seek. So many times she'd been caught because she'd given herself away by making too much noise. She was determined that wouldn't happen now.

"Anna? Ruth? Where are you?" Martha's voice sounded farther and farther away, and Ruth figured they were safe—at least for the moment. She relaxed a bit and was about to whisper something in Anna's ear, when someone tapped her on the shoulder. She whirled around. Martin Gingerich was staring at her.

"What are you doing down there?" he asked with a crooked grin. "Looking for bugs, are you?"

Anna giggled, and Ruth snickered as she put her finger to her lips. "We're hiding from Martha."

He tipped his head and looked at her as if she'd taken leave of her senses. "Why would you be hiding from your sister?"

"We're playin' hide-and-seek," Anna said before Ruth could respond. "Aunt Martha's it, and if you're not quiet, she's gonna find us."

Martin nodded and dropped to his knees beside them. "I won't say another word."

The three of them crouched there for several more minutes until Martha jumped out from behind a tree and hollered, "Found you!"

When she spotted Martin, she planted her hands on her hips and stared at him. "Now where on earth did you come from?"

"Came from home, same as you." He winked at Anna and offered Ruth a heart-melting smile. In that moment, she realized how easily she could fall in love with this man. Martin was nothing like Luke. He was steady, polite, and attentive, not impetuous, flippant, or brash. She felt certain that Martin was trustworthy, which was more than could be said for Luke.

"I don't know about the rest of you, but I'm hungry as a mule," Martha announced. "I say we head back to the pond and eat our picnic lunch." She nodded at Martin. "We made plenty of food, so you're welcome to join us if you like."

"I appreciate the offer, but I left my brother waiting in the buggy where the road cuts by the pond. The only reason I came into the woods was because I heard you hollering and thought someone might be in trouble." Martin turned and smiled at Ruth again. "Maybe some other time I can join you for a picnic."

Her cheeks heated up. "That'd be nice."

"See you later then," Martin said and dashed away.

Martha nudged Ruth's arm as they started back toward the pond. "I can tell he's smitten with you."

Ruth just kept her gaze straight ahead.

"What's 'smitten'?" Anna asked, looking up at Martha.

Martha chuckled. "It means he can't take his eyes off my sister."

"How come he wants his eyes on her?"

Martha's laughter escalated, and Ruth joined in, too. She hadn't felt this carefree since she was a little girl.

As they stepped out from the darkened trees and into the clearing where they'd left their food, Ruth gasped. "Our picnic basket—it's gone!"

Chapter 39

Whatin all the world?" Martha planted her hands on her hips and stared at the quilt where they'd left the picnic basket. "Where did our lunch run off to?"

Ruth squinted. "It sure couldn't have walked off by itself."

"Maybe some animal came along and took it," Anna said, looking up at Martha with a frown.

"More than likely it was some human playing a trick on us," Ruth said with a shake of her head.

"You don't suppose Martin did this, do you?"

Ruth looked at Martha as if she'd gone daffy. "Martin?"

"He snuck up on you in the woods, so what's to say he didn't hide the picnic basket, too?"

"I'm sure he wouldn't have done something like that."

"How do you know?"

"I just do, that's all."

"You said you're only beginning to know him, so I doubt you'd be able to tell what he's capable of doing."

Ruth's eyebrows drew together. "It's not like I just met Martin. I've known him since we were kinner."

"We've known Luke that long, too, yet you seem to think he's capable of doing all sorts of terrible things."

Ruth motioned toward Anna, who had taken a seat on the quilt. "Let's not argue about this, okay?"

Martha nodded. "You're right. We should be looking for that

picnic basket, not trying to figure out who took it." She glanced around. "Which direction should we look first?"

Ruth shrugged. "Makes no difference to me. I'm getting hungry and I want to eat."

"Me, too," Anna said in a whiny voice.

"Then let's get busy looking. We can start on this side of the pond, and if we don't find it here, we'll walk around to the other side." Martha reached for the little girl's hand, pulling her gently to her feet.

They broke through a clump of bushes, rounded the bend, and had only gone a short distance when Martha spotted the wicker basket sitting near a pile of men's clothes not far from the water. "There it is!" she and Ruth shouted at the same time.

Martha dropped to her knees and opened the basket lid. Nothing remained except a bunch of empty wrappers and a half-full jug of lemonade. "This makes me so mad," she muttered.

"Look there!" Ruth pointed to the pond. Several young English men floated in inner tubes. "I'll bet they're the ones who took our picnic basket."

Martha shielded her eyes from the glare of the sun and squinted. "I think one of those fellows was with Luke when we saw him talking to some Englishers outside the market several months back. Do you remember?"

Ruth shrugged. "Can't say for sure since they're so far away, but they're obviously the ones who took our food, so I think we should teach them a lesson."

"What kind of lesson?"

"One that's going to leave those fellows with some sore feet on their trip home and probably feeling pretty chilly if the wind picks up." Ruth bent down, grabbed the shirts and shoes, and turned toward the woods.

Martha reached for Anna's hand and followed. They stumbled through a tangle of bushes, past a grove of spindly trees, and went deeper into the forest. As Ruth scurried along, she hung the shoes and shirts on various branches, hiding some under shrubs and inside a hollow log. "That ought to teach them not to take what doesn't belong to them." Her forehead wrinkled as she shook her head. "If they're the ones responsible for the terrible things that have happened at our place lately, then maybe this will make 'em think twice about that, too."

Martha stood, too dumbfounded to say a word. This act of retaliation wasn't like her normally placid sister. It wasn't the Amish way, either, and it wasn't a good example to be setting for Anna. "Do you think you should have done that, sister?"

Ruth folded her arms and gave one quick nod.

"If those English fellows are behind the break-ins and other things that have been done at our place, they may decide to do something worse in order to get even."

Ruth shrugged. "Well, I'm not going to put their clothes back, but if you want to, I won't stop you."

Martha looked overhead at a black and white sneaker flopping in the breeze and shook her head. "I say we take our picnic basket and hightail it out of here before those fellows get out of the water."

"Sure seems quiet around here with everyone gone for the day, doesn't it?" Judith asked Roman, who sat in the wicker chair beside her on their front porch.

He nodded. "Jah. Quiet and peaceful."

"I hope Anna has a good time with the girls."

"I'm sure she will."

"Haven't seen anything of Grace or Cleon, so I'm hoping they're enjoying their day together, too." She reached for his hand. "I'm enjoying my time spent with you, as well, husband."

He smiled. "Same here."

"Things have been so crazy around here for the last couple of months. It's nice to finally have some peace."

"Let's hope it stays peaceful." Roman's eyebrows drew together. "We still don't know who's responsible for the attacks, but I keep praying that whoever's behind it will realize what they did was wrong and that it won't happen again."

Judith nodded. "I wish I knew why we seem to be the only ones under attack. It's as if someone has deliberately singled us out."

"I agree, and I'm fairly sure it's someone who wants to get even with me."

"You? But what could you have done that would make someone angry enough to do such horrible things to our property?"

Roman's forehead wrinkled. "Let's see now. Steven Bates could be trying to make me pay for ruining his wife's birthday present. Or Luke could be getting even because I fired him."

"Grace still thinks that reporter fellow might be trying to get even with her for breaking up with him and marrying his friend."

"I doubt he'd be carrying a grudge that long." He tugged his earlobe. "It could even be that land developer who seemed so determined to get me to sell off our land."

"He did seem determined, but I guess he must have taken no for an answer, because he hasn't been around."

"I heard he's bought some land up near Kidron, so maybe he's given up trying to buy our place."

"Could be that no one has a grudge against us at all. Maybe it was just some wild kids stirring up trouble, like you thought in the beginning. Say, isn't that Cleon walking up our driveway from the main road?"

Roman squinted and stared across the yard. "I believe it is."

"Wonder where he's coming from and why Grace isn't with him."

"Could be she's takin' a nap, and he decided to go for a walk."

Judith wrinkled her forehead. "It's strange we didn't see him leave his house."

"Maybe he left before we came outside."

"But we've been here for some time."

Roman patted her arm. "Is it really so important?"

"I thought one of the reasons the girls took Anna on a picnic was so Grace and Cleon could spend time together. They can't do that if she's in the house sleeping and he's taking a walk by himself."

As Cleon came to the end of the driveway, he turned toward their home. When he reached the porch steps, he stepped up and nodded at Roman. "I. . .uh. . .need to speak with you about something."

"Jah, sure. What's is it?"

Cleon looked over at Judith and shuffled his feet.

"I think I'll go inside and get a jug of iced tea while you menfolk talk," she said, grasping the arms of the chair and rising to her feet. "Would either of you like some?"

"Nothing for me," Cleon was quick to say.

Roman shook his head. "Not right now; maybe later."

She disappeared into the house. *Guess if Cleon had wanted me to hear what he had to say, he would have invited me to stay.*

"Have a seat," Roman said, motioning to the chair Judith had been sitting in.

Cleon sat down and cleared his throat.

"What's on your mind?"

"I've been wanting to get my beekeeping business going again, and my brother Ivan's offered to loan me some money. So I was wondering if it would be okay with you if I took a few days off from work to see about buying some bees, boxes, and other supplies from a fellow who lives near Harrisburg, Pennsylvania, not far from where I grew up."

"I'd thought maybe since you'd come to work for me that you'd decided to quit the bee business."

"I'll keep working for you as long as you want me to, but I enjoyed what I was doing with the bees, and I could use the extra money now that we have a boppli on the way. Since Ivan will probably be helping me part-time, maybe I can tend to the bees when I'm not working for you."

Roman's eyes narrowed. "Workin' two jobs won't give you much time to spend at home with your wife and kinner."

"Taking care of the bees isn't a full-time job, so I'll be around home enough, I expect."

"What's Grace think about this?"

"She. . .uh. . .doesn't know yet."

Roman rubbed the bridge of his nose. "I guess it'll be all right if you're gone a few days, but I hope you'll be back by Friday. It's Grace's birthday, you know, and she'd be mighty disappointed if you weren't there to help celebrate."

Cleon clamped his lips together. He didn't want to appear like a thoughtless husband, but he needed to get those bee boxes and other supplies before someone else got to them. "I can't promise I'll be back by Friday, but I'll try."

After Cleon left for his folks' place, Grace rested awhile. Then she decided to spend some time reading her Bible. She'd been negligent about doing her devotions every day and knew that getting into God's Word might help her depression.

Curling up on the sofa, she opened the Bible to Isaiah chapter 50. When she read verse 7, words of scripture seemed to jump right off the page. "For the Lord GOD will help me; therefore shall I not be confounded: therefore have I set my face like a flint, and I know that I shall not be ashamed."

Tears coursed down Grace's cheeks, and she sniffed. She needed to rely on God to help her as she set her face like a flint. She had done some wrong things, but she no longer needed to be ashamed of them, because she'd asked God for forgiveness. Even though Cleon hadn't forgiven her, God had, and for that she felt grateful.

When the back door opened and clicked shut, Grace dried her eyes and sat up. "Who's there?"

"It's me," Cleon said as he stepped into the living room.

"Did you have a nice visit with your folks?"

He nodded. "Didn't visit with 'em long, though. Spent most of my time talking with Ivan about the possibility of getting some more bees, boxes, and other supplies."

"I see."

Cleon took a seat in the rocking chair across from her. "When I got back, I spoke with your daed about letting me have a few days off."

She tipped her head. "How come?"

"I read an ad in *The Budget* from some fellow who lives near

Harrisburg, Pennsylvania. He's got a bunch of bee things for sale at a pretty good price, so I want to see about buying them."

"When would you be leaving?"

"Tomorrow morning."

Grace moistened her lips with the tip of her tongue. She didn't want Cleon to think she was trying to tell him what to do, and she wasn't going to mention that she wanted him home to celebrate her birthday. Cleon knew when her birthday was. If he didn't remember this year or didn't want to spend it with her, then she wouldn't bring up the subject. "I—I guess if you feel you need to go, then that's what you should do."

He nodded and stood. "Think I'll walk over to the Larsons' and see if Ray can give me a ride to Dover in the morning so I can catch the bus to Pennsylvania."

Grace stared at him. He finally shrugged and left the room.

She released a sigh that turned into a strangled sob. *Dear Lord, please give me the strength to endure my husband's rejection.*

Chapter 40

Roman was about to close up shop for the day and take Grace and the family to dinner, when John Peterson showed up.

"I was driving by and thought I'd stop in and see how things were going," John said, leaning against the desk where Roman sat.

"I'm keeping busy enough. How 'bout you?"

"Same here. Seems to be a lot more folks in the area who want quality furniture."

Roman nodded. "How are things working out with Luke as your new apprentice? Is he coming to work on time and working steady?"

"So far he's done okay, but I'm keeping an eye on him all the same."

"I gave that young man plenty of chances, but he didn't seem to care enough about his job to do as I asked." Roman gritted his teeth. "I'm glad my daughter broke up with him, because to tell you the truth, I don't trust that fellow."

"Do you make a habit of firing your employees?"

"What's that supposed to mean?"

"I just wondered if Luke was the first employee you've had to fire."

Roman shrugged. "May have had to let a few others go over the years, but it was only because they wouldn't listen to me and wanted to run things their own way."

"Luke thinks you believe he had something to do with the break-ins you folks had awhile back."

"I wouldn't be surprised." Roman shrugged as he ran his fingers through the back of his hair. "Martha found Luke's hat outside in the dirt after that brick went through the kitchen window. Then Judith found his sunglasses not far from the clothesline that somebody cut."

John's dark eyebrows drew together. "That does make him seem guilty. Guess I'd better keep a closer watch on Luke. Sure wouldn't want him tearing things up at my place."

"As long as you don't give him an ultimatum, he probably won't bother your place. It wasn't until I jumped him about being late a couple of times and docked his pay for being careless that things started happening." Roman shook his head. "We've had a couple of incidents since Luke quit working for me, too. Makes me wonder if he might be trying to get even because I fired him."

"I'll be sure and let you know if I hear or see anything suspicious."

Roman glanced at the clock on the wall, and realizing what time it was, he pushed his chair aside and stood. "Sorry to cut this visit short, but I need to head up to the house and get washed and changed. Today's my oldest daughter's birthday, and we're taking her to dinner at Der Dutchman in Walnut Creek."

John smiled and moved toward the door. "Don't let me hold you up. Tell Grace I said happy birthday, and I hope you all have a pleasant evening." Just as he got to the door, he glanced around the room and his forehead wrinkled. "I thought I'd heard that you'd hired your son-in-law to work for you."

"That's right. Cleon started working here a few weeks ago after he got home from a trip and discovered that all his bees, boxes, and supplies had been burned."

"I heard about that, too. The fellow who told me said he thought it was probably done by some kids playing a prank."

Roman nodded. "Could be."

"So if Cleon's working for you now, where is he?"

"Went to Pennsylvania to look at some items for his beekeeping business, which means I'm on my own for a few days."

"He won't be here for his wife's birthday?"

"Nope, afraid not."

The strange look on John's face made Roman wish he hadn't said anything. It was bad enough that Cleon wouldn't be here for Grace's birthday; he didn't need John making something of it.

"Well, guess I'd better get going." John lifted his hand in a wave. "See you around, Roman, and don't hesitate to call if you need anything."

Grace wasn't looking forward to her birthday dinner, but her folks had insisted on hiring a driver and taking the family to Der Dutchman. She didn't want to disappoint them. Besides, a meal out with her family was better than sitting home alone with Anna. Grace would have spent the evening wishing Cleon could be with her and that their relationship was on track. If only there was something she could do to earn back his trust and his love.

As Grace sat in the backseat of Ray Larson's van, she realized that at times she actually felt relieved that her husband wasn't around, looking at her as if she were a terrible person and making her feel guilty for the secret she'd kept.

When Ray pulled into the restaurant's parking lot, he turned to look at Grace's father. "I've got some errands to run, so I'll be back to get you folks in a couple of hours. Is that okay?"

Dad nodded. "You're welcome to join us for supper if you like."

"No, thanks. I'd better get my errands run, or I'll have to answer to Donna."

"Okay then," Dad said as he and the rest of the family climbed out of the van.

Grace took Anna's hand and followed her family inside the building. A long line of people waited for service. Anna and Martha busied themselves at the revolving rack near the checkout counter. It featured lots of postcards and books about the Amish, as well as some novels and a few children's books. Several English people, who were obviously tourists, commented on how cute Anna was as she squatted down to look at the books.

Any other time, it probably wouldn't have bothered Grace, but this evening her nerves were taut. She resisted the urge to tell everyone to quit staring at her daughter. Instead, she sat on a bench with her hands clenched in her lap, hoping they would soon have a table.

After thirty minutes of waiting, they were ushered into the dining room. Soon after they'd placed their orders and the waitress had brought beverages and rolls, Anna announced that she needed to use the restroom.

"Want me to take her?" Martha asked, looking over at Grace.

"I'll do it." Grace pushed her chair aside and reached for Anna's hand.

When they stepped out of the ladies' restroom a short time later, Grace collided with a man. Her heart thumped erratically when she realized it was Gary.

"Well, now, isn't this a pleasant surprise?" he drawled. "It's been a while since I've seen you, Gracie. Where have you been keeping yourself?"

Grace opened her mouth to respond, but before she could get a word out, Anna looked up at Gary and announced that today was her mama's birthday. "We're having supper to celebrate," she added.

A look of recognition registered on his face as he stared at Anna. "Oh, that's right—I remember you. Aren't you the little girl I saw at the Hostettlers' house a while back?"

Anna nodded. "I'm Anna, and this is my mamm."

Grace squeezed her daughter's hand. "Haven't I told you not to talk to strangers?"

"Come now, Gracie. I'm hardly a stranger—at least not to you." Gary offered Grace a lopsided smile, and it fueled her anger.

"I want you to go back to the table now," she said, giving Anna a nudge in that direction.

"What about you? Aren't you comin', too?"

"I. . .uh. . .need to use the ladies' room, but I'll be there as soon as I'm done."

"You didn't have to go before."

Grace gave Anna another nudge. "Go on now. Tell Grandpa and Grandma I'll be there soon."

Gary winked at Anna, and she gave him a quick smile, then darted off toward the dining room.

Grace turned back to face Gary. "How much longer will you be staying in Holmes County?"

He rubbed his chin and looked at her in a most disconcerting way. "Well, now, that all depends."

"On what?"

"On how many more interesting stories I find here."

"Are you sure you're not hanging around just to make trouble?"

He chuckled. "You're really direct and to the point these days, aren't you, Gracie? Not like the timid young woman I used to date, that's for sure. Must be those years you spent living among the English that made you so bold."

She grimaced. This man certainly had a way of getting under her skin.

He folded his arms and leaned against the wall. "I remember spending one of your birthdays with you, Gracie. Let's see now—which one was that?"

She glanced back at the table to be sure Anna had joined her family again.

"Say, here's an idea. Why don't I join your little birthday party? While I'm there, maybe I can get someone in your family to open up and tell me more about the vandalism at your place. I really need to get that story wrapped up, you know."

"You wouldn't dare follow me back to the table."

"Wanna bet?"

He started in that direction, but she reached out and touched his arm. "What information do you want that you don't already have?"

His eyebrows jiggled up and down. "I'd like to know why you left me for that simpleton, Wade Davis."

"Why would you talk about Wade like that? I thought he was your friend."

"He was until he snatched you away." Gary frowned. "What I'd really like to know is how come you gave up the English way of life for this." He motioned to her plain dress and eyed her up and down.

"I chose to return to my Amish roots after Wade died because I knew that's where I really belonged. I should never have left home in the first place."

He motioned toward the dining room. "I only see one man sitting at your table. Where's that new husband of yours?"

Grace could hardly swallow around the lump in her throat. She would never admit to Gary that her husband cared more about starting up his beekeeping business than celebrating her birthday. "Not that it's any of your concern, but my husband is away on business right now. Now, if you'll excuse me, I need to get back to my family."

"Sure, Gracie. Don't let me stop you." He snickered. "Oh, and happy birthday."

"What's wrong?" Ruth asked, taking Grace's hand when she returned to the table. "Are you having a wave of nausea? Is that why you went back to the restroom?"

Grace shook her head. "I'm fine."

"Are you sure?"

Grace gave a quick nod.

"Anna said you were talking to a man in the hallway outside the restroom," Mom put in. "Was it someone we know?"

Grace's face paled as she shook her head. "Can't we talk about this later?"

Their father nodded. "Grace is right. Let's pray so we can eat."

All heads bowed for silent prayer, and then everyone dug in. Everyone but Grace. She toyed with the piece of chicken on her plate.

"For one who was supposed to be hungry, you're sure not eating much," Dad said, reaching for another biscuit from the basket in the center of the table. "Are you feeling bad because Cleon couldn't be here to help celebrate your birthday?"

Grace shrugged. "It would have been nice, but he's got important business to tend to."

"It'll be good when he gets his bee boxes set up again," Mom put in from across the table. "Nice for us to have some fresh honey again, too."

"That's for sure." Dad lifted a drumstick off his plate and had just taken a bite, when he scrunched up his nose and released a moan.

"What's wrong, Roman?" Mom's eyebrows furrowed, and she reached over to touch his arm.

He opened his mouth, stuck two fingers inside, and withdrew a porcelain crown.

"Oh, no." Mom clicked her tongue noisily. "Looks like you'll be making a trip to the dentist tomorrow morning."

"No, I won't," he said with a shake of his head. "You know how much I hate going to the dentist."

"But, Dad, you can't go around with the nub of your tooth exposed." Ruth grimaced. "You'll need to get that crown cemented on right away."

"I've got some epoxy cement in my shop. Maybe I'll use that."

Martha's mouth dropped open, and she looked at their father as if he'd taken leave of his senses. "You wouldn't."

He nodded. "Sure would. It'll save me a chunk of money."

Ruth couldn't believe how stubborn her father could be at times. She glanced over at Grace, who had been unusually quiet all evening. Grace stared at her half-eaten food as if she didn't care that Dad had lost a crown. Something was going on with Grace, and Ruth hoped it wasn't anything serious.

Chapter 41

I don't see why you felt the need to follow me out here," Roman said to his wife as they stepped into his shop after they'd returned home from dinner.

"Because I know what you plan to do, and I'm hoping to talk you out of it. It's just plain *eefeldich* to try and glue your crown back in place." She frowned. "It won't hold, you know."

"It may seem silly to you, but I know what I'm doing, and this will save us some money." Roman ignited one of the gas lamps.

Judith pulled out the chair at his desk and took a seat. "If you insist on doing this, then at least let me help so you don't get it glued on crooked or put glue where it doesn't belong."

He shrugged and started toward his supplies. Most women worried too much, especially his wife.

"Grace seemed sad tonight, didn't she?" Judith said.

"Guess she was missing Cleon," he called over his shoulder.

"I still don't see why he couldn't have waited to make that trip until after her birthday."

"I'm heading into the back room now, so can we talk about this later?"

"Jah, sure."

Roman stepped into the room and turned on another gas lamp. When he opened his toolbox to retrieve the epoxy cement, several things were missing. "Now that's sure strange."

"What's strange?"

Roman whirled around. Judith had followed him into the room. "Some things in this case are missing, including the epoxy cement."

Her forehead wrinkled. "What all is missing?"

"A hammer, a couple of screwdrivers, a pair of pliers, and two tubes of cement."

"Maybe you put them somewhere and forgot."

"Don't remember puttin' them anywhere but here."

She covered her mouth with one hand. "I hope someone hasn't broken into your shop again. I'm getting so tired of these attacks."

"If it is another attack, we just need to hold steady and keep trusting the Lord." He looked around the room. "We don't know if the missing tools really are part of an attack, and I don't see anything else missing. The front door was locked when we came in, so it doesn't seem as though anyone broke into the place while we were gone."

"You think maybe Cleon borrowed the tools and forgot to tell you?"

Roman leaned against the workbench. "I suppose that's possible. I'll ask when he gets back." He closed the lid on the toolbox and turned down the gas lamp. "Guess I'll have to see the dentist whether I like it or not, because without that cement, I can't glue my crown back on."

Judith smiled. "At least one good thing came out of your supplies being gone."

He grunted and touched his mouth. "Jah, right."

As Cleon entered a café on the outskirts of Harrisburg, he noticed a small calendar sitting on the counter near the cash register. *Oh, no, today was Grace's birthday, and I didn't even send her a card.*

He seated himself at a booth near the window and reflected on his wife's last birthday, when he'd been invited to her folks' house for supper. They'd made homemade ice cream after the meal, and he and Grace had spent the rest of the evening sitting on the porch swing, talking about their future and holding hands. Cleon had hung around until almost midnight, wishing he could be with Grace forever. Things had sure turned out differently than he'd imagined they would.

He wondered what Grace had done to celebrate her birthday, and as he reached for the menu the waitress had placed on the table, a feeling of guilt swept over him like a raging waterfall. Even if he was Grace's husband in name only, the least he could do was to acknowledge her birthday.

Cleon thought about a verse from Matthew 6 he had read in his hotel room: *"For if ye forgive men their trespasses, your heavenly Father will also forgive you."* He still loved Grace, and he needed to forgive her. But if he couldn't trust her, then how could he fully forgive and open his heart to her again?

Maybe I'll buy her a gift before I head for home. At least that way she can't say I didn't care enough to do something for her birthday. And when she finds out that I've bought enough bees, boxes, and supplies to start my business again, maybe she'll realize that I'm not going to shirk my duties, and that I plan to take care of her and the baby.

A lump formed in Cleon's throat, and he swallowed a couple of times, trying to dislodge it. God had put Grace in his life for a reason. It wouldn't be enough to give her a gift and let her know he didn't plan to wriggle out of his duties to her and their unborn child. Grace's secret wasn't the problem. His unforgiving actions and refusal to trust her were keeping them apart.

Truth be told, he hadn't given Grace a chance to tell him about the boppli and then had blamed her for not telling him the news. He had to give his hurts over to the Lord, for only God could break down the barriers Cleon had erected between him and his wife. He'd been running from what he wanted the most. He and Grace belonged together. He needed not only to forgive Grace, but to seek Anna's forgiveness, as well. Cleon resolved to do that as soon as he returned home.

As Grace and Anna headed for their house, Anna chattered about how Ruth had hid somebody's clothes in the woods when they'd gone on a picnic the other day. Grace barely let the words sink in. She was still feeling flustered over her encounter with Gary, and she wasn't looking forward to spending the rest of the night in an empty house, knowing Cleon wouldn't be coming home. A lump formed in her throat. He hadn't even bothered to give her a card, much less a gift.

"Look, Mama, somebody must have left you a birthday gift," Anna said as they stepped onto the back porch.

Grace bent down and picked up a small package wrapped in plain brown paper. She wondered if it could be from Cleon. Maybe he'd bought it before he left for Pennsylvania and asked someone from his family to deliver it to Grace on her birthday.

"Open it! Open it!" Anna shouted, hopping up and down.

"Calm down. I'll open it when we get inside."

Grace pushed the door open and stepped into the kitchen. She placed the package on the table, turned on a gas lamp, and pulled out chairs for Anna and herself.

"Can I open it?" Anna asked.

"Jah, sure, go ahead."

Anna ripped off the paper, pulled open the lid, and screeched with horror. "Dead mouse! Dead mouse!"

Thinking the child must be joking, Grace reached for the box and peered inside. "Ach! It is a dead *maus*!" She shuddered and tossed the package to the floor.

Anna started to sob, and Grace gathered the child into her arms. "It's okay. I'm sure someone's just playing a trick on Mama."

As Grace sat rocking Anna back and forth, the bitter taste of bile rose in her throat, and she swallowed to push it down. Who could have done something so horrible? Who could hate her so much that they would want to ruin her birthday?

Her thoughts turned immediately to Gary. When she'd seen him at the restaurant tonight, she'd mentioned that it was her birthday. Could he have driven over here and put the dead mouse on her doorstep?

Chapter 42

When Grace awoke the following morning, she looked out the window. Large droplets of water splattered against the glass, and a streak of lightning zigzagged through the dreary sky. Her stomach twisted as she thought about the night before—missing Cleon, encountering Gary, finding the package with the dead mouse on her porch.

She moved back across the room and sank to the edge of her bed as a wave of nausea hit. Her head pounded, and her hands shook. Maybe yesterday's doings had taken more of a toll on her than she'd realized. If only she could be free of the pain. If she could just let go of the past and release her fears to God. If she could keep her focus on the good times she and Cleon used to have, maybe she could find the strength to go on.

"For the Lord GOD will help me; therefore shall I not be confounded: therefore have I set my face like a flint; and I know that I shall not be ashamed."

"Thank You, Lord," Grace whispered. "I needed the reminder that You're here to help me." She rose from the bed and, with a sense of renewed determination, left the room and headed downstairs to fix breakfast.

Anna sat at the kitchen table with a piece of paper and a pencil. Her faceless doll lay in her lap. It was good to see her taking an interest in things again.

"Good morning, daughter." Grace bent to kiss Anna's forehead. "What are you doing?"

"Me and Martha with no face are drawin' a picture for Poppy. We want him to come see us soon."

Grace took a seat beside Anna. "You still miss your Grandpa Davis, don't you?"

Anna nodded, and tears welled in her eyes.

"The last letter we had from your poppy said he's feeling some better but isn't up to traveling just yet."

"Can we go see him?"

"I don't think so, Anna."

"How come?"

"We're busy with things here." Grace pressed her hand against her stomach. "And I'm not feeling well myself these days, so a long trip isn't a good idea."

Anna's eyes opened wide. "Are you gonna die like Grandma Davis and my puppy?"

"No, dear one, I'm not sick; I'm pregnant." Grace reached for Anna's hand and gave it a gentle squeeze. "That means in a few months you'll have a little sister or brother to play with."

The child's mouth fell open. "You're gonna have a boppli?"

Grace nodded and smiled. It pleased her to hear Anna speaking German-Dutch.

"A baby sister would be better'n havin' a puppy," Anna said with a grin. "Can I name her?"

"Don't you think we'd better wait and see whether it's a boy or a girl?"

Anna giggled. "Guess it would be kinda silly if a boy had a girl's name, huh?"

"Jah. We'll also have to wait and see what the baby's daadi has to say about choosing a name."

Anna's eyebrows drew together. "Who's the baby's daddy gonna be?"

"Why, Cleon, of course. He's my husband."

Anna shook her head forcibly. "My daddy's name was Wade. Poppy said so."

"I used to be married to Wade, and he was your daadi. But now I'm married to Cleon. He's the daadi of the boppli I'm carrying."

Grace placed Anna's hand against her slightly protruding stomach.

"I don't like Cleon. He don't like me, neither."

Grace sat dumbfounded, not knowing how to respond. She'd seen the way Cleon reacted to Anna—seeming to barely tolerate her. He wasn't Anna's father, but he was her stepfather, whether he liked it or not. Just because he was angry at Grace gave him no right to ignore Anna the way he did.

"I'm sure Cleon doesn't dislike you, Anna," she said, wrapping her arms around the child. "It's going to take some time for the two of you to get better acquainted."

Anna sat staring at the table.

Grace finally pushed her chair aside and stood. "What would you like for breakfast?"

No comment.

"How about pancakes and maple syrup?"

A little grunt escaped the child's lips as she shrugged her slim shoulders.

"All right, then. Pancakes, it is."

As Judith prepared breakfast for her family, she thought about the missing items in her husband's toolbox. Could Roman have misplaced them, or was it possible that Cleon had borrowed some things and forgotten to mention it? She grimaced as she stared out the window. Rain rattled against the roof. Maybe someone had been in Roman's shop and stolen the tools. But if that were so, how did they get in without breaking a window or tampering with the lock on the door?

Thunder clapped. Judith gasped. "Oh, how I dislike *dunner* and *wedderleech*. Haven't liked it since I was a girl."

Roman stepped up behind Judith and put his arms around her waist. "No need for you to fear. I'm here to protect you."

She leaned against his chest and sighed. "I wish we were safe from all outside forces."

"We need to trust God with every area of our lives—the weather included."

"I wasn't thinking about the weather. I was thinking about the attacks and wishing they would stop."

"We can't be sure those missing things from my toolbox were stolen, if that's what you're thinking."

Judith turned to face him. "Have you remembered where you put them?"

"No, but I'm pretty sure Cleon must have borrowed them." Roman shrugged. "We'll know soon enough, because I'm certain he'll be home soon."

"It isn't good for him and Grace and to be apart like this. They're newlyweds, and they shouldn't be sleeping in separate bedrooms."

"Give them time to work things out, and whatever you do, don't meddle."

"Jah, I know." She nodded toward the window. "Sure hope this rain lets up. I've got some washing to do today, and I was counting on hanging the clothes outside on the line. I also need to go down to the phone shed to make that dental appointment for you."

He shook his head. "You stay put in the house. I'll make the call myself."

She nodded as another clap of thunder rumbled, shaking the house. "Sure hope no one's barn or house gets struck by lightning today."

Grace spent the rest of her day cleaning, mending, and trying to keep Anna occupied. The rain hadn't let up, and the child was anxious to go outside and play. At the moment, she was taking a nap, which gave Grace enough time to get some baking done. She'd just put two rhubarb pies in the oven when she heard footsteps on the porch, and the back door creaked open.

"You busy?" Martha asked as she stepped into the room, holding a black umbrella in her hands.

"Just put a couple of pies in the oven. Come on in. We can have a cup of tea."

Martha placed the umbrella in the old metal milk can sitting near the back door, removed her lightweight shawl, and took a seat at the table.

"Sure is nasty weather we're having," Grace commented.

Martha nodded and glanced around the room. "Where's Anna?"

"Upstairs taking a much-needed nap."

"I'm glad she's not about, because I don't think it would be good for her to hear what I have to say."

Chills ran up Grace's spine as she took a seat across from her sister. "What's wrong? Has something happened to another one of Heidi's pups?"

Martha shook her head. "The dogs are fine, but I can't say the same for poor Alma Wengerd."

"Ach! What's wrong with Alma?"

"She's dead. Dad got the news when Bishop King dropped by his shop this morning."

"What happened to Alma?"

"She'd gone out to feed the chickens, and when she didn't come back to the house, Abe went looking. He found her on the ground a few feet from the chicken coop. She'd been struck by a bolt of lightning."

Grace gasped. "Oh, that's baremlich!"

Martha nodded soberly. "I know it's terrible. Alma was a friend of Mom's, and she's terribly broken up over this."

Grace stared at the table as tears gathered in her eyes. "After last night, I didn't think things could get much worse around here, but I guess I was wrong."

"What happened last night?"

"First, I ran into Gary Walker in the hallway outside the women's restroom at the restaurant."

"Did he say something to upset you?"

"Gary always says things to upset me." Grace swallowed hard. "I wish he'd leave Holmes County and never come back."

"I've been praying for that—not just because you think he's the one responsible for the attacks, but because I know that seeing him makes you think about the past."

Grace sniffed and turned to reach for a tissue from the box sitting on the counter behind her. "Something else happened last night that upset me, too."

"What was it?"

"When Anna and I got home, we found a package on the porch."

"A birthday present?"

"I thought so at first." Grace blew her nose and dabbed at the corners of her eyes. "I made the mistake of letting Anna open it, and—"

"And what, Grace? What was inside the package?"

"A dead maus."

"That's *ekelhaft*! Who in their right mind would do such a disgusting thing?"

"Gary Walker, that's who."

"You really think he's responsible?"

Grace nodded. "As I've told you before, he said he would get even with me someday."

"That was several years ago. Surely the man's not still angry because you married his friend."

The back door opened, and Ruth stepped into the room. "Whew, this is some weather we've been having. You should have seen all the water on the road. I had a hard time seeing out the front buggy window on my way home." She set her umbrella in the milk can next to Martha's, hung her shawl on a wall peg, and hurried over to the table. "Have you got any tea made? I could sure use some about now."

Grace reached for the pot sitting on the table and poured her sister a cup of tea.

"Have you heard about Abe's Alma? Is that why you're here?" Martha asked as Ruth took the offered cup.

"Haven't heard a thing about Alma. What about her?"

"She's dead. Struck down by a lightning bolt right there in her yard."

Ruth's eyes widened. "Ach, what a shame!"

"That leaves Abe with six kinner to raise. He's surely going to need some help in the days ahead," Grace put in.

Ruth nodded with a somber expression. "I'm sure their relatives will pitch in."

Grace moaned. "So much sadness going on around us these days. Sometimes I wonder how much more we can take."

Ruth set her cup down and reached over to touch Grace's hand. "Despite the sad news about Alma, I've got another piece of news that might bring a smile to your face."

"What news is that?"

Martha leaned forward. "I'd be interested in hearing some good news for a change, too."

"That reporter you used to date came into the bakeshop today, and he mentioned that his work was done here and that he'd be heading to Wisconsin soon to do some stories about the Amish there." Ruth squeezed Grace's fingers. "Now you can quit worrying about running into him every time you go to town. And if the attacks on us should quit, we'll know he was responsible."

Grace sighed as a feeling of relief flooded over her. Maybe now they could stop worrying about being attacked and concentrate on helping Abe and his family plan Alma's funeral and make it through the days ahead.

Chapter 43

The sky was a dismal gray, and the air felt much too chilly for a spring morning, but at least there was no rain on the day of Alma Wengerd's funeral. As family and friends gathered at the cemetery to say their final good-byes to Alma, Ruth's heart ached for the six children Alma had left behind. Molly, age two; Owen, who was four; six-year-old Willis; Esta, age eight; ten-year-old Josh; and the oldest, Gideon, who was twelve, huddled close to their father as they stood near Alma's coffin.

Alma had been only thirty-two years old when she'd been snatched from the world so unexpectedly. The sweet-tempered woman, still in the prime of her life, would never see her children raised or enjoy becoming a grandmother someday. It tore at Ruth's heartstrings to think of these little ones without a mother, and she wondered how Abe would manage to take care of the house, do all his chores, watch out for the children, and run his harness shop.

She glanced over at Martin, who stood near his parents. He hadn't attended the main funeral that was held at Abe's house, but he'd shown up in time for the graveside service. Ruth wondered if he would be expected to do more work at the harness shop now, since Abe would have additional family responsibilities. Martin seemed like such a kind young man, and she felt sure he would do all he could to help lighten Abe's load.

If Ruth didn't already have a job at the bakeshop in town, she might offer to work for Abe as his maid, but she'd heard that his unmarried sister who lived in Illinois would be coming to care for his children.

As Alma's four pallbearers lifted the long, felt straps that had been placed around each end of the coffin and lowered it slowly into the ground, Ruth drew her attention back to the gravesite. Death was a horrible thing, and she couldn't imagine how Abe must feel after losing his wife of thirteen years. The closest people Ruth had ever lost were her grandparents, and she couldn't conceive of how it would be to lose a mate.

As short boards were placed over the casket by one of the men, Abe bent down and scooped his youngest child into his arms. Maybe Molly had become fussy, or perhaps Abe had picked her up in order to offer himself some measure of comfort. The tall man with reddish-brown hair and a full beard to match showed no outward signs of grief other than the somber expression on his face.

Gideon leaned over and whispered something in Josh's ear, and little Esta moaned as she clasped her two younger brothers' hands.

Ruth wanted to dash across the space between them and gather the children into her arms. Instead, she reached one hand out to Martha, who stood to her left, and the other hand out to Anna, who stood on her right, looking as though she might break into tears. Was Grace's daughter thinking about the passing of her English grandmother? Had Alma's death been a reminder of what Anna had lost? Grace looked on the verge of tears, too. Perhaps her greatest sorrow came from the fact that her husband wasn't at her side, for Cleon hadn't returned home yet and probably didn't even know about Alma's death.

As the pallbearers filled in the grave, the bishop read a hymn from the Ausbund, a few lines at a time, and a singing group followed. Then the grave was filled in and the soil mounded. Everyone turned away, wearing solemn expressions, and moved slowly toward their buggies.

Everyone but Esta, that is. The young girl dashed across the grass and, sobbing as though her heart would break, threw herself on the ground next to her mother's grave.

Abe stood as if he was torn between getting his other children into the buggy and going back to offer comfort to his grieving daughter.

No one else was close enough to notice the child. Even Ruth's family had left the gravesite, but she'd stayed put, waiting to see what Abe would do. Finally, when she saw him move toward his buggy again, she rushed over to Esta and knelt on the ground beside her. Gathering the little girl into her arms, she rocked back and forth, gently patting her back.

"Mamma. . .Mamma. . .why'd you have to leave us?" the child sobbed. "Don't you know how much we all need you?"

Tears coursed down Esta's face, wetting the front of Ruth's dress and mingling with her own tears. At that moment, Ruth promised herself that she would not only pray for the Wengerd family, but she would also drop by their place as often as possible and offer to help in any way she could.

As Grace directed her horse and buggy down the road after she and Anna had left Alma's funeral, she was filled with concern—not only for Abe and his children, but also for Anna, who hadn't spoken a word since they'd left the burial site. The child was shaken by the death of Esta's mother, but she'd refused to talk about it. Due to Anna's melancholy behavior, Grace had decided to get Anna home as quickly as possible, rather than stay for the dinner at Abe's house.

She glanced over at the child, who sat in the seat beside her with her arms folded and her eyes downcast. If only she knew what was going on in her daughter's head.

Grace was glad her parents and sisters had stayed for the funeral dinner, for the women's help was needed serving the meal. Dad and Abe had done a lot of business with each other, as well as sending customers one another's way, so she knew Dad would want to hang around and offer encouragement to Abe. Grace had noticed that Ruth had taken Esta Wengerd under her wing, and that she'd even been the one to walk the crying child to Abe's buggy after the graveside service.

Ruth would make a good mother someday, and Grace hoped her sister would find a nice Amish man to marry when the time was right.

Maybe it would be Martin Gingerich. He'd certainly shown an interest in Ruth. Martin was rather quiet and shy—nothing like Luke Freisen—but he seemed like a kind man, and from what Abe had told Dad a few weeks ago, Martin was a hard worker.

Grace's thoughts went to Cleon as she placed one hand against her stomach. *He'll be sorry when he hears of Alma's passing. Sorry for Abe and sorry he wasn't here for the funeral.* She swallowed against the burning lump clogging her throat. *Would Cleon mourn if something were to happen to me, or would he be relieved to have me out of his life?*

She shook her head. She shouldn't allow herself to think this way. It wasn't good for her to focus on the negative. It wasn't good for the baby she carried to have its mother feeling so distraught.

As they came down a slight incline, the buggy horse whinnied, halted, and pawed at the ground.

"What's the matter with you, Ben?" Grace snapped the reins, but the horse refused to move, shaking his head from side to side. His behavior made no sense. Cars weren't whizzing past, and from what she could see, nothing in the road signaled danger.

She snapped the reins again and reached for the buggy whip. "Giddy-up there, Ben. Move along now, schnell!"

The horse finally moved forward, but he acted skittish, and Grace had to keep prompting him with the buggy whip. Finally, they reached the driveway leading to her folks' home, and when she turned Ben to the right, he tried to rear up. She pulled back on the reins. "Whoa, now. Steady, boy."

The horse finally calmed enough so she could get him moving again, but they'd only made it halfway up the driveway when she smelled smoke. Grace forced the horse to keep moving until her Dad's shop came into view. Nothing wrong there; it looked the same as it had this morning. Past Mom and Dad's house they went; it looked fine, and so did the barn. She'd just started up the incline to the second driveway when she saw it—smoke and flames coming from her and Cleon's house!

At first, Grace wasn't sure what to do. Should she run for the hose and try to put out the fire on her own, or turn the buggy around and head to the closest English neighbors' to call the fire department? Trying to put out the fire by herself was ridiculous. However, it would take some time for the fire trucks to get there, and the house could be gone by then. If only Dad or Cleon were here, she could go for help while they fought the fire.

Anna squealed and crawled over the seat just as Grace halted the buggy. She turned to reach for the child, but Anna scooted away, climbed out the back opening, and ran toward the burning building.

Grace opened her door and jumped down, too. "Anna, stop! Don't go near the house!"

The child kept running, and by the time Grace reached the front porch, Anna had already opened the door and slipped inside.

"Oh, dear Lord, no," Grace panted as she raced in after the child. "Please don't let anything happen to my little girl!"

When Cleon's bus arrived in Dover, Henry Rawlings, one of the English drivers he sometimes used, picked him up. But Henry needed to make a stop in Berlin, and since Cleon was anxious to get home and make things right with Grace, he headed there on foot.

As he trudged along the shoulder of the road, he thought about his trip to Pennsylvania and how well things had gone. Not only were some bees and hives being shipped home, but also he'd purchased a honey extractor, some goat-hide gloves, a bee veil, a smoker, and a hive tool that would be used to pry frames out of the beehives. He'd also found a couple of outlets that wanted to buy his honey. If things went well, by this time next year, he could have a thriving business again.

He'd also bought Grace a package of stationery with bluebirds scattered along the top of each page. It wasn't much, but at least it would let her know that he hadn't forgotten her birthday.

About halfway home, Cleon heard a horn honk. He turned and saw John Peterson's SUV pull onto the shoulder of the road behind him. "Need a lift?" John called through his open window.

"I'd appreciate that." Cleon pulled the door open on the passenger's side and climbed in.

"Heard you'd been on a trip to buy some bees," John said as he pulled onto the road again.

Cleon nodded. "Bees and boxes, both."

"Did you have any luck?"

"Sure did. Had the bees, boxes, and beekeeping supplies shipped to my folks' place. They should be there by now, I'm guessing."

"Is that where you're headed then—to see your folks'?"

Cleon shook his head. "Figured I should stop by my own house first and let Grace know I'm home."

John gave the steering wheel a couple of taps. "There's been some excitement in the area since you've been gone."

"What kind of excitement—good or bad?"

"Afraid it's not good. We had a pretty rough storm a few days ago, and Alma Wengerd was hit by a bolt of lightning."

"I'm real sorry to hear that. Was she hurt bad?"

"She's dead. Her funeral was today, although I didn't attend. Since I'm not Amish and haven't been in the community very long, I wasn't sure I'd be welcomed." John shook his head. "Your neighbor Ray Larson wasn't there, either. I saw him at the pharmacy in Berlin not long ago."

A chill ran up Cleon's spine, and he shivered. Abe's wife was dead—struck down in the prime of her life. He couldn't imagine how he would feel if something like that happened to Grace.

"You okay?" John asked, nudging Cleon's arm. "You look kind of pale."

Cleon popped a couple of knuckles and reached both hands around to rub the kinks in his neck. "I was thinking about Abe losing his wife like that. Must have been some shock for him."

John nodded. "I heard he was the one to find her not far from the chicken coop where she'd gone to gather eggs."

"How terrible. Abe's got six kids, you know, and it won't be easy for him to raise them on his own."

"He'll probably be looking for another wife soon. That's what most Amish men do when they lose a mate, isn't it?"

Cleon shrugged. "Some do; some don't. All depends on the

circumstances." *Would I be looking for another wife if Grace died? Could anyone make me as happy as she does? How would I feel if Grace was taken from me before I had a chance to ask for her forgiveness?*

When they turned onto the Hostettlers' driveway, Cleon noticed a thick cloud of smoke hanging in the air. The acrid smell stung his nostrils, and when they began the climb to his driveway, he realized that his house was on fire. His spine went rigid, and his heart pounded. *Dear God, don't let them be in there. Don't let it be too late for us, please.*

He turned to John. "Can you call the fire department for me?"

"Of course." John fumbled in his shirt pocket and frowned. "Rats! Must have left my cell phone at home. I'll go there now and make the call."

Cleon opened the door, jumped out of the vehicle, and raced up the driveway. He spotted Grace's horse and buggy parked nearby. *She must be home. She could even be in the house.*

"Grace, where are you?"

Silence except for the crackle of flames shooting into the air.

"Anna! Anna, come back here! No, don't go upstairs!"

Cleon halted. That was Grace's voice coming from inside their house. Apparently Anna was there, too. His heart nearly stopped beating. If he lost Grace now, without making things right between them, he didn't think he could go on living.

Noting that the fire seemed to be coming from the second story, where it shot out the bedroom windows and through the roof, Cleon pulled a quilt from the buggy, wet it in the horses' watering trough, and threw it over his head. He jumped onto the porch, flung open the door, and raced inside.

Chapter 44

Rather than helping the other women serve the funeral dinner, Ruth decided it would be best to stay with Abe's children, especially Esta, who had refused to eat anything.

"If you promise to eat a little something," Ruth coaxed as she sat on a bench beside Esta, "then I'll ask your daed if you can come over to our place tomorrow so you can see how my sister's puppies are growing." She smiled. "I'm sure Anna would enjoy having someone to play with, too."

Esta stared up at Ruth, her dark eyes looking ever so serious and her long lashes sweeping across her cheeks with each steady blink. "You think Martha might let me have one of them hundlin?"

Ruth knew Martha had given Anna one of Heidi's puppies, but that pup had died, and Martha was counting on getting paid for the other two she still hoped to sell. She took hold of Esta's hand. "If they were my hundlin to give, I'd say, jah, but I'm pretty sure Martha's planning to sell the others."

Esta's lower lip protruded. "I've got no money, and I'm sure Papa won't give me none, neither. He always says we can buy only what we need."

Ruth had some money saved up from her job, and she couldn't think of a thing she needed it for right now. "I'll tell you what, Esta," she said, gently squeezing the little girl's fingers, "If your daed says it's okay, then I'll buy you one of Heidi's hundlin."

Esta's eyes opened wide. "Really?"

"Jah."

"Okay." Esta grabbed a sandwich off her plate and took a bite.

Ruth smiled and turned her attention to her own plate of food. *I hope I have a child as sweet as Esta some day.*

After the meal, the men and women gathered in groups to visit, while the children and young people visited with friends. Since Esta seemed content to play with one of the other children who'd brought along her faceless doll, Ruth decided it was a good time to go off by herself for a while to think and pray.

As she wandered through the yard, heading for the stream near the back of Abe's property, her thoughts went to Grace, who had taken Anna home some time ago. The sad expression on her sister's face concerned Ruth, and she was sure it wasn't only due to Alma's death. Grace anguished over her strained marriage and worried about the assaults against their family over the last several months.

If there's something I can do to help my sister deal with this, please show me how, Lord, Ruth prayed as she dropped to a seat on the grass not far from the stream. She lifted her face to savor the warmth of the sun and closed her eyes. *And help me know what to do to help Esta and her brothers and sisters in the days ahead.*

"Are you sleepin'?" a male voice asked.

Ruth's eyes snapped open. Toby King and Sadie Esh stared down at her.

"I didn't realize anyone else was here."

"We weren't. I mean, we just got here," Toby mumbled.

"Too many people were milling about the Wengerds' yard, so we decided to take a walk by ourselves," Sadie said, her cheeks turning rosy.

Ruth nodded.

"Seems like nearly everyone in our community came out for Alma's funeral. Everyone but Luke." Toby shook his head. "I wouldn't be surprised if he isn't spending the day with his English buddies. Seems to have more time for them than he does his Amish friends these days, uh-huh."

Ruth made no comment, preferring not to discuss her ex-boyfriend.

She had other, more important things on her mind. Things like how she could help little Esta and her siblings cope with the loss of their mother.

Toby gave Sadie's arm a tug. "Are we goin' for a walk or not?"

"Jah, sure," she said with a nod. "See you at work tomorrow, Ruth."

Ruth lifted her hand in a wave and closed her eyes again as she leaned back in the grass. A few minutes later, she heard a man clear his throat, and her eyes snapped open.

Her insides quivered when she saw Martin standing over her.

"Saw you heading this way awhile ago and thought I'd come talk to you," he said, his face turning a light shade of red.

She patted the ground beside her. "Would you like to have a seat?"

"Jah, sure." Once Martin was seated, he removed his hat and flopped it over his bent knees. "Sure was a sad funeral, wasn't it?"

She nodded, afraid if she voiced her thoughts, she might dissolve into a puddle of tears.

"Just goes to show that no one knows what the future holds. You can be going along fine one minute, and the next minute some unexpected tragedy occurs." He shook his head. "I'll bet Abe never dreamed when Alma went out to feed the chickens that he'd never see her again—leastways not in this life."

She nodded again.

"I couldn't help but notice the way you were comforting Abe's kinner—especially Esta when she was so upset."

Ruth swallowed around the lump in her throat. "They're all going to miss their mamm, that's for sure."

"Seemed like you got her calmed down, though."

"I did my best."

Martin pulled up one blade of grass after another. Finally, he turned to Ruth, cleared his throat a couple of times, and said, "I enjoyed the time we spent with each other at the young people's gathering the other night."

"Me, too."

"I was wondering. . .that is. . .would it be all right if I came calling on you at your home sometime next week?"

Ruth didn't want to appear too anxious, but the thought of being courted by this kind, gentle man made her feel so giddy she could barely breathe. "Jah, Martin. I'd be happy to have you come calling," she said with a nod.

"I'm sure sorry about Alma," Roman said as he clasped Abe's shoulder. "If there's anything I can do, please let me know."

Abe nodded. "I appreciate that."

"Will someone from your family help with the kinner?"

"My youngest sister, Sue, who isn't yet married, said she'd move in and take over their care." Abe ran his fingers through the back of his reddish-brown hair as he leaned against the barn door. Tears welled in his eyes. "Alma was only thirty-two when she died. Don't seem right for one so young to be snatched away from her family, does it?"

Roman shook his head. Judith was forty-four, and he couldn't imagine losing her.

Abe groaned. "We celebrated thirteen years of marriage a few weeks ago. Alma was nineteen, and I'd just turned twenty when we tied the knot."

Roman clasped his friend's shoulder again. "From what I knew of Alma, she was a fine Christian woman."

"You're right about that, and she was a good mudder to our six kinner." Abe stared across the yard where his two oldest boys played a game of tug-of-war with some of the other children. "Losing Alma is gonna be hard on us all, but I'm especially worried about Esta. At the end there, I was torn between helping her and getting my other five back to the buggy. I finally decided to tend to them first and then see about Esta, but when I caught sight of your daughter Ruth comforting Esta, I figured I'd let her handle things."

He turned to face Roman. "Esta's the oldest of my girls, you know, and the truth is she got along with her mamm better than she did me. I'm thinking now that Alma's gone, Esta will need the hand of a woman to guide her along."

"I'm sure my wife and daughters will be willing to do whatever they can to help, along with your sister, of course."

"We'll appreciate any help we get." Abe turned away from the barn. "Guess I'd better go visit some of the others for a bit. Although, if I had my druthers, I'd go in the house, climb into bed, and pull the covers over my head."

Roman nodded in understanding. Ever since the attacks on his family had begun, he'd felt the same way.

As Grace dashed through the house screaming for Anna, her eyes stung with tears, and her lungs filled with smoke. "Anna! Anna, where are you?"

All she heard was the crackle of flames lapping against the wooden structure of her home. Unless help came soon, they would lose everything. But Grace couldn't worry about that right now. She had to find Anna and get her out of this inferno.

Coughing and choking, Grace looked everywhere, hoping for some sign of her daughter. She could barely see for all the smoke and worried that Anna might have gone upstairs. "Anna! Anna, where are you?"

The front door *swooshed* open, and Cleon burst into the room. Grace gulped on a sob and threw herself into his arms.

"Thank the Lord, you're all right," he panted, squeezing her so tightly she could hardly breathe. "When I got home and saw the place was on fire, I was afraid you were inside and had been—"

Grace pulled away and hiccupped on a sob. "Anna's missing, Cleon. I'm afraid she may have gone upstairs."

Cleon motioned to the door. "It's not safe for you to be in here with all this smoke. Go outside, and I'll search for Anna."

Grace hesitated, but the intense heat from the flames made her realize that she needed to get out of the house. They all did—especially Anna, her precious little girl. "Oh, Cleon, I—I don't think I could stand it if something happened to Anna. I need to find her—to be sure she's all right."

"I promise I'll find her," he said, practically pushing Grace out the door. "I love you, Grace, and right now you need to take care of yourself so that boppli you're carrying has a chance at life, too."

Grace blinked a couple of times as she let Cleon's words sink in. He'd said he loved her and was concerned about the child she carried. Did that mean he'd forgiven her, too? There was no time for questions, and Grace didn't argue further, for she knew Cleon was right. He had helped on the volunteer department and would have a better chance of saving Anna than she ever could.

Moments later as Grace knelt on the grass in their front yard, she whispered a prayer. "Help us, Lord. Help Cleon find Anna, and keep them both safe."

With each passing second, she struggled against the desire to run back into the house and help search for her little girl. What if Cleon couldn't find the child? What if he and Anna both perished in the flames?

She stood on trembling legs and was about to head back to the house when Cleon emerged from the building, Anna in his arms.

"Oh, thank the Lord!" Grace rushed forward and reached for her daughter, who clutched her faceless doll in her hands. "Where was she?"

"Found her upstairs in her room, trying to rescue her dolly."

"Is she hurt?"

"I think she breathed in quite a bit of smoke, but I didn't see any burns, and I think she's gonna be—"

Before Cleon could finish his sentence, Anna buried her face against Grace's neck and cried, "Poppy saved me from the fire!"

"Oh, no, daughter," Grace said, as she patted the child's back. "It was Cleon who went into the burning house to rescue you."

Anna turned her head toward Cleon as tears rolled down her flushed cheeks. "Can I call you Papa?"

"I'd like that." Tears welled in Cleon's eyes. "I owe you an apology, Anna. I've been selfish, thinking of my own needs, and never considering what it must be like for you coming here to live with people you didn't know and trying to adjust to a new way of life."

Anna reached out and touched Cleon's damp face. Then she leaned forward and kissed his cheek.

His gaze turned to Grace. The look of tenderness she saw on his face caused her to choke on a sob.

"One day while I was off buying some beekeeping supplies, I thought about a verse of scripture, and it made me realize—" He gulped in a deep breath. "I love you, Grace. That's never changed. And I'm sorry for my unforgiving spirit. Will you forgive me for being such a stubborn *narr*?"

"You're not a fool," Grace said with a shake of her head. "You were just deeply hurt by my deception."

"That doesn't make it right," he said, leaning down to kiss her lips. "I promise to be a better husband from now on."

Tears pooled in Grace's eyes, clouding her vision. "And I'll try to be the best wife I can be." She sank to the ground, placing Anna in her lap; then pointed to the house as angry flames lapped at the sides and shot through the roof. "Oh, Cleon, if help doesn't come soon, we're going to lose the whole house."

He knelt beside Grace and reached for her hand. "John Peterson gave me a lift home, and when we realized the house was on fire, he said he'd call for help. The fire trucks should be here soon, but even if we should lose the house, it doesn't matter."

She blinked several times. "What do you mean, 'it doesn't matter'? We've worked hard to build our home, and if we lose it—"

"The house doesn't matter; it can be rebuilt. What counts is you and Anna—that you're both unharmed."

"You're right," she murmured. "God has given us a second chance, and all that matters is that we obey Him and try to do what's right."

Sirens blared in the distance, and Cleon took Anna from Grace as they clambered to their feet. Two fire trucks roared up the driveway, followed by John's rig. Several firemen hopped out of the vehicles and set right to work, but the house was nearly gone. It looked hopeless.

"Do you have any idea how the fire got started?" the fire chief asked Cleon.

He shook his head as he put his arm around Grace's shoulders.

"There's been no more lightning since the day one of our Amish women was struck down, so it couldn't have been that," she replied. "Were any of your gas lamps left burning inside the house?"

"I thought I had turned them off before my daughter and I left for Alma Wengerd's funeral this morning, but then I've been so upset about Alma's death, I guess I might have left one on without realizing it."

"Once the fire is out, we'll conduct an investigation," the fire chief said. "In the meantime, you all need to let the paramedics check you over."

Cleon nodded, and his arm tightened around Grace's shoulders as they headed for the rescue vehicles. "When I think how close I came to losing you, I feel sick all over." He grimaced. "And I feel even sicker when I think how terrible I treated you after Anna arrived and I learned the truth about the secret you'd been keeping."

"As Bishop King said to me the night Anna showed up on our doorstep, 'The past is in the past, and nothing's going to change what's been done.'"

Cleon stopped walking and turned to stare at their home. The fire was out now, but the house was burned beyond recognition.

Grace leaned her head on his shoulder and sighed. "It's going to be all right. We have a boppli to look forward to, and with the love and support of each other and with God as the head of our home, I know we can face whatever might come in the days ahead."

"You're right, my blessed gift." He kissed her tenderly on the mouth, then leaned down to kiss the top of Anna's head. The little girl smiled up at him.

Grace's heart filled with joy. "And from now on," she promised, "we won't have any more secrets."

About the Author

WANDA E. BRUNSTETTER enjoys writing about the Amish because they live a peaceful, simple life. Wanda's interest in the Amish and other Plain communities began when she married her husband, Richard, who grew up in a Mennonite church in Pennsylvania. Wanda has made numerous trips to Lancaster County and has several friends and family members living near that area. She and her husband have also traveled to other parts of the country, meeting various Amish families and getting to know them personally. She hopes her readers will learn to love the wonderful Amish people as much as she does.

Wanda and her husband, Richard, have been married forty-four years. They have two grown children and six grandchildren. In her spare time, Wanda enjoys reading, ventriloquism, gardening, stamping, and having fun with her family.

Wanda has written several novels, novellas, stories, articles, poems, and puppet scripts.

To learn more about Wanda, visit her Web site at www.wandabrunstetter.com and feel free to e-mail her at wanda@wandabrunstetter.com.